BISHOP'S QUEEN

CRISTIN HARBER

ISBN-10: 1-942236-69-7
ISBN-13: 978-1-942236-69-6

www.CristinHarber.com

Published in the United States of America

Books by Cristin Harber

The Titan Series:

Book 1: Winters Heat (Colby Winters)

Book 1.5: Sweet Girl (Prequel to Garrison's Creed)

Book 2: Garrison's Creed (Cash Garrison)

Book 3: Westin's Chase (Jared Westin)

Book 4: Gambled (Brock Gamble)

Book 5: Chased (Asher McIntyre)

Book 6: Savage Secrets (Rocco Savage)

Book 7: Hart Attack (Roman Hart)

Book 8: Black Dawn (Parker Black)

Book 8.5: Live Wire (Jared & Sugar Westin)

Book 9: Bishop's Queen (Bishop O'Kane)

Book 10: Locke and Key (Locke Oliver)

The Delta Series:

Book 1: Delta: Retribution

Book 2: Delta: Revenge

Book 3: Delta: Rescue

Delta novella in Liliana Hart's MacKenzie Family Collection

The Only Series:

Book 1: Only for Him

Book 2: Only for Her

Book 3: Only for Us

Book 4: Only Forever

Each Titan and Delta book can be read as a standalone (except for Sweet Girl), but readers will likely best enjoy the series in order. The Only series must be read in order.

Acknowledgments

This book would not be made possible without the steadfast support of my family! I am blessed.

Also, thank you to my wonderful friends and crit partners who helped when I needed it the most: Claudia Connor, Sharon Kay, Patricia Patti, and Sara Shone.

There's always so much that goes on behind the scenes, and huge "thank you"s go to Amber Noffke and Tara Gonzalez from InkSlinger PR, Lynn McNamee and Neila Forssberg from Red Adept Editing, Amy Atwell from Author E.M.S., and Hot Damn Designs for the amazing cover design. Thank you to my industry friends, the "reps", and people who have taught me so much and push me to make each book better than the last.

As always, I wouldn't be anywhere without Team Titan. We're Titan Strong, baby! LYH.

To Tara Gonzalez, my publicist,
who is *nothing* like the Tara in this book.

Thanks for always being awesome.

PROLOGUE

Fifteen Years Ago

SOME NIGHTS WERE WORTH REMEMBERING, and this was one of them. Laughter flowed in the car as Eloise leaned against the backseat window, unable to keep her Captain Morgan-infused lovey-dovey eyes to herself. "Hey, hot stuff."

Bishop threw her a sexy smile from the front passenger seat. "What's up, babe?"

"Hey!" Brie giggled from the driver's seat. "How do you know she was talking to you? I think I'm the better-looking O'Kane."

"Shut it." Bishop play-shoved his hand in his sister's face as she slowed for a stop sign. "You don't look better to El."

Eloise laughed as they turned and accelerated onto a two-lane highway. "He's got you there."

"She loves me more," Brie said. "Besties for life."

"Or does she?" Bishop gave Eloise a look that made her fly, and that had nothing to do with the Captain.

Brie fake-gagged. "Oh, puke."

"Hey, hey!" Eloise threw her hands in the air, erupting into a fit of laughter. "Don't make me fight over you two."

Brie grabbed her phone, and Eloise's chimed a minute later.

BRIE: I know who your real favorite is. ;)

Bishop grabbed Brie's cell, read it, and scoffed. "Yeah, me."

"*Bishop!* Don't read Brie's phone." Despite the teasing, everyone knew Eloise belonged on his arm. Brie had nearly orchestrated the whole thing.

"Give me that." Brie fired off another text.

BRIE: Such a JERK. Run for your life.

ELOISE: He's in rare form tonight!! <3

"I brought this upon myself." Brie giggled. "You two…"

"Are you two still texting about me?" Bishop eyeballed his sister and made a play for her cell.

"Touch it and die." Brie swatted his hand then grabbed her phone. Steering with her knee, keeping an eye on both the road and her brother, she sent another message.

BRIE: Ask hm abt ihih

Eloise made a face. "What? That made no sense. It was all jibber-jabberish."

Brie laughed. "Hang on—"

Tires screeched. Eloise's arms and legs flew forward, while her torso stayed pinned to the seat. The seat belt ripped into her neck, and she slammed against the window, thrown back and forth as metal and glass crunched. The car rolled, and she slumped over.

Pain radiated as adrenaline surged, and Eloise couldn't hold her head upright. The heavy weight lulled back and forth. Her ears rang. Blood seeped in her mouth. Painfully, she blinked until she could see straight, but that did nothing to take away the vibration in her temple.

She brought her fingers to her lips, which were wet, then slid them up her cheeks and into her hair. "Bishop."

God, what had happened? They'd been in an accident. *Shit.* How bad were they hurt?

"Brie. El." Bishop's voice sounded so far away.

"We're okay?" She swallowed bloody saliva. "What...are we..." Oh, her head hurt. Eloise unbuckled her seat belt, shaking the glass off of her, trying to see in the shadowed dark.

Oh...no. Brie was partly sprawled across the center console, an arm angled awkwardly overhead and another across her hip. Bishop was perched in the front passenger seat, angled over his sister.

"What's that noise?" Eloise asked.

"That's *her*," he said. "Find your phone. Call 9-1-1."

All Eloise could do was stare at Brie. Her friend didn't scream, but how could she not be in pain? Her wheezing clamor gurgled, but she didn't cough. It sounded as though she was drowning but without water.

"What's wrong with her?" Eloise couldn't look away; she had never seen nor heard anything so terrifying. Was this her fault? She had asked Brie to resend the text. *Oh, God. No. Did I do this to her?*

"Where's your phone, El? Call 9-1-1!" Bishop sounded frantic.

Eloise reached for the ground, numbly searching for her cell. Everything was strewn. This was bad. "She needs help."

"No shit, El."

This was her fault. Bishop knew it too. Eloise still couldn't find the phone she'd just held in her hand. "I can't find it—"

"Hey, who's in there?" someone shouted from outside the shattered windows. "Fuck yeah. Couple people in there, Mary. Call the cops."

"Bishop." Eloise grabbed onto Brie's hand and let the strangers call for help. She didn't know where her phone was, and she didn't want to let go of Brie to find it. "What's happening?"

"Fuck if I know." He took Brie's other hand. "Come on, Brie."

The way she was lying wasn't right. It looked too awkward. Half of Brie was out of the seat belt, and half of her was still in the driver's seat.

"Can she breathe?" Eloise asked.

"I don't know. Don't think so." Terror hung on to his every word.

"What should we do? CPR?" She was still breathing. Eloise moved closer to Brie's side.

"Don't touch her!"

"I wasn't going to," Eloise cried. But Brie was in trouble. They had to do something.

A flash of light scanned through the car. "You kids okay? Shit, don't move. Dispatch says an ambulance is already on its way."

Blood covered Brie's face, and with the light on her, she seemed a thousand times worse.

Loose glass fell off of Bishop as he leaned closer. "Brie."

Eloise looked to Bishop. There wasn't a situation he couldn't fix. But his terrified stare didn't offer a solution. Sirens howled in the distance. The flashlight bearer opened Eloise's back door, but she wasn't going anywhere until help came for Brie.

"Hang on, sis." Glass shards on Bishop's face caught the flashlight's reflection. "Almost here."

Brie's face was anguished. Blood seeped out of the corners of her mouth along with her wheezing, gurgling gasps. Her hand didn't grip.

No, no, no… "Please, Brie." Tears trickled down Eloise's cheeks, but the nonexistent hold of Brie's hand became frailer. "No. Hang on."

The flashing lights arrived, and Eloise shifted closer. "They're here, sweetie, coming to help." Beads of glass bit into her knees as she bent closer, whispering, "Bishop, *Bishop*!" Eloise pleaded as if he could do something to help. "Tell her it'll be okay."

"Damn it, Brie. Hang on!"

The gasping slowed. Oh, Brie's tortured face looked pained for a breath.

"Say it nicely," Eloise cried. "Brie, don't."

Don't stop.

Don't die.

Don't leave us.

The wheezing faded. Brie's lifeless hand hung in Eloise's.

"No, Brie." Bishop's voice broke. "You've got it."

Lights filled the car. First responders opened the door. Bishop yelled that he wanted to stay with his sister. Eloise wouldn't let go of her best friend. She couldn't. "Help her!"

A radio crackled as paramedics forced them apart. Bishop went one way, shouting that he needed to stay close to his sister. Eloise was torn another direction.

A medic flashed light into her eyes. They made her lie down then wrapped a neck brace around her. No one would listen. "I need to stay with her. She's scared."

Eloise was scared too. She needed Bishop. The ambulance doors slammed, and the radio crackled again.

"Roger that. We're headed to Meadow Brook," another voice in the ambulance answered. Then they read Eloise's stats. "Second victim's right behind us."

A garbled response returned.

A third voice broke in and cut off the radio. "That's a negative on the second female." From the front seat, someone mumbled, "Damn shame when we have a DOA."

It hadn't been for her to hear, but Eloise's world shattered. *Dead on arrival*. She had killed her best friend.

CHAPTER 1

Present Day

ELLA LEIGHTON KNEW THERE WASN'T someone following her. *Simple paranoia.* That was all this urge to turn and look over her shoulder was. But the shadows seemed to wave at her, and Washington, DC's streets seemed emptier than normal.

"Chill out, Ella," she whispered to herself. "You're losing your cool."

And not for the first time.

Ever since her publicist had clued her in to those creepy messages and fan mail that had gone from oddball to absurd, she'd been feeling as if there were constantly a pair of eyeballs following her—and not in a hired-security kind of way.

Everyone blamed *Under the Roof* for the onslaught of attention, but blaming a reality TV show was the easy answer. She was now grouped into a weird category of social media personalities and reality celebrities, which was hard for her to compute, seeing as she'd actually made her claim to fame as an environmentalist and blogger. Her website, Eco-Ella, had hit the viral lotto. But the cops didn't care when she tried to explain that. They knew her from TV, and her job was to "rile people up when she wasn't calming them down."

How about that for boiling down her career into a one-sentence snapshot?

The late-night light shed little help as Ella jaywalked across the street. No one was out on this lonely night, and she shivered.

Another quick glance over her shoulder confirmed she was still alone. "Hello?"

No response.

Paranoia. Again. Her stomach twisted, and the hairs on the back of her neck stood like suspicious defenders, trying to awaken her enough to run. She picked up her pace, though it felt as though she was wading through wet sand.

Having actually faced off with desperate excuses for humans—the type who would leave her dead in their search to make a dollar—she would rather deal with threats she could see, not the unknown that made her feel as if she were losing her mind.

"Pull it together," Ella mumbled as she slowed to cross another street. "Nothing scares you."

A yowling cry pricked at her ears. But this wasn't a soft sound. The loud mewling was enough to break through her worried preoccupation. Her eyes dropped to the empty street, and triangulating the distress, Ella carefully followed the curb a few short feet.

Meow. She dropped to inspect. Trapped in the plastic rings from a six-pack and caught on the spike of a metal grate was a tired, malnourished, terrified kitten. "Oh, dang."

It was nothing but a scrap of fur and ribs, though it housed powerful lungs and fierce claws that came out as she tried to set it free.

"I've got you. Hang on." *Ouch.* "One more second."

Once untied, the kitten gave up the fight and let Ella pet its head. Together they sat, the two of them finding solace in each other. Still, unease sat at the back of her mind. “I don’t know what to believe anymore.”

The kitten meowed. What was she going to do? Leave it on the side of the road? Of course not. “We should get going.”

Giving in to her suspicions again, she tucked the kitten into her elbow and hurried down the center of the street, taking no chances if there was actually somebody following her.

“There’s my car. We’re fine,” she promised the kitten.

A few rushed strides later, Ella opened her car door and slipped them both inside, petting the shaking kitten as she settled the little thing into the passenger seat.

“You felt it too, little kitty. But we’re okay now. Just stay put.” Once she was sure that her purse would keep the kitten somewhat in place, Ella grabbed her seat belt and sank into the seat, finally taking a safe breath. Hands on the steering wheel, she looked up to see a note on the windshield, pinned underneath the windshield wiper.

The writing was in block letters:

MEOW! ECO-ELLA SAVES THE DAY!

I’M ALWAYS WATCHING.

CHAPTER 2

JAY GRAFF LICKED HIS LIPS as he leaned against the oak tree. There Ella was, inside an all-natural grocery store, oblivious and irritating. He could sense her distress through the storefront window as he sipped his coffee. She would benefit from a back rub, something she was missing out on since breaking up with him.

Her loss—*shit.* Jay ducked out of view. Ella didn't take nearly as long as he'd expected. She grabbed whatever she'd purchased and spun toward the door.

Now, his morning fun would really start. Ella would be a few yards behind him as he started his leisurely stroll. Toying with her made his blood race faster than the double shot he nursed.

It had been thirty-seven days since she claimed they were *just* friends. Ella had lied her ass off and said they didn't have a spark, that she didn't want to be his girlfriend, that they should only work together—*didn't he feel that way too*?

Screw her.

He swallowed his frustration. Ella was a game, like chess, and involved strategy. One move meant a great deal. Every action had a consequence, and he needed patience.

Jay sipped out of the mug he'd purchased when they left Congo. Side by side in Virunga Forest, he and Ella had fought against gorilla poachers. They'd had a spark then, and they still had it now. He would *force* her to remember that, so help him…

"Hey, Jay," Ella called from behind him.

He smirked. Baited, Ella couldn't stay away. This game was intense, exhilarating. Each time she crawled back to him, she fed his Ella-addiction.

Ironic how Ella, who railed against poachers and triumphed for the environment, would one day amount to nothing but a trophy on his wall. It served her right.

"Jay." Ella touched his bicep as she pulled alongside him. "Hey."

He paused, readying for the close-up inspection he'd spent hours imagining—bloodshot red eyes and dark circles.

She looked fine! Anger slammed into his heart. She showed no signs of being scared—no worry or sleepless nights.

What the hell? His fingers tightened on his coffee mug, and he consciously decided not to crush the plastic.

He bristled. "Good morning."

"Wake up on the wrong side of the bed?" She laughed light as air.

"Not a chance," Jay snapped. "You're doing well?"

"I can't complain."

"*Really?*" She couldn't complain about the note on her car when she shouldn't have been walking around DC alone at night?

Everything about her radiated with sunshine and positivity. He couldn't stand it, and his mind was swinging. He missed her; he hated her. He wanted her back; he wished she would go away.

DC commuters in business suits brushed by as they rounded the corner to Ella's publicist's office, pausing at the crosswalk. Her airy skirt and tight tank stood out like a beacon of hope in the humdrum of traffic and pollution. The traffic light flashed, and Jay put his hand at the small of her back at they stepped into the crosswalk.

Ella shifted out of his touch. "Have you talked to Tara this morning?"

"No." He ignored the urge to throw her into oncoming traffic. That flowy skirt would flare if he pushed her hard enough.

Once they were safe on the sidewalk, she pivoted. "Jay…"

Damn her and that voice, that sweet *you're my friend, but don't touch my back* voice.

"Old habits, Ella." Which would be new habits again when she got over herself and fell back into their old routine.

How long would it take Ella to come back to her senses? Ella was his job, his obsession. She used to be his woman, and so much like a possession, it was simple.

She was his.

CHAPTER 3

AS DAYS WENT, THIS MONDAY had been a long one. After walking into Tara's office that morning, Ella and Jay hadn't left until they broke for dinner. At least now with a belly full of roasted veggie vegan naan, Ella felt reinvigorated, which was good because Jay was hell-bent on mapping out the rest of her blog's calendar tonight if it killed them. All he'd wanted to talk about during dinner was logistics.

"If you don't need me…" Tara knew she wasn't needed for the nitty-gritty. The promo had long since been hashed out. "You two have fun and lock up again when you leave."

Ella turned to Jay, hoping the good food had put him in a decent mood. "Let's finish this tomorrow."

"Slacker." He turned to Tara. "Might as well start pitching her to TV execs again, because she's done with the hard stuff."

"Jay." Ella's jaw dropped. "Are you kidding me?"

"Just saying. When have you ever been one to not finish what you started."

Tara pressed her perfectly lined lips together and shook her head. "Call if you need me. I'm gone."

"My phone's dead," Jay muttered.

"Then Ella can. Have fun." Tara hugged her and waved at Jay then left them in front of the restaurant.

He was already walking toward Tara's office. "Let's get it done already."

Her big project now focused on lavender and mint, semi-hard to kill, easy to transfer in real life. Jay's concern was that Ella wanted to bring real people into the blog's posts. Logistically, what she wanted was a "nightmare" as Jay had explained a dozen times over dinner.

"Coming," she mumbled, catching up.

They closed in on Tara's office, and he twisted his key in the door.

"Telling Tara to pitch me to TV was a low blow."

"Got you back to where you were supposed to be."

"Nice," she snipped.

They tromped the familiar path up the stairs and into the conference room. "What's your problem lately?" Ella asked.

Jay walked in, slamming the conference room door so hard, the walls shook. "My problem is you, Ella."

Her phone rang, and Jay grumbled while she grabbed it. "It's my dad. Chill out for a second." Accepting the call, she put the phone to her ear. "Hey, Dad."

A picture waited for them in the center of the conference table, and her blood went cold. "Oh no." Ella stepped closer, unable to look away, and Jay's eyes caught it at the same time.

"Hey, El. We were just checking in," Dad said.

Jay stepped in front of her, trying to keep her from seeing what she was certain she already had.

"Jay, move."

"El?" Dad tried again. "Are you there?"

This was clearly the work of her stalker. A picture of her and everything she hated, things she railed against, had been

Photoshopped into a collage—rainforests that had been mowed down, smashed turtle eggs, and a rhino or an elephant, she couldn't tell which, that was missing part of its tusk or horn. *So much blood.*

"El, are you there?" Dad's worried voice called to her.

"It happened again, Daddy."

When she had first turned over the sick photos, scary mail, and recapped her *feelings* to the police, they hadn't taken her seriously. She had millions of fans. The police had told her that TV personalities attracted creepy people. Issue activists brought out the crazies, they explained. Surely some of them would be overly excited, especially because her message was semi-political and very emotional. There would be people who grabbed onto her message with their whole hearts, as well as those who rejected it with fervor. Passion bred reaction.

"Are you okay, El?—Yes, it's El. Pick up; she had a problem again."

A second later, her mom clicked on. "Hi, honey bear."

"There's another picture, Mom."

"Call the cops, El," Dad ordered.

Right. Ella walked toward the conference room phone.

"What are you doing?" Jay asked.

She looked at him. "Calling 9-1-1."

"Are you stupid?"

She recoiled. "What?"

"Are you going to say a picture scared you? We've been down that road."

"The picture…" She glanced at the conference table but couldn't quite look at the collage. "Someone obviously broke in and put it here."

Jay reached for the conference table phone. "This is *not* an emergency. It's a picture. Where do you see any signs of a break-in?"

"This isn't an emergency?" She balked, but then again, he was right. "Why does everyone play this down?"

"El," Dad snapped. "Stop listening to him."

She focused back on her parents. "I'm here."

"That guy is not right sometimes," Dad said. "Now let me get this straight. Where are you?"

"Tara's office."

"And someone broke in?"

"Well, there's a picture here. I don't know how it got here." It's not like the door was busted or a window was broken.

"Let me talk to your dad," Jay said.

She shooed his hand away. That was all kinds of a bad idea.

Maybe she was overreacting. An intern could've received it in the mail and tossed it on the conference table, assuming Ella or Jay would be back and thinking one of them should see it. Okay, calling 9-1-1 seemed like overkill. The collage was totally screwed up, but maybe not an emergency.

"Hang up already so we can deal with this," Jay snapped.

Ella pulled the phone away from her mouth. "You're being a dick."

He grumbled. "Yeah, well, you're not dealing with this exactly how I think you should either, Ella."

"Glad you have a script written." She rolled her eyes, going back to her call. "What should we do?"

"Ignore it and go home," Jay answered for her parents. "If you're that worried, stay with me."

"Jeez, Jay." She spun away from him, needing to talk to the reasonable people in this conversation. Ella wanted to approach the situation as calmly as she would any other activist-environmentalist problem when she was in danger.

"Jay's a piece of work," Dad lectured. "You know who we should talk to? Where's that email from your parents? The one about that man going to Spain and the business card…" Her dad's voice faded away, and in the background, her parents lobbed a conversation back and forth.

"From Gamma and Pop-Pop?" Ella asked, confused about how her grandparents had been brought into the conversation.

"El," Mom said. "They know somebody in private security we're going to ask."

"Good. Can you ask them and not the *cops*?" She gave Jay a look to appease him. "I want to go home, but I feel like we can't just walk away. Maybe we'll call Tara too."

"A man named Rocco Savage, that's a name you don't forget, gave them a business card at the airport once, and said if there was ever a problem, he could help out. It was one of those stories your Gamma likes to tell about her travels. This situation constitutes a problem—Yes, that's it," Mom said to her dad. "*Titan Group*. That's right. From everything she said, they're the type of people who would know what to do. We'll make a quick phone call and get another perspective."

What kind of folks were her grandparents hanging out with? "Thanks. I appreciate it, Mom."

"Call you back. We love you, sweet pea."

"Love you too." Ella hung up and turned to see Jay's pissed-off face. It was as if he thought she had planned this night and the picture. "Honestly, you can leave if you want."

"Like hell, Ella."

She pulled out a chair, refusing to look at the picture, and waited for her parents' advice. Whatever they said, she trusted. Jay had said too much, and she was tired of hearing his opinion.

Jay sighed. "This is only going to get worse before it gets better."

CHAPTER 4

ELLA RECEIVED ONE TEXT MESSAGE from her dad, which said to stay put. Someone he now trusted was coming to talk to her. Jay had brooded since she hung up with her parents, and he exploded over the text. Granted, he'd always been moody, but as the minutes ticked by, he was being borderline passive-aggressive.

"You know, I'm perfectly capable of taking care of myself," Ella said.

He glanced purposefully at the picture. "I can see that."

Jay stood and paced again then dropped into his chair. "Your people are slow."

"My people? People who know my grandparents are not my people. Your vote was to stick around, remember? My vote involved fast, with blue-and-white flashing lights. Someone's going to offer an opinion without judging me. You can leave."

He muttered something under his breath.

Exasperated, Ella jumped up. "Excuse me? What is your problem?"

"I don't have a problem."

"Yes, you do. Which is ridiculous because *you're not the one with the problem.*"

He scoffed. "Trust me. I deal with your problems." He said it as though *she* were the problem.

Ella crossed her arms. "That's rich."

What environmental issue had she touched on that was so bad, it had created a stalker? Or was this because she'd gone on reality TV? She spent all of her time live steaming and vlogging on her website, Eco-Ella—maybe that was why some very concerning people had sometimes fixated on her. She'd gotten even more exposure because Tara cross-posted to other social media sites like Monarch, YouTube, Twitter, and Facebook.

Had Ella said the wrong thing or commented in a way that had triggered this? Had she encouraged a person that was hanging on by a thread to simply snip that string and lose their marbles? Sometimes, it seemed as though the line was so blurred between entertainer and fan that it didn't actually exist.

Ella talked to her fans all day long. That was one of the reasons TV and Hollywood threw legitimate offers to her on a regular basis. She had street cred, and they wanted that viral power.

The conference room door opened, and Ella sucked in a breath. She had assumed this *Titan Group* would call or knock, but no. They let themselves in.

"Ma'am."

Ella stood, staring at men who, even in streetwear, looked as if they would be more comfortable in SWAT gear. She steadied on her feet, breathing easier at just the sight of them than she had during any conversation with Jay. "Hi."

"My name is Jared Westin." Three men flanked his sides. "We're friends of your family."

"Thanks for coming by." She sounded flustered. She hadn't expected that several people as large and in charge as them would show up. They were not quite normal men. They seemed more like machines sent to protect her, and they were *clearly* in security.

That type of person made her wary. She'd never met any person who carried a gun and acted tough who didn't abuse that power. Poachers and pilferers were perfect examples. Her automatic reaction was not to trust badgeless gun carriers, but her dad had said they could be trusted.

Jared's eyes darted to Jay then to the picture on the table. "With that said, I'd like to speak with you privately."

Jay heaved, acting like an ungrateful child. "So I'll just, what, sit here?"

OMG. She gave him a sideways glance to telecommunicate her bit of embarrassment, but he missed her mortified telepathic vibes.

Jared crossed his arms. "Yes. Why don't you sit your ass still for a minute, *my friend*."

Ella froze as if she were one of the statues decorating Capitol Hill. Some people were not to be ignored. And Mr. Jared Westin was one of them.

He pivoted back. "Ella." It was not a question, not much of anything, and gave no indication of what he wanted.

"What Jay is trying to say is thank you for coming to talk about this," she said. "I didn't know what my parents meant. But any advice would be awesome, and—"

"Hang on." Jared gave her a once-over then turned his entire body in one slow, deliberate motion and stared at Jay, assessing him, before he came back to her. "Winters, Roman, check the office building. Find out what we need to know. Rocco, talk with the boyfriend. Miss Leighton and I will chat privately."

"He's not my boyfriend." The words wouldn't come fast enough, as two of the men peeled out of the room. Ella would *never* take ownership of her relationship with Jay after he had been that rude and showed no plans to check his attitude.

"Very close friends." Jay's lips pinched. "We work together.

And there's nothing to see in this building other than the picture on the table."

Jared didn't look at Jay. "Ready?"

"Ella, if you'd rather me sit in with you," Jay snipped.

Jared tilted his head. "Rocco, the non-boyfriend. Now."

"Why would we talk separately?" Jay asked.

"Jay." Ella bugged her eyes at him. "They're here to help me. They're part of our team. They're *not* the people we have to team up against and fight off."

Jared's eyebrow eased up. "You *routinely* team up and face off with people like us?"

"Sort of." Feeling as though she'd maybe impressed him, she hid her smile, but she was pretty proud of her work. "Most recently in Congo, Costa Rica, and then there was that time in the Amazonian jungle."

Both of Jared's brows went up. "Interesting."

Jay huffed, and the man named Rocco hovered between them. Ella shifted, deciding it was best to let those two have their own pissing contest.

She and Jared left the conference room, and Jared found a desk for them to sit at as though he'd been in Tara's office a hundred times. "So, Ella. Let's break down what's been happening and what you need to do moving forward."

Please, please don't say make an appointment with the police and explain. While she loved the boys in blue, the ones she had talked to so far hadn't taken anything seriously. This conversation was about to be disappointing. "Okay."

"My night was like a game of telephone. Ever play that?"

She nodded. "A long time ago."

"Thought so." He cracked his knuckles. "Your grandparents met my guy, Rocco, at an airport a couple years ago, and they agreed if there was ever an emergency, he owed them a favor.

Your grandmother had emailed the story to your parents—and I have to admit that it's a hell of a story—because I got a phone call from your father. He said he had a problem and was cashing in the favor."

"I'm the favor." She dropped her head, hating the fact that she was anyone's responsibility, but she also paused. How had no one told her that Gamma and the man who'd just been identified as Rocco had had a situation at an airport that resulted in a favor years later?

"Ella? You with me?"

"Yes." She focused. "I'm the favor."

"Yes." He nodded, eyes crinkling at the corners as his ever-assessing once-over paused. "And good thing for you, as it turns out, Rocco also watches a lot of TV."

Ella raised her eyebrows. "He does?"

"The reality crap, particularly."

Her eyebrows arched higher. "Okay."

"And from what he said, you're level-headed in a sea of bullshit."

"Oh, okay." While that was true, in her opinion, normally people didn't outright say that. "Thank you?"

Jared cracked his knuckles against the table. "You're a favor. You're a known entity. You're in deep over your head."

Over her head? "Well—"

"You"—Jared scowled—"are going to get yourself killed over a fucking clean-the-planet blog. Do you know that?"

Her spine went rod-iron straight, and her jaw dropped. "Excuse me?" *Good-bye warm fuzzies from safety patrol.* If this Jared Westin character was going to attack Eco-Ella, he had another thing coming. She was officially back on duty. "Or in the process of talking to people on the blog, on all social media, and in real life, I will save lives, animals, marine life, insects, and basically nature's life cycle." She met his gruff stare. "Mr. Westin, it's more than a *clean-the-planet* blog."

"And you talk to yourself on videos."

Ella balked. "I vlog."

"Whatever it's called. The TV thing is where you probably picked up the whacked-out nutjobs."

Ella rubbed her temples. "Honestly, that's all just a medium."

"Meaning?"

"I didn't set out to be on television. I didn't wake up and say 'I want to be famous' or whatever." It felt so weird to even say that. More often than not, people didn't recognize her. Actually, they did, but she dropped her head and tried not to be noticed. It wasn't as though she was Hollywood-famous; she was just Eco-Ella-famous. She thought of it as if Martha Stewart *Living* and Katy Perry were smashed into a celebrity sandwich and spouted out an environmentally focused spawn. Everything about her was still in the infantile stages, but it was growing exponentially.

"Explain it to me, Ella." Jared leaned back, crossing his arms. "Because from my point of view? The fans, millions of people up on your shit? I'd say that would be the driving force behind what most anyone would do." He paused. "We're behind closed doors, and I give no fucks about your answer. But the truth matters."

"Of course it does."

"No one's going to hear what you say. You're going to have to convince me that you're not selling me a line of bullshit. Between that jackass ex-boyfriend of yours—"

Ella leaned forward. "I ran Eco-Ella before the website went viral and the TV cameras showed up because it's important. And if they go away tomorrow, that's fine. But it would break my heart, because my message is important."

He looked *so* unconvinced.

"Everything's about the air. It's a finite commodity." She stood up. "In China, *right now*, not decades from now, where there aren't regulations, where environmentalists like me don't exist without major repercussions, people—kids, grandmas, even dogs—they have little masks they wear every day because pollution is as thick as fog."

His glower didn't change.

"You don't get it, and that's fine. It's hard to, maybe, unless you have kids or a dog, so whatever. My point is *they can't breathe*. When you can't breathe, you die. If you could ever imagine something like that." Ella smoothed her long, wispy skirt, hating where he'd forced her to go in her explanation. She drank in a mind-clearing breath and sat in her chair again. "It's horrific. Watching someone die who can't breathe..."

Still, he didn't utter a word.

"My work is more than just a blog, and what's grown from simply protecting the air has been amazing: Protecting animals and taking down corporate asshats who would rather save a buck and poison a community than tell the world they're responsible for cancer clusters."

Jared smirked—or was that a smile? "You certainly grow a set when your buzzwords are touched, don't you?"

Now, it was her turn to size up the mountain of a man before her. "Maybe."

He gave an imperceptible grin that lasted as long as a blink—though maybe she'd imagined it. Definitely she'd imagined it.

Jared grumbled. "Back to business. You've had death threats."

She crossed her arms just like him. "No one threatened my life."

He tilted his head. "What do you call pictures with your face sliced and diced? The carcasses that were—"

"All right, okay. Those things would all kill me."

"Slowly and painfully."

Ella tried to hide the swallow that seemed hard to take. Better that than to have lost her dinner on the guy. "Understood."

"And the language. *Always watching*. Variations of that."

"Throwbacks to the TV show? Watching to see what position I take on an issue?"

"You don't believe that, but you do put up a strong show." He shrugged. "Look, we're not investigators, though in our own way, at times, we hunt people and organizations."

That sounded ominous. "The police didn't really think that I had much to investigate."

He nodded as though he knew or expected that. "We're going to loop you in with our FBI folks."

Oh. *His* FBI folks. She squared her shoulders, readying to explain that while she didn't appreciate not being taken seriously, the Feds sounded as though he was going overboard. "Well, as it turns out, something has to happen *to* you before someone can help. I have a *situation* where someone is antagonizing me."

He pinched the bridge of his nose. "You have a stalker."

"According to some of the cops, not technically, I don't." She smiled weakly. "I have an overly eager fan or online hater."

"The FBI is better equipped to handle your situation, especially given the jurisdiction hopping. What do your haters do?"

"Down vote, report, troll, nastygram, comment stuff that is pretty shitty, pardon my language."

He gave her a look, and she guessed that her apology wasn't needed. Jared placed his elbows on the table. "I perused your Eco-Ella website on the way over here. You're no angel."

"Well, thank you." She couldn't tell if that impressed him or pissed him off. "It's a talent."

He doubled down on his glare, which she was toughening up to, but it still made her shake. "You're a hot button, viral-spewing, ratings-driven dream. You need to be more cognizant of your situation."

"I *am.*" And where was Tara when someone said something like that? She would have an orgasm over his compliment.

Jared bumped his fist on the table. "And that brings us to the end of this conversation. You need to work with us. At least until this situation wraps."

"I don't understand. I'm not an organization or whatever you protect."

"It's simple. Law enforcement will get your stalker. We will keep you safe until that point."

"Like…how?" Images of her in beach chic, surrounded by masked men straight out of an action movie, sprang to mind. If calling 9-1-1 made Jay yell at her, this would give him an aneurysm.

"You need a security detail."

Wait, what? "Like a bodyguard."

He gave a curt nod.

"I'm not really at that point in life." Nor would she ever be. That was for movie stars and politicians. Her stalker was absolutely crazy, but he was also lazy. He liked to take his time. He only struck on weekends and the occasional workday. Granted, he was scary. But he wasn't consistent, and the threats weren't daily. This was nothing like when she went into actual danger zones to try to stop illegal hunters or jungle harvesters. In those cases, round-the-clock security would've been smart, but she had Jay, and all had worked out fine.

"You need Titan."

She needed Titan? Maybe.

"Miss Leighton?"

"I'm not sure what to do."

"Wrong." Jared took on a surprisingly father-like protective tone. "You were smart enough to have this conversation with me. You know the answer."

She stared over his shoulder at the door.

"It's simple." He pulled his phone off his hip and typed away. "Bullet points have now been emailed to you. That's the gist of the services we'll provide. Basically, we'll keep you alive so you can protect your precious oxygen and watch out for sea turtles or whatever. I included an attachment that boils down the bullshit: I get you; you get me. If you want Titan, you've got us."

"It's everyone's oxygen."

"More or less, I think you'll realize we're on the same page." He slapped the table and walked out of the room. "Have a good night, Miss Leighton."

Drained, Ella leaned back in the office chair. Honestly, would it be so bad to have someone hold her hand and walk her through the process of convincing the FBI she had a serious threat? Her parents trusted Titan.

Rocco, the man who'd been with Jay, knocked on the doorframe. "Your ex skedaddled. Here's your purse. Boss man says check your email, and we'll get you to your car."

She took the handmade purse from him. "Thanks."

He gave a curt chin lift as a good-bye. All in all, they were a little cold, but that was how a private security firm should be, right? They should be tough and run like a machine…with guns. *Machine guns.* Her stomach turned. Okay, maybe that was a bit much.

Ella took out her phone and read the email, and it said exactly what Jared had detailed. Then she opened the attachment as directed, not wanting to misstep on his orders already. Failing as a client seemed as though it was a distinct possibility, and—

Whoa.

A picture appeared on her screen. Jared Westin stood with a beautiful woman snuggled under his arm and a grade-school-age kid leaning over what had to be a newborn in their arms. An English bulldog curled next to the family on the couch.

He had a family. Kids. A *baby*. A dog. The works. The guy understood the need for oxygen in the future.

Ella let the phone rest in her lap. Never had she realized how badly she made assumptions before. Shaking the shocked bits from her head, she typed a quick response and read it back before she hit send:

I get you. You get me. I need help. Titan is hired.

CHAPTER 5

"A REALITY TV STAR?" BISHOP tossed the closed folder onto the briefing table. This was hazing. It had to be. "She needs a bodyguard? That's what you're saying?"

"The woman has a stalker." Jared nodded. "Simple enough. You won't get yourself killed on the first week of work, which makes my life easier." The bulldog perched on Bishop's new boss's boot groaned as she rolled over, signaling that even she was in on the big joke.

He picked up the folder again, flipping past the first page of magazine highlights from red carpets, TV shows, and website screenshots. They all looked about the same—fancy dresses and paparazzi. One picture caught his eye. A sun-kissed brunette, barely looking over her shoulder, was in an evening gown on a red carpet. Earthy eye makeup and cascades of wavy hair almost obscured her face. But it was less her face he noticed, and more the contrast of that sexy-ass dress. Dark sleeves covered every inch of her shoulders and arms, but it plunged down her back, almost to her ass. That dress was a distraction—in the most sinful of ways. That was his first clue that this job was BS.

"Protective detail for celebs?" He flipped to the next page. "Lots of people know who she is, huh? I don't."

"You and Jared," Rocco added. "That would make sense for you, given that you've been ass-deep in the Hindu Kush mountains, smoking out ISIS for the last few years." He shook his head. "This guy? No excuse."

Talk about a brutal job that few wanted. Bishop had had no connection to the world. He and a select band of special forces had used everything from armored vehicles to horses and donkeys to crawl through the nooks and crannies of those Afghani mountains. They'd trudged through the snowcaps of Kunar Province only to find themselves passing intel in the valleys of Bala Murghab months later. Truth was, he missed it, and going from that to *this* had to be a joke.

Jared's brows furrowed. "Little early in your career here to start questioning the assignments and clients, isn't it?"

Bishop opened the folder and skimmed her bio. Blogger. *What does a blogger do?* Reality TV star. Environmentalist. They were fucking with him. "For a woman who protects *trees*?"

Rocco leaned forward, resting his elbows on the table. "No, bro. She doesn't protect *trees*. The lady specializes in air and baby turtle eggs if that makes a difference to you."

He snorted. "Oh, good. *Air*."

"She's prime-time powerful, and she's ours to keep alive."

Jared broke in. "Basically, she riles up most everyone with an iPhone and a Smart Car—which there are a lot of—and she has someone lobbing threats at her."

Bishop grumbled. How dangerous was the Smart Car crowd?

Rocco's forehead furrowed. "You're two seconds from losing a job that most men would cut their nuts off to have."

Bishop turned back to the page with the sexy dress but didn't want to eyeball it in front of his new bosses. Something about the woman struck him as familiar. He turned back to her details. She was local to the area. Great, so was he. They were about the same age, so he wasn't dealing with a teeny bopper.

Blah, blah, beaches.

Blah, blah, blah, videos.

The woman was anti-everything dangerous, yet she earned a living raising hell online. She was pro-everything nice, safe, and sane, yet somehow, she had people wanting to kill her. Well, that seemed a contradiction. He turned the page to read more of her background.

"FBI has assigned an agent. Just keep her alive," Rocco said.

Bishop glanced at Jared and Rocco. "Anything on the threats I should keep her from?"

"The way this woman collects enemies?" Jared whistled. "Anyone high-profile will have their share of whackos. But a specific escalation began a few weeks ago."

Rocco pointed to the folder. "Flip all the way back, last pages."

Bishop turned to the photocopies of letters, and damn, they were legitimately freaky. "Just to screw with her?"

Jared shrugged. "We're not investigating. Motive is the Fed's problem."

Rocco pushed back in the rolling chair. "Parker had a new surveillance system installed at her place already, and she's met Locke. He'll be your relief, but you're the primary."

"Got it. I didn't know Titan did celebs."

"Sit tight until I make sure she's settled. Then you can head to the war room." Jared stood. "Read up on her file. All that activist, famous-person-for-her-cause stuff is important. Time to immerse yourself in the online world of Eco-Ella. The girl's a blogging champ."

A person could be a blogging champion? He still wasn't sure how blogging could be a career, or what made reality stars into celebrities, much less one that was at this apparent level.

Jared laughed. "Bishop's going to be posting videos and going live before we know it."

"Hashtag trucks and tree huggers," Rocco said.

Jared smirked. "Hashtag Titan does TV."

"What are you guys talking about?" They didn't have this shit up in the mountains. He hadn't even had a cell phone for years. That was the way he liked it.

They laughed as the heavy door shut, closing him in a room that was as dangerous as it was a safety cocoon. Social media and an environmental-loving Internet sensation? Okay, not a problem. It wasn't as though they had to have a conversation. But his eyelids hung heavy as he stared at the file folder in front of him. *Damn it...*

This wasn't what Bishop had signed up for. Where were the grenade launchers and attack choppers? Pure, one-hundred-percent boredom mixed with a solid dose of he-didn't-get-it loomed ahead.

Operational assessment: not good.

CHAPTER 6

"BISHOP!"

His eyes widened, and his head snapped up. *Shit.*

Rocco glared over at him from the other side of the war room table. "Tell me you were not fucking *sleeping* instead of reading that file."

"No, sir." Though he had seriously zoned out…and maybe slept. "Processing."

Reading that file would've been like paging through a gossip magazine—if he had done it. *Painful.*

He flipped the folder back open, ready to start again. "I'm back on it."

"No need. The eco-princess is waiting."

"All right." Bishop rubbed his face to get the blood flowing again.

"Give me this." Rocco snatched the folder. "Hit the head. Whatever you have to do. Meet her in the second conference room on the north side of the building."

"Right." He prayed the next assignment would involve explosives. But for now, he would stay in the area, do the security gig, and earn his stripes.

As quiet as Rocco had stormed in, the hurricane left the room.

Bishop pushed back from his rolling chair and let it drift to a standstill. He lumbered up and grabbed a beef jerky stick from a side table, tearing at the wrapper. Jerky cured all, and he ripped into a bite.

Titan headquarters was a labyrinth, and as he ambled down the hall, Bishop figured it would take only a week, maybe two, for FBI investigators to clean up the threats against this Eco-Ella personality, then Titan would be off security.

He twisted the conference room door handle and a woman slammed into his chest, squeaking in surprise. Her face hit his hand, sandwiching the jerky to his chest.

"Sorry." He fumbled back, trying to make apologies, knowing that a handshake would've been better. Damn, maybe he was better suited for the field rather than this private security bullshit, but hell if he wasn't getting older and wanted to keep the action going and—

"Oh, God." The woman made a gagging noise. "Could you tell me where the restroom is?"

"What? Are you, um, okay?" They'd run into each other; he hadn't manhandled her. Was she sick? *Wait—what the hell?* His mind jumped fifteen years into history—*his* history—as he took in the red-faced beauty, who looked as if she were close to vomiting. "El?"

Eloise Lewandowski. No way.

Bishop took a cautious step back as the woman's hands covered her contorted face. He would know everything about Eloise anywhere. Except, it couldn't be her.

"Bathroom?" This doppelganger was spastic and…dry heaving—or something—as she spun away.

"Down the hall. To the right."

She took off, wiping at her tongue as her long snow-white skirt trailed.

Bishop dropped his gaze to the beef jerky then back to the empty hall. "What the hell just happened?"

That woman was his protective detail? That crazy lady?

He didn't know what to do, standing there, looking around as if it were a joke. And he was now certain this was part of a Titan newbie hazing plan. *Goddamn it.*

It was a sucker punch that the brief glance made him think the woman looked so much like Eloise. Now there was a memory he hated to remember, as much as he could never forget.

Bishop nodded to himself. "Titan hazing is a go." *All right, Rocco and Jared. Not a problem.* He could handle this. Before Crazy could make her way back, Bishop stomached the rest of his jerky and chucked the wrapper into a trash can.

He took a seat, waiting for her to come out of the ladies' room. One minute passed, then two. He blew out a breath and locked his knuckles, stretching and waiting. Was it hazing or a test?

Five more minutes passed.

Maybe it was a test. Then again, did Titan mess around with crap like hazing? And they had already seen him in the field, had already recruited him and signed him on. Okay, so Eco-Ella was either dead in the bathroom, and he'd lost his job at Titan—death by jerky—and he would never work at a private security firm again, or in their one-point-five-second-long interaction, she'd determined that she didn't want to work with him.

Screw it. He powered out in search of the ladies' room. He walked down the hall and to the right then stood there like an asshole, thumbs in his pockets, having no fucking clue what to do.

If someone gave him a gun and an enemy, no problem. *Bang, bang, dead.*

A mission objective? Consider that gig complete.

He was one of the best and usually didn't have any questions on the job. Except this *was* the job, and he was standing outside a women's bathroom door, lost on what to do.

"Hey." *Eco* popped into his head like a jingle. "Ella, you okay in there?"

No answer.

He knocked on the door with his boot. Maybe she wasn't in there. But this was Titan HQ. She couldn't exactly wander around without a fingerprint and retina scanner allowing her passage.

What would a bodyguard do? Well, he would go in after his client. But, hell. What if he'd been the one who sent the client running…while gagging? "I'm coming in." *Eco*. "Ella."

Bishop pushed the door open with his foot as if he were entering The Twilight Zone, toeing it open an inch, then another. "Hello?"

The bathroom was nice, as bathrooms went, complete with a little sitting spot before the down-to-business area. And there Crazy was, ignoring him, pink-faced, and somehow pissed, upset, disgusted, and nauseated all at once.

And without question, it was a time-hop to the pain and memories that he would never forget. That was his Eloise.

CHAPTER 7

ELLA WATCHED HER PAST WALK into the room, and time froze. All of a sudden, she was just a college kid who could stare into those green eyes and feel safe. Too much time had passed, but in a breath of a second, she recalled what it had felt like to run her fingers along the scruff of his jaw. She remembered how he would rub her bare back, walking his fingers up and down her spine until she drifted to sleep in the pillow of his chest, their naked legs tangled.

They had history heavy enough to make a moonless night moan. Their baggage was deep and devastating. Pain had forced them apart. She had agonizingly ignored the tears in his words and in her heart, until she never saw him again.

Her chest ached for one quick second as he leveled her with the same shocked stare. The glance hit so fast and so hard, slamming so deep and true, that she couldn't breathe. Her mouth fell open, but words abandoned their purpose and wouldn't form.

Bishop O'Kane stood large and broad. Life looked as though it had been as good to him as it had been hard. He'd roughened, hardened. But those eyes, the poignant greenness, were a well to his soul, counteracting the attitude that rolled off him.

He was the same type as the Titan men who'd swept into

Tara's office—machine-like, *mountain*-like, with muscles made of boulders, and a corded neck. Long ago, Ella had touched and kissed those same spots, never noticing even the tendons that demanded her attention now.

Everything was noticeable as he stood in front of her, stunned—the veins on his arms; the way he hulked.

"Eloise?" Boots planted to the bathroom floor, Bishop stood his ground, showing a flash of uncertainty as though he needed permission to be in the ladies' room.

"Bishop." Was he as confused about the situation as she was about him? Likely so. Because the last time he'd seen her, she'd simply been a kid.

She'd been a kid who hadn't dealt with trauma and loss well, who had panicked, *who had hurt him.* Because when they'd ended—no, they'd never ended. They had simply stopped. Ella had walked away because she was too broken-heartened, unable to deal with life. She just couldn't…

He snapped out of his trance before she did and stepped forward in a way that smacked of menace and anger. "Who the hell is Ella Leighton?"

At that moment, the disgusting jerky taste roared back, its ugly presence on her tongue. The revolting meat taste stirred up her gag reflex again. With the damp paper towel, she mopped at the side of her mouth. "That's me. It's like a pen name, except I used it online. It was supposed to help me with being anonymous, like a social safety net. But a lot of good that's done."

"El—" He stopped mid-word, mid-step, and rubbed his hand over his face as if he could erase his disbelief. When he dropped his arm, his palpable frustration had softened. "What happened back there?"

She shrugged.

"Eloise…"

She couldn't do this. She couldn't stand there, feeling so different than how she used to be, saddled with guilt and…curious about who he was and how he'd been. "You know, pretty much everybody calls me Ella. I just use it. It's who I've become. Eco-Ella. You know my real last name. But Ella? That's who I am. Call me Ella." She offered an explanation that she knew he wouldn't get. "And I'm a vegan; jerky's disgusting."

"You're a vegan, and jerky is disgusting." He repeated as though her words had been gibberish.

She wanted to push him away. Wasn't that what had worked last time? Inwardly, she cringed at her cowardly ways when everyone thought she was so strong. Outwardly, Ella lifted her chin and faked the strength. "I'm not who you think I am. So whoever you think you used to know, forget her. She's gone."

"Obviously." His eyes searched her up and down, landing on her face. "That old girl's forgotten. No worries." His raw words somehow stung. "So, *Eco-Ella*. Shall we start over?"

"Please," she whispered then cleared her throat. "Ella Leighton. I run Eco-Ella. I'm an environmentalist with a stalker problem."

"Bishop O'Kane. I'm with the Titan Group, and I'm the guy who will keep your stalker problems at bay."

AT LEAST BISHOP'S OFFERING OF introductions seemed to take Ella's edge down a notch. Because damn, that wasn't just a wall. That was a solid fortress of fuck-you, all of which, he deserved.

And now Eloise was Ella.

Ohhh-kay. Weird, but doable. So long as Titan signed his paychecks, his ex-girlfriend could demand to be called a space cadet and have "celebrity" tattooed on her forehead, and he would be good with it—whatever it took for Bishop to keep his job with Titan.

Eloise... Ella...was a *famous* person, not that he'd heard of Eco-Ella or *Under the Roof* before. But she was famous to someone. Hell, he hadn't heard the term "Internet celebrity" before today. Lots of people loved the woman he'd once loved, and that was odd. But not to know that she was well-known at all? That put into perspective how off-the-grid he'd been for the past few years.

The military had been his world, the only thing he'd needed for what had been almost half his life. He'd gone deep—lived it and breathed it. Then it was time to be done. Re-acclimating back to the United States and all of its viral, political, commercial-driven bullshit hadn't been on his to-do list.

"Now that we're acquainted," he joked, not necessarily landing it by the way she tilted her head and smiled. *Okay, tough crowd.* Ella put the wet paper towel on her tongue. "Did you bite your tongue?"

She arched an eyebrow accusingly. "I accidentally licked your jerky."

He laughed, and that bending eyebrow of hers almost jumped across the room and smacked him. He rolled his lips together to hide his humor—because honestly, she'd said that all wrong. Stifling his laugh didn't work, so he cleared his throat. That was the stupidest, dirtiest, unintentionally hysterical thing he'd heard all day.

"Are you *laughing*?" Ella's angry eyebrow dropped, flattening and taking a whole new line of aggressive positioning.

He ran a hand over his mouth. "No."

"You are!"

"Come on. You have a paper towel on your tongue."

"Jerky is disgusting," she mumbled over the towel.

"Or delicious." He stepped closer. "I'm a fan of it."

Pulling the paper away, she folded it neatly into a tiny, compact square before walking to the trash to throw it away. "You've developed a few poor eating habits since the last time we crossed paths."

Last time they crossed paths... That seemed a little harsh, considering their history, but fair. He'd been a dick. He hadn't meant to be, but now he could see that. Age had given him perspective. Walking—or running—away from her at the shittiest low of their lives had been immature, and if Ella wanted to be a first-class bitch to him, no problem. She could get a couple of solid sucker punches in without his complaint.

"So..." He shifted in his boots, uncomfortable on a dozen levels. "Do you want to head back to the war room?"

She looked around the tiny sitting area and folded back onto the couch. "I like it better in here."

He blanched. "You *want* to stay in here?"

"Yes."

"The ladies' room?"

"*Yes.*"

"Not where we were?" Because that would be logical, and clearly, Ella had dropped logic from her repertoire when she'd picked up superstar.

"Really?" She shook her head, eyeballs popping out. "The *war* room?"

"Yeah." His skin itched to get out of the bathroom. But, semi-amused, he also wanted to watch the shit show that was this crazy-*but*-interesting woman he used to know. Maybe that was why she made such a good reality star. He would have to ask Rocco.

Her little nose wrinkled. "I don't think I like any room called the war room."

"Huh." Ironic.

"Huh, what?"

"I like *any* room called a war room." Bishop crossed his arms, and they stayed silent, assessing the other for what had to be forever. "All right." He walked across the tiny sitting area to take a seat, and—*shit*—unexpectedly, the chair moved, sliding back and forth. *A glider*. Man, that was kind of sweet.

She giggled, and he jolted his head up to see her watching him check out the side of the chair. "Glides." He pointed out the obvious.

"It does."

Yeah, he was going to have to check out the men's room to see what kind of hidden gems were in there. Maybe it had a foosball table or something. Bishop shifted, trying to stop the chair from moving so much. It was comfortable, but not good for authoritative conversations.

He cleared his throat, planted his boots on the ground, and slowed the chair. Time hung, though they were now both on equal footing.

"Can we start over?" he asked. *Again.*

Ella wasn't going to give up easily, it seemed. Radio silence came from the pretty girl who had mental breakdowns over jerky.

It was *almost* amusing…if she weren't so damn crazy. With all of her turtle- and air-loving, maybe the sun had fried her brain. It had certainly lightened her hair and tanned her shoulders.

They teeter-tottered in a silent showdown. He almost said something again—almost, because even in the quiet, she looked as if she had something she wanted to say, and he was curious about what it might be.

If only she would acknowledge this was a game of who would give in first. If he could get her to say that… But then he would lose, and Bishop O'Kane never lost. That was a fact. Then her lips quirked. Ella was a breath away from giving him the win, and if this arrangement were to work—him watching out for her—there had to be some semblance of respect and give-and-take between them. There also had to be a winner at the moment. Though *why,* he had no idea.

Still, with Crazy, he would keep score. That nickname fit her better than Eco-Ella any day of the week.

Pretty pink lips, which could've been a distraction, turned upward, and he *knew* he had the win. Whatever she was about to say would work in his favor. Mentally, Bishop readied to give himself a high five.

"Yes," she said. "We can start over—"

The bathroom door swung open, and Beth and Nicola, two Titan agents he had met in passing, walked in and stared at them. Whatever the women's conversation had been, it was now muted. All Bishop could do was thank God that Crazy had ditched the paper towel she'd been licking.

To Beth and Nicola's credit, neither agent gawked for too long. One of them mumbled over her shoulder, "Hey, new guy."

Both ladies hit bathroom stalls around the corner. The doors opened, the locks slid into place, and they *started to pee*.

He tried, really tried to maintain a blank face. Then he tried to imagine they were in combat. He didn't give a shit if there were women in the battlefield or if they were mucking through a jungle. He didn't care when people had to go. But those agents were the wives of some of his teammates, and he *could hear them peeing*.

His molars ground down as he tried to focus his unwavering attention on Ella. "Can we leave?"

"Are you uncomfortable?" Ella was apparently aware they were keeping score in their newfound situation. She was on the hunt for a point of her own. "Truthfully, I think we should hang out here a bit longer. I like people watching, and this is a comfy couch."

She wiggled back as though she needed to get more comfortable then took out her phone. Her fingers flew on the screen, and for the moment, it looked as though she'd set up shop—checking emails or blog posts or whatever Internet celebrities did.

"What are you doing?" he asked.

"Seeing what time I told my publicist I'd post my vlog."

"What the fuck is a *vlog*?"

"A video blog post." Her forehead scrunched as if he'd asked the eco-girl whether she'd seen the color green before. Then, as serious as the threats that had been made against her, Ella asked, "Do you think we can have lunch delivered here?"

They were in a bathroom. *A bathroom.* Had she lost her ever-loving mind? There was no way. Fifteen years, or however long it had been, might have changed her, but just...*no*. He prayed she didn't actually want to eat in there. "Are you screwing with me?"

She cracked a smile, and for a moment, he saw the silly girl playing with the carefree guy, just like they used to be. "Maybe."

He choked on a chuckle, shaking his head, because this was all a joke. Titan was the best in the world at pretty much everything. Why wouldn't they dig into his past, find an ex-girlfriend, and throw him into the bathroom with her. It was epic. "You're in on this thing with the guys, aren't you?"

Ella's eyes narrowed, twinkling with a dose of curiosity. "I have no idea what you're talking about."

"This is a *beast* hazing job." He would give them that. Sugar had to have something to do with this, and it was total payback for tying her up with a jump rope at the job he'd completed before starting at Titan. "And—"

"No one is hazing you," one of the women said from the stalls.

Gah. Bishop dropped his head into his hands and rubbed the shit out of his face, trying, for the life of him, to not feel as if this was an insane moment as he heard Beth and Nicola flush and exit their stalls.

"All right." He dropped his voice several octaves lower. "Ready?"

He pushed out of his glider and extended his hand. Ella eyeballed his hand, analyzing the peace treaty that it was. *Come on, babe...* Their distance hung, unsteady for a moment, and hell if he was going to let this waif of an uncertainty dangle without an anchor. "Take my hand, *Ella*."

He'd said her name the way she liked it and left his hand outstretched. There wasn't much more he was going to offer, and that included lunch in the bathroom. Saying "Ella" brought her eyes to his, and it was that simple. They'd always had a connection, and it was good to know the lines of communication had never truly disappeared.

Ella placed her much smaller, surprisingly familiar, hand in his, and he pulled Crazy Eco-Ella to her feet.

"Come on." Bishop tugged her fingers that cautiously wrapped around his, and the touch triggered a faint memory, tickling deep in his chest. Before her hand fell away, his mind cataloged several startling unknowns. Her handhold exuded strength and confidence, even though it was a passing touch. For everything eco-this and enviro-that, he would've thought she'd blossomed into some kind of delicate flower—but no. Ella was decidedly, *unpredictably*, powerful.

He cleared the eco-miscalculation from his head and turned toward the sinks, where Nicola and Beth were involved in the slowest handwashing process known to man, also known as obvious spying. "We're out of here, ladies. The bathroom is all yours."

Two good-byes mixed with laughter rang out.

Bishop grumbled, but focused on controlling the situation. On the upside, he no longer had a running, crying, paper-towel-licking Ella. On the downside, where the hell should they go if not the war room? He didn't know this building, and even the conference rooms looked lethal. "If not the war room, where to?"

She stopped in the hallway. "This seems benign enough."

Annoyance ticked at his patience. No way would she want to set up shop there. No way would anything that had happened in the last twenty minutes have actually happened, but it had. He gritted his teeth. "If we could just go over the day, then we can get a move on."

She dropped her line of sight to the gun holstered on his hip, as if she had just noticed it, then dug through her purse as her phone rang. "If you think I dislike jerky, I have a running list of things—" She stared at the screen before silencing it. "I forget what I was saying. Never mind."

"Not an important call?"

"I don't talk to numbers I don't know."

That sounded pretentious as fuck, just as pretentious as choosing a new name. "What happened to you?" He turned and walked away before spinning back. "You aren't the girl I knew."

And why had he opened his mouth? He shouldn't broach the topic of their past with everything that had happened to them.

Surprise rounded her eyes because, finally, one of them had said it. Her lip curled as though indignation and disgust battled to take a swing at him. "You think I expected to see you like this?"

"I don't care," he lied, but they both knew his nonchalance was total bullcrap. How was this what his Eloise had become? A television princess mixed with an Internet goddess. A new name without a past.

"The girl you knew was young and lost. She didn't have a way to make sense of how unfair life could be, and she was lonely. So damn alone, you have no idea."

"Now look at you." Guilt and anger spiked in his throat. "Not alone anymore, are you?"

"Yeah. Look at me, Bishop." She stepped even closer, throwing out her arms. "Happy and formidable."

"In danger and stupid about it—" Her phone rang again, cutting him off, and he shook his head. "That thing is going to kill you *too*."

Ella slapped him instead of silencing the ringer. "It only took you an hour to get that out. Bet you've been waiting for your opening."

Stunned, Bishop could have outlined her hand mark on his cheek. The sting bit into his flesh almost as sharply as it reminded him he had no ground to respond. "Screw this gig." He stormed away, done with all this—her, Titan, everything. Screw it all.

"You used to like me," she shouted. "You weren't such a jerk."

Bishop seethed and charged back until he was inches away from her. "Hell, Eloise, I used to *love you*."

Her mouth hung open. "Don't call me that."

The hallway walls closed in, and he moved a head's distance from her lips—lips that he knew the taste and feel of, how they melted and came alive. His heart surged as he closed the distance between them, but then his boots stepped away from her, somehow thinking on his behalf. Almost every part of him wanted to be up against her. Thank God for boots that had experience running like all hell.

His gaze swept down. Where the hell had he just gone? Nowhere he was supposed to, that was for damn sure. Knowing he'd crossed the line on just about every topic between them, he bottled it up and faced her.

Ella's bottom lip trembled.

Shit.

He dropped his chin, vowing to tamp down their past and any

memory that wanted to unfurl its ugly head. He needed this job like he needed a purpose in life. Titan was an end goal, and in truth, he wanted Eloise—*Ella*—safe. She deserved that. This would work if he boxed any loose reactions.

Bishop slowed his mind and reached for her arm, trying to offer some manner of compassion that was subpar and long past due. "I shouldn't have brought that up, shouldn't have gone there."

"I, uh. We…we never really talked about…" She closed her eyes and took a deep breath. "It's been a long time."

"Yeah." He rubbed her arm once then dropped his hand, knowing he shouldn't touch her. "You okay?"

Beth and Nicola crept quietly down the hall. As they passed, Ella painted on a perfect smile. Fascinating how well she could put up a fake wall.

"I'm okay…" She shifted her shoulder bag to the other arm. "Is this going to work?"

"Do you want it to?" he asked.

Ella chewed on her bottom lip then nodded.

He gave her a nod as well. "All right, then." Talk about a change of plans. First thing he needed to do was loop his new boss in about his old girlfriend. So much for having a good first week. "Go back into the bathroom, El. I'll find you when it's time to rock and roll. Then we can figure out what our day's like. Deal?"

Her eyes bounced up and down, assessing him as though she were fitting a suit. Not checking him out, but more like…measuring. "I have things to do. Then we can just do that and get going?"

Finally. Something they could agree on, *after* he talked to Titan about his history with Ella. "Absolutely."

His gut churned, and he didn't know if that uncomfortable sensation stemmed from her sane suggestion or the fact that he had to go explain how he didn't recognize his hot ex in a file folder. "Give me ten to grab my gear, and we'll head out."

"I'll be in there." She gestured to the bathroom that he'd just wrangled her from. "I like it."

"Right." Ella was nuts. "I'll knock. You'll answer. It will work that way. It can be like your home away from home if you're here at Titan for any reason. Deal?"

Her grin was less fake than any he'd seen thus far. "Deal."

Turning, he wanted to find a piece of jerky and down it in private before Eco-Ella freaked out again. "See you in ten."

"One more thing."

Bishop pivoted but kept walking backward toward the jerky. "Yeah?"

"I have to drive. I have herbs in my car. The plants are important; I'm working my way through the neighborhood, handing them out—"

"I can move them. No problem."

"I'd really prefer not to move them."

"Why?"

"I've had success in cultivating an urban garden program. Arlington went really well, and we vlogged about it like crazy. People loved it. But now…" Her eyes lit as though she was waiting on a mouthwatering dessert. Even her voice jumped an octave to match her smile. "There are these local beekeepers that the DC Parks and Rec department partnered with. But I thought that it would be great to focus segments on pollen sources. Pollenating plants are basically bee protein and—"

"That's not why I can't move them."

She pursed her lips. "My plants are fragile. You're not."

"That would've been a much faster explanation." For a half-pint size of a woman, she didn't waver when she decided she wanted her way, which was, as his luck would have it, every damn time.

"I can carry your plants, Ella."

"They're herbs," she corrected.

He dropped his eyebrows. "Aren't herbs plants?"

"Well, the lavender—"

"And isn't that a flower?" Not that he knew shit about that.

"You don't want me to get into the explanation of the nearly forty known species of lavender and how it's both an herb and a flower, do you? Since your preference was for my more expedient explanation."

Bishop smirked. "They're green. Have roots. Drink water. Sprouted from a damn seed. We'll call them plants."

"They're important. And you have to be careful with them."

"Do you fight over everything these days?" he asked.

"I'm protective over things I care about."

He could relate to that. But seriously, they were battling over garden items that he generally ate. "I'll be careful while carrying your *herbs*."

"Honestly," she pushed. "We should just take my car."

He waved an internal white flag, not pleased at the loss. Though it was only this round. "Fine."

"Good."

"Great." Bishop ground his teeth, remembering she was part of the Jared Westin family-and-friends plan. "We'll take your ride. No problem." She was going to be a pick-a-battle type person, and he wasn't jackass enough to demand to drive every time. *Whatever.* He would survive.

She tilted her chin in a move so opposite the stubborn behavior she'd just displayed that it struck him as...*delicate*. Decidedly *not* Ella-esque. *Damn it.* He could not get a read on her. One minute, she was tough, and the next minute, soft.

"But"—the corners of her lips quirked—"don't sneak any jerky before we go. It'll stink and make me sick."

Then she had to go and open her mouth. Bishop turned, ignoring her and heading straight for his next ration of beef jerky.

This job would kill him—not from high-flying bullets or enemy tangos, just a woman who drove him mad. But he was going to die with a full belly of beef jerky.

"ROCCO, HEY, BOSS." BISHOP JOGGED down the hall to catch his team leader, who didn't stop.

"What?" Rocco asked as he continued on.

"I have a situation."

"Deal with her. She's hot. A model. A vegan. A tree hugger. Whatever. Deal with it, O'Kane. Don't make me deal with you instead." They rounded a corner, and Rocco never even looked his way.

This wasn't going to be easy. "Right. I get all that—"

Rocco stopped abruptly, aggravation oozing from every pore. "Then what is it?"

Yeah, this wasn't going to be an easy conversation. "I didn't connect the dots because she didn't go by Ella."

Lines deepened across Rocco's brow as he groaned. "Excuse me?"

"Ella Leighton was Eloise Lewandowski, and I used to date her when we were in high school and college."

Intel like that seemed best to throw out all at once. Though Bishop hadn't known Rocco for long, so maybe his ass should be ready to duck and cover.

"You and the tree hugger?" Rocco's face scored through shock to annoyance in a millisecond. "Were a thing?"

"We were *drastically* different people back then, as evidenced by the fact that she used to use a different name." That counted for something, right?

"Did you not read any of that file?" his boss snapped. "*Eloise Lewandowski* was in there. Listed under birth name."

"I read the first few pages..." Or the first one...or two.

Bishop rubbed the back of his neck. On top of this, he wasn't sure about his comfort level that everyone had likely checked out Eloise—or Ella, or whatever this crazy lady wanted to be called. For whatever this crazy anti-meat, anti-normal food, possibly anti-common sense—albeit still extraordinarily attractive—woman was, she was in his dating history.

"Dated, how?" Rocco grilled him.

Bishop blanked. "Excuse me?"

"Dated, and you fucked her a few times? Some one-night stands, promising her true love? And now that she's seen your ugly mug, she's on her way to Jared's office, *traumatized*, and will be sending us a bill for her therapy?" Rocco paused to let the full effect of that scenario weigh heavy. "Or are we talking dated, she wanted to marry you, but you, I don't know, joined up?"

"Err..." Bishop cleared his throat. "Closer to the latter, but, um, I think that..." He rubbed his hand over his jawline. "I..."

Rocco's jaw tightened. "Does she hate you?"

"The...well...it's complicated."

"Shit. I am low on men this second," Rocco growled. "Do you want this job?"

"Yes, sir."

"Good. This is your job. Do not lose this job. Do not get fired. And do not, under any circumstances, repeat history. Do you understand me, O'Kane?"

Bishop nodded. "I don't plan on it. Just wanted to offer up everything in terms of full disclosure."

"I appreciate that." Rocco crossed his arms over his chest and leaned against the wall. "Locke will be more available by the end of the week. He's going to be number two on this assignment.

Work your schedules together with him so when you need a break from Ella, he's on her. If you need to do something to keep your sanity, Locke is your man. If you need to do anything to keep this job, if you need any R&R, he is your guy."

Bishop tilted his chin up. "Thanks for understanding."

"Do not screw the job."

"I won't screw up," Bishop pledged.

Rocco took a step forward. "Not what I said, O'Kane."

Bishop ran the words back in his head. *Don't screw* Ella. Those were the instructions. "Ten-four."

With this version of that woman, sex wasn't on the table, or anywhere else.

Chapter 8

The plants took up half of the space in Ella's car. Literally. That was how small her car was, and as Bishop stared at the contents of her ride in Titan's parking lot, he wondered if anyone of his size had ever been in one of these tiny-ass cars. Forget that they were death traps; he wasn't sure he could fit.

"All right, Muscles. In we go."

Bishop's arms crossed his chest. There were some lines that couldn't be crossed. This was one of them. "No."

Ella's nose wrinkled as she dangled her key ring on her finger. "Get in. We had a deal."

"I don't think I *can* get in." Bishop stared at the Smart Car. His arm span could reach both sides, and without a doubt, he could toss the thing. She hadn't been checking him out in the hallway; she'd been measuring him. "This thing's a death trap. You have a better chance of someone smashing you to death on the Beltway than some angry anti-Ella hater finding you and smothering you with wheatgrass."

Ella rolled her eyes. "Well, no shit, Bishop. No death threats mentioned wheatgrass. Get in the car."

"I'll follow behind."

"*Get in.*"

He dropped his head back, trying to regain his composure, then focused on her. "We can put your car in the bed of my truck."

She smirked. "Very funny."

"You can sit in the driver's seat. Pretend you're driving, and I'll just drive us there. Your *herbs* will be fine. Your car will get to where we need to go. Problem solved. Everyone will be happy."

"You're being an asshole."

"There's no fucking way I can fold myself into that car."

Her pink lips pressed together, matching the irritation in her light-blue eyes. "I don't think I like you very much, Bishop."

"Lady, you don't have to like me. You don't even have to thank me. But each breath you get to take, that's on me. My job is to apparently keep you alive since you've pissed off *tree huggers* to the point that they want to kill you." He leaned into her space, throwing his arms out. "In what world does that happen?"

She ducked under his arm. "I'm done. You're fired. This is ridiculous."

"Oh no, you don't." Bishop hooked her with an arm around her waist. For as short as she was, she hid some muscles under her hippie-hempy, flowy clothes. "You're ten shades of off your rocker if you think I'm losing my dream gig over this. In you go." He opened the driver's door, deposited her inside, and semi-ignored how her lacy white skirt caught with the wind as he let her go. Her hands fought to smooth it into place as he slammed the door shut. Cursing every step on his way to the passenger seat, he shook his head. "Someone somewhere is making a YouTube video about this right now."

And what the mother hell? Ella pulled her phone out and was talking into it before he reached his seat. He threw his door open. "What were you doing?"

"Vlogging. I told you; I'm documenting the process."

"Right." He reached for a button on the side of the car seat, and they listened to the tiny whir as the seat moved as far back as the car allowed.

Ella beamed. "I could put that on my blog too."

With one eyebrow up, he silenced her amusement with a glare and forced his frame to fit into the little car. "Honest to God…"

A sly smile lit her face, and her giggle came back. Even his death glare didn't silence her this time. "Honest to God, you fit."

"I don't," he shot back.

"You're in my car."

"Barely."

"The door shut."

"*Ella.*" He dropped his voice, which wasn't hard with his knees up to his chest.

"Yes?" she asked sweetly.

"What is your deal? No bullshit."

"I—"

"*No. Bullshit.*"

"I try to live with as little of a negative carbon footprint each day as possible, and two cars, or your truck…that leaves a larger one."

"That's why we're packed like sardines?"

"Yup," she quipped.

"Isn't there a quality of life that you'd like to also live?" He hoped to whatever her higher authority was that she said yes.

Her chin dropped as she fidgeted with the keys. "My quality of life is fine."

The way she said it…where had all the sass gone? He recalibrated his approach, obviously hitting on something that wasn't in her file, like a mental health check. "Well, mine might be a little better if we took my ride."

The stoic look worked for her as she remained silent. He could see how thousands of people would follow her all around the world, trusting her when she leveled her serious stare. Even trapped like a gorilla in a hamster cage, he almost wanted to put up with their planned forty-five-minute drive. His leg cramps said otherwise. "I'm getting a charley horse, babe."

She grimaced on his behalf, and there it was. He was making a little bit of headway with her, even if he couldn't get her to say it. Whatever her issue was, she wasn't a cramp-giving client from hell—just a crazy one.

"I just looked at your blog." He tried again, hoping to find common ground. It was the truth too, even if it had only been two minutes of fast skimming, solely for the purpose of opposition research. "You don't want people to live and suffer. You want them to adjust their lifestyle so the world is a better place. *This. Sucks*. I'm not adjusting anything based off this."

"You were on Eco-Ella?"

"Bits." He tried to shift, and the mouth to the seat belt dug into his side. "You wouldn't video this and put it on there. You'd be off message."

Her mouth dropped.

"It'd be against everything you say you want."

Pink lips dropped a little more.

Bishop went in for the final offer. "Two cars, or I'm more than happy to drive with that eco-button pushed in my truck." Who knew that thing would ever come in handy? "Eco-button for Eco-Ella?" She slid him a sideways glance, but was a moment away from giving in, he could tell. "Who knows? Maybe I should've had it pushed in all the time. I never thought about it before now. Come on, better than two cars. Or your car in the bed of my truck."

She laughed quietly. "You know it won't really fit."

"I know." Though it might.

With a tiny breath, she slumped back. "You win round one, Muscles."

"Didn't know we were playing games." But inside, he was running around the car, giving high fives, throwing the football in the end zone, and doing a damn touchdown dance.

A flash of awareness danced in her eyes. "You did too."

He leaned closer, letting the seat belt bite into his side. "I win round two. Round one went to you and the jerky-paper-towel fiasco."

Blue eyes lit—all the confirmation he needed—and Ella pulled her buzzing handbag from behind her seat. "You're right."

Bishop reached for his door, and she pressed a button on her remote to pop the trunk.

"We should keep better score," Ella said as she hopped out of her micro car and shut him in alone.

Yeah, sure. It was all a game. No death threats or stalker, who apparently wanted her dead. "You got it, Crazy."

CHAPTER 9

JAY PRESSED THE REWIND ICON on his computer screen and tapped it to pause, zooming in on Ella. With a few quick snips and snaps, gone were her pristine picture and the beautiful background he'd snagged from Eco-Ella's homepage.

He leaned back to analyze his creation and scrolled through the last few pics: Ella in the middle of commercialized hell, surrounded by neon lights. Then she was in a landfill mecca. Gone was her recyclable water bottle, professionally replaced with a Styrofoam container from some fast food chain. He smirked. That would make Ella sick. As he paged to the next picture, disgusted with the images, he knew Eco-Ella fans would go insane. One picture showed her next to an ashtray overfilled with non-biodegradable cigarette butts, while she casually chatted to Wall Street-looking suits. "Yeah, this is the money shot."

Tara would go ballistic, and Jay couldn't contain a chuckle as he imagined her going into uber-publicist mode when these surfaced. He'd already posted one picture to see how folks would react, and true to the Internet behavior, those who saw it believed it without so much as a questionable comment. Tara had said that his Photoshop skills were subpar. "Well, subpar this, Tara."

He uploaded the new photos through another Monarch account,

using an undetectable profile. Each picture had spectacular file names too.

Ella Does Wall Street. Ella Does Corporate CEOs. Ella Makes Friends with Corporate Greed. Ella Loves Styrofoam—the upload was complete. Using the torrent side of Monarch was almost too easy, and normal users would see the photos and have a PR field day. Tara and Ella's day was going to suck.

Proud of his accomplishments, Jay leaned back in his chair and stretched, eying his chessboard. All morning, he had played against himself, strategizing and analyzing his skills, determining which positions were the best offense and defense. It took a special kind of talent to be the grand master of his own games, internally challenging and initiating moves to outwit his own psyche. Chess was a thinking man's game, one that pushed Jay to be brilliant in all things that he endeavored.

Speaking of brilliance…

"How's that little addition looking?" he mumbled, flipping back to check the comment he'd left after he uploaded his trial picture.

Wow. That one afterthought had 174 likes, proving people knew what they needed to do.

"Time to go viral." He swiped the screen to see his current uploads, adding the same comment to each newly uploaded picture. Ella's cell phone number.

BISHOP THREW HIS HAND OVER the back of the passenger seat headrest, easing his truck into the parallel parking spot—the tiny one that Ella waved him away from—reversing, then dropping the gearshift into park. The drive to her condo had been filled with an odd, one-sided conversation of Ella talking to her phone, explaining to whoever was watching on a live video cell phone feed that his big, *awful,* gas-guzzling, earth-ruining ride wasn't that depraved.

If he rolled his eyes once, he'd done it fifty times. When she threatened to show the world her *driver* at one of his grumblings, he gave a strong enough glare that she quickly shut down that idea, instead flipping around and zooming in for an up-close-and-personal conversation with the ECO button next to his radio. All in all, it was an educational broadcast, though if he'd known the inside of his truck was going to be on display, maybe he would've shined her up a bit.

"So, warriors, you know the drill. Post your comments, and I'll get to them later." Ella dropped the phone. "I didn't think you'd fit in this spot."

"I did." Now that she wasn't talking to the folks posting questions, her phone buzzed and rang incessantly, grating his nerves. "I'm not your driver, babe."

She eyed him, the steering wheel, then back to his face again. "Well, I lost out on the driving opportunity. So *I'm* not the driver."

"Warriors?"

"We have causes and a fight."

All right, Internet Badass. He stifled another eye roll and hopefully avoided a lecture about the definition of a warrior.

"The word has more than one connotation, Bishop. You and your soldier buddies don't have a lock on it." Her phone vibrated in her purse, and with a slamming hand, she silenced it. "Ready?" She was a warrior secretly pissed off at that potato sack purse of hers.

"Always."

Her phone buzzed again, and with another slap at it, she opened her door and hopped out, heading to the front door of her condominium.

Crazy was on the move. She strutted as if she owned the world, white skirt drifting. Bishop liked her dark-blue tank top, mostly because, when her hair moved, he got peeks of her back and shoulder blades. When he'd hooked an arm around them earlier, he was struck with how deceptively forceful she was. It reminded him that long ago, he'd spent an inordinate amount of time with his hands on her back.

Ella glided on the sidewalk, confident and carefree. Everything about her cadence and her easy nature-chic was picture perfect, except how she wrapped her arms around her bag. It didn't hang on her shoulder. No, she was strangling it to her breasts.

She twisted, staring at him in the truck. "Hey! Coming?"

That was his cue to stop gawking. He pushed out and opened the dually's door. "Hang on. Here I come with your skid of vegetation."

"We don't have to bring it all in. Just a couple for me and my neighbors."

"Got it." He pulled the first box from the truck bed and smelled the mint. Yup, he could see why she didn't want to move these babies out of her car. They were tiny air fresheners. Even out in the open, they had a strong scent. He juggled them and a few of the lavenders as he caught up to Ella, finding his key fob to lock the truck.

"Stop calling," she mumbled.

"Hey," he said to the doorman as they stepped into her building. Her mumbling alternated with a dose of looking at her phone and shoving it back into her purse. Bishop eased closer to her side as they moved from the open entryway to a wall. "I thought you loved that thing."

"Sometimes, it goes a little nuts." Her cell buzzed nonstop, and Bishop watched the screen pop up with phone calls that she swiped to ignore, slowing down as she pulled up her text messages and typed something that, from what he could eyeball, included a ton of exclamation points.

A response pinged, and Ella stopped and stared, before angry-typing back.

"Or you can tell me what's going on." He put his hand on her back, urging forward momentum. At the elevators, he pressed the call button. "Floor?"

"Three." But she didn't take her eyes off her phone, fighting or whatever, with someone.

Ella's building was modern to a fault, almost lifeless. Everything was metal and harsh. The natural light had bled into the entryway through a glass wall, but there was a harshness. The entire building had a contemporary feel.

He hated cold, unfeeling buildings. Though, bonus, he appreciated the high-tech security and doorman. That made his job easier. Titan would know who came in and out, and Parker, the genius behind all things tech-related at Titan, had already outfitted her condo with upgrades.

"This way." She led them out when the elevator door opened, never once looking at her surroundings. Not the best moves for someone with a stalker. Then again, that was why he was there. He looked both ways, doing what she should have. At her door, she slipped the phone into her purse, pulling a key out.

With one twist, she let him in. "Home sweet home."

She didn't bother disarming the security system. It was set to DISARMED. Irritation ground at his nerves. There was only so much that could be done if she chose not to use the damn thing. He set the lavender and mint down as carefully as he could.

Ella fretted over her plants. "Easy with those, please."

Hell. "Really?" If she wouldn't be careful with her life, damned if he was worried about banging up some plants.

"What?" she asked.

"Not smart, babe." He gave Ella a look, and she gave one right back. They'd been back in each other's lives for a few hours and had figured out how to communicate with eyeball bulges and eyebrow lifts. Not bad. Except what hers said was something along the lines of *bite me.*

"It's a pain in the ass, Muscles. I'm sick of it going off for no reason. Speaking of which…" A little dog and kitten ran into the room. "Meet no reason. This is Furry Baby and Little Kitty. My other security system."

Her dog, mostly made of cotton balls, didn't bark. Not what Bishop would deem a help-to-the-cause when he was an unknown in Ella's condo. Brick, his mutt of a dog, would have smelled, growled, and barked loud enough that the neighbors a mile away would have been aware of the meet-and-greet process. "I think this system isn't engaged either."

Her dog rolled over on its belly, asking for tummy rubs, and Bishop couldn't have had a better example of what a guard dog shouldn't do.

"Oh, be nice, Bishop." Ella dropped down and snuggled the rolling dog. "Furry Baby knows. If you were bad, he'd just love you to death."

The dog jumped up and smacked her with a kiss as if to agree. Bishop wasn't going to call any animal Furry Baby or Little Kitty out loud. They clobbered her face, making her squeal, and Bishop laughed. "Another battle for another day."

"Enough! Enough." Gasping in laughter, Ella rolled as both animals crawled over her. "Wait—Is that a gun tucked under your shirt?"

His eyes dropped to his side. "That would be a gun. Yeah." The same one that had been there all day.

"Why do you have a gun on still?" She batted the dog and kitten away, staring at the concealed carry that hadn't been overly intrusive, but he sure as hell wouldn't have left it in his truck or at work.

He offered her a hand to help her off the floor. "Why do you worry about fledgling bee populations?"

"Ha, ha." She gripped his hand, letting him tug her up. "I mean, I get it. Bodyguard work or whatever. But we were just coming here. So…you always have a gun on you?"

"Yes."

Ella scooped up the kitten and gave it a kiss before setting it down. "Always?"

"Yes."

"Movie theater?"

"Yes."

"Grocery store?"

"Yes." He walked farther into her condo and turned. This wasn't how he'd pictured Eloise—Ella—as an adult. Not that he'd pictured her. Well, he *had* had a thought or two, or ten, about her over the years. Who didn't think about an ex? Especially when they broke off under circumstances like theirs. But this was Ella as a very *green* adult whose living space was *perfect*. Every cushion and picture frame looked expertly placed. All things matched and, oddly enough, reminded him of Eco-Ella. The woman took branding to a whole new level. She lived it. "I'm armed at all the times."

Her eyes narrowed as she watched him assess her collection of knickknacks from what had to be many different trips to various parts of the world.

"What about during sex, Muscles? Bet you're not armed then." She didn't even bat an eye. Not a wink. Not a blush.

Nothing like the choked laugh lodged in his throat. "You win. Not on me."

He turned back to the wall of travel memorabilia, because he wasn't one to put his hot cheeks on display. Ella had made him blush? He *could* blush? That was news on several levels.

"I don't like guns," she explained. "Actually, I loathe them."

"Well, I don't like to shoot people, El, but there's a time and a place for everything."

"Well, this is my home," she murmured. "No shooting in here please."

Time for a subject change. Guns could be a hot-button issue with certain people, and he had a feeling Ella was the leader of that group. Besides, he was more interested in her cell hidden in her purse. "What's the deal with the calls?"

She groaned, taking his invitation for a shift in topics, and dropped her head back. "Some asshole gave my phone number out." She twirled, and her skirt flared as she flopped down on her couch. "I hate calls to begin with. So having my phone ring nonstop is maddening."

Instinct on high alert, Bishop shifted his weight and rubbed a hand over his jaw, catching the scent of lavender and mint. He tried to hold that herb-scented breath in for a five-count as his patience had officially worn thin. *One, two, three, fuck it...* "Think that's something you should mention?"

"To you?" She pushed upright on the couch, and her dog jumped next to her. "You're upset about the calls?"

"Uh, yeah." Maybe they needed a roadmap or a strict set of rules that she needed to follow.

Use your security system.

Report harassing phone calls.

Somehow, the woman in front of him seemed unable to see what he clearly could.

"First, stalker boy isn't calling me." Ella ticked off while pointing on a finger.

A headache scratched at his temples. "You don't know that."

"I do know that. I've been doing this Eco-Ella thing longer than you know."

"I know exactly how long you've been doing Eco-Ella. I read your damn file, El." *Mostly.*

"Well, not in enough depth to realize who I was, genius. Second—"

Round three, point goes to Eloise—Ella. "When death threats are involved, you and your people are not the ones who filter threats anymore."

"Bishop," she snapped. "Someone put my phone number on the Internet. That's it. It's out there. It happens *all the time*. I've changed my number before, but I'd rather wait it out. Updating the people who should have my number with the new one is a pain in the ass. This is my life."

"That you brought on yourself."

She threw her arms out. "Have I given you the impression that I don't like it? Because I do. I love it. More than you can ever imagine. It's taken me places, brought me my dreams, saved me from a hell that you don't know about, and I'm *not* changing it because some asshole out there doesn't like what I'm doing!"

"Damn it, Ella." Truth was, he didn't know the woman in front of him. He didn't know her wants or goals, and he had no clue what her dreams were. No idea what Eco-Ella had saved her from. Bishop cleared his throat. She was a Titan VIP. That's the only thing that mattered. "Fine. Agreed. I don't get this."

She nodded, the coloring on her cheeks fading. "Fine."

The kitten and dog sat on either side of her, and Bishop stood awkwardly in her living room. "Why don't you turn the volume off and vibrate off?"

"I might miss a notification I need." Her dog licked her neck, and for one vulnerable second, the pissed-off chick, who was having none of this conversation, relaxed and lay down on her couch.

"Only on phone calls," he countered.

"Yeah." She laughed as the dog tickled her until she shoved him away. "I'll go into my settings and auto-reject any call from unknown numbers."

Good. Compromise. Teamwork. They were heading in the right direction. This was something they could do. "Second, I need to know these things so we can rule out that it's *not* who you're calling stalker boy."

She propped up on an elbow, ready to protest, but he shook his head. "Ella, I know you've been doing this on your own."

"I have a team."

"Then with your team. And that you have a gut feeling on it, but now you have my team too." *The* team. The best in the world. Didn't she know that? "We need to be looped in for no other reason than to take out the noise as we monitor the chatter."

She focused on the dog. "It's not him."

"Glad you're an expert on stalkers and all—"

"*You're* not an expert. You're mister military gun-strapping, jerky-eating guy. With big muscles and stupid hair."

"What is your problem? Did we not just say team?" He cracked his neck. "And what the hell is wrong with my hair?"

"I don't know. The first part of my list, I hate. The second two just came out."

Chapter 10

Bishop sucked in his cheeks, semi-self-conscious, no matter how she'd meant it. He'd already mentally given her permission to throw cheap shots and be a jerk. He'd earned it, one of the reasons he would put up with it. She wouldn't be in this situation if he hadn't left her. They'd likely both have very different lives. But he didn't see the angle of her backhanded compliment and didn't like the way it settled in his chest.

He ran a hand into his *stupid* hair, needing to bring the conversation back to the *expert* talk. "Touché. But I *am* more versed with the criminal sect than you. I know the experts. So we play by my rules until no rules are needed."

Ella didn't budge.

Stifling the urge to pinch the bridge of his nose, Bishop moved to the edge of her couch, lifted her feet off, and dropped them. "Sit up a sec."

"Those were my feet," she said, pointing out the obvious.

"Give me a break." But point made. That was probably far too personal a touch than he should've made. But he was drawn to do it again, damn it.

"I would rather lie here with Furry Baby and Little Kitty."

He patted her skirt-covered knees, that half-hung off the

couch, then pulled his hand back. "What aren't you telling me?"

She shrugged. Demanding that she spit it out wouldn't work, and his temples throbbed. Bishop rubbed his forehead, and the instant scent of lavender and mint met his nose. He brought his hands closer and inhaled. They'd scent-stained his hands but now offered somewhat of a calming effect or, at the very least, a distracting one.

He wasn't a shrink and didn't know the first thing about getting Crazy to talk. But he knew that she had to say it. Whatever *it* was. "Do you want a beer, babe?"

"Ha!" Ella dropped her elbow over her face as her dog heard something imaginary and took off, the kitten chasing after it. "I could probably use one."

"You're wound a little tight. I'd say you could use a six-pack."

"I'd die if I drank a six-pack. Then you'd get fired."

"No six-pack for the lady." He patted her knee again, drawn to touching her. The soft skirt smoothed against his palm, and he let his hand rest.

Across the room, her kitten rolled over itself and a little toy, and her dog watched him. Ella hadn't removed her arm, which acted as a blindfold, and the whole scene was like a circus. Maybe he was the one who really needed the beer. He stood and walked toward the kitchen attached to her living room.

Ella hummed. "You're about to be very disappointed."

He pulled the obviously energy-efficient fridge open, and—*No. Shit.* Not only was there a lack of beer. There was also a lack of what he would call *food.* "I'm all for healthy eating and all, but…"

"I could use a trip to the grocery store. And I eat out."

That surprised him. He eyeballed the lack of edible options and unrecognizable labels. "Probably not where I do."

The fridge wasn't just filled with organic packages and the expected tofu. There was actually grass in her refrigerator. Ella had a patch of live, growing *grass* on the top shelf. Some parts were snipped down as though she'd…eaten it?

Bishop was a gym rat. It wasn't a moniker he owned, but he wasn't stupid. He clocked enough hours at enough gyms, lifted enough weights, worked out enough, traveled in enough circles, and ate healthy enough that he knew what wheatgrass was. But never in his life had he known someone who actually owned what he assumed was wheatgrass and actually cultivated it in their fridge.

She laughed. "Nope. Probably not where I shop."

"And you do not have beer."

"We can both agree that's a tragedy."

"Ella…?"

"Hmm?"

"There's grass in your fridge."

"High-quality grass."

All right, then. Bishop shut the fridge and went to her cabinets, inspecting them more out of curiosity than anything else. Everything had a place, and it was labeled. The Container Store could show up that second and do a photo shoot. No prep time or need to bring a label maker. Eco-Ella had them beat to the punch. Everything was organized, labeled, and…*hell.*

He spun, doing a slow look around her condo unit as two and two collided with such force that his stomach churned. Of course this place looked familiar. He might've paged through her file folder and her blog at the speed of a bullet, but this was her live *studio*—the home of Eco-Ella stock photos. Her condo was the basis for several pictures, backgrounds, and videos. Bishop stood in the center of Eco-Ella's home base, and a big-ass red flag crept higher and higher as he hoped he was wrong. "Hey…"

He checked under her sink. There were two receptacles, clearly labeled RECYCLING and LANDFILL. Inside of both, the trash and recycling had been smashed, compacted, or folded to make them as small as possible. Odd, but inconsequential.

"Crazy," he mumbled under his breath. "El... Do your fans know that you post pictures and do live video from your place? That this is your actual home?"

She shifted on the couch, pulling her arm free. "Yes. Live the lifestyle. The warriors know."

He shut the cabinet door. The public had a blueprint of her condo. Did Parker and Rocco know that? Surely someone would've mentioned it. Had that FBI realized that? Had *anyone* actually seen what Ella was doing and realized how much information she had provided to the public? Given the level of intel he'd read, even in the file folder he'd glanced through, the answer was no. The police reports, the FBI's take, everything was very surface level, assuming she was a potent cocktail of celebrity and activist, conjuring up angry fans and small obsessions. Nothing like what might come from this type of access. He could only assume that given this much personal information, the lines quickly blurred between reality and performance, fan and entertainer.

Bishop pulled his phone off his hip and shot Rocco a text message. *Eco-Ella shoots video from inside her home. All viewers have an all-access plan of the place.* His boss could disseminate that however he saw fit.

Finished perusing her kitchen for anything to drink or snack on, he gave up and returned to the living room. "Let's chat about the calls. When did they start?"

"The other day."

"And what did you think the source is?"

"The voice mails said something about—"

"*Oh.*" He lifted his eyebrows and gave her a look. "There are voice mails?"

"Not stalker-related. Tara's in uber-publicist-handling mode."

Why hadn't her publicist roped in Titan or the FBI? "Again, you guys have no idea."

"*Again*, I've been doing this for years. You're new to the Eco-Ella scene. It happens. It's called crazy grassroots people. This is what Tara is paid to do."

Comical, her calling people crazy, but now wasn't the time to address that. "Titan can handle the voice mails in question, and we'll go grab a beer."

"I deleted them."

"Right." He pinched the bridge of his nose, lavender and mint trying like all hell to come to the rescue with a little peace and calm. This time, Bishop inhaled deeply, relying on their soothing scents. He let the breath trail out. "Don't do that anymore. Okay?"

"Fine." Ella petted her dog, who'd nestled at her feet instead of looking at Bishop. "Maybe there are new ones since the calls kept coming."

"I'll loop Titan in, and they'll put an end to that in addition to you changing your phone settings. Okay?"

She nodded.

Bishop rubbed his face. "Ella… Is there anything else that maybe you should tell me that you haven't?"

All of her attention was on her dog. "Not that I can think of."

Not an overly convincing response. "Great. Well, if something pops up, let me know. Deal?"

She sighed, finally turning to him. The dog crawled into her lap, and the kitten used her talons to crawl up Ella's skirt. Once both animals were nestled in her lap, she gave them a quick squeeze. "Deal."

The front door clicked and flew open. "Girl! You would not believe my day!"

Bishop spun at the sound of a man's voice and reached for his weapon. In ran two fluffy, tiny dogs that were identical to the one in Ella's lap—and a squirrel. They were all followed by a skinny hipster kid sporting a utility belt of neon-colored dog waste bags.

Bishop's eyes narrowed on the squirrel, who wore a little tiny harness and leash. Free of the hipster, the rodent scampered into the room and jumped onto Ella.

"Hi, Tiny Tyke!" she squeaked. "Hey, guys!"

The kitten mewed, and Ella let the dogs run amok over her as she carefully petted the squirrel.

"Uh…" If there was a circus before, this was the very definition of a shit show. There were no words for the fury spinning around him and the questionable sanity of two people who didn't notice—one who had access to Ella's place. And Bishop didn't know who he was. *"Hello?"*

"You must be the new muscle around here." Hipster kid shot his hand out. "Manny, assistant to the stars, at your service."

"Oh, brother," Ella mumbled, nuzzling the squirrel.

"To the stars?" Bishop didn't know who to focus on. Maybe Ella had an Eco-Ella camera set up to catch this craziness, and he didn't know it. Wouldn't her fans go nuts for this? Or would that be more reality TV?

"Well," Manny said, "I'm also Ella's number one fan, and she's my biggest star. But my clientele is growing. Would you like my card? Do you have any pets?"

"A dog. But Brick's good."

Ella beamed. "You have a dog?"

"His name is Brick?" Manny questioned but shook Bishop's hand. "Who names their dog Brick?"

Surrounded by Little Kitty, Tiny Tike, and Furry Baby, Bishop could ask the same thing about names but decided not to. "There's been other muscle?"

Manny laughed with an amused smirk. "Jay would like to think so."

"The scrawny surfer guy?" Bishop asked, referring to the guy who was featured in some Eco-Ella post. "*He* was the muscle around here?"

"The boyfriend," Manny offered.

"*Ex*-boyfriend and *associate*," Ella piped up, focusing her attention on the squirrel. "My pets are my only significant others in my life, thank you very much. And Jay works at Eco-Ella. Let's not forget that. He actually has a job."

"So this is your…*squirrel,* and you have more dogs too?" Bishop took in the size of the condo. It was a one-level, apartment-style home—nice, spacious, and environmentally friendly. But large enough for a zoo?

"Nope," Ella said.

"They're her neighbors'." Manny offered the squirrel a treat. "She talked them into adopting the dogs so they wouldn't be far apart."

"These cuties are obviously related," Ella pointed out.

"Obviously." The place was immaculate for the number of animals that were in there. His place…maybe Brick slobbered more than her pets. How was her apartment so clean?

She held out the rodent as it gnawed on the treat Manny had given it. "Would you like to meet Tiny Tike?"

"I've met squirrels before. Thanks." *That* was not in her folder. Crazy was well beyond the cat-level of nuts, seeing as she had a varmint on a leash.

"He doesn't understand." Ella sat up, and finished with the treat, Tiny perched on her knee. "Just like you didn't get the bees. Which is why I quit explaining."

"He doesn't get the bees?" Manny repeated, looking dumbfounded.

"You're right. I don't. I wouldn't." Bishop clapped to

punctuate his agreement, but that sent the dogs whirling around him. “Easy. Okay. Stop. Down.”

Manny stepped forward. “Down.”

The fluffy white dogs stopped and obeyed the hipster’s one quiet word. The kitten meowed as though it was having a good laugh at him.

Manny picked Tiny up. “We need to get going. Oh, and nice job firing everyone up over Vamanato last night. I could hear the interwebs sharpening their pitchforks.”

What? Bishop pulled his phone out, quickly Googling to see what kind of online, riot-inducing post Ella had done to take on a corporate behemoth like Vamanato.

VAMANATO POISONS YOUR CHILDREN. AGAIN.

Nice headline… He clicked on the post as Manny and his animal crew made their way to the door. Ella followed, chatting about how successful last night’s post had been.

Bishop’s screen switched to the post their conversation was about, and there was Ella, sitting on a bed, frozen in a video thumbnail, ready to talk. There were tens of thousands of likes, and hundreds of comments and shares.

His gaze went back to the image of her sitting, almost innocently, in the middle of a king-size bed on her white comforter, surrounded by bright-turquoise pillows.

He was feet away from that bedroom, and his eyes drifted down the hall, wondering how intimately the world knew about her private space.

And was that when the calls had started…? Maybe she did know what she was talking about. But still, he wanted to be in the know. How could he protect her from a corporate giant if she didn’t let him?

Bishop’s gaze fell back to his phone. Sitting on the bed, she wore another tank top and skirt, seemingly her trademark outfit, and barely a smidge of makeup. Her eyes were bright, and her face looked freshly washed and rosy. Ella looked ready for time alone at home—not ready to go live and record a video about a business giant and talk about how their corporate behavior would hurt children. The powerful imaging and headline both haunted him and promised a solution even from a thumbnail, and he wasn't even the intended demographic. The post was masterful.

She rounded the corner. "Still game for a beer? We could stop somewhere for a drink first, before we drop off the herbs."

"I can always eat too." Nothing in her house would be considered edible, and he was hungry. "Works for me."

Ella pulled a bowl from a cabinet, filling it with water from a bottle. Then she whistled before placing it on the floor. "Furry Baby, water."

Meanwhile, Brick drank water from the tap or outside at a creek on the far side of his property. "If your kitten and dog are set—"

"Give me one minute, and I'll be ready."

"No problem. I'm going to call in, and maybe something will pop from the voice mails." Rocco's phone rang once as Bishop watched Ella head over to the window with a container of mint in hand. Filling his boss in and watching her simultaneously wasn't easy. She held out her phone and announced to the world *exactly* what she was about to go do.

"Hey, boss," Bishop cut off Rocco's response, none of which he had heard, anyway. "I gotta jump." He ended the call and had a thousand things to worry about as he walked directly in front of Ella.

Her gaze jumped, but she went back to the screen. Bishop cleared his throat, needing her to end what she was doing *now* and not wanting to cause a scene. He assumed she was livestreaming.

He *hated* people's need to stay connected via phone, no matter the cost. But maybe if he stared hard enough, she would realize that her topic of choice was problematic.

"So if you're in the area, swing on by! We'll be there."

Bishop threw his arms out, mouthing, "Ella!"

There was no way to avoid that. She saw him and wrapped up her stream. "What?"

"Why did you do that?" he snapped.

Her eyes were wide. *"What?"* She may have been flabbergasted, but more likely, she was shocked. Sweet, charismatic Ella likely didn't have people yelling at her. Or she did, but not out of sheer aggravation.

"I can't believe you did that. The things you do..." Bishop snatched the phone from her. The screen showed that a few hundred people had watched the impromptu appearance live, but that number was climbing fast as people saw it in replay. He shook the phone. "*With. Your. Phone*. You were holding that plant. I thought you were talking about stupid—"

"It's not *stupid*," she growled out. "And I reminded everyone to compost after dinner. I wanted them to see the mint, and I pimped the bee project in DC. If other cities took initiative like that, it'd be *freaking amazing*."

Was she getting in his face about bees? Why yes, she was. What the hell? Bees.

She took a step closer. Her head jutted as though explaining those things were beyond driving her to the point of madness. "It's my job, Bishop. Get over it."

He had to put the bees to the side because, no, just like she and Manny had pointed out, he didn't get them. "What else did you say?"

"That I was going out. Pics to come from my new favorite place." She bugged her eyes. "It's the job. It's a lifestyle job. I lived the life on TV, and now it's transferred to the blog. That's how the bills get paid, Bishop. I *am* the job. Do you get that? Or are we going to keep rehashing this? How else do sponsorships come in? Where else do ad dollars come from?"

"Telling people what you do and where you do it, in real time, is *stupid* when you have someone stalking you. And fuck yes, we will keep rehashing it."

"I…" She gave him a side eye, turned, and paced.

"Go huff some herbs, babe. You've got to see that I'm right on this one."

She threw her shoulders back and ignored him, letting her skirt spin as she power walked tiny circles in the living room until the march slowed to a thoughtful crusade. Her dog followed the dizzying circles, and the kitten clung to her skirt, hanging on for the ride. Ella didn't seem to notice either.

She went to the window, placed her hands on the sill, and took what had to be some deep yoga-infused breaths, because the only other people that had lung power like that were deep-sea divers. Her breath drifted out as slow and long as she pulled it in. Maybe she was about to drop an "ohm" or something. Hell, he didn't know. But the angry waves that rippled off her had lessened. For that, Bishop would give yoga a thumbs-up.

"Fine." Her shoulders relaxed until she balled her fists and rubbed her eyes, until she dropped her kneading knuckles. Her arms hung limp as she turned to him. "You made your point."

"I wasn't trying to make a point, El."

"Yes, you were."

"Okay. Yeah. I was. But I'd rather you just realize you're not a moron. Stupidity isn't something you can catch. And from my point of view, what you just did was stupid as shit."

Her chin dropped. "Easy, killer."

He pulled back, recalibrating. "Not the best move, all things considered."

"I just talk to people. I did it when there was nobody there, and then there was one person, then two. It was me, chatting about what I hoped for and what I knew was possible. I needed a…distraction and desperately needed to focus on something that was…important to me."

The defeat on her face cut straight to his chest. "You're not the girl with ten followers anymore. You've got, like, ten million."

"Boom," she whispered, tossing her hands up. "I had some. A lot, I guess. But not that many. And then, there they were. Just kind of blew up."

"*Under the Roof* was a tipping point, maybe." Reality TV would do that.

She closed her eyes as though maybe her popularity was something she hadn't come to grips with. "Talking candidly is a habit. And it's what I do. I want to be authentic."

Now that was a stretch. "What's authentic in this room?"

Bristling, she opened her eyes and became a fortress again. "You don't know me anymore, Bishop. This is all me. I like everything about this place. It has order. It is where it is, how it should be."

Completely in control…okay, so he could appreciate that. A lack of control had, in one way or another, ruined their lives. "Fair. Being authentic, staying true to yourself? That, babe? All that won't matter if you're not here to keep your stuff going. There's no Eco-Ella without Ella. Figure out how to balance the truth and your lifestyle with your reality."

"And what's my reality?" she asked.

He couldn't tell if that was sarcastic or genuine, so he ran with it the way he needed the conversation to go. "The world is messy. Trust but verify, and when you can't, which you can't with millions of fans, have no faith. Zero. Zip. Zilch."

Her blue eyes lost their shine, and her lashes fluttered down. "That's awful."

"That's the path you've chosen if this is how you want to keep going." He wished it was more black and white for her. She had such a good heart, always had.

"I can't look at the world that way."

"Ella—"

"But… I can keep my faith. Do what I do, and you, Locke, Titan… *Jared*," she said in a tone that Bishop totally could appreciate. "All of you can see humanity for what it is, and I can see it for what it *can be*, and desperately protect it from where we're headed."

No wonder the woman had an army of followers behind her. She didn't give up. All she needed was a level of protection. Bishop took a step closer, wondering how wild of a ride it would be to guard this eco-trailblazer. "How about this?"

Her chin tilted up, hope flickering.

"Put yourself on delay or be generic. If we're headed out for a beer, that's all you need to say. No '*come and meet me*' or maybe 'I'm posting it when I get back *tonight.*' Just post the pictures after you've left."

She looked to the side as though she were considering what seemed so simple.

"If you have to say a specific place, say it as you leave. That way you're there, but we get in the car and roll out."

She nodded, rolling her lower lip into her mouth. "Makes sense."

"Will you delete it?"

"What I just posted?"

"Yeah."

"Okay."

"Then later you can be as authentic as it gets *and* safe." Okay, that was about as deep as Bishop could go. "Let's go."

He turned for the door, wishing he had the ability to down a six-pack, but the woman kept him on his toes, and he was on the clock. His drink would be a nice, tall glass of nothing with a kick.

"Bishop?"

He turned. She hadn't moved.

"I'm sorry. I don't think of the world the way you do. I put too much trust in people I can't see who have said they think like me, and maybe I shouldn't do that."

Finally, they were on the same page. "Maybe you shouldn't."

"And sometimes, it seems pretend. I live here, just me in Virginia. Not Hollywood, not NYC. Nothing flashy."

"It's real, babe." He shifted, and she did too.

Her tongue darted out, licking her bottom lip. "And honestly…forget it." She laughed quietly. "Can we make it liquor instead?"

"Is there something eco-friendlier about liquor over beer?" Because if there was, he was about to love his beer even more.

"No." A genuine smile warmed her eyes, replaced by an edge of amusement. "I just like the way it feels, especially after a conversation like this."

Not a crazy-girl answer. That was as all-American as he could've wanted. "Now you're talking my language." He walked back to her, grabbed her hand, and pulled her toward the door. "Let's go. You've had a shitty few days."

"Weeks," she corrected him. "And I need a drink."

"Hell yeah, you do."

She brushed against him, leaning on him and not letting go. The scent of her lavender plants caught in the air as she stepped to the door. It was the closest they'd been in years, and at that moment, he was hyperaware of her skin on his and her soft hair touching him. The front hallway was too small for them to pause side by side. But they did.

Lavender and mint clung to them, and she lingered against him. The day had been emotional. Maybe it justified their closeness. He didn't know. And the job would never allow such things. But they had a history. If they hadn't known each other, though, that conversation would never have happened.

Ella let go of the arm that had needlessly guided her to the door. Her fingers drifted down his forearm, their tips not quite breaking contact, skimming over his arm hair that spiked to attention. Awareness crested as their touch finally broke.

When she turned, the white skirt swayed. The material was softer than air and light enough that even with the slightest change of direction, it swished. He swallowed over the lump in his throat. Once the alarm was set, they had only seconds to vacate, but in his mind, the dark-blue tank top and long white skirt were a sudden tease.

With crystal clear clarity, it was easy to imagine her pressed against her front door instead of setting the alarm. Not an appropriate thought for him to have as she readied to punch in the code. At least she was doing that…but that wasn't where his mind was. He was wondering how it would feel to spread her sandaled feet apart. One hand on her back, holding her still, and with the other hand, he could reach all the way down to her ankle. Had a long skirt ever been so sexy? It covered so much and made him so curious. If he ran his palm up her calf, dragging that fabric up, how would her skin feel? If her legs were anything like her arms and shoulders, they would be smooth and athletic, something to hold on to, to flex his fingers into.

His mouth watered. If he wasn't working, if she weren't his to watch out for…if this wasn't an arrangement like it were, he would keep walking, press her breasts against the door, and his erection against her ass.

It'd been years since he last stole her breath, yet he could remember the sound as if it was last week. The sighs she made. The way her chest would heave and her eyes would flutter when they were in bed, as he readied to take her. *Hell…*

He let out a breath, and it shook. The alarm beeped, signaling they had to leave, and Ella turned around, unaware of the knot in his throat and his semi-hardening cock, but she met his hungry stare and had to have known in a hot second where his mind had been.

Damn it.

A quick fire hit her cheeks, and Bishop backed away, swallowing away urges that should have been more hidden, impulses that should've been non-existent.

"Ready?" He twisted the knob and exited into the hall first, giving a quick sweep that didn't distract him, but at least toned down his arousal.

She followed behind, turning a key in the lock. "We'll grab the herbs after dinner." Her eyes were everywhere but near him, and without a doubt, the woman was a mind reader. "And—"

Shit. Damn it. He needed to fix this now. "Hey, wait." Bishop stood in the hallway. Ella's pink cheeks and lack of eye contact were all the confirmation he needed to know he'd been busted checking her out. "Part of my gig with you is you have to always feel safe with me."

She moved her purse from one shoulder to the next. "I know."

"I'm here to watch out for you, no questions asked. You have to rely on me, without hesitation. That's the way it works. You have to trust me."

She lifted her chin, finally meeting his gaze. "I know. Jared explained that to me."

"We're good?"

"Yes."

"No matter the past." Or no matter if he had just ogled her, which would never happen again.

"No matter what happened all those years ago."

"Or..." How did he word this without sounding like a crass pervert?

"You're like the asshole older brother I never had, making sure I do what I'm supposed to do. Right?"

Asshole older brother. *Brother*. Couldn't get any less sexy than that, could he? "Right. Just like that," he agreed, hating the description and embracing it simultaneously.

"Great!" She marched toward the elevator, and he let her lead. Ella punched the button for the elevator, and she was almost chipper. "Drinking with my grumpy, grouchy, older brother babysitter. Then we get to run errands. Fun."

CHAPTER 11

ELLA'S NERVES WERE IN HER throat as Bishop opened the door to the Bistro Lounge. How stupid could she have been? Clinging to him at the front door of her condo? She squeezed her eyes shut for the thousandth time. When he had grabbed her hand to leave, she'd lost her mind. She'd simply forgotten anything except for the simple art of breathing.

And those breaths…they felt delicious. The kind that tickled her pressure points and slipped up and down in her throat. They made her heart race with each step toward the front door, and when they stopped, she was drunk on Bishop.

That was absurd—being aroused without doing a thing. He didn't touch her seductively, didn't even have anything that nice to say. But what he did do was something that hadn't happened in a long time. He told her the truth. He acted with what felt like her best interest in mind. Not her blog or her business, but her safety. Ella hadn't thought about that in…ever.

Then he walked her across the room, like a man.

So simple.

But her nipples hardened and surely, he had to notice.

Her cheeks heated again, and she couldn't look him in the eye. Was she so easy to fall for such domineering commands? But there was a selflessness to Bishop, which made him even more attractive—except he absolutely didn't want to be there.

And there was that small part in which he was *paid* to be by her side.

Ugh.

The Bistro Lounge was one of her favorite vegan spots, and bonus, it was within walking distance to her condo. Those were the only two things she had in mind when she picked the location. But with Bishop at her side, she noticed the lights were dark, a stark contrast to the sunshine that had warmed her back. Jazz played low. This bistro was a place to get in the mood, and she didn't mean for that to happen at all. Another strike against her. They had been playing games earlier. Three rounds to her, one to him. Did he think this was a setup? That she was trying to seduce him or make up for what had happened before?

"Trendy, huh?" He took the lead to the bar, where she couldn't have been more out of place if she had tried.

"Something like that. Closest place for a vodka soda."

He pulled the barstool out for her, and she hopped up. As he lumbered himself onto the velvet-covered seat, he leaned back, looking at ease, but taking in the room. Was he inspecting it or judging it? Watching for stalker boy or making an assessment of where she had chosen?

And why did she care?

Ha.

The man in charge of her safety had given her the warm fuzzies. Except they were the hot tinglies. They had a boatload of unaddressed things to say that neither were apparently going to touch, and he had said a *ton* about what Eco-Ella had become. Celebrity culture, no matter what niche corner it was, was still hard to embrace. She hadn't figured it out, and he was judgmental.

He shifted, still eyeing the various parts of the bar and table section, then put his hand on her back. "You good?"

A thousand nerve endings jumped up and down, screaming *yes,* while her mind shook a scolding finger at them all to stand down. "Can you flag the bartender?"

He laughed and grabbed a menu. "Easy, Thirsty."

The bartender appeared a blink of a second later, tossing two cocktail napkins out with a tip-winning grin. "*Hey, Ella.* It's nice to have you stop in again. Last time was great for business. Thanks!"

Bishop gave her a look.

"Hi. I'm glad you remember." She ignored Bishop. That wouldn't be happening tonight since she'd deleted the post. "It's hard to get good vegan food sometimes."

"We try. What'll you start with?"

"Grey Goose and soda."

The bartender turned to Bishop. "Anything for you?"

He flipped the menu back and forth. "Are the burgers any good?"

"Nope." The bartender shook his head, waiting expectantly.

She agreed, mostly because she didn't want to smell it, though she knew this place did order from a sustainable, animal-friendly producer. "But the shiitake Nori rolls are to die for."

The bartender pointed at Ella. "Our fave girl is correct."

Bishop lifted a brow. "When in Rome. And a water."

"Water?" she asked.

"On the clock, babe."

Oh. Right. She was work. "Ah, right."

"Give me a few, and it'll be right out." The bartender smiled and left.

Bishop twisted her way. "Doubtful that rolled-up mushrooms are better than a burger. But yeah, okay, if you're wrong, I'm grabbing a point in our game."

"Our game is back on?"

"Never stopped, babe." His gaze pivoted through the room, landed on her—lingered—then went back on patrol.

Bishop casually rotated on his stool. The night-watch act was methodical and unhurried as it breezed across the bar. A chance observer wouldn't pick up on his actions, but every few minutes in their conversation, the rotation hit all points of the room and landed back on her face. Silly, but Ella found herself eagerly awaiting his organized, premeditated cycle. Here his glance came. On her again.

Mmmm. Her reaction was unintentional. Everything about him annoyed her. His too-large muscles were obvious, and his hair looked as if she shouldn't touch it, though she wanted to. The dark room was in shadows, but she could still tell how his green eyes held a fire. One that brightened…

And when his head pivoted, his gaze stayed with her, holding onto her for one micro-blink of a second too long. It felt so familiar…just like it had before, when she hadn't let go of him, when he'd freely given her that same look but let it linger.

Or was it in her head?

Maybe it was a combination of both. Something had to be uncontrollable when a man was that virile, that manly. All muscle and girth and width, and…strength. Someone like Bishop had to have a deadly, intoxicating amount of testosterone pumping through his veins.

His rotating observation stopped on her again. "Your hair's longer." His simple observation made her shiver, prickling until her nipples hardened. "Your skirts are too."

Ella pushed a stray strand of hair off her cheek. "I like how it feels."

He rolled his lip into his mouth. "I like them both too."

It was just conversation, but her lungs took every word and

made it hard to breathe. "I—oh, thanks." She focused on the vodka soda that arrived and gulped a sip, then another.

"Easy, Ella," Bishop teased. "Bad day and all, but I think we opted for lightly toasted. Not slammed."

She put it down, and he pushed the drink back an inch. Part of her wanted to elbow him for the alpha dick move. She could take care of herself, thank you very much, and the presumptuous bodyguard act could keep to the parameters of stalkers, not alcohol, except he was correct. She needed to slow down.

"Guess I was thirsty." Or seeking refuge under the deceptively protective arm of liquid courage.

"Did you want to order a water and..." Bishop grabbed the menu and perused, clearly at a loss for what some items were. "Some of these falafel things as well? The tahini sauce sounds solid. And vegan."

Might not be a bad idea. "In a few."

He'd thought about her food preferences. That struck her as sweet. *Oh, come on.* She was searching for cutesy actions, thinking like she had when they were younger—what a bittersweet memory.

"Right." He tossed the menu, and she scooted her drink closer, slugging another sip.

"Seriously," he said. "I promise it's not going anywhere."

Correct, and it was also starting to hit her empty stomach. That was both a good and bad thing as she started to relax. "How'd you get stuck babysitting me?"

The bartender placed Bishop's water in front of him.

"She'll have a water also," Bishop added.

"Bossy." She eased back, dropping her head and letting the liquor warm her from the inside out. "But thanks."

The effect was marvelous, if just for the moment. He was right, though. She needed to chill, lest she puke on his jeans.

"A water for Ella," the bartender said. "Anything else?"

"Double the order of nori rolls. And throw in some bread or something."

"We don't have bread."

Ella's laugh slipped out when she saw Bishop's expression. She could imagine what he thought at that revelation.

"Oh, really?" he muttered.

The bartender didn't laugh.

Bishop patted her hand. "Falafel us."

With a quick nod, the bartender went to punch in their order.

She giggled. "Your face was comical."

He smiled. "When?"

"Just now. No bread, and it was like your world shattered."

"Nah." He tilted his head, a questioning look loosening his face. "Though, really? No bread."

"I promise." She finished her drink and reveled in the buzz from slamming her cocktail. "If I had known you were such a carb guy—"

"It was for you, babe." He rotated on his quick check through the bar. "You warned me; I was prepared for a lightweight. Though a pleasant, giggling Ella has me off guard."

"I just…" She sighed, now feeling the vodka in her blood. Both false courage and the uncanny inability to shut up were edging close. She wished the falafel or nori rolls had arrived as soon as he ordered, but magic was impossible. "Truth is…"

He didn't say a word.

"The stalker thing…sucks."

Bishop nodded.

"I don't let anyone know. Everyone thinks I'm rock solid. But it's all…" She shrugged. "How do you know what you're looking for when you do that thing?"

"Thing?" he asked.

"When you check the room. Look over here and there, but casually. You have a pattern."

A moment of surprise washed away, and Bishop studied her. He rolled his bottom lip into his mouth and let it go. "Sometimes, people behave certain ways. Sit or act in a particular manner. But primarily, I'm a solid reader of people."

She narrowed her eyes and leaned forward, curling her finger for him to lean in.

He chuckled but inched closer. "What?"

"I heard you call me Crazy under your breath. You can't be *that* good."

He laughed, tossing his head back. "You do some crazy-ass shit, Ella." But then he put an arm around her shoulder and huddled them close again. "I can tell you have a strong backbone, stronger will, and an inner strength that some men I've served alongside would kill to have."

Her mouth parted, and a tingle of electricity ran along her neck.

"That's why you have the following you do." Bishop ran his hand up and down her back before sitting upright. "You're the real deal."

His belief in her sent tingles cascading across her skin. Even the little hairs on her arms stood up, as though they believed him too. Bishop needed to give a few of these lines to Tara. She hadn't called or texted with any *helpful* advice in the last two days.

Bishop winked. "I didn't expect to leave you speechless."

She shut her mouth and squared herself. "You didn't, Muscles." But he *so* had. "I haven't told anyone that the stalker thing has me spooked."

Their food arrived, and her mouth watered. "Smells amazing."

"I can't smell a thing." Wary would be the best way to describe Bishop, though. But after a questioning look, he turned his attention back to her. "You were always hypersensitive with your senses."

"Including how my heeby-jeeby alert is in overdrive."

"I won't tell a soul. As long as you promise to trust me."

"Of course." She should say more, but whatever it was wouldn't come.

"Time to try my first mushroom wrap."

Painting on her best face, she grabbed one too. "If you don't love it, I'll take you anyplace else, your choice, my treat. You can have anything you want until you're completely satisfied."

He paused, dark-green eyes burrowing into hers until she needed to squirm. What she said was innocent, but his look was loaded. It wasn't dirty, but damn…

He stabbed a bite of the nori roll and put it in his mouth. "Tasty."

"Good. I'm glad." Ella let out a breath she hadn't realized she'd been holding. Her heart pounded in her ears.

"El…" He took a sip of his water and leaned forward as if to tell her a secret. They were cheek to cheek, and Bishop's warm skin grazed hers as his hand touched her back.

His touch was more intoxicating than the vodka on an empty stomach, better than any memory of sex. Just his touch, his lips and breath tickling her skin, caused her stomach to flutter. Ella leaned into him, bracing herself with a hand on his hard, denim-covered thigh. Even relaxed, the muscle was so broad and cut that it surprised her. What kind of power could Bishop unfurl in bed?

Heart racing, she tilted toward his chest, and her hair fell, a curtain hiding them from the dark world.

"Your three o'clock, babe. Is that your ex-slash-assistant sitting at a table, eyeballing the shit out of you?" Bishop eased back.

Devastated that it was a diversion and shocked at her sheer visceral reaction, Ella crashed as though she couldn't let go of her lead-lined disappointment. But as she twisted to see Jay actually sitting at a table in the bar, watching them, a new wave of irritation quickly cropped up.

For a moment, she had pretended this was real—that Bishop cared about her without being paid, and the chemistry and body positioning were more than him scanning for threats. And for all that was holy on this green planet, what was Jay doing there?

Bishop put a hand on her cheek, directing her attention to him. "Yes or no?"

"That's Jay."

Bishop pulled back. "That is one angry-looking assistant you have."

"Well…" She gave Bishop a pointed look, dropped her eyes back and forth between them, then raised her eyebrows. "We used to date. This looks…not what it is. No one's a perfect saint."

"Something's off," Bishop countered.

Ella almost laughed, inching back, but Bishop huddled them close again. Her stomach dropped at the ruse. "Jay's harmless. We work together. Our schedules match up; our eating habits do too. Not a lot of places serve awesome vegan. So"—she shrugged—"no conspiracy."

Bishop stood up. "He's your ex and coworker, and lucky us, he's here."

"Don't cause a problem." Ella placed her hand on Bishop's side to stop him and—whoa, not the time to notice a solid sheet of muscle—she stood up too. "We'll go say hi. No big deal."

"Let's."

"Oh, brother," she groused.

"For the sake of argument, no explanation as to who I am." With his hand on her back, he guided her to a glaring Jay.

"All right." A few steps later, they were beside the table of her displeased friend. "Hi, Jay."

Jay stood, staring at Bishop as though his buck-fifty frame could take the man who had his hand on Ella's back. Not a chance.

Not even if Bishop were twenty sheets to the wind and didn't see it coming. But leave it to Jay to act like an asshole.

Bishop threw his hand out to shake. "Hey, man. Ella said you were a friend of hers."

"I am." His tone of voice could've frozen the Kalahari Desert.

"The name's Bishop." His hand remained out.

"*Jay*," Ella hissed.

Jay darted his eyes to her then met Bishop's grip and didn't say a word. Only then did she realize that in all the time she had dated Jay, they'd never talked about meaningful life outside of work, never talked about growing up, about old flames or whatnot, because the name Bishop would've stuck out to Jay, and she would've remembered telling *anyone* about what had happened. But no. If she had realized that before now, it would have been a clue that they were nowhere near as serious as the amount of time they'd spent together would indicate.

"Nice to meet you," Bishop continued. "Do you want to join us?"

"No."

"All right, then. You were staring like you wanted an invite." Now it was Bishop's turn to change his tone of voice. Though it wasn't cold, it was a warning. "If you change your mind, walk over and pull up a stool. I'd love to get to know you."

Jay dropped to his chair as his good-bye. "I'll see you later, Ella."

Jeez, Jay. "See you at work."

Bishop turned them toward the bar, placed his hand on her back, and out of the corner of her eye, she saw Jay throw cash on the table and leave. "What's his problem?"

Bishop's jaw flexed. "That dude is a problem."

"He's not used to seeing me around other guys—not that…obviously you're another guy. I mean—"

"I'm aware how we looked to him."

"Right." Bishop gave a hand as she lifted herself onto her barstool, annoyed that Jay had worked his way into her time with Bishop—not *her* time with Bishop. What was she thinking? This was not a get-to-know-him-again date. This was food before errands with her brother-like protector. Alpha extraordinaire, who happened to be hot…and nice…and many of the things she remembered from before.

"You okay?" he asked.

"Sure." She brushed off his question. Bishop hadn't changed like she had. He'd always been caring; that quality defined him. It might not have been apparent, but she'd had behind-the-stage access. He'd always been the first one to stand up and say something. Judging by his introduction to Jay tonight, that hadn't changed.

And she vividly remembered Bishop's lips. Not that his lips had anything to do with who he was or what he had to say. But they were powerful in many, *many* ways.

His words and kisses had held meaning. They both had the ability to drive her wild. Now his lips were just as full, as pink, and as delicious as she had ever seen. With years of growing up on their side, they were likely more talented than she knew.

A flush ran to her core.

Back on his stool, Bishop was closer than before, and she chose to power down her water rather than concentrate on what it would feel like to kiss him. She pushed her vodka soda glass farther back.

She motioned to the water. "I think I need to order another one of these babies."

Bishop's doubtful once-over didn't earn her a quick drink order. "Or we could wrap up and go deliver your plants."

"Herbs."

Bishop's brows bit together as his stare focused over her shoulder. His hand went possessively to her thigh, and before she could read his face, a harsh hand landed on her shoulder.

"Ella," Jay snapped.

She twisted to see Jay's tight face. "*What*?"

His fingers flexed into her bare skin. "I was checking if you need anything before I leave."

Ella pulled out of his grip. "No."

"No," Jay repeated. He glared at Bishop. "Is this a date?"

"*Jay!*"

Bishop tossed his arm over her shoulder. "Why don't you go home, buddy."

"Is it?" Jay asked.

"It's none of your business," she snapped, leaning into Bishop. "Really."

Jay's face darkened, but he turned, shoving a barstool out of the way and grumbling loudly as he left.

She turned into Bishop, close to his face, close to everything she liked about him, and whispered, "I'm sorry. I don't know what got into him."

Bishop's green eyes had darkened. "He's not ready to let you go."

"I've been old news." With the slightest of head shakes, Ella wondered out loud. "I'm so blown away by his behavior right now. And embarrassed."

"Old news, only for one of you."

Ella inched back on her barstool, mortified. "I'm sorry. You have, I'm sure, a real job. And here you are, stuck with me and *this* drama. I've literally never seen him behave like this."

Bishop put his hand on her back. "Don't worry about it."

Still, she shook her head. "When Titan showed up at Tara's office, they wore SWAT gear. Face masks and guns and vests and things strapped to all their body parts. That's what you do, and this has to be the worst job ever."

"It's fine."

"And I'm the biggest headache ever."

"I like a little crazy sometimes. Nothing I can't deal with." He elbowed her then pulled her close. "Kidding, kidding."

"Seriously, you've got what I'm sure is a stellar military career, and here you are, eating nori rolls and dealing with my ex."

"Honestly, it's fine."

"It's not."

"Ella—"

She closed the distance and pressed her lips to his. His lips were fuller than she ever would've dreamed, and his mouth more potent than she could've imagined a man's being.

Bishop edged away, but she leaned in, unable to break from the kiss. A tiny, remorseful sigh started at the back of her throat as she pulled away—but Bishop kissed back. *Finally*. His lips melted, and his tongue sliced to hers. He pulled her closer. Her blood rushed, and her mind raced—all of her did. It was a kiss in the middle of a bar, but the room drifted until she would have sworn they were alone.

Then he stilled again, slowly giving her a squeeze. It was a hug that said so much. She squeezed her eyes shut as his lips left hers, and gently, he gave a careful peck before letting their foreheads touch.

"Ella..." He breathed her name.

For those few seconds, he had her, held her, their foreheads kissing. Then he broke away with another squeeze.

God, she was so stupid.

"I shouldn't have done that." He brought his bottom lip into his mouth and shook his head, looking away, but then came back stronger than before. Classic Bishop. "If you want someone else on the job, I'll have him here in twenty minutes. No questions."

"That was me." Heart in her throat, she wanted to cry. "I'm sorry."

"No. Don't say that."

How bad did she just screw everything up? "Really—"

"El, come on. No big deal."

No tears! But they welled. "*I* shouldn't have done that, and you shouldn't have offered what you just did."

He didn't respond.

"I won't do that again. I swear." *Please don't leave.* She hadn't told a soul she was scared and didn't want to trust anyone else with that.

His eyes were unreadable, and his jaw flexed. The sinew in his neck showed when he turned away, and her heart sank. Bishop reached for his water and took a long drink. "Your falafel are cold."

"I don't think it matters," she whispered.

He grabbed a bite from the ignored plate. "Not quite beef jerky level of delicious, but it'll make do."

She buried her face in her hand. "You're trying to make me feel better."

"Ease up. Here. Wait."

She unburied her face and watched him slug back the rest of his water. "What?"

With a hand on her cheek, he pushed a strand of rogue hair back into place and dipped his head to hers. Bishop pressed his mouth to hers, kissing her, giving her a tease of what had happened before, enough to steal her breath and show her who was in charge.

His hand cupped the back of her head, tilting it where he wanted. Then, just as startling and perfunctory as it started, he ended the kiss. "Now we're even."

Chapter 12

With late summer crawling into fall in Virginia, sometimes the days were hot, and sometimes Ella froze. But nights were another story. The temperature had dropped, and so had Bishop's arm as they walked out of the bar. If she'd been thinking about anything besides her distraction-worthy ex-boyfriend bodyguard, then she would've remembered a sweater. Though at the moment, she wasn't complaining as he rubbed her arm.

He guided her through the gaggle of people crushed together at the front of the trendy bistro, but as they hit the open sidewalk, he put a regrettable amount of space between them. Which was what he should have done. This was not a date, no matter what Jay's impressions were or where her mind went.

But that kiss…

Ugh. That kiss. It was a pity kiss, an even-the-score kiss. The damn thing had singed her lips and scorched her mind. Ella had nearly melted to the barstool. The fire alarms were lucky they hadn't blared for how much smokin' hot heat had to have rolled off of her when he cupped her cheek. Could there be a worse reason for a man to press his lips to hers?

"I didn't get you toasted," he said, trying to break through the awkward tension that pulsed between them on the empty sidewalk.

Did she want his hands on her or not? Did *he?* Did the kiss count toward their back-and-forth game?

"No. But I did get you fed." They rounded the corner. "We both accomplished our goals—*Oh!*"

A man jumped toward them.

Bishop reacted before she could process what was happening. He pushed her against the wall, stepping between her and the fast-moving man. Bricks abraded her arm as her elbow hit, funny bone stinging. Stars shined, while her temple throbbed.

The sound of splashes and a pop rained around her, and Ella stumbled, lost her footing in her long skirt, her sandal catching on the cotton. But she spun, still on her feet, and Bishop's strong hands caught her, twirling her in a fluid motion, so fast and fierce that she wasn't in control. One shoe on, the other bare, Ella's face was pressed to his back, and her shoulders were pushed against the wall all before she could gasp out, "What the hell!"

"Hands in the air," Bishop growled out, grabbing his gun. He looked as if he were right out of a movie, though he was so broad, and she was so pinned, that she couldn't see. But his stance was deadly, and his weapon was in play.

"Hey! Hey!" The first *hey* had been playful, the second one concerned. "What are you doing?"

Ella had no idea who the young guy was, nor why *he* was confused. Bishop's tense body relaxed, and his arms dropped enough that she could tell he was assessing the situation rather than reacting in a defending role.

"Put your hands in the air," he ordered again, stepping away from her.

Only then did she see the dark, wet marks on the sidewalk. Ella took a cursory step to the side. *Oh!* Even in the early night light and streetlamp glow, she could see that Bishop was covered in green goo.

Across from him was a messy-headed guy with a messenger bag, easily college-aged, who had his hands semi-tossed up.

Bishop holstered the gun back on his hip. "Geez, I'm not getting paid enough to do this."

The guy dipped his hand into the bag and pulled out what looked like a water balloon.

Bishop's fist flew before the guy could take aim, knocking the green-blob-throwing jerk on his butt in one solid punch. The balloon bounced and popped on the sidewalk. The same thick green goo that covered Bishop now formed a circle of demarcation between the men.

"What is going on?" she shrieked.

Bishop grabbed the guy by his T-shirt collar, lifted him, then slammed him against the wall. He removed the bag from the guy's shoulder and tossed it. Two additional balloons rolled out of the bag's flap.

"Ella." Bishop ran his hands along the man's pockets, from his stomach to armpits, then along his shorts. "Call the cops."

"Hey, man," their attacker whined. "Don't do that. That wasn't part of the gig. Come on."

Part of what? Her mind reeled to make sense of what was happening.

"Why wouldn't I?" Bishop spun the man to face Ella and him then pushed the guy back against the wall. "What are you talking about?"

"*The game*."

"What game?" Bishop took a step forward, and when he was in protector mode, there was nothing sweet and gentle about him. Scary and lethal were the two best descriptors that came to mind.

"Are you not playing? I thought you were who I was supposed to..." The guy's confusion scored across his forehead. "No. You are. I saw her picture."

"Explain," he growled.

"I don't know, seemed like your buddy was cheating, but whatever, easy cash."

"For what?" Bishop roared.

"Whatever you guys called it, hand-to-hand paintball. Or whatever this crap is."

Bishop snarled. His chest rumbled low and deadly. She watched his eyes dart around the empty street, and if she'd been on the receiving end of his wrath, she might've peed or passed out. Part of her wanted to chirp up that violence wasn't the answer, but she wasn't the one covered in who-knew-what, and the cops were the reasonable answer.

Bishop inched closer to the man. "I don't know what you're talking about."

"The other team paid me," he sputtered. "I thought it was all fun." He looked at her, his eyes narrowing. "And…games."

"Eyes on me." Bishop leaned even closer. "Keep explaining."

"On Monarch. I grabbed the gig in the DC-Northern Virginia IRL forum."

"IRL?" Bishop asked.

"In real life," she said.

The guy nodded. "Moolah came through up front." His voice wavered. "With directions and where to get her." He paused. "Sorry. I thought it was a thing. A game."

"How much?"

"Hundred bucks."

"How?"

"MonarchMoney," their goo-thrower volunteered.

Ella bit her lip. Again with the untraceable cash sent through social media.

"Christ," Bishop grumbled.

"Call your FBI contact, Ella."

"*What*?" The guy's eyes bulged. "I honestly just thought it was fun times. I read the whole thing wrong. Look, I'm sorry. Your name is Ella? Ella, I'm sorry. I—oh my freakin' God. Are you Eco-Ella?" He took a step forward. "*You're Ella Leighton.*"

Bishop dropped his head back. "This is happening?"

She was hesitant and didn't know how to react. The guy was paid to slime her, but he just morphed into an okay fan. "Hi, yes. That's me."

"I'm, like, a huge fan. Seriously. I'm so sorry. So sorry."

"Not a big deal." She bit her lip, having no idea what the right response was. People played Pokémon Go, they married after meeting online, so surely they would take online money and agree to play paintball. Why would anyone think it was nefarious? Right? The guy was a college kid. This was their world…how they grew up. She tried to put herself in his shoes and understand.

"It is a big deal, El," Bishop added, not putting himself in anyone's shoes but his own. "It's a big fucking deal. You, asshole, threw crap on a stranger for cash. Do you realize how screwed up that is?" He shook his head, backing up, and mumbled, "What kind of world do we live in right now?"

The kid pulled his phone from his back pocket. "Could I get a picture with you?"

"Are you shitting me?" Bishop snapped.

"Um…" She grinned uncomfortably. "It's been a really crazy night. I'm not sure."

Bishop pivoted to her, and his hardened jaw hung slack. "This is not okay. Do you not know that, Ella? The answer is *no.* No pictures."

She tried to turn on some sort of telepathic portal between them that screamed this was her job and she was trying to figure out what the right move was. Him yelling like a protective buffoon wasn't it. But, obviously, they didn't have their telepathic wavelengths set up yet.

Awkwardly, Ella shifted between the two men. "He didn't know." Really, what she needed to do was manage how this conversation went before it ended up on a Monarch forum. Ella had one chance to control how the story would be presented to the public. "Sure, one picture would be sweet."

"He took money to slime a stranger. He's lucky he's living."

"*Bishop*, give me a minute." She stepped closer to the man. "What's your name?"

"Stan, and dude, I'm sorry." The guy was sidling up to her for a selfie. "This is really epic. I can't believe this is what—oh! And I was supposed to tell you good luck this weekend."

Bishop mopped at his face with his sleeve, unsuccessfully wiping away the green smears. "Good luck?"

"I guess at the Bloggies, right?" Stan asked. "You're up for *everything*." He snapped a pic and shrugged. "It's going to be so rad. Win everything, Ella. Win it all."

"No, wait. That was awful. One more." She cheesed it for another pic. "I plan to."

"What else did he say to say?" Bishop pushed.

"That's it."

"Make sure to tag me, okay?" Because she wanted Tara looped in on the comments in case anything sketch was said.

"And don't mention the sliming part," Bishop added. "Okay?"

Ella countered Bishop's grumbling, trying to lighten up his death-and-destruction disposition. "I'll make sure to say something on your pic too." Yes, she agreed that the sliming part shouldn't be mentioned, but they were on opposite ends of the spectrum on how to make that happen.

Bishop handed Stan his card. "This is my number. If anyone gets in touch with you about this, makes you another offer, follows up, whatever, you get in touch. Deal?"

Stan nodded.

"It's important."

"I get it, man."

Bishop didn't look convinced. "It'll keep her from pressing charges."

"Bishop!"

"Hey!" Stan balked. "I said I was sorry."

"And give me your phone *now*."

Few people in the world wouldn't have complied given the tone of that order, but if Bishop so much as deleted a single picture from that kid's phone, Ella would have his gonads in a jar.

Instead, Bishop punched numbers, and a moment later, his phone rang. "I have your number. My number is programmed into yours. You have my card. There's no excuse."

"Got it."

Bishop eyed Stan until he apparently believed it. "Anyone contacts you about Ella, you call me. Immediately. Read me?"

"Loud and clear, officer sir."

"Christ," he mumbled.

"It was great to meet you, Stan," Ella offered. "Circumstances aside."

Bishop seemed to ignore the remainder of the conversation, instead nudging the guy to leave.

"Don't forget to tag me." As soon as there was enough distance between them and Stan, she turned to Bishop. "You didn't have to be rude."

"Are you nice and accommodating to everyone but me?" he challenged. "Because really, it's your life. I'm the one trying to keep you in one piece."

She walked the remaining block and headed for the door, waving to the doorman as they passed. "You need a shower and to start making your calls, I'm sure. Or I can call Agent Byrd. I'm sure she'd love to hear about my goo incident. This will go far in having my case treated seriously." Ella rolled her eyes. "I have to make sure *you* don't wind up as part of the story. Tara is going to love that."

He trailed behind. "Don't you think the picture was pushing it too far?"

"He wanted a picture, Bishop. An inconsequential picture." She closed her eyes, recounting the entire scene. "And you pulled a gun on him."

Slamming to a stop, he glared at the front entryway as though it was a danger zone. "We rounded a corner, and a lunatic was waiting, ready to come at you."

"It was a water balloon filled with gunk."

Bishop closed the distance, towering over her. "Do you think I had time to process what was in his hand?" Even with a sheen of drying green film over his skin and clothes, his serious attitude was inescapable. "Action, reaction. Incoming assault? You bet your ass I was prepared to defend what was mine to protect."

His to protect?

Bishop took her hand, lifting her wrist, inspecting her arm, turning it enough to see that her elbow had been scraped. "I'm sorry that I manhandled you." For as angry as his lecture had been, his fingertips were feather light. "I had to get between you and the unknown."

He didn't think, simply put himself in the line of danger. Talk about perspective. Gone was the embarrassment from kissing him and the adrenaline from the ambush. Emotionally tapped, all she could manage was, "Thanks."

Had she said that yet? Had she said it enough?

"I have to keep you safe," Bishop whispered. "It's what I do, Ella."

A waterless, legless lightness ran through her. Each breath, each thought reminded her that his sacrifice was on a level of selflessness that she didn't deserve.

Wow.

Bishop was ready to give so much when she deserved so little. Served her right for being aroused simply by the blink of his green eyes and getting nothing in return but a pity kiss.

"So…" She hated how her insides craved him. "Errands tonight are shot."

He broke away, turning his head. "Yeah, I'd say so."

"You can shower real quick while I wash your shirt. Your jeans seem fine. Just get it out of your hair."

"I'm good." Bishop took a step back, running his hand into his hair, but his fingers got stuck in the tangle of dried goo.

Ew. She made a face. "That's disgusting. Shower. My shower doesn't have cooties, and don't worry, nothing I have is fruity-tooty-foo-foo. You'll walk out, still smelling like a man. No guy-card-stealing soap, I promise."

"I'm fine."

"You're a pain in the ass. Whatever, I don't care. Don't let Furry Baby and Little Kitty lick you. No telling what's in that stuff."

"*Ella*." He threw his head back and rubbed his temples. "My point exactly. No telling what was in it. Okay. Fine."

"All right—wait. Hold on." Ella pulled out her keys as they passed the row of mailboxes.

Bishop rubbed his face, and some of the dried slime flaked off like she had predicted. "You're checking your mail?"

"It'll take two seconds." She twisted the key in the box. Truth was, she wanted to check her mail, needing to find some junk mail to be preoccupied with. But that wasn't something she would loop him in on. "Cool your jets, Muscles."

"Nice place you have here, by the way, excluding the slime-throwing asshole." Bishop brushed past her in the hallway after she had collected the mail. He led the way to the elevators as though he had been in her building a thousand times. "A little overly modern. Even the mailboxes are…artful."

They didn't look like mailboxes, more like a piece of seamless metal that opened.

"What's your place like?" *Junk mail!* She knew she would have it, despite the amount of times she requested off lists. "Look, this is all unneeded stuff. I need something to be upset about besides me. Do you know how many times I've told companies not to do this? How many trees didn't need to die so I wouldn't have to recycle it?"

"You do have a focus," he mumbled.

She shuffled through the papers and envelopes. "Bills, bills, more bills. All of this stuff is on direct debit for a reason. I don't want the mail. But no, they have to mail me to say they've been paid."

There was a flyer for a Chinese take-out place she would likely never eat at, and—oh, something interesting. An envelope addressed to her, and it was on stationary. Her parents traveled the world—that was where she'd picked up her nomad gene—and treasures and notes came from them in the mail. Even when she'd been a little girl, they'd traveled and sent her letters and gifts, things she'd always treasured.

"Scoot boots, babe."

"I'm coming." She shuffled the envelope to the front of her pile as she walked in front of Bishop. "My building, thank you very much. I can call my own elevator."

She punched the button. The elevator came quickly, and the doors opened.

"Then you should walk faster." He snagged the Chinese food menu she had mentally labeled for the recycling bin. "This might come in handy if I keep hanging in these parts."

That was a nice thought—him hanging around, making himself at home—and Ella grinned as they walked inside the elevator. "If you insist. One day, we can talk about how animals are treated." She tore the envelope open, and pulled out the homemade card. As she opened it, something struck her as wrong. Homemade? Her mom didn't do homemade. "And there *are* ethical options, free…range…"

Confetti scattered to the ground.

Not confetti. Dime-sized cutouts *of her face* interspersed with circular cutouts of graphically mutilated animals. Her stomach dropped as she jumped back. "Oh, God."

"What the…" Bishop dropped forward as she pushed back to the elevator wall, letting it catch her.

Vomit teased the back of her throat, and watery acid coated her tongue. There was so much violence and blood captured in the bite-size photos scattered on the floor. Ella's weak grip slipped from the railing, and she slumped, her weak knees propped against the wall. "It's…that's *me* mixed in there."

When she leaned closer, she saw that the eyes had been poked from each of her pictures.

"I'm going to be sick." Surrounded by the grotesque images, she couldn't understand why her eyes had been gouged out, why there was such depravity, or why people had done such horrific things and taken the time for pictures. She collapsed, bile slushing in her stomach.

Eyes closed, crying maybe, hyperventilating for sure, Ella felt Bishop's powerful arms scooping her off the floor as the elevator stopped. He pressed the Stop Elevator button so the door would stay open, then he took off. Down the hall they went, him cradling her to his chest. She hadn't been sick, but her entire body had gone numb, except for the tears. They flowed freely. "Where were my eyes? And why was there so much blood?"

He didn't answer. At her door, he dropped to his knee, supporting her against the wall, still clinging her to his chest as he went through her purse. With her keys in hand, he unlocked the door, turned off the alarm, and moved through her unit before placing her on the couch. "Ella, I'll be back in two minutes. Don't answer the door for anyone but me."

Chapter 13

As soon as the door clicked shut behind him, Bishop had the phone pressed to his ear. With each ring, he wanted to rip apart a man he didn't know. Heaven help the bastard, because when Bishop got his hands on the man, it would be game over.

The elevator doors remained wide open, and Ella's confetti face covered the floor.

"Someone's going to pay." He wanted to punch the wall and crush his phone. Screw that. Bishop wanted to *hunt*. He wanted to scour the *green, green earth* that Ella so desperately wanted to protect. But for the moment, he waited for somebody at Titan HQ to answer the phone.

An automated voice picked up, irritatingly offering a variety of options. He punched the one that would process this headache and return the most amount of intel in record speed.

Parker answered. "Whatcha got for me, buddy?"

"A problem." Bishop seethed, staring at the cutouts. "The police aren't doing anything. The FBI isn't doing a damn thing. And I don't know what to do. I can't protect her from her goddamn *mail*."

"Whoa, all right. Slow down, man. What's going on?"

Bishop couldn't slow his roll. This wasn't bodyguard work. This was personal, for both Ella, *and for him*. A complete mindfuck.

"I can save her from bullets. I can take out fuckers with slime bombs. I can do a whole hell of a lot. This is…" He stared at the tortured animal and eyeless pictures. "It's fucked up."

"Start with what's happening."

Bishop took a deep breath and let it out slowly. "Parker, man. Ella opened her mail, and *confetti* made out of her face and dead animals fell out of the envelope."

"Damn."

"The eyes have been gouged. The animals…" Bishop dropped to a knee, and his stomach turned. "Sick stuff. That's not the kind of thing I can protect her from; that's the kind of thing that law enforcement, the investigators have to find the fucker for. To make this stop."

Parker blew deep into the phone. "Shit."

"It came right after someone tried to throw crap at her." Bishop pulled his phone from his ear and quickly snapped a few pictures, texting them to Parker's cell phone. "Check your phone. It's messed up. She's in a bad place, and this isn't helping."

Immediately, Parker whistled. "That's screwed up."

"Can you pull the video surveillance outside her building? You'll get the incident before we came inside. Then send it over to her FBI POC?" And if her point of contact didn't have a fire lit under his ass after two instances, Bishop wanted heads to roll.

"Yeah, right now. We'll get them out there ASAP."

"What do we have on the stalker?" Bishop pushed.

"Nothing, man. We're not an investigative arm. Whatever we see, we're sending their way."

"That's bullshit."

"We're not contracted for it." Parker sighed. "She's got you and Locke to keep her safe. FBI'll figure it out. Hang tight a minute."

Bishop stared at the mindscrew on the floor; his rage only building.

A minute later, Parker came back on the phone. "All right, wait there. Someone from the Bureau will be there ASAP."

"Thanks."

"I'll relay it to Rocco too. Call back if you need anything."

Bishop ended the call and called Ella.

She answered on the first ring. "Caught the bad guy?"

He shut his eyes, wishing like hell he could tell her yes. "Hang tight. I'm going to call your doorman and wait for the crime scene team to arrive."

Her good-bye was soft and sad, a gut shot that made him hurt. The FBI techs arrived thirty minutes later, which was apparently their version of ASAP. It was probably a reasonable amount of time. He was just being a dick.

Bishop stood back and watched them process the scene, then ground his teeth after he led them to Ella's unit and watched two damn good investigators do their job. An hour and a half later, all statements had been given and all signs of the mail were gone.

What an awful damn night.

Except for kissing her. That'd damn near been a career highlight.

Ella had curled onto the couch with FB and LK, which is what he'd decided to call her dog and kitten.

"Rough night." Bishop sat on the opposite end of the couch and listened to the kitten purr. "Need anything?"

"I should probably call Tara."

He rolled his bottom lip into his mouth, keeping his disagreement to himself. To Ella's credit, she hadn't broadcast the night's troubles to the world.

"She's pissed I went silent tonight."

He turned, ready to change his stance on keeping quiet. "She told you that?"

"No. I just know. No time to go quiet. But I'm sure she had things scheduled, or posted something on my behalf. So it's fine."

"Good. That's her job." Ella trusted everybody. She trusted her team. Tara, he hadn't met, and Jay, he didn't get a good read on. Bishop didn't trust any of them, and hell, right now, he blamed each and every one of them for letting this situation spiral.

They were all at fault. Ella had put herself in this predicament, surrounding herself with crazy people and a team that couldn't see logic or reason. Her life was documented on the Internet—her condo, where she ate breakfast, where she went out to dinner. She showed people how she dressed and where she went on almost a twenty-four-hour basis. It wasn't safe. Was it a big surprise that someone had found her home mailing address?

"Tara is…" *A piranha. Or a leech. Actually, much more like a leech.*

Bishop wanted to see her face when she learned about this latest incident. Would she be excited that it was newsworthy, which would mean bigger ratings?

Yeah, Bishop wanted to talk to the FBI and see what they thought about little Miss Tara, the publicist. For that matter, he wanted to talk to them and see what they thought about Jay. He wanted access to the investigative file. He wanted to be read-in on everything. This was too close to home. This was too close to his girl—or someone who used to be his girl. She was somebody he cared for, regardless. Somebody he *worked* for. Someone he had just kissed.

THE SHOWER WAS HOT, BUT it couldn't wash away his irritation. The soap did its job, and the slime was gone. Breathing in the steam, Bishop tried to ignore how Ella pushed his buttons and his memories, but he couldn't. The soft towel smelled like her, and that served only to irritate him. This was a job. Titan was his dream. Distraction made him useless. Kissing her was stupid. *And hot.* He pulled his jeans back on and slung the towel around his neck. *Damn it.*

"Ella?"

Padding down the hall, he didn't see her. There was a bottle of all-natural cleaner on the counter, an emptied landfill can without a liner, and a bright-pink Post-it with Ella's cursive scrawl.

Had to walk Furry Baby. Potty emergency. DON'T BE MAD. Things were happening everywhere. Be back.

He crumbled the note and threw it. "Are you kidding me?" What was the point of trying to keep her safe? He pinched the bridge of his nose. She was hell-bent on doing whatever she wanted.

"Screw it." In five minutes, he would know if he'd lost his client to the dark world of pet walking and stalkers. Or she would bop back in as if venturing out was no big thing. Either way, she was calling the shots at the moment.

DON'T BE MAD.

He shook his head. *Not mad. Furious!* Her dog had the shits, and Ella might die. All because he took a shower.

Bishop pulled his towel off his neck and stomped down the hall, slamming doors open. Why not? Everyone else on earth had seen this place. Where the hell was her washer-dryer? He would throw his shirt in the dryer and decide if this job was too much for his sanity, with all the back and forth.

He twisted a doorknob and discovered a room that was all new to him, completely sight unseen. *Never on her blog.* Relief slammed over him as he took in the second bedroom, as did an insatiable curiosity. This was the real Ella? Private life, uncensored?

Holding his breath, Bishop took a barefoot step into her sanctuary. The space wasn't as matched as the rest of the condo, and it looked lived in. His skin tingled as if the air had shifted, as if the air inside her hideaway was in and of itself, sweeter. He gulped.

This was messed up.

Him. In here.

But still, he crept in until he had no excuse. He stood in the middle of Ella's private escape, uninvited. And it was nothing like the rest of her condo. A doggie bed and cat tower lined one wall, and he ran his fingers along a weathered white dresser, stopping in front of a bookshelf filled with DVD cases. They were labeled with locations and years, arranged chronologically on the shelf.

"Busted." Ella's voice made him jump.

He spun around, feeling guiltier than hell at being caught red-handed. "Shit, sorry." His cheeks heated. He was surprised to have been so lost that he didn't hear her approach. "I wasn't snooping."

Her blue eyes narrowed. "You totally were."

He totally was. "I mean…sorry." He scrubbed a hand over his face. "Is FB doing better?"

"I think so. He's knocked out with Little Kitty on the couch."

"You can't run out, El. Just because he has to go—"

"I—"

"I'm serious." He gave her a once-over, and surprisingly, she looked better than she did before he'd gotten in the shower. "You're feeling better, I guess?"

Ella shrugged. "It's not the worst thing I've seen. Just caught me off guard, while at home. You know? I didn't expect it."

Bishop chewed the inside of his cheek. "I didn't expect to see this."

"What? A real space that wasn't perfect and ready to go live on video?"

He shifted, taking in the comfortably uncoordinated room. "Well, yeah."

"My job is a lifestyle. I live it. But I also need some time off too. You're not always Titan, are you?"

He raised an eyebrow.

She put up her hand as if she couldn't handle his world. "Don't answer that."

"You don't sleep in that other bedroom?"

"It's a guest room. Technically, the master. Even though people think it's my room. I never outright say it's mine. I don't know..." She bit her lip.

Their conversation about authenticity came to mind. "El. That's safe and smart. And it makes me ten kinds of thrilled."

She looked up. Her eyes dropped to his bare chest, and her cheeks heated. Then her gaze shot back to his again. "Well...good. Thanks."

He'd forgotten that he was half-dressed, but he hadn't missed the way her eyes raked across his chest. He didn't work out for anyone but himself. But for the hungry look she had just fought, he would do it every day. Too bad she now looked everywhere but at him. Color pinkened her cheeks, making her irresistible. Even her nipples had pearled against the front of her shirt. Her distraction-worthy breasts were a weakness of his, and the thought of them in her personal space with just that thin shirt as a barrier? Torture.

Years ago...it had been so long. She would sit in his lap, and he could have her chest in his face. He would lick and love her tits, letting the hard tips roll on his tongue. He vividly remembered how she sounded when his teeth tugged.

He inhaled deeply, not needing to go there. "Is...my shirt dry yet? I can throw it in—"

"I just threw it in. So no."

"Right." God, she was beautiful and *off limits*—a reminder he needed to say over and over, apparently. He took another deep breath and searched for a new direction, turning to look at her DVD collection. "Which video to watch first?"

"Oh! None." Her cheeks reheated for an entirely different reason.

He grinned. "Now we're definitely going to watch one. Let's see, we can start at the beginning."

He scanned row after row of DVD dustjackets with homemade labels. Each listed a location and a year. His eyes went to the far corner, to the one that looked to be the oldest. Bishop wondered what Costa Rica almost a decade ago would have in store for him.

"That's so old," she protested.

"That's why we're starting here." He popped the plastic open and flipped on the television. Then he slid the disc into a DVD player and hit play.

The tropics lit up the screen, exactly like he could've guessed. Water and sand. Boring enough.

Bishop hit the fast-forward button until he caught a glimpse of Ella *in a bikini*. She was clearly working, and it wasn't the right time to gawk. Still, he hit play to slow the fast-forward. The screen lit with her smile, and the speakers trilled to life with magic that could only be her laughter. Bishop watched, mesmerized as she danced in the water.

The beauty on the screen rocked his world. That Ella was so close to the one he'd been in love with before. It reminded him of that quality that made him want to walk through hell for her. He hadn't been able to place his finger on it…until now.

Ella was on fire.

With passion.

With determination.

She still had that inner determination he had known and loved, and she'd applied it to this world. *That* was more attractive than her sun-kissed shoulders or beach-bleached hair. Though he wouldn't lie, that bikini was nice. But not as arousing as the fight she conveyed on-screen with just a glance.

He was in way more trouble than he'd initially realized.

"Where are you?" an off-screen voice asked.

"Costa Rica."

"And what are you doing?"

"Saving the sea turtles."

Bishop grumbled to himself. The environmentalist saving sea turtles struck him as cliché, except he was mesmerized by the screen—her smile, the light in her eyes, the *passion* they held. But more than just that, it was—

"And how are you going to do that?"

She threaded her fingers into her much lighter, sun-bleached hair, not answering. Instead, she was tying her hair into a bun on her head.

"Ella?"

Bishop knew that voice.

On screen, Ella turned. "I'm going to take them down. Destroy them. I'm going to tell the world that grown men are destroying babies so they can make a quick buck. I'm going to fight them. With my words. Maybe with my fists. And one day, I'm going to win."

Shivers ran down Bishop's back. Her words, her fire, were wildly intoxicating. He blindly stared at the woman on the TV and couldn't have respected her any more. He couldn't have *wanted* her any more, and it had nothing to do with the swell of her tan breasts in her bathing suit top or the nice shot of her ass when she spun.

Ella self-consciously took the remote from his hand. "Well, enough of these old things. Why are you looking at me like that?"

His heart beat in his throat, and Bishop wanted to listen to her talk *now*. About bees or herbs or whatever would make her dance in the water and level him with a stare so fierce he would be able to feel it years later on a video. "What makes you fight, Ella?"

Her head tilted as her laughter and words carried in the background as the video continued. "What do you mean?"

Swallowing away the need to touch her, he stood his ground and clarified his question. "What makes you as fiery as this video?"

She looked over his shoulder. "Everything does. Nothing. I don't..." She shrugged, but he saw through her self-effacing downplay. "I fight for the cause."

"Bullshit." He took a step forward, needing to pull back, needing to run away, but doing no such thing. "What makes you want it so bad?"

"It's an incredible job. I'm lucky to have this opportunity—"

"What about your work makes you like *that*." He snatched the remote back and hit fast-forward until he saw her burning passion again, then he hit play.

Carefully, as though she were unsure of how to watch, she sidled next to him. The screen panned close to a cordoned-off area with a sign that she'd marked: STAY AWAY. SEA TURTLE EGGS. UNDER SURVEILLANCE.

"You have to tell me." His throat hurt from how quiet his words were.

"The innocent," she whispered. "They can't help the monsters who want to hurt them."

He nodded, understanding more about her in the last fifteen seconds than he ever had. "No, they can't."

What she fought for had nothing to do with air quality or bees or Smart Cars. He could put aside all of her sass and veganism for right now, because the woman on the screen and the woman in front of him were the same person. She was his innocent, who had a monster hunting her in the wild. And she had found her own innocents to care for. For as much as he and Ella had grown as opposites, they were the same as protectors.

"You put your life in danger to rescue turtles." His quiet voice didn't ask what he knew, more like repeated what he wanted to remember.

"It's more than that, Bishop. Whatever I could, and that's what I do now with the videos and blog. It's just different. That's how you need to see Eco-Ella." She leaned against his arm, reminding him again he was still bare-chested.

Everything he knew and assumed about Eloise-turned-Ella was wrong. "Maybe I'm starting to."

Chapter 14

One week had gone by without any incidents, but today was her big day. The *Bloggies* were a big deal in Ella's world, and as Bishop took a bite of his hoagie, he watched Ella pace. Her publicist had reminded her too many times to count that the awards show was *huge*, and he wanted to shove the foot-long sub down Tara's throat if she mentioned one more thing that could go wrong and that Ella should be prepared for.

"I'm not nervous."

He took another bite. "I didn't say you were."

"Tara thinks I might be."

"That's because Tara told you that you were nervous seventy-five times." He pointed the sandwich at her. "There's being prepared, over-preparing, and then there's Tara."

Ding. Ding.

"What's that?" Ella spun toward the front door, and FB didn't move. Not the greatest guard dog. Brick would've torn down the wall to search and destroy that noise.

"The intercom on your souped-up security system. Take a deep breath, babe."

"Right." She walked to the wall and pressed the touchscreen that connected to the doorman. "Hi, there. Can I help you?"

"Miss Leighton." The scratch of the man's voice immediately made Bishop's senses prickle. He dropped the sandwich onto the wrapper and met Ella by the speaker in a few short strides as she listened. "You have a delivery. But I think it's one of these things that's better left down here."

"What is it?" he asked.

"Flowers…?" the man offered.

Shit. That didn't sound good. "I'll be down in a minute." Bishop raised his brows. "You stay here. Let no one in until I'm back. I don't care if it's Manny, *pet walker to the stars—*"

"Manny has a key."

He groaned. "Deadbolt the door, Ella. *No one* comes in. Not Tara. Not Jay. Not a person with dying animals and a corporate truce from Vamanato. Don't live blog. Just sit still. I don't care if FB gets the runs and has to go outside. Can you stay put?"

"Yes." She bit her lip. "Of course I can."

Thank God. He shouldn't have asked a question he didn't know the answer to. He put his hands on her shoulders. "Ella, I'm not joking about your team. Please understand the seriousness here. They show up, they wait in the hall."

"I heard you." Her chin jutted out. "Just because you disagree with *everyone* I work with doesn't mean I'm not going to listen."

On top of that, he wasn't pleased with the FBI's lack of arrests this week. He let his hands slide down her biceps. "I'm going downstairs to check out your flowers."

"And then what?"

"If you have a nice delivery, I'll come bearing roses."

She smirked. "And if not?"

"Then we call back your FBI friend."

Ella took her wheatgrass smoothie from the counter and got comfy on her couch. Bishop locked her in, inspected her hall, and took off for the stairs. The look on the doorman's face said enough, but as he stepped to the side, Bishop smelled the problem as soon as he saw her delivery. A dozen dead roses, covered in a stench he could only attribute to a sewer, waited on the counter, wrapped in twisted plastic.

All right, they had cameras everywhere now. Surely, one of the angles had picked up the courier. "Make sure not to touch them—"

"I can't leave them here."

"It's an active crime scene investigation." Bishop cracked his knuckles and crossed his arms over his chest. "Do you want me to sit here until someone shows up? Or can you follow the simple instructions not to touch them again?"

The doorman's wrinkled nose matched his green pallor. "They stink."

"Sometimes, life stinks." Bishop pointed to two cameras. "Do something stupid with those flowers, I'll have your ass for obstruction."

Not that he could…seeing as Titan wasn't law enforcement. But the doorman didn't know that. Bishop wanted to get back to Ella, and this guy wasn't a bad dude. This arrangement just stunk.

The doorman hemmed and hawed but didn't touch the stinking flowers. "Did you want to see the card?"

"It came with a card?"

Using a pen to shove over a piece of paper on the desk, the guy sent it Bishop's way. He'd assumed the delivery had been couriered for a specific name. Maybe this was why he wasn't an investigator. Stepping forward, his stomach dropped at the message.

Good luck at the Bloggies. Tonight will be your best awards show ever.

It wasn't an outright threat, but in his mind, hell yeah, it was. "Thanks."

Bishop ground his molars together and called the situation into Titan along with a couple of pictures. Rocco and Parker could contact the FBI.

Whatever was going on with Ella's stalker, Bishop didn't get it. Psychobabble wasn't anywhere near his expertise, but whoever wanted to mess with her was doing a decent job of creeping him out.

And for that, Bishop wanted to nail the fucker.

CHAPTER 15

"IF WE DON'T LEAVE THIS second, we will never leave," Tara demanded from the hallway of the hotel suite living room.

Ella looked in the mirror affixed to the wall, staring at Manny, who sat on the king-size bed. "My marching orders are at an all-time high."

"Demanding, but she means well." Manny pushed off the bed and stood. "Everything about this is perfect. Makeup, hair, and dress. All flawless. I wouldn't have let the stylist leave if I didn't agree. And Tara would have killed her. That sweet makeup artist too." He clucked. "Just go have fun. I've got your babies taken care of; just text me when you're home."

"Seriously, Ella!" Tara yelled.

"Coming," she returned at a lesser volume, giving Manny *the look,* which he returned.

"Kiss me," he demanded. "I'll go first and feed her some lines to keep her happy. *Ella's so pretty. Ella's gonna win.*"

"Ella's going to kick your pretty butt if you don't stop." Laughing, she shooed him out and turned back to the mirror, listening to them chat down the hall. "Tonight will be fine."

With that, she headed to the living area, balancing in the heavy dress and killer shoes. Her hair looked au naturel, though it took hours to make it stay *exactly* that way. "I'm ready."

"Finally. Let me run next door to check on another client." Tara was halfway out the hotel hallway door as Bishop walked in.

And everything slowed—except for her heart, which sped to the point that it might have been hatching a plan to escape and throw itself at his feet. There he stood, a towering force of nature, clad in a tuxedo with a simple black tie in place of a bowtie. His broad shoulders were covered in what had to be tailor-made perfection, and she didn't know men's fashion, but she did know that what Bishop wore *worked.* Freshly shaven, and more handsome than she could possibly have imagined, Ella froze in place and watched him do the same.

Maybe ten empty feet stood between them, and he was the first one to take a step forward. "Ella…"

"Hi." A blush tinged the word as much as it did her cheeks.

Bishop licked his lips, and he tore his eyes away, only to steal them back to her. "It's one thing to see you pictured in a magazine like this. Damn, it's another when you walk out."

The pulsing thumps in her neck jumped. "Thanks. You look…" Was there even a word that could do him justice?

"Like I'll blend in," he finished for her.

Not if his life counted on it. "More like—"

"Are we ready?" Tara popped her head in the door. "Because by my watch, *we're late*. Are you following or riding with us, Bishop?"

Bishop checked his watch. "Riding with. My truck's already on-site."

They made their way to the elevator, Tara standing in between them. Ella couldn't look away from the tips of her toes that popped out from the bottom of her dress. Because if she did, all she would see would be Bishop.

The doors opened, and Tara led the charge.

"You know who she reminds me of?" he asked as they crossed the hotel lobby.

"Who?"

"Our P.E. teacher, senior year."

Ella laughed. "That bitch."

"Right?" He chuckled, holding his hand out as they passed through the automatic doors and arrived at the side of a waiting Escalade. "Give her a whistle, and they might be one and the same."

Relaxed, Ella climbed in first. They all rode in silence for the short drive to the awards show location. She tried to hide her clammy palms against her dress as the driver pulled up next to the curb for their grand entrance.

There they were at the Bloggies. *Deep breath in.* It was time to go to work.

Tara turned from the front passenger seat. "Smile, Ella." She snapped a quick picture and posted it to her social media outlets. "Done. Good, okay. The comments are rolling in; people are already *spotting* you." She pivoted to check the window. "I'm hopping out here. You look golden."

Her phone buzzed with a thumbs-up text from Jay. He was already inside, working the crowd, revving up her fans, and making sure all was a well-oiled machine on the inside.

Tara held out her hand. "Give me your phone, Ella."

Ella put her phone in the purse and handed it over. The driver paused, and Tara bound out. Ella knew the plan. Two car lengths away, Tara was out first. When they pulled up, red-carpet staff would open her door. Tara would be in front of her, working the reporters and crowd. Bishop, who sat quietly next to her, would exit street side as she made her entrance, go deep around the back of the car, and trail her. Tara had her front from a PR point of view, and Bishop had eyes on her security. She was covered in all things.

Bishop shifted on the leather seats. "Ella?"

"Hmm?"

"You ready?"

"Always."

"Take a deep breath and don't give me the bullshit Tara-answer." He leaned close to her in the backseat. "Are you ready?"

She drew in a shaky breath and let her eyes sink closed. "I'm nervous." The words she'd been repeating all day that she was *not* nervous. "But you're with me, so it will be fine."

His large hand took hers, and her eyes fluttered open. It was an unexpected touch. A personal one, unlike anything they'd had since she made a fool out of herself and kissed him the week before. "I'm with you, and it will be fine." He squeezed her hand. "And you look *amazing*—"

The door of the Escalade swung open, and there was the mouth of the red-carpet entrance. The loud calls of paparazzi filled the noisy air. The constant sound of people shouting names and camera lenses clicking were a rich cacophony that Ella had always thought didn't blend well.

A hand reached in to help her out.

"This crowd is fine," Bishop reassured her. "The press has been vetted, screened, and patted down. The fan section is fine."

She swallowed away a note of unease, taking reassurance from his steady voice and the firm hand at her back.

"Go do your thing. I'm a few feet away."

She smiled weakly, knowing a feeble grin like that would earn the wrath of Tara. "Thanks."

"Hey, Ella."

She turned slightly. "Hm?"

A head ducked in. "Ma'am?"

Bishop urged her on. "You're safe."

Surely, underneath his black jacket was enough ammo to start a coup, but for the moment, he looked like a large, overbearing, slightly out-of-place better half instead of a bodyguard.

"You look beautiful. Stunning. Relax."

Her cheeks heated.

"Now you're camera-ready. Go."

All part of the job. Nicely done. He winked. *Holy wow.*

"Ready?" Tara, her publicist, appeared out of nowhere, sticking her head in the Escalade. Dressed all in black with her publicist credentials hanging down, she gave Bishop a sideways glance. "Is there a problem?"

"No," Ella said.

"Give me ten seconds to back away so you have a clean exit out of the car for photos."

Ella inhaled slowly, letting it drift out. "Got it."

Tara didn't leave. "This will be a piece of cake. You owe thirty seconds to GreenTV and whatever E! wants. Deal?"

Another deep breath. "Of course."

"Ten seconds, then off you go."

"*Tara*," Bishop growled. "She's got it.

Once Tara stepped away, Ella took a breath, counted to ten, painted on her smile, and made an entrance worthy of the red carpet. She concentrated on not tripping over her dress. The skirt wasn't the problem. She wore maxi-length dresses all the time. It was the damn heels.

It wasn't her first entrance. She moved along in front of the backdrop covered in sponsorships and the Bloggie logo. *Walk, wave, pose, repeat.* She pivoted, looking over her shoulder and waiting. Bishop watched. Ella angled her face, changed directions, then did the same thing. Every time she saw Bishop, his eyes were trained on the crowd, rotating the way they had that night in the bistro.

At the end of the step-and-repeat, Tara pushed her around the corner, and the cheers from the rope line started.

"Eco-Ella!"

"Ella Leighton!"

Click. Click. Click.

"Ella! Big *Under the Roof* fans over here!"

"Ella! Over here!"

The lights and cameras glared as she walked the line. She'd done it before, and with Hollywood in town for the award ceremony and dinner, she knew she would see her favorite and not-so-favorite reporters.

Hellos were said. Talking points were done. Over-the-shoulder looks were ordered and given. But with each passing step, her anxiety grew. The slime, the flowers, whoever was messing with her knew she would be there tonight. Was he there? What did he want? Could he see her now? Had she talked to him already on the rope line? Her breaths became shorter and tighter.

At the end of the red carpet, after she'd done every possible pose on the step-and-repeat, every inch of forward momentum became a challenge. Her heels felt heavy. She couldn't make it to the end. Was this a panic attack?

Bishop locked eyes on her, mouthing, "Come here."

He was a lifeline, exactly what she needed while Tara was bitching and moaning about who knew what. He didn't even notice Tara at his side. The strength of his intense stare was Ella's oxygen.

He didn't break eye contact as though she were the most precious thing in the world—*of course* she was. She was his job. How did she keep forgetting? Her stomach fell like an A-lister who had committed social suicide. But his reasons didn't matter. Bishop did what it took to get her out of the line of sight, where no photographers could catch a glimpse of her panic. For that, she should be grateful.

As soon as she was safe, Tara led the way, oblivious to the

disaster Ella had almost brought on herself. Bishop followed. Ella could sense his proximity even as she tried to ignore him. With a quick glance over her shoulder, she saw his green eyes hunting, searching.

The three of them crossed a threshold into the auditorium, which had been transformed into a banquet hall for the awards show. Circles of tables covered the impressive room. Music played, and the stage was close. Ella had a primo seat. Their VIP table had seats for other industry folks joining them, who Tara had expertly arranged. The night would be perfect.

The crowd of who's who buzzed with flocks of people, but Ella didn't fit in at all. Though she did. It was her night. Apparently, even Vegas had bet on her to win big. Her palms sweat at the thought, and she closed her fists. Where was Jay? Having her friends around felt like a security blanket, especially in this crowd.

"Here we go," Tara chirped. She pulled her phone from her bag and scanned a few video clips that they would use for B-roll. "Ready?"

"Sure." She took the phone that Tara handed her and drank in a deep breath, pressing the button to go live. The screen counted down—three, two, one…

"I'm here, warriors!" Ella rotated partially to show the enormity of the room. "Before the Bloggies start. Another night where I throw the flip-flops to the side and step into the limelight"—she made a face—"which is *really not* my thing, to bring to light everything we've done. Thanks for doing the heavy lifting for our cause, and I promise that no matter what happens tonight, I'll keep up the fight. So, signing off…"

Dang.

There were a lot of questions and comments about Jay. He'd always popped into the awards show videos and most of the other ones too. Since when was a lack of Jay on the red carpet conversation-worthy? When did her *social life* become part of the topic list?

"Sorry, everyone. Jay's working the room somewhere." She read the scrolling comments and questions then looked off camera. "No, I don't see him." Though Bishop was there, and if her fans wanted to see a handsome man in a tux, he knocked Jay out of the arena. "But there's plenty of things to look at."

She slowly panned, walking in a circle, eyes on Bishop. Until he realized what she was doing. His hand shot out, and that man moved *fast*.

"Well, you'll just have to trust me. I have to go. Chat with you later. Like, comment, and share." She ended the feed.

Bishop scowled. "*What the hell—*"

Tara clapped her hands together. "That was *amazing*!"

"It was just an idea."

"Brilliant." Tara took the phone back. "If he's part of the team, he has to contribute."

The tightness in his jaw was enough to strangle Tara. "She's insane. Your publicist is fucking bonkers."

"All right, you two. It was a spur-of-the-moment idea that, with the benefit of hindsight, was maybe questionable." She rubbed her nose. Something foul lingered very faintly in the air. "I won't do it again. Sorry, Bishop."

Tara rolled her eyes. "Pussy."

Ella's eyes popped so hard, she was sure her fake lashes would fall off. "*Tara*."

Palpable restraint deepened the tension in Bishop's jaw. His lips flattened, and his hand slapped down on a chair, pulling it out. "Ella. Your chair, babe."

Oh no. This was bad. He was going to sit her down and strangle Tara, for good reason too.

"You and I need to have a word," he ground out before giving

Ella a curt nod, excusing them. Then he all but physically moved Tara aside with a glare.

Even Tara paused, maybe oblivious that her brash attitude problem had gone a step too far. All-business-Bishop took three powerful steps forward, and Tara backed up with every one, until her retreat was stopped by another table. Dang it, Ella couldn't hear their conversation. But she could see Tara's face. The woman didn't get a word in.

Oh, yes she did. One word. *Sorry.*

So was that…a miracle that Ella had just witnessed? Yes, it was. But… God! What was the putrid smell? Faint enough to be indistinguishable amidst thousands of peoples' perfume and cologne, mixed with the scent of coffee and champagne being served by waiters, but still present enough to bother her hyper-senses.

The lights flickered to signal a start time of so many minutes away, but Ella wasn't sure how many.

Her tablemates joined her, distracting her from the Bishop-Tara show. As soon as she did the polite hellos, she turned to see Tara coming over.

"I won't be a bitch to him."

Well, wow. What had he said? "That's good."

"I have to go run and check on my other clients. You good for a bit?"

"Sure." She hadn't expected Tara to stick around this long. Just like at the hotel, she usually hopped around but always came back. Ella was one of her top clients. "I'm fine."

Bishop took a seat next to her and shooed away a waiter offering wine for dinner. Tara took off, and Ella said please to the vino.

She downed a big sip and turned to Bishop. "Did you hear back from anyone about my flowers?"

His face darkened, giving her a *no*.

"I was just wondering, since you all had so much technology, and the Feds were all like *thanks*."

"Feds and Titan talked. Our tech guy talked to theirs."

"*And…?*"

"It wasn't a flower company. No one in their right mind would sell that shit, anyway. Someone posted and paid anonymously through Monarch on a local forum." He made a face. "IRL again."

"Oh…" She knew enough about Monarch profiles. People either used them legitimately or not. And when they didn't, it was troll heaven.

"They're tracing IPs and whatever," Bishop continued.

"It's not going to turn anything up, will it?"

He pursed his lips together. "Internet ghosts with burner phones, Visa prepaid cards to fund Monarch Money, and accounts that last for five minutes? Nah."

Her stomach turned. Not great news, but she shrugged—and her stomach turned again.

Whatever the food option was for tonight had to be disgusting. Where was the smell coming from? It smelled as if they were readying to wheel hunks of meat out, completely overpowering. Tara would've signed her up for the vegan option, but it didn't mean that she could handle the foul aromas overwhelming her now. Whatever was on the menu was too much.

The music shifted, and the emcee bound onstage and took the mic. "Welcome to the international blogger awards! The Bloggies! The world's most exciting, most daring, most enigmatic people are in this room! And tonight, we're going too…"

Salad plates were collected, and Ella sipped her water, ignoring the wine. Maybe that would help. The room was uncomfortably warm. The smell of dinner was uncharacteristically robust.

Bishop leaned close. "Are you okay?"

"Yes," she whispered, rubbing her temple.

His arm draped over the back of her chair. She liked having him around her, but at the moment, not so much. Her clammy, sweaty hands were back. Maybe her dress was too tight. She couldn't think. Her head spun, and it wasn't her schoolgirl crush on Bishop that had her feeling queasy.

"So dig in to dinner—one that is worthy of a few blog posts and videos! We've done our best to create a great show for the people who know entertainment. As you watch the best video bloopers the Internet has to offer—"

All around them, waiters emerged with giant slabs of meat on large sticks. The crowd oohed and aahed at the visual delight. Each waiter was partnered with another, carrying the equivalent of kitchen swords.

The aroma hit Ella like a tsunami. Where was Tara? How hadn't she known this was coming?

"Oh…" Ella gagged quietly and queasily, turning into Bishop.

Right now, she needed him to fortify her, protect her from this as much as from the stalker. It was a reaction she couldn't help, and he wouldn't understand. But it was visceral. She took mouth-breaths to avoid the smell. The taste plastered itself to her tongue. This wasn't good.

"Bishop," she whispered, faltering in her seat.

He leaned closer. "You doing okay?"

"Yes, of course." Even though the answer was *absolutely not.* The smell of animal flesh that had been seared, seasoned, sliced, and skewered made her ten shades of woozy. He wouldn't understand, and now wasn't the time to explain. "But…"

He took her hand, and she tried to focus on how large it was, how protective the gesture. She squeezed it, and her eyes shut, feeling a migraine coming on yet knowing that she needed to make it through this award dinner. Eco-Ella had come too far. *She* had worked too hard. And tonight, she wanted to nab every award she was nominated for, including best of bloggers.

This was work. Mister Rough Around the Edges had manned up and put on a tuxedo, and the mental picture of that first image was deliciously scored into her mind. That was what she would concentrate on.

"Hey, Ella." Bishop leaned forward, and his hot breath on her ear should have done something magical. But it didn't lesson the urge to vomit. "You're not looking so hot. I mean, you're hot. Just that—are you going to hurl?"

"Maybe."

A waiter with a tower of meat walked to their table, gesturing for them to choose their fresh cuts.

"Please make him go away," she begged.

Bishop waved the waiter off. "We're good, thanks."

But the others at the table weren't clued in on her problem. They laughed and took pictures of the offerings. One wanted "the rarest" part. Another, not so much. Ella's head spun, and with a shaking hand, she reached for her water.

"Ella?"

The waiters and their chunks of meat left. The scent, the sight—everything—was like nails on a chalkboard except it made her ill. How had Tara not known?

Then it hit her. Of course Tara had known. But Ella wouldn't have come if she'd known the meal was going to be a show centered around skewered meat, and Tara knew that.

"Ma'am," a waiter said. "Your vegan option." He placed a plate in front of her. "Sir, did you order that too?"

Bishop shook his head. "No."

"We missed you? So sorry!" Looking flustered that there was a problem at the VIP table, the waiter turned, hissing, "Over here."

"No, it's okay," Bishop said.

The other waiter with a skewered slab spun from the table behind them, making a genuine apologetic face—and he tripped. As he dropped to his knees, the skewer fell, and a bright, bloody piece of meat slapped on the table between Bishop and Ella with such force that juice splattered all over her.

Her stomach roiled. Ella pushed out of her chair and bolted, needing to run from the red flesh and wash it away.

She ran through the maze of tables in the crowded hall, certainly catching the attention of those around her. She needed to find the restroom, but mostly she needed to breathe. Too many people. Too hot. Too much of a smell that she couldn't stand, and it was *on* her.

No! This was the way out, not the way to the bathrooms. But her flight reaction had overpowered reason, and she continued to rush toward where she hoped the cool night's air might be.

Bishop was hot on her tail. "Ella."

Whether he was clued into her mindset or not, he did his job. In a second, he was on her, moving her through the back of the auditorium as though she didn't have to walk on her own. Her heel caught on an electrical cord, and his arm carried her those final few feet until *finally*, the fresh, clean air hit her.

She gasped. Her head dropped back, and her mouth hung open.

Outside was better, but she *still* smelled the stench in her hair and on her skin. Not wanting to gag, hating to be this out of control, she stepped away from Bishop, when his large hand pulled her to a stop.

"What just happened?" he asked, warily eyeing her. "This is like the jerky, all over again."

Panting, she felt the tears in her eyes. She couldn't hide them and didn't want him to see. She turned, mumbling, "Nothing. I need a second."

He spun her back around, assessing the tears and taking a step closer as though he needed to protect her from the world. "The hell it's nothing."

"I'm fine."

"One second, you're finally loosening up, trying to get me on a stupid video; the next, you're nothing but a blur of a dress, running for the hills."

God. Mortification painted her cheeks. "I'm sorry."

"Don't apologize. I'd just like to know before you haul ass—"

"I don't eat meat."

"I know that, Ella." His jaw went slack as he processed that. "No one asked you to."

"The smell got to me. When it fell, I lost it."

He laughed. "The mortified waiter who just tripped?"

"Bishop!"

"I didn't realize it would mean that you'd have a nervous breakdown at the table. All right, so what are—"

"*Ella!*"

"Shoot," she grumbled, hearing Tara's warpath before she could see her.

Tara strode up in full PR mode. "What. Is. Happening. Here?"

"She needed some air," Bishop offered.

Tara's narrowed eyes sliced through them.

"I got a little choked up," Ella offered.

"Obviously. My notifications went crazy before I realized you had run from the building. If you want to pull a stunt, clue me in so I have the right eyes on you at the right moment."

"I didn't do it on purpose, Tara." She needed some water, and her nose wrinkled as she could still smell the splatter on her. "Not something we can plan for."

Tara's fingers sped across her phone. "So you say."

Bishop put his hand on Ella's back. "Ladies."

"Are we ready to go back in?" Tara snipped.

Ella groaned. Surely people were still eating, and the place still had to reek. Her stomach turned. "I need another couple of minutes."

They stood in a quiet holding area where, only an hour ago, people had milled after coming off of the red carpet. They were outdoors but the area was tented, and a cool breeze thankfully drifted by. Bishop walked over to a table set up with water glasses and two pitchers of water. Lemons floated in one, and the other contained cucumbers. He filled a glass and grabbed a handful of napkins. "Did any of that get on you?"

Her heart slowed at the simple gesture. "Yes. Thanks."

She dabbed the cocktail napkin in the water and tried to wipe where she thought the waiter had left his mark—her forearm, neck, cheek—

"Don't mess up your makeup."

"Tara, really—"

"Give me this." Tara grabbed the napkin and dabbed at Ella's face. "There. Are you good now?"

She took a breath and cringed. Tara squeezed her lips.

"I have an idea," Bishop volunteered. "Ella, hang tight a minute. There's a drugstore across the street."

Tara's jaw dropped. "You're leaving? Aren't you sworn to protect her or something?"

"Are you going to off our girl?" He shot back. "Because frankly, I'm tired of your bullshit tonight."

Stunned, Tara shook her head. "Well, no."

"Good. It's a secure area; everyone's vetted. Security is there and there." He pointed to the armed guards on either side of where they were. "Stand with her for five minutes." Bishop put his hand on Ella's shoulder. Warmth from his palm radiated down her arm. Tingles slipped down her spine, and her head spun for an entirely different reason. "Ella, you okay for a sec?"

She nodded, unsure of her voice.

"Good. Don't move."

The massive man gave her shoulder a squeeze and held her eyes as he nodded. Then, in a tux that looked tailor-made for his God-gifted body, he took off at a jog.

Both she and Tara stood and watched him disappear.

Tara huffed. "Obviously, no one is going to try to *off you* here. I'll be inside. Unless you need me?"

Week after week, Tara had been harder to work with. "No. I'm fine."

Then Tara gave her a once-over, and Ella braced for whatever scrutiny was coming. "Are you sure?"

That follow-up was unexpected. "Yes. I'm sure."

"This actually works well. Upping the drama factor really does great things for your Google hits. Good thinking." Pleased, Tara spun on her designer heel and left.

Right...always about publicity. Ella looked up. They were outside but in a cordoned-off area. She couldn't see the street, as they were standing behind the partition used for the red carpet. The actual road had been closed for standing room, the press, and risers. The sky was barely recognizable with so much light pollution from the city. The stars barely shone. The half-hidden moon was not nearly as vibrant as she knew it could be. Still, for the first time in a few hours, she was by herself, minus event staff and the security guards that milled nearby, and her mind was quiet.

Bishop caught her attention as he jogged up with a white plastic bag in his hand. That was fast, and she had no doubt he'd likely run the whole way to the drugstore and back and hadn't broken a sweat.

He lifted the bag. "Here's the plan."

"In there?" She ignored the urge to explain that plastic bags were the devil.

"Yup." He pulled out a small bag of coffee and a container of Vicks VapoRub.

Laughing, she had no idea what his plan was. "Well, you've got me."

"Trust me." He pocketed the bag and the jar of Vicks then tore open the coffee. "Stick your nose in here. Breathe deep."

She watched for any sign he was screwing with her, but there were none. "French Roast?"

"Only the best for my favorite blogger."

She took the coffee. "You know others?"

"Breathe already."

He had a point, and she dipped her head to smell the coffee, keeping her eyes on him.

He shook his head. "Forget the ladylike BS, Ella. Stick your nose in there and *huff* the coffee beans."

Self-consciously, she raised her eyebrows. "*I did.*"

"Try again," he urged.

"Why?"

"Breathe deep, babe."

When she didn't move, he did for her. Before she could say, "what the what," Bishop had her nose deep in the bag of coffee. And with a mocha-blast to the nasal passages, the meat scent that had taken up residence in her nose was gone.

With that, she even relaxed a little despite the forced beans in her nose. Then, slowly, she moved back. Her eyelashes fluttered, and she expected the sick feeling from the meat to come back. It didn't.

"Old cop's trick," Bishop said.

Ella raised her eyebrow. "You were never a cop."

"Go with it. If you get a whiff of a dead body that's been waiting to be found for a few days, well, I guess it's like a vegan surrounded by meat skewers."

Resourceful and oddly, very thoughtful. "Thanks."

"Give it a go again."

Nose in the bag again, she *huffed*. She let out the coffee bean exhale and noticed she didn't have the disgusting leftover meat smell stuck in her nose anymore. She gave him an approving chuckle and did it again.

"Now she gets how well it works."

Nodding, she took one more sniff then folded the bag closed. "Wow. That really helped."

"Now." He took the coffee, set it down by his well-polished shoes, and cracked open the Vicks. "You have awards to go win. Put this under your nose. Not *in* your nostrils. It might burn." He offered her the container. "And don't touch your eyes. That'll definitely burn."

Not one to question him twice, she did as he said. He handed her a napkin to wipe her fingers. Her nose felt menthol-fresh, maybe a little too tingly as though some Vicks had travelled a little too high.

Bishop watched, holding his hand out for the used napkin. "What'd you think?"

"I think…" She wrinkled her nose. "Can you tell that I have anything under my nose?"

He shook his head.

"I think that you're a miracle worker." A kind-hearted, out-of-the-box, never-saw-it-coming, miracle worker.

"Come on. I want to watch you win." Wrapping a strong arm around her waist, Bishop turned her. His hand drifted slowly across the small of her back until he let her go.

The moment he lost contact with her, a tinge of disappointment made her arms hang heavy and her steps feel as though the red carpet clung to her heels, slowing her entrance.

Bishop took her elbow. "Careful."

Absurdly enough, that step felt perfect. "Thanks."

She cast a glance up. Whether she won any of the awards tonight or not, the coffee-and-Vicks moment would likely be her favorite.

The lights were down as they started to make their way back to the table. The emcee onstage ran through the teleprompter's lines, announcing a winner for whichever random category. What had they missed?

Jay appeared from the shadowed side of the hall. "Ella, are you okay? I was on my way to find you." His eyes shifted to Bishop, who stood to the side, remaining in his job role. "Tara said you needed me."

The day after the Bishop-Jay run-in at the Bistro had been awkward, but Jay got over it when she eventually, with Bishop's blessing, explained that she'd had to hire security. With that in mind, Jay appreciated that Titan was on the job. Still, there was no love between the men.

"I'm fine. I'd like to sit and watch." And avoid more of an awkward scene.

Their threesome moved front and center to their table. Tara's seat was still empty, not surprisingly, and dinner had been cleared.

"Bishop," Jay asked, leaning over, as they sat down. "Do you play chess?"

"*What?*" Ella hissed, surprised. "Not the time, Jay."

"It's important."

"Your timing is off."

"It's—"

"Easy answer." Bishop cut their bickering off. "Not really."

"Figures," Jay added.

Ella shot daggers at Jay. "Oh, come on. Really?"

Musicians played a drumroll. "And for the category that everyone has been waiting for…the best of!"

Ella's nerves tornadoed and focused back on the reason for being there. Winning wasn't everything. It would be amazing. She wanted it. Losing would hurt. Tara would die. Jay would sulk. She would too. But more importantly, the acknowledgement of a win would further her work.

Jay reached for her hand. *Shit. God, no.* She batted it away, not wanting his support like that.

The names were listed, and the bios were read, including hers. Their video clips played, then the drumroll started. In the dark room, she couldn't breathe. Her lungs hammered for each breath. *Please, please...*

Bishop put his hand on her back.

Oh, she wanted this win so badly. Was that wrong?

"Ella Leighton from Eco-Ella!"

"Oh!" She won! She did it! Her hand slapped to her mouth. Really! It happened! Ella threw herself into Bishop's arms as he hugged her. "Oh my God, I can't believe it."

"Good job, babe."

She pulled back in tears. All around her, people stood and clapped. Suddenly, Tara was by her side, and on the big screen was *her*. She stood, pushing out of her chair, having no idea what she would say. Tara pressed her speech into her hand.

"Thank you," Ella mouthed, giving her a hug. "For pushing me."

Her publicist beamed. "I do it because I love you."

"I know." She turned and saw that Jay remained seated. Clapping, but seated. Ella leaned down and kissed his cheek. "Thanks, Jay."

"I do everything because of you too. I've invested too much to forget."

CHAPTER 16

THE TROPHIES HANDED OUT ONSTAGE were not actually the trophies that were for keeps. Didn't matter, though. Ella won each of her categories, though she had apparently missed a couple presentations. Thankfully, Tara had gleefully given her speeches. The best of the best award was what sent Tara over the edge of happy to thrilled. Interview upon interview had been lined up afterward, all live-broadcasted on every possible social media source.

Ella was exhausted, and even though Bishop had kept the Vicks fresh and discreet, she was in desperate need of a shower. More than that, for the last hour, she had felt a cold chill—the same feeling that came with every stalker incident. Whoever had caused her problems was in the room; she was sure of it. But looking around, there was nothing to pinpoint.

"I want to get out of here," she said to Tara. Ella eyed Bishop and tried to flag him over. The few feet of distance might have been miles as Tara stood between the two of them, trying to snag every person she could to cover any angle on Eco-Ella.

"No can do." Tara shook her head. "We have five more—"

"Nope." Bishop must have bio-enhanced ears. He took a step around her publicist. "We're out."

"I don't think you call the shots here, buddy," Tara snipped.

"I think *I* do." Ella grabbed onto his outstretched hand. "And I'm done, Tara. Honestly. My voice is gone. My answers sound canned. No one left here even cares about what I say anymore; they won't post or air my interviews."

Tara didn't disagree.

Bishop urged her a few steps. "Let's blow this place."

Jay stepped closer. "What's the problem?"

"I'm tired. Done with all of this."

"I'll—"

"We're headed out," she said, standing closer to Bishop. "I will touch base with you both tomorrow. Thanks for everything."

If she had one more ounce of energy, she would tell them to go celebrate the enormous success they had just achieved instead of trying to land one more iota of coverage. But then again, it was their job.

With Jay and Tara bitching in the background, Bishop parted the crowd like Tara never could. Ella suspected it had something to do with that menacing-handsome combination he managed to work so well in a tuxedo.

"This way." They ducked out the back side of the overhead tunnel made from tents and exited into an alleyway.

She picked up her skirt and tried to keep pace in her heels. Finally, they reached a parking garage, and he led the way to the elevators.

"You'll have to survive a ride in the eco-gas guzzler."

"If you recall, I handle your ride fine."

He looked down, letting his eyes linger on her face long enough to make her feel an uncertain scrutiny. "I know."

The elevator dinged, and the doors opened. Holding them for her with one arm, he swept the other arm out, gesturing with a bow. "Eco-Ella. Winner extraordinaire."

"Stop it."

He laughed and followed her into the elevator. "You racked up tonight."

"We did."

He tilted his head back as they ascended floors. "You know, I'm aware that you're actually the only person who does the whole blogging-vlogging-posting thing. Everyone else takes their marching orders and works part-time, but you—" The doors opened, and he did the grand gesture thing again, holding them at bay.

She shrugged. "Maybe."

"You do everything. You're the brains of the operation."

"Don't blow too much smoke my way."

He caught her shoulder, swinging her around to face him. "Congratulations. From someone who had little idea what you've done but has clued in pretty quickly. It's impressive. *You're* impressive."

"You're making me blush."

He ran his tongue over his bottom lip, rolling it into his mouth. He had more to say. She had more that she wanted to hear. Not that impressive stuff. But the way he said it. The way he looked at her. Ella wanted him to know…

His eyes tracked over her head, and he spun her around him, pressing her to his back. *This again?* It had happened before, and he hadn't been wrong. Her pulse picked up, and adrenaline spiked as she gripped the back of his tuxedo jacket.

"Let's go. Time to get in the truck." He picked up the pace.

"What's wrong?"

"Call it a bad feeling."

Her heels clicked with each step.

"Over here." Bishop rotated her and put his hand on the small of her back, leading her farther into the garage.

Two voices screeched through the parking level. "Oh my God!"

Bishop moved her again, securing her safely as though she were in danger. But those were the familiar squeals of a fangirl. The sound echoed and bounced off the low garage ceiling and floors, reverberating. It was a cacophony of "Oh my God, there she is." But the way that Bishop had tensed, they might as well have said, "There is our target; go grab her."

"Stop right there," he ordered. He had one arm outstretched, and the other arm was bent, his hand reaching for his weapon.

"No, no, wait." Ella stepped to his side, panic seeping into her words that he would unwittingly take excitement for derangement.

The girls' squealing didn't stop as they ran. There was no reason for her fans to assume she had armed security. And from the way they carried on, Ella guessed they'd pregamed the Bloggies with a bottle of something strong, hoping to drink up the courage to approach their idols. Now that they'd stumbled across someone they deemed worthy at the end of the night? Disaster was unfolding in three, two, one… She grabbed Bishop's *shooting* arm. "Wait."

"Are you crazy?" If looks could kill, he would have to explain why she was in a body bag too. He tried to gather her behind him.

She tugged on his arm. "Look! They're fans!"

The truth registered on his face, and a frustrated kill-the-world, protect-the-girl growl matched the irritation set in his jaw.

"They're my people." Ella reached her arm toward them as they reached for her. "Harmless. And *drunk*."

He studied the girls then backed down. "Why the hell are your people standing in a garage?"

"Coincidence. We're all parked in the same place."

"Nothing is coincidence."

"Sometimes—"

The two girls squeed in unison. "We *cannot* believe it's you!"

Bishop's hand rested on his weapon, but he took a wary step back.

"Hi!" Ella chimed in the high-octave conversation.

"Oh my God. He is *so* much hotter than Jay, the sidekick!" The girl on the right with deep-blue streaks dyed in her hair leaned against the other girl, pointing at Bishop. "We saw your video. You should've showed him. So much hotter."

Ella turned, amused. "True."

"I'm not her sidekick," he grumbled.

The other girl shifted an overstuffed bag from one shoulder to the other in order to support her slightly more drunk friend. "But he is way hotter."

They both giggled, and Ella watched Bishop blush. "Are you going to dispute that?"

"Ella," he warned.

"*Oh*, he's so cute!"

"He is! You should put him on!"

"I like his voice. *It's very low*." Blue Streaks made a deep wannabe-baritone. "*Manly*."

"He doesn't like to be on the videos," Ella volunteered, giving Bishop a wink. "I tried."

"Sidekicks do the videos."

He raised an eyebrow. "I'm not a sidekick."

Ella laughed. "He's my muscle. Aren't you, Muscles?"

That made his blush deepen! She loved it. Who knew Mister Tough Guy could get a little rosy-cheeked?

Bishop backed away to give them space. "I'll let you guys do your thing."

"He's got a really cute ass too." Bag Girl gave Ella a you-go-girl approving look.

"Super," Blue Streaks slurred. "Tight. I bet he works out."

Ella couldn't stop her laughter. "The tux shows it off nicely, huh?"

Bishop paced. "*I can hear you three.*"

Blue Streaks and Bag Girl erupted into a fit of giggles.

Ella couldn't help but join them. "All right. I'll see what I can do about getting him on a video sometime."

Two minutes later, after the girls had listed their favorite videos, posts, and places she'd gone that they had loved and treasured, Ella's heart was full. The two girls had adequately turned their attention from a very good-looking Bishop O'Kane, which Ella admitted was hard to do, to talk about Eco-Ella posts. She had a heart-to-heart with the girls, who confirmed that they wanted to be warriors for the world.

They weren't discussing just the blog or the videos. Eco-Ella was only the catalyst and the vehicle for getting their message out. For all the headaches, *the stalker*, and everything that came with moving Eco-Ella to the next level, it was worth it.

The two girls staggered away, drunk dialing their sober friend, giggling into the phone about who they'd just met. Bishop hadn't batted an eye when asked to take pictures with both their phones despite for, what he'd explained, was his complete disdain for cell phones in general.

Ella and Bishop walked to his truck in silence. He opened her door and helped her in, lifting the train of her skirt and tucking it on the floorboard. He started to shut the door but caught it before it closed and leaned against the frame.

"Everything okay?" she asked.

He glanced through the quiet garage. The lights were low, the spaces sporadically taken. "I called that one wrong. Sorry."

She shrugged. "In the military, you were a…?"

"Army Ranger."

"An Army Ranger." Wow, how their lives had gone separate

ways once they'd parted. "And you mentioned Titan is a new gig?"

"That's affirmative, babe. One I'd like to keep."

"My dad explained, and Jared also, that this isn't normally what Titan Group does."

"No, it's not. But you're important, and your father did something for my boss when he was in a pinch. Now we're returning the favor. Truth is, our protective detail runs the lot of heads of nations, not celebrities. Everything is a threat until deemed otherwise."

"I'd rather you be too protective of me than not at all." She would rather he be anything with her at this point than not at all.

"I promise you, El. You're safe."

"I didn't doubt that. I never doubt you."

"You have."

She looked away and shook her head. "It's not you I doubted, Bishop. I promise you."

He touched her chin and brought her face back toward him, letting his green eyes hold hers. "Good."

This was a moment when she wanted him to step closer, to dissolve the distance and put his strong hands on her bare shoulders and slide them down. Ella wanted the power and strength he exuded over the most mundane things to be worked over her. She would die to feel the starched crunch of his tuxedo shirt pressed against her silky dress, to run her fingertips along his shirt buttons, to push her hands into the warmth of his jacket and slide it away.

Ella brushed her hair away from her face and—*oh*. She sniffed and realized the Vicks was wearing off. *Buzzkill*.

"Still stinks?" he asked.

She nodded. "Can I have my bottle?"

He patted his pocket. "Damn. I'm pretty sure that's somewhere in the interview room."

"Oh. Okay."

"The meat is back, huh?"

"Laugh all you want. It's in the dress. At least I could wipe it off my skin and pull my hair back. But the dress and no Vicks?" She fake-gagged. Not the most attractive thing, but definitely the most real. "Best case, it stinks. Worst case, I'll have a migraine all weekend long and puke on you."

"Change of plan." He laughed, shutting her in the truck, and she watched him hustle to the driver's seat. "We're not headed home yet. That'll take an hour, and I'd like to avoid worst-case scenarios."

He meant *her* home. But headed home with him wouldn't be so bad. Except she couldn't stand how she smelled. *Not sexy.* And she was so tired. "I just said I was—"

"Trust me." They pulled out of the parking garage. He turned down a maze of streets then floored it before sliding his big truck into a tiny street spot with no effort. "Let's go."

Bishop jumped out of his truck, rounded the hood, and opened her door before she could process where they were or what was open on the Georgetown strip of bars and restaurants.

"Grab your skirt." He took her hand, dragging her the opposite way of his car. "Come on, slowpoke. I saw how fast you could hustle out of a packed auditorium in those heels. Move your ass, babe. One, two. One, two."

"I—"

"Smell like a shish kebab. We've been over that."

Jutting across traffic, she trotted behind him in the killer heels, trying to keep up. "You're supposed to keep me alive."

"Hurry, and that won't be a problem."

Her heel hooked on a mini-pothole, and right when he expected her to speed up, she went down. Almost.

Her hand was still in his, and his other hand wrapped around her lightning fast. Before her knees hit the asphalt and she became roadkill, Bishop lifted her. He had one powerful forearm under her butt, and the dress that stunk like a vegan's nightmare hung down over his arm. Now was the time for paparazzi. If there ever was a picture to be taken, it was this one. Her knight in shining armor carried her, while she was dressed like royalty, and her expensive clothing trailed in the night.

Every pitter-patter of her heart raced. Her mouth went dry, and her mind shattered as he held her close and jogged them to the safety of a nearby sidewalk.

The late-night crowd milled, and some clapped. What an entrance. But with her head ducked close to him, no one had recognized her, and the applause were for the save and chivalry displayed by Bishop. He didn't notice.

"There." He pulled her from the tuxedoed cover of his chest and put her down gently. His hands lingered on her sides as though neither one of them trusted her to remain standing.

The word *thanks* should have rolled off her tongue, but her pounding heart had simply stopped all semblance of manners. Cool, confident Eco-Ella was tongue-tied. But if he took a step forward and wrapped his arms around her again, she would melt away from this crowded bar scene.

He took a step back, dropping his hands, then tilted his head. "Time to teeter-totter your cute vegan butt in there."

His words sliced the tension. She turned to take in the coffee shop's sign. "More coffee?"

"Like I said, trust me. And go sit down at a table. Try not to get yourself into any trouble. No videos. No check-ins. No whatever else."

"Ha, ha. Tara had my purse stashed when we left, and I didn't grab it. *No phone*. Didn't you notice?"

His gaze raked across her. "That thing's like an appendage, and somehow not what I was looking at. *No*. I didn't."

Whoa. What?

Stunned from whatever this rollercoaster was, she turned and pulled the twenty-four-hour coffee shop's door open, walked in, and sat down as Bishop went to the counter. What exactly had he meant by that? What else could he mean?

His tuxedo creases showed wear from the day and night's hours on the job, but that did nothing to dampen how absurdly attractive he was. The two garage girls had been right. He was hot with a tight ass.

Tearing her eyes away from him, she realized they were in an *all-organic* coffee shop. There were a half dozen national chain coffee shops within a stone's throw from here. She knew them by heart, having blogged about them on a fairly regular basis, questioning the carcinogen levels of their additives. Had he picked this place on purpose? She glanced out the window, and saw they had parked adjacent to a coffee shop with a MADE HOT AND FRESH sign glowing in the window before he'd carried her across the street.

He'd chosen this place on purpose.

"Hey." He approached the table. "I didn't check in and status update my GPS coordinates. Thought you should know how most normal folks roll."

"Ha, ha. Very funny." She rolled her eyes, shaking her head. A cascade of her meat-scented hair fell over her face. "God, I've got to strip out of this dress and get in a shower."

Bishop was silent, but his face wasn't.

Shower. Naked. Sex. The words were written all over the color in his face and the hunger in her eyes. There was something addictive about his protection, about how he claimed to know best and then *did*, about how he wanted to take care of her. But it wasn't just an act. He'd literally carried her like some sort of pothole-saving kamikaze street-crosser.

His chiseled jaw set and didn't budge, and his green eyes were a pool of emotion. It seemed as though they always warmed when she made him angry, when she irritated him, when she turned him on…

Right now, they were very, very green. And her heartbeat matched the fast pace of the deepening hue. For all of her concern that what she felt was one-sided, his eyes said otherwise.

"Don't look at me like that, Ella." His words rumbled so quietly, they scratched across her senses.

He'd said it so quietly that she felt the rumble of each word graze down her neckline. "I'm sorry."

"Don't apologize, either." He pulled out a chair, dropping into it.

"We're here for more coffee?"

Bishop shook his head. "Almost."

She hadn't realized he had something tucked under his arm until he put it on the counter. "Go change."

"Um, what?" She studied it. "You bought me a T-shirt?"

"I thought it might help. If the dress is holding on to the smell, then ditch the dress."

"This is a thousand-dollar dress." Or something like that.

"And *this* is a twenty-dollar shirt. Put it on. No one cares what you're wearing anymore, babe. You'd be beautiful in a trash bag, so who cares?"

"Bishop, that's…"

"Go change. Heels and an oversize shirt. Kinda hot, if you ask me. But I'm not a Bloggie red-carpet dude." He leaned back, balancing the chair on two legs. "We'll grab a cup of coffee beans to go. I'm pulling out all my tricks tonight. We have an hour's drive out of town, so might as well get as comfortable as you can. Right?"

Ella stood up, clutching her new shirt. His thoughtfulness gave her a moment of heart pangs that she didn't want to admit, and she pecked him on the cheek. "Thanks."

He leaned into her, and she let her lips linger, dragging them against his cheek.

The air zipped and zapped. She wanted him to turn his head, to let his mouth linger against hers again, and not because he wanted to make things even. But they were in the middle of a coffee shop and, together, they smelled like the dinner-scented auditorium. Though that was starting to be forgettable…

"Go change, Ella." Bishop turned her around and patted her upper back.

Damn. Cringing, she backed away, disgusted with herself. Flirting with him again! And shut down again!

Yes, there'd been a look. But so what! Or maybe she'd dreamt it. He couldn't have been more clear. She was work. He loved his job, and Bishop was the opposite of her entire world. Yet with each footstep away from him, she dreaded the space.

Finding the bathroom down the hall, Ella stripped off the scent-stained dress and pulled on the double-XL T-shirt. The massive tent swallowed her in black cotton. From far away, no one would be able to tell it was a T-shirt. Her eyes dropped to the front of the shirt.

"Organic Lovers Do It Better."

God. It was funny. Bishop was funny. He was witty and smart on his feet. She couldn't hide the smile tugging on her cheeks.

A rap sounded on the door. "Let's see it, Crazy."

Might as well own the title he had bestowed upon her. She threw the door open, grabbed her stinky dress, and tossed it to him as she strutted her stuff past Bishop, swinging her hips and catwalking as though she was on a Milan runway.

The oversized shirt easily hung to her knees, but she bunched it in one hand and turned. "What do you think, Muscles?"

A one-sided grin played on his lips, and his green eyes danced. "Best. Dress. Ever."

A blush hit her cheeks, and it seemed like ages ago that the guy had attacked her with a stick of beef jerky. He'd certainly made up for all things meat-related tonight. "Do it better, huh?"

"Don't you?" They turned to leave the coffee shop. Bishop was already holding a to-go cup of coffee beans. Her rolled-up dress was tucked under his elbow, and he guided her toward the door, a hand placed low on her back. "At least in my experience, that's been the case."

Chapter 17

The city lights fell behind them as they sped down Interstate 66, leaving Washington, DC and heading west. Her condo was nestled in a booming part of northern Virginia. The area's growth was planned and smart. Very green. Very Eco-Ella. Bishop preferred more space than she had. Everything of Ella's was tiny—small dog, small cat, little condo. She even boxed up her trash into tiny-ass pieces to fit into her already microscopic trash—*landfill*—can.

"Your schedule is clear this weekend, right?"

No answer.

He glanced over, and… Ella was asleep. How about that?

For as lost in thought as he was over her, she had simply fallen asleep. Hell, she'd had a big night. Draping his wrist over the steering wheel, he took it as a compliment that she could relax enough to zone out. And she had to be tired after being on point all night. Her acceptance speech had been funny, almost self-deprecating in a good-natured way, and had genuinely pushed her cause. She was definitely a true believer. Not many of them out there anymore, especially once they reached a certain level of success.

Did she even realize the success she'd achieved?

Realistically, she knew she had done well. But had it really occurred to her? He took his eyes off the road and stared at her. Ella's heels were kicked off, and the T-shirt-turned-dress rode high on her legs. Maybe not. Maybe she was naive to it all. Simply oblivious to the force she'd created around her.

Bishop's chest tightened. Good for her for staying grounded, but damn, she needed to be more careful. The people around her were no help.

Bishop changed lanes, looking for her exit.

Jay was a classic dickhead, whether Ella wanted to admit it or not. Bishop was going to have a long discussion with her FBI agent. Jay had stalker practically tattooed on his forehead. Tara cared less about Ella and more about success than any publicist he'd ever come across. Though, truthfully, he didn't know many.

Bishop slowed as he pulled off the highway. A few turns into the trendy ex-urban neighborhood, and he decelerated onto her street. It was late, and the lack of street parking was expected. Bishop's eyes roamed, looking for another option.

"Hey, babe. Which one is your parking garage?" There were two entrances ahead, so it was heads or tails.

Ella murmured and sleepily batted his words away with her hand.

"Cute. Not helpful, but cute." He circled around the block and double-parked in front of her building. Green slime coated the front door, the brick facade, and the sidewalk.

What the hell? More of the slime. Hadn't they been through that before?

He pulled his phone from his hip, dialing the kid who had slimed him before. No answer. Bishop redialed, and the guy answered on the third ring.

"Hello?" He sounded sleepy and annoyed.

"Bishop O'Kane here. Did you visit Ella Leighton's building again?"

"What?" He cleared his throat. "No, sir."

"Who did?"

"I don't know." The guy was now awake and sounded as though he could be believed. "I haven't seen other messages on the boards, either. No one private messaged me. Nothing."

"Then who did this?"

"I don't know!"

Bishop ended the call and called the front desk at Ella's building, watching the doorman answer.

"Good evening—"

"Bishop O'Kane calling on behalf of Ella Leighton."

"Yes, sir."

"What happened outside?"

"We're sorry, sir. Maintenance will be here in the morning to clean it up."

"What happened?"

"Er, we don't know. Paintball? But it will be clean first thing in the morning. Ms. Leighton did have a message."

He cringed. "What does it say?"

"Congratulations on your big night."

"Thank you." Bishop ended the call.

She wasn't going inside there, and Bishop wasn't high enough on the chain of command to drop the hand of God into the FBI investigation. He didn't want to be part of the investigative arm, and he was certainly not thrilled to report a second problem at her residence.

He swiped the screen on his phone and hit Rocco's number. His boss picked up on the second ring. "It's quarter past two in the morning. What's wrong?"

After an awkward explanation of the second slime situation, Rocco remained quiet.

"Yeah, so, what do you want me to do with her?" Bishop pushed.

"Where is she?"

"Asleep in the passenger seat of my truck."

"Right. Okay. So, two options. Give me an hour to make arrangements for a safe house or find a hotel, following alpha-red protocol."

Easy enough. Check in. Cash only. False name. And get some shut-eye. "Roger that. Option number two."

"All right. Check in tomorrow. We'll hash things out with her FBI POC."

"Thanks." Bishop eased his truck out of Park and headed south, exiting on a random thoroughfare. He crisscrossed traffic a half dozen times, ensuring he wasn't followed, then pulled into the nicest hotel the town had. *Not too shabby.*

After doing a drive around the perimeter, he decided that it would more than work for the night. The place looked safe, and there were good cars in the parking lot. All around, a decent place to crash. He unbuckled his seat belt and carefully brushed her arm. "Ella. Time to wake up."

She stirred but didn't rise.

"Ella. Hey, babe. Eyes open." This girl could sleep through a tornado. He unbuckled her seat belt, hoping the shift would jostle her. *No.* She readjusted, apparently pleased with less restriction. He chuckled and, with a firmer grasp, ran his hand along her forearm. "Rise and shine."

"Hmm?"

Her drowsy, sweet sound struck him in the gut with the strength of a mortar explosion. It was innocent, sweet, and breathy, pulling him all the way back to the years when she used to wake up in his arms. He hadn't realized it was a sound he liked, or one that he missed, until he heard it again, and it knocked him sideways. With his hand frozen on her arm, he regrouped and calmed the hard crescendo of his heart. "Change of plan. Eyes open."

She blinked awake. "What's—" Ella stretched, leaning against the door, and her T-shirt dress slipped up to the top of her thighs. "Why aren't we at my condo?"

Staring at her bare thighs wasn't right. But all the blood in his body diverted to his cock the second he focused on her legs and began to wonder if that shirt would move higher, what it would take to *move it* higher. Would she balk if he leaned across and dragged his tongue up her leg? Would she moan if he shouldered her legs wide, spreading her thighs? And what would he find under that shirt? Would her panties be wet? Would he feel her arousal through the fabric that rubbed against her clit, against that pussy that had driven him to distraction?

Growing erect, he throbbed. All night, he'd tried to ignore her, and now there was nothing to think about except burying his face between her legs. He wanted to tear whatever shred of underwear off that served as a barrier, and he wanted to feast. *Damn it. What would she say...*

"Bishop?" She twisted in the seat, oblivious that the shirt inched just a little higher. "What do you want to do?"

Everything. He wanted to kiss her until he choked on her moans. He wanted to shove his hands down her underwear and feel her ride his hand, fingers inside her, pumping her sweet canal until she exploded. He needed it—to crush the climax out of her, kissing her while she tried to cry his name. And when she was panting and spent, incapable of begging for more, he wanted to tell Ella that he would do the same thing with his tongue and then his cock. They wouldn't stop until she looked at him the way she had once before.

Bishop pulled back. That was the problem. He'd hurt her, and he didn't deserve another chance. *Damn it.* He opened the door, needing the cool air's help. "I can explain later." Pushing out of the truck only did the bare minimum to alleviate his hard-on. "But more slime, basically."

"Oh."

"Until we figure it out, room service and housekeeping." He offered her a smile that was meant to be encouraging; one to offer comfort. But it was dark, and his attempt failed because her demeanor didn't change. "It's the middle of the night, so we missed the good perks."

Her eyes went to his. "Um…"

"I'll be right next door. You need anything, just knock. Kick the wall. Whatever. It'll be fine."

She nodded. "No slime problems." As if breaking through her sleepy fog, she tugged at her shirt-dress. "Fine. Okay." Then she laughed. "Heels and a T-shirt. People are going to love my outfit."

"It's like two a.m. No one is going to be around."

He rounded his truck and helped her out as she held the shirt down, shivering. "Wow, it got cold."

He grabbed his tuxedo jacket from where he'd thrown it in the backseat. "Wear this." He draped it over her shoulders and rubbed her arms, creating friction. "Better?"

"Much." Ella leaned into him, fitting perfectly under his arm. "You don't want it?"

He laughed, not even answering. An arctic blast could have chilled the parking lot, and he wouldn't have been any less hot to trot for the woman under his arm. As soon as they had a wall between them, he would finally be able to function. Until then, he would let himself fall into the fantasy that he and she were still a "they."

CHAPTER 18

"WHAT DO YOU MEAN THAT you don't have any other rooms?" Bishop evil-eyed the lady at the counter. She was asking him to tempt the devil by putting him and Ella in the same room. There was only so much he could handle.

"I'm sorry," the desk clerk said. "You're lucky. We had someone go home, and one happens to be available. A big convention is in our neck of the woods, and every hotel in town is booked."

They could hop back in the truck and drive down the next exit. Or—

"It's fine," Ella mumbled. "I'm exhausted. We don't have cooties and have obviously slept in the same room before."

The sane, rational thing to do was go to the room and sleep. He could control himself. It was pure selfishness that he wanted a little breathing room. "Yeah. Of course."

He paid in cash, using fake identification, and took the key. Rocco's name appeared on his phone as they walked through the door to their room, and Bishop listened to the recount of everything Titan had learned by hacking Ella's building security and talking to the FBI.

It wasn't great. But the good news was that Titan and the FBI were now on the same page. Unfortunately, they were still one step behind. This was more than a juvenile delinquent with an attitude problem. It was a smart, calculating sadist.

Bishop threw the phone on the king-size bed, loosened his tie, and let it hang. He unbuttoned his top button and watched Ella crawl next to the phone. "What did they tell you?"

"We can talk about it in the morning. You're spent."

"Agreed. But I'm… I stink. I'm jumping in the shower." She kicked off the bed and left him alone. The water turned on, and he finally had time to think. Hell, there wasn't anything to think about. Nothing to decide. The job was the job. Ella was Ella. He was hot for her—if the erection he'd been sporting since the day they crashed back together was any indication. But Rocco had clearly said not to fuck her.

The way his boss had said that… Bishop balled his fists. That order had downplayed their history and didn't do justice to his reaction to her now. As much as he wanted to get her naked, he had enjoyed taking her to that coffee shop tonight.

Bishop rubbed his chest. He wanted to protect Ella far more than he wanted to kiss her again. All of this—the history, the emotions, the possibilities of a job he would die for, and a girl he would die for regardless of payment—all of that rolled together. And his mind spun in circles.

The water shut off. He paced, knowing she was dripping wet and drying off and that he wanted in there too. He was torn in too many directions.

The door slipped open, and steam wafted out. "I hate this."

His ears prickled as he turned to Ella. That wasn't the voice of a relaxed woman coming out of a shower. A white towel was wrapped around her breasts, and her semi-dried hair hung on her bare shoulders. She had a hint of makeup under her eyes, which were red and tearing.

"El?"

"I hate this. I hate this. I hate this," Ella whispered. "I brought this on myself. I know. I get it. You told me. But now I can't even go home." She sniffed and had clearly cried in the shower. "I'm tired. So exhausted. And stressed. And I don't tell anyone ever. And I'm just done. I want my own bed."

"I know, babe. You can get through this."

"Why? Tara yells at me. Jay yells at me. You're none too pleased with things I do."

Well, hell. Not the group he wanted to be lumped into. "I'm not them. I'm on your team."

She threw her head back. "Ha! They *are* my team!"

"Ella," he warned. "I'm different."

"I just want to go home and sleep in my bed. I don't want to have a panic attack in the shower that Manny might not have Furry Baby and Little Kitty handled for breakfast—"

"He has them all weekend until you say otherwise."

"I know. But I forgot. I'm just stressed. And I'm scared. I want this all done." She let out a little sob.

His inability to protect her tore at his insides. He carefully stepped closer, knowing that it was a danger zone—her in a towel and crying. She was his weakness, and he couldn't handle her seemingly so vulnerable and hurt. "We'll get it figured out."

"No. We won't. No one takes this seriously." She covered her face.

Bishop gathered her into his arms. Her skin was semi-damp and warm from the shower, and Ella smelled like soap. She leaned into his arms, dropping her hands, and clung to him as though no one had hugged her in ages.

"You're getting worked up. It's fine. Get some shut-eye. It'll seem less overwhelming in the morning." He kissed the top of her head, wishing he could dissolve her fear. If only there were a way to drop-kick away every bad memory, every fear. He wanted to just absorb her pain and, *God*, he wanted to keep her close.

Shit. He was in deep. The tighter she held onto him, the more he needed to make it right.

She burrowed against him, her wet hair dampening his shirt. "I don't want to sleep."

He stifled a groan. Now wasn't the time to follow through on every urge. *Never* was actually the time. But with her rubbing and swaying against him, this was painful. Maybe when everything cooled down. But for damn sure, not when she was a breath away from tears and clinging to him for support and friendship.

"Titan will keep you safe."

"You will keep me safe," she corrected.

Hell yeah, he would. Selfishly, he dropped a kiss on top of her head…and another one. It was the only thing he would allow himself to do. He shouldn't. But damn it, some things were out of his control. He kept his lips there, breathing her in.

"I want more of you than that, Bishop." She shifted so that his mouth moved against her forehead.

He groaned, inwardly at war. Ella hugged him tighter, her fists grabbing onto his shirt, delving back and forth against his chest, and taunting him with only her towel and his shirt as barriers.

"El." Her name caught in his throat. "Ella."

Arousal choked his airway, keeping a stronghold on his lungs. Each breath teased and tortured him as though every inhalation was an exercise in staying alive.

"Don't let go of me, Bishop." She squeezed. "Whatever you do tonight, don't take your arms off me."

Fucking hell. "El, you're in a bad spot. You need to sleep."

"I'm spent. Upset. And I'm telling you, I need *you* to make it better." She eased back, and her fingers started at the top of his shirt, unbuttoning on a nimble search-and-destroy mission. The last of the buttons loosened, and Ella lifted her chin. "Do you understand?"

Damn it, he was going down this road. He untucked the shirt and gathered her into his hold. Then he backed into a chair, carefully dropping himself into it and holding her against him. His palms grazed against her bare bottom, and his dick jumped to life, as though it were not already wide awake.

"Do you remember that shirt I got you?" she asked, her hands running beneath the inside of his white undershirt.

A smile crackled onto his face. How could he forget? Both their parents had about killed them. "The one that said 'I liked to spoon'?"

Her sexy laughter brightened her face, and the red eyes began to soften. "Yes."

"I had to explain a few things to my mom after yours called."

She laughed again. "Sorry."

"You're not sorry."

"Not one bit."

The air danced around them, heavy with want and wishes, sparks and sizzle. He shifted, unable to hide his erection, unable to keep his hands from holding her in place.

"A lot of time has passed, El."

She nodded slowly, her lips parting.

"What do you want?" It was obvious what they both were after. As soon as he'd held her in a towel on his lap, Ella had been drawing imaginary doodles on his chest. But there were some things people couldn't recover from. They had one of those things.

Ella's hand froze on his shirt. "Take off the dress shirt."

He shrugged, letting his unbuttoned shirt fall behind him.

Her fingers bit into his undershirt. "Take off this shirt too."

Rolling his bottom lip into his mouth, he let it go, enjoying how his cock turned to steel under her orders. "Can do." He pulled it over his head, barely breaking their eyelock. "That's all you want, babe?"

Ella inhaled, maybe to fortify herself, then loosened her towel. She didn't unwrap it, just slackened it enough to drive him insane.

"I want your mouth," she whispered. "All over me. Kissing me hard and deep until I can't remember the difference between light and sound, and hot and cold."

His possessive hand splayed on her side, and her short breaths burned in his ears.

"I want you to hold me, control me, take over this night. Bishop, I want you to own everything about us right now." Ella leaned close to his ear. "That's what I want. To forget about this day, to be treated like you need me."

"El, if there was ever a doubt…" He pulled the corner of the loosened towel, baring her breasts and stomach, letting the cotton pool in her lap. "I've had too many dirty thoughts about you."

Her eyes shot to his.

"And now you'll have to indulge me." He peeled back the rest of the towel, unwrapping her like a present.

The hardened tips of Ella's nipples reached for him, and the heavy mounds of her breasts were swollen. A trim triangle of hair led to the pussy he'd wanted in a hundred different ways, and now she lay in his arms, naked, flushed, and beautiful.

With his hand behind her neck, he brought her to meet his kiss. Sweeping her mouth with his tongue, he explored, listening to her mew and moan, feeling her rock and writhe as their slow burn heated.

Bishop massaged her breast, squeezing and making her back arch. Ella bit his bottom lip, sucking it into her mouth.

"Yeah?" he asked.

"Mm-hmm."

That sound, this woman. He pinched her nipple, twisting and

tugging. Her reaction was exactly what he wanted. Ella writhed as he smoothed his palm down her stomach, smoothing over her soft skin.

"More, Bishop."

"Trust me. I've got you." Deftly, he brushed his fingers between her legs, urging her thighs wider with a whisper soft touch.

She panted. "More of that."

He delved two fingers along the seam of her slick juncture, and she grinded against him.

"Yes, yes. That, yes."

He growled as his tongue forced her mouth open when his fingers speared her tight entrance, knuckles deep. Ella's most sensitive muscles gripped. A gasp fell from her lips, and he claimed it with a soul-stealing kiss as he withdrew and slowly sank his fingers in again. "I'm going to do this all night long. Slow and steady."

"No. I need more, please." But she thrashed and tightened.

Slow and steady was his plan, no changing that. As though twisting a vice, Bishop worked her until she couldn't take any more, then he pressed his thumb to her clit, circling the tight bundle of nerves. She threw her head back, clamped her legs down, and cried his name.

CHAPTER 19

***TRUST THE MAN.* ELLA HAD** screamed for him to hurry up, and he forced her to wait—*hallelujah.* They hadn't had sex yet, but that was a top-ten orgasm.

He'd had her hanging onto her sanity by a fingernail since he walked in all tuxed out. This was so much more.

Arms numb, lips tingling, and mind spinning, she wouldn't let a climax-coma slow them down. She needed more of him, more of everything, and it had been too long since she'd had anything from Bishop.

"Damn, El." His hungry eyes burned, and his chin dropped as he took in her bare body recovering from the ricochets. "You're…perfect."

"Oh, be quiet."

"I'm glad you can still take a compliment."

The reminder that he knew her so well squeezed her racing heart. Instead of finding words to acknowledge the truth, she pushed up to taste his kiss again.

He didn't move. Didn't open his mouth for more. But a growl, *a groan* collided against her lips in the minute fraction of space of their almost kiss.

Ella pulled back. What had Bishop expected? For her to take

her climax and run to bed? Go nod off to sleep? No, thank you.

His green eyes had her mesmerized, making a fever run rapid down her spine. He'd never made a decision that wasn't in her best interest. Was this him, offering her security and safety? Holding back until she gave whatever green light he might deem appropriate?

Ella shivered.

"Cold?" he asked.

"No." Her breath shook, and she pressed her mouth to his again, needing everything he could give her. Not a kiss, more like a touch she couldn't stay away from, and she whispered against his skin, "Don't stop now. I already explicitly explained what I wanted."

He tore the towel from underneath her and quickly sat her upright. Ella put her legs on either side of his black-pants-covered thighs.

"That's better," she said. "Cut the good guy routine."

Bishop flexed his cock against her and dropped a kiss on her lips that possessed her soul. His tongue slid, and he sucked hers until her core clenched.

"Promise." He bit her lip. "Nothing good guy is coming from me."

Her reward was a hand threaded possessively into her hair, knotting its hold. His other arm wrapped around her waist.

"Thank you."

He pressed her to his bare chest, letting her breasts sway against his smattering of light chest hair. God in heaven, he was built like a wall. Solid as a mountain, skin as hot as a fiery day.

"I like your muscles, Muscles," she breathed against his cheek, letting his five o'clock shadow scrape roughly.

"I like your mouth, Crazy." He flicked her lip with his tongue, lapping it with a gentle kiss.

Ella's nipples were so tight they hurt, and she rubbed them

over his course chest hair. The sensation had her rocking against his hard-on. Delirious for more friction, more Bishop, she let her nails dig into his biceps. "You still have on pants."

"We'll let me be in charge."

She bit his bottom lip like he'd just done to her, tugging it with her teeth, then letting go and kissing it sweetly.

"Trying to leave a mark?" He tugged her hair lightly, exposing her neck.

She gasped, the vulnerability and control making her desperate to submit. "Maybe."

He pulled her hair again and sucked behind her earlobe. "Two can play that game."

Wriggling and feeling the sting of her hair being pulled as she moved, she couldn't get away and never wanted it to stop. "God, Bishop."

"You like that?" His tongue licked down to her collarbone and back. "Because I love that sound."

"What"—she gasped—"sound?"

He chuckled again then raked his teeth where his tongue had just run. "Do you know how wet you were for me?"

"Bishop," she whimpered. They had never been that direct when they were younger. Now they'd both said things they wouldn't have dreamed of back then. Just thinking the words were erotic, but to experience this? She could hardly stand it.

"Just for my fingers, babe? *Soaking*."

Her cheeks burned as he crooned the truth. So hot, and she was still as wet as she had been.

"Do you want more than that, Ella?"

"Mm-hmm."

"You want my cock?"

"Yes," she murmured, drunk on the idea. "But it's not fair. *You're still in pants.*"

"I don't care." He rubbed her thighs straddled over him. "You need me in charge."

Hell, Bishop didn't just stare. He devoured. He consumed. His gaze did a million things. It was slow and sweeping, stealing her breath and making her feel like the most revered woman who had ever walked the planet she loved so much.

"And I need that too, El."

"I'm the only one naked, Bishop." She tried again, her voice shaking. "Let me unbutton your pants."

He licked his lips and placed strong hands on her thighs.

"You don't want to?" she asked.

"That's not it."

Ah, there they were. The problem. Or problems. But mostly, she'd left him. Or was it that she was a job now? Hours ago, she would have cringed, but somehow, knowing that at least he wanted her as much as she wanted him made the *Should they? Shouldn't they?* conversation more an intellectual one, and less an emotional one. Ella tried to find reason in what he might be thinking and came up empty. They were both turned on with too much baggage and a legitimate reason to go to bed.

"Somewhere along the line, I think I was going to tell you not much had changed"—she motioned between their naked chests—"with us in bed."

His eyes narrowed.

"But," she continued. "You've got some pretty rock-star moves."

His face froze for a moment before he threw his head back and laughed. "I had rock star moves before."

"No woman on the planet has come like I just did."

"I made you come like that before."

She kissed his cheek, and his hand gripped her chin, redirecting her lips onto his. "Maybe."

"Don't rewrite history." He kissed her back, reminding her that there may have been truth to his statement.

So they were semi-naked and kissing. Why did he still have pants on? "It was a long time ago."

Bishop trailed his fingertips down her spine. "True."

"We were younger." *Screw it.* She wanted him naked, so she was getting him naked. He could pull all the alpha-in-charge BS later. She unfastened the top button of his pants, taking extra care to stroke him as she did.

His eyes slipped shut, and he leaned back in his chair. "You sure, Elo—Ella?"

She dropped her chin, hating that sadness had unexpectedly crept into place. Ella had replaced Eloise as much as she had run away from Bishop. Even hearing the name hurt. Bishop had never been a guy to shy away from owning his feelings. Until it had ended. Until they couldn't stand being together when they'd needed each other.

"El?"

Smiling to cover up where her mind had gone, she didn't want it to ruin what was here and now—something that felt amazing and had saved a crappy day. "Sorry."

"It slipped," he said, referencing the almost name. "Happens sometimes, but I'm catching myself."

What could she say? Before she had cut and run, they'd both realized they wouldn't talk about his sister. Ella had left him mentally before she had literally—just stopped talking to him. Ella, the girl now who couldn't live without the phone in her hand and talked nonstop to strangers, which he had to be painfully aware of, hadn't been able to talk to him when he'd probably needed her the most.

No wonder his pants were still on. She categorically sucked as a human being, forget how she ranked as a girlfriend.

Ella bit her lip, lost in her thoughts, when he rubbed his hands on her arms.

"Come back to me," he half-joked.

She dragged her mind back to reality, to the man that deserved better, who sat in front of her. Maybe she'd been a pain in his side since they reconnected in order to avoid this exact moment. Putting him in her Smart Car? She cringed. Bishop was too good for her. How he wasn't married with a brood of babies, she didn't know. Oh yeah. She'd literally chased him off to war.

Well hell...

Bishop dropped his head back and sighed. "You want to get dressed?"

This would be even more awkward than she'd thought, and they hadn't even had sex. Her heart sank as she slid back.

"Nope." Bishop caught her wrist. "No. No way, Crazy."

"No, *what*?"

He pulled her closer. "You can't give me sad eyes like *I'm* the one who doesn't want to."

"You're a guy. You always want to." But did he really? His *pants* were still on.

He scoffed. "You know me better than that when it comes to you."

Visions of his restraint, of his walking away, of his offers to find a replacement after she kissed him replayed in her head. She couldn't explain what she understood.

"What I want to know"—he grabbed the towel, covering her shoulders as though that was what needed covering, then dropped his palms to her bare waist—"is why do you, *did you*, say all that tonight? About us hooking up?"

Her mouth moved, but nothing intelligent came out, just something that sounded similar to "Ah-um..."

"Old times' sake?" His dull green eyes narrowed. "Or was

it just needing something to get over this stalker shit?"

He had to have known that wasn't why she would do this.

"Okay, okay." He smiled and shrugged. "That was an awkward question. We'll just go with I'm a stud, you're attracted to me, horny as hell and—"

"Bishop!" When he broke down his uber-serious routine, his funny-guy act killed and made her laugh. She batted his chest, and he laughed too.

"Seriously, Ella." He caught her hand and threaded his fingers into hers. "You've been scared, and I'm your security blanket. It's all good. Okay?"

The towel didn't cover anything, and the vulnerability of this conversation exposed her more than spreading her legs. She stared over his shoulder, letting her gaze drift to the carpet.

"El, look at me."

"I'd rather not." It would be much easier to keep the rawness inside, where he couldn't get first-hand knowledge of it.

"Ella," he growled.

She jumped, and their eyes locked.

"I will always keep you safe, babe."

Her eyes bugged. "I know."

"Good." He squeezed her hand. "Go get dressed. I still like to spoon." He shifted. "We'll, I don't know, order room service and watch movies until you fall asleep."

Again, her heart tumbled, and her eyes brimmed with tears she didn't want to explain to him. Mostly because she couldn't.

"El—"

She kissed him—hard—with everything she had pent up. The heartache from leaving him too long ago. The disappointment from not chasing him down. The panic that had surged when she saw him at Titan for the first time. And the fear that he was pushing her away now.

Tears slipped down her cheeks, and he kissed her back, gripping her face and holding her as if she would run.

She wiped her eyes and put her palms over his hands, panting as she stopped kissing him. "*Please* get undressed with me. Take off your stupid pants."

He nodded, letting their hands fall to the side, then he lifted Ella up and on her feet as her towel fell. Bishop stood, removed the remainder of his clothes, then took a condom from his wallet and placed it on a side table. "There. Now I'm naked with you."

Warmth hit her cheeks. "About time."

She sniffled. How unbelievably *not* sexy was that? *God.* She laughed, covering her face, but then she peeked between her fingers to see him smiling. When he did that, she was sure angels sighed. He was breathtaking, and now that he was naked, every muscle was on display. He was lean and corded, bulked and shredded, statuesque…and *well-hung.* Her face had turned magenta, and he took it in stride, even as she gawked and blushed, and would likely have to find her eyeballs on the floor.

Bishop took her hand. "All right, back to our chair."

"You want to do dirty things to me on this chair?" Ella giggled because she couldn't think straight. She was an overly exhausted, emotional basket case, dealing with the past and present. Silliness was the only thing her mind could comprehend at the moment.

Bishop's eyes had intensified. "I want to do dirty things to you everywhere."

Her stomach catapulted and would've kept spinning, but he yanked her back onto his lap.

"Where did we leave off?"

"I think—"

"You were just kissing me."

She nodded.

"Rock-star kiss."

Ella smiled. "You think so?"

"Try me again, babe. Just to be sure."

"That was an emotional kiss." She rolled her eyes. "Spontaneous things like that can't be replicated."

"Christ. You live to challenge me." He grabbed her face and gave her a repeat performance of her emo-kiss, minus her tears. His tongue danced with hers; his mouth consumed and devoured her in a way that made her core clench with every devastating sweep of his kiss.

His well-hung dick rubbed against her inner thigh and between her legs where she grew slick again. As he hardened, Bishop ran his hands into her hair, pulling just enough to make her moan into his mouth, beg into his kiss. Ella arched her back and rocked against his cock. Thick and swollen for her, he flexed his hips up and stroked his shaft against her wetness, teasing her clit as he spread her folds.

"I'm no longer challenging you." Legs spread wide over his thighs, arms draped on his shoulders, she leaned forward so that their foreheads pressed together.

Bishop wrapped an arm around her waist, pulling her close. "You feel good." His lips moved to her neck, his tongue licking its way to her earlobe. He gave it a tiny, sharp bite. "You have no idea how good it feels just to stroke against you."

She slid her palms to his pecs. The rapid beat of his heart urged her on. "I need more." Her thumbs outlined the dark disks of his hard nipples, and he sucked in a deep breath at the touch. "You like that?"

His chest rumbled, and the head of his cock teased her opening before sliding forward again. "Do it again."

She did, and he grabbed her ass so tightly, so possessively that she almost climaxed. Ella rubbed against his shaft, gasping at the deep sensations of pain and pleasure, want and need. "God."

"One of my favorite memories of you"—his rough grip moved to her waist and squeezed her hips—"was how you would slide down on my cock. Tight." His chest heaved. "Slow. Like you couldn't."

That was how it had felt. Bishop stretching into her, thick and long, beautiful and strong. She remembered all those years ago. "But I did." Her words caught. "And I loved it." Because she had loved him.

"Eyes open, Ella."

She didn't realize they were closed. "I thought of you. Before. After you and I…we were apart. Remembering how you felt."

"How did I feel?" His voice graveled, and his fingers flexed, rocking her back and forth, riding her against him.

Her juices coated his cock. Without searching back for the memory, she was aroused. But thinking about him pressing into her? A weight wrapped around her ribcage, tightening, strumming her to a whole new level of OMG.

"That first touch, that first thrust." Her breathy whispers were nothing more than a gasp of words, but he heard them and shut his eyes.

"Open your eyes, Bishop."

"Hell of a feeling." He reached for the condom, tore it open, and scooted her back.

The moment she lost contact, her body inwardly cried despite the fact that he had separated them to sheath himself. Her mouth watered as he stroked himself once before rolling on protection.

His gaze lifted, one hand cupping her hip, and Ella moved over his shaft. She guided the crown to her opening. Gently, delicately, his other hand splayed on her thigh. Patience and desire colored his face. "Easy…"

Ella sighed as he inched inside her. His erection stole her breath and seared her lungs. Foreplay and fun had readied her, but his intrusion would always be demanding. Bishop O'Kane had a big fucking cock.

She withdrew and took more of him, and his jaw flexed. "God, Bishop."

Again with the visible restraint, yet his soft fingers didn't dig in, didn't demand more. She loved that about him, how in control of himself he was—body and mind.

Following his gaze, they watched her body swallow his shaft, letting her arousal coat him as she paused. The stretch was nice and worthy of so many late-night memories. Ella pressed down on him again, and Bishop thrust up.

Her fingernails bit into his chest. "Yes."

His gruff breath fell in time with hers. He wrapped her into a bear hug and began to thrust up until her head fell back. Lost in euphoria, she let him take over.

Inch by mind-stealing inch, she rocked her hips. He thrust into her, until gasping and panting, Ella was fully seated. Then his mouth sealed on hers.

"Better than I remember." Bishop squeezed her, delving her mouth with his, lashing his tongue, and she was lost.

Her breasts bounced, scratching against his chest hair, and her orgasm came faster than she could scream his name. Ella bucked, arching in his arms as he held her still, keeping his cadence. Deep and strong.

But his mouth went to her ear. "Come, Ella. Now, babe."

She exploded, her inner muscles rippling, almost painfully as intense as the climax was. "Yes!"

"Ella, my Ella," he growled in her ear. "I want to hear that again."

He stood, still deep inside her pulsing, rippling pussy, and walked them to the bed as she caught her breath against his neck, drowning in the familiar taste of his skin.

Slowly, he withdrew and slid back inside, holding himself on top of her.

"So..." she drew out. "Sensitive."

"Easy," he whispered again. Long and slow. Deep and...meaningful. His mouth found her neck, and she languidly knotted a hand in his hair.

Mmmmm. This was heaven. Her head dropped to the side, and the mirror caught her eye. Bishop's powerful body over her, making love to her. His sculpted ass rhythmically moving, his corded back flexing. He was a work of art, and draped together...they were beautiful.

Bishop stilled, his fast breath in her ear. "You okay?"

His panting breaths tickled, and slowly, she nodded, not turning away from the mirror. She couldn't take her eyes off him, off them. He was gorgeous. She was fine with how she looked, but it wasn't that. It was *them.*

His tongue caressed her ear. "What is it?"

"Look," she whispered.

He kissed down her neck before turning his head, then his body went rigid. Every muscle tightened. His dark-green eyes found hers in the mirror, and they locked in a silent conversation before he kissed her neck. "Don't take your eyes off mine."

Bishop rolled his hips, flexing his shaft deep inside. Moaning, she couldn't look away, couldn't keep from staring at the powerful man making love to her.

"Wrap your legs around me, Ella."

She did, and he went deeper. Her mouth hung open, wanton, watching in the mirror.

"See that?" he asked.

Barely. Ecstasy made her blind. "Yes."

"That's what I dreamt of."

Her face shot to his, abandoning the mirror and their erotic show. Slowly, he turned to face her. In and out, long and slow, Bishop fucked her to the brink of insanity. Tears burned her eyelids. The impending orgasm tightened, but she didn't want to come, because then this moment would be over. Two old lovers reconnecting.

"Oh..." She couldn't help it. Knees pinching to his sides, fingernails raking his back, she cried, "Please."

He pistoned, pumping short and harsh, grunting. His growling kisses bit her lips and clashed with her tongue.

Her sight slipped away as sparks exploded. "Bishop, God!"

Ella came, and he strained, coming with her. Bishop knotted a hand in her hair and wrapped the other around her in a hug that sent her flying higher than her climax. Together, they gasped and clung, lost in each other.

One by one, her muscles relaxed, and his hug loosened until they were a cuddling mass of arms and legs. His lips pressed to her temple. Her eyes fluttered as she realized that this was exactly how she wanted to go to sleep.

Chapter 20

Bishop woke with one arm numb and a face full of Ella's hair. Despite what had to be mid-morning light shining into the hotel room, he could have easily fallen back asleep, breathing her in after gathering her closer.

But instead, he remained still. When had he slept past the break of dawn? He couldn't remember. Running his tongue along his raw lips, he replayed the night before—all the way to when they had said good night and he'd kissed the top of her head—he wouldn't have changed a thing.

Ella, though? No telling how she would wake, and he would brace for that storm. They'd needed last night. For stress relief. Maybe he would get a reprieve from the ultimate dick move he'd pulled fifteen years ago. *Hell.* Who was he kidding? If they ever came to that bridge, he would have to figure out what was involved in a fucking grovel.

There was likely an email on his phone with an update from Titan. Whoever was messing with Ella had better hope that the FBI found him first. With each passing day, Bishop wanted to play bodyguard less and hunter more. That was in his blood, not this wait-and-react bullshit.

Anxious to see what Titan had learned, he shifted to reach the nightstand. Ella snored quietly and went back to her peaceful sleep as he failed to dislodge himself. Now *that* was funny, and he stifled a laugh. If someone would make that a video, her little snore would get mega hits, though who knew if Tara-publicist-from-hell would shit for a lack of flawless makeup and perfect talking points.

On second thought, it would go viral, and her publicist would finally be on Team Bishop. But then the entire world would have access to the sleeping beauty in his arms, and territorial pride wanted this view for his own. So that would be a no-go.

She stirred again and nuzzled against him. She'd always had a crazy streak, had always been passionate. How had he not seen the woman she would become? Did he know the last time they were in bed that it would be the last time?

No. *Maybe…*

He'd lied. He should've called her or done something to show he wasn't an unfeeling asshole, running off like he had. Little did she know it was to fucking hide. However, if someone was going to be a bitch and hide, the army was a good place to do it—though the Rangers would've kicked his ass for ever thinking about the word hide. Bishop closed his eyes and thought about the last day he saw her.

"What are you doing here?" Eloise stared with dark circles under her eyes from across the bursar's office.

"Paperwork." Of all the people and all the places, Bishop couldn't handle her there. He'd signed his life away to the army and needed to pull out of school. But he couldn't look at her, couldn't tell her that or explain how angry he was at the world. He wouldn't tell her he was leaving—not now.

"Sorry I haven't called," she said, biting her lip. "I'll make it up to you."

They were the worst couple on the planet. "Sure."

Eloise wrapped her arms across her chest and didn't say good-bye as she drifted away, in a current of students.

Ella's eyelashes fluttered, and she snuggled into him again. The girl still woke up slowly, and he still loved the show. That hadn't changed, reminding him of first kisses that they'd promised would be their last. First nights spent together, first mornings. *Damn it.* Didn't matter, though. Could time heal all?

No. Not everything. Some hurts were still as raw as they were fifteen years ago.

"Hi." Ella repositioned, letting blood flow to his arm, and tugged the sheets higher on her chest. "Should we do awkward morning after or pretend nothing happened and go for brunch?"

He curled his fingers, making a fist, as the fresh blood flowed strong into his arm. "Gee, I was hoping for a vegan brunch."

Her sleepy smile was pretty fucking cute. "I've broken you of your jerky ways."

"Don't make me call you Crazy again." He stretched, now that all the feeling was back in his arm, then reached for his phone. It was after ten. Wow, that was something. Thumbing his email open, he saw that there was additional intel from HQ about what had happened last night. But he wasn't ready to get out of bed and didn't want to talk business now that Ella was awake.

"You were staring at me."

He tossed the phone down and went with a bold-face lie. "Nope, I was checking emails."

"When I woke up."

"I had lost all feeling in my extremity and was contemplating moving your head and shoulders."

They were both buck-ass naked, raw as hell from mind-blowing sex, and neither were acknowledging that anything had shifted. Or had it?

"I need some coffee." She rolled away from him and sat up. "And more clothes."

It had not, according to her mannerisms and tone. Straight-laced and serious. Her hair was a testament to their night in bed even though she'd finger-combed it for the thirty seconds it had taken him to get up and throw the condom away. Last night ended on an easy note.

This…this would be work. *But hell.* Bishop killed every job he ever had. Eco-Ella was work to begin with, and Awkward-Ella was no different than Crazy-Ella. All were the same girl he was once in love with long ago… His-Ella.

Problem was, was that what he wanted?

For sure, he wanted Titan. The job would understand if eventually this girl became *his* girl. But that wasn't the basis of their real problem, the one never dealt with. Enlisting in the army hadn't done shit but bury feelings, and—

"I can't function without coffee," she repeated—as though maybe he'd missed her mention of caffeine—while also doing her best to wrap the sheet around her. "We should go do something about that."

He rolled to her side of the bed, both their naked legs dangling, her bicep now touching his. "You're all morning-after awkward."

She elbowed him. "I am not!"

His side eye earned him another elbow, but he caught it that time and held her in place. "Chill out with the sheet."

"I am chill."

"You're questionable at the moment."

She rolled her eyes, and he stood up. Her eyes dropped to his junk then shot up, looking over his shoulder.

"El, you've seen it before. Think you can again."

Her cheeks flared red. "Oh-kay."

"You actually did *way* more than see it." He bobbed his

eyebrows, laughing quietly. "Last night and from back in the day. You've seen my goods, maybe more than any other person, ever. Cumulatively speaking."

Cheeks and neck blotchy with embarrassment, she glued her eyeballs to the ceiling. "Got it."

"I'm staring at you, babe. You can—" She tugged the rumpled comforter as though she wanted to bury herself in it, and he caught it. "Don't hide on me."

"Oh, come on. This is silly."

"You want to see silly, Ella? Because I think in saving all the turtles and taking down Wall Street with a stalker breathing down your neck and a publicist who needs to chill the fuck out, you've forgotten what the hell *silly* looks like."

"Yeah, yeah. Silly." Rolling her eyes and sticking her tongue out, she made a decent attempt at a face to appease him.

"Amateur silly."

Her mouth gaped. "*No way*."

"You, babe." He let go of the covers and stood up. "Are too high-strung."

"Says Mister Badass Army Ranger, *Sir*."

"Trust me." He shook his hips. "Soldiers know how to get down."

Her wide eyes matched her still-gaping mouth. "What are you doing?"

He had no fucking clue, but damn it to hell, the woman needed some fun in her life that wasn't programmed, publicity-driven, planned, or because of ratings. Bishop arched his eyebrow, rolled his hips, and watched her eyes drop, fight back up, and drop again.

"Would you stop!" she snapped, her hands covering her mouth.

He laughed, flexing his muscles for her and watching her nipples harden. What was this? Kind of a mix between Magic Mike and the Arnold bodybuilding competition? Hip shake, flex, cock thrust. What a pattern…

Her fingers splayed. "You are an *awful* dancer."

"You're hiding a smile." He thrust his hips, making his hardening cock reach for her.

"Bishop O'Kane!"

The point of this *wasn't* to turn her on, but those dark cherry nipples were beaded tight. He stroked his cock and rolled his hips. "Fuck it, Ella. When you let go…" He moved bedside and tilted her head back with a light tug of her hair. "You're you. Not the girl you are for everyone else."

She drew back. "*What*?"

"Be the real girl in the bedroom with me. Not the one you put on display."

She recoiled. "I need coffee."

"Bullshit." He dropped between her thighs, pushing them wide.

"Bishop—*Bishop*."

He wasted no pleasantries in getting what he wanted, her clit on his tongue, her taste searing his senses. Bishop groaned against her skin, sucking her clit until her ass lifted off the bed, then he ran circles and kisses over the delicate skin.

Listening to her try to control herself was a treat—hell, *a challenge*. His tongue ran along her seam, and he shouldered her legs wide open.

"God," Ella gasped.

"Whatever you say." His fingers and tongue stroked her open. She writhed on the edge of the bed, and her wetness tasted like coming home.

She wriggled and moaned, and he hadn't even finger-fucked her yet, but maybe she was close.

"Bishop," she gasped. Quiet. Too quiet.

"Ella." Bishop buried his face into her, lapping and kissing, holding her down before he paused. "If I don't hear you screaming like a banshee, I don't want you getting off."

Then he went back to work to prove his point. He kissed her until the hotel room neighbors would complain, until her hands ripped into his hair. And as she let loose, she screamed his name as loud as a full war cry.

Ella collapsed onto the bed, and—

Bam. Bam. Bam. "We get it. He's great! Shut up!"

"Oh my God!" Ella covered her face with a pillow, and Bishop fell back on his butt, laughing.

He crawled onto the bed with her, pulling her pillow-covered face into his arms. "We should escape for coffee."

"I'm never leaving this room or taking this pillow off my face," she mumbled. "Ever."

He leaned over and kissed her breast.

"*Bishop!*"

Laughing, he rolled his eyes at the people next door. "Screw 'em."

Ella peeled the pillow back and eased herself onto him, draping her body across his chest. "How about me instead?"

Damn... "Sorry, babe. I didn't come fully stocked for a hotel room funfest."

She raised her eyebrows.

"No more condoms," he painfully confirmed.

"Oh." She slunk down his chest, dropping wet kisses and raking her nails. "Guess we should see if you can scream like a banshee too."

CHAPTER 21

JAY WALKED IN STEP WITH Manny after volunteering to help with the pet-walking. He wrapped and unwrapped Furry Baby's leash around his hand, annoyed that Manny loved to do this, and that this was the second walk of the day he'd had to do. Jay did *not love* to do this, and Ella still wasn't home.

The sun was high overhead, reaching toward noon, and Manny was still chattering about all of the coverage that Eco-Ella had had. "It was on every single channel! And this morning, it was on every single blog. Every single website. Ella was trending. Did you see how beautiful she looked? And her speech," he gushed.

Jay agreed for the thousandth time. Ella had been perfect. Everything about last night was a career culmination. Together, he and Ella had been waiting for this moment. It was everything they had dreamed about, and she had thrown herself into Bishop's arms to celebrate—in the middle of the auditorium, surrounded by thousands of their peers, surrounded by media, surrounded by industry and publicists and reporters and journalists and bloggers. She'd embarrassed him.

His temples pounded. A headache he hadn't been able to shake since that moment wanted to explode in his head. White rage colored Jay's peripheral vision. Some moments in his game with

Ella were about teaching her a lesson. Sometimes, his actions were simply about getting back together.

Right now? This was different.

Right now, he wanted to teach Bishop a lesson.

Bishop O'Kane was shit. He was nothing more than a guy hiding behind muscles and a gun.

Manny dropped down to give the dog a hug. "We are so lucky your mama is the most famous person in the world."

"She isn't the most famous person in the world, Manny. Give it some perspective."

"Ha." Manny laughed as if Jay was joking. "Can you believe that we are a part of the Eco-Ella team? I even called my mom."

Speaking of parents, Jay still had to call Ella's father. He hadn't quite mapped out the right words to explain the Bishop problem. But he realized something as they were standing outside of her condo. He watched maintenance men clean up the mess that he'd paid some random kid on MonarchMoney to make last night, hoping to scare Ella into his arms. And he realized the games weren't working anymore. The flowers, the scary pictures—none of it was working. And why would it when she had a bodyguard?

If Ella couldn't be with Jay, then she shouldn't be with anybody. Though she wasn't *with* Bishop. That asshole was just impeding their relationship.

Bishop.

Damn it, Jay was becoming as obsessed with Bishop as he was Ella.

"I'll go upstairs with you," Jay said. "Check on Little Kitty."

"Oh, no way." Manny shook his head, wagging his finger. "No can do, Jay. You know that."

"Excuse me?"

"You know I can't let anybody into her condo. I've never been able to let anybody into her condo." Manny whistled through his teeth. "And Bishop? He would fire me."

"*Bishop cannot fire you.*"

"Not only could Bishop fire me, I would let him. He's crazy hot." Manny faux-swooned. "Bonus points if he did it while growling."

"Come the hell on. First, Bishop can't fire you. Second, do not discuss how that man looks—"

Manny fanned himself. "Hot. H-O-T."

"Enough, Manny." Jay threw the leash at the dog walker and stormed around the corner as Manny's confused questions fell on his back.

He pulled out his cell phone and hit redial again. And again. Now it just went straight to voice mail. Earlier at least, his calls had rung through. "This is bullshit."

Obviously, she was still with Bishop, because where else would she be? Jay knew all of her friends. She wasn't with Tara. Where was she? Wouldn't Tara tell him if Ella was with her?

He scrolled to Tara's name and hit send. It rang twice before she picked up.

"What in God's name do you need, Jay?" Tara snipped.

He balked, pulling the phone away, before coming back. "What do you mean?"

"You called Ella's phone until it died. I would've put it on the charger except you kept calling, and it was driving me nutty." Tara groaned. "If you actually needed something, you would've called me first. So what is it that you need?"

Jay gawked. Ella didn't have her phone on her? And Tara allowed this? Things as Jay understood them had been changing since Bishop had come around. But this was different. "Where is she?"

"Jay, I am not her keeper. And neither are you. I know everything we've talked about—"

"*Not on the phone*, Tara."

"Fine, whatever. But neither one of us are her keepers. She's safe. She's a grown woman. She took a day off after a really big event. She's our boss; we work for her. Not vice versa. Whether I like it or not, she calls the shots."

The whole world had gone insane. Tara had lost her ever-loving mind. Ella didn't have her phone. What would happen next? Freaking monkeys would fall from the sky, and the street would break open with lava spouts? Nothing logical was happening. "Screw off, Tara."

He hung up, more determined to call Ella's father.

BISHOP HAD DOWNED MEAT AND potatoes and listened about *the bees*. All last week, Ella had talked about them, with Manny piping up in excitement whenever he'd been around. That, on top of the lavender and mint, had been and continued to be her favorite things to talk about. Finally, Ella had a day off, and all through a decidedly lopsided order of his meal and her fruit and oatmeal—*water only, please*—she had determined the day would be spent catching up on herb and insect errands.

Fun...

But it hadn't been half bad. It started by breezing in and out of her condo. The green shit on the side of her building was gone. Manny had come and gone twice, leaving her dog and cat happy campers.

Now Bishop and Ella, with her pets, were all loaded into his truck. They'd run the course of Ella's list, dropping off containers of herbs. Bishop likened the process to an adult version of a girl scout on her cookie run. People were stoked to see her.

The afternoon crept by, and they were at the end of her to-do list, scouting locations for her to film a couple of videos. They had made their way through several parks and nature preserves in northern Virginia. Who knew there were so many?

This last stop was as good as all the rest in his mind, but this park spoke to Ella in some fashion. Her dog ran circles in the park, and the kitten was stuck to Ella's skirt. All in all, Bishop had to admit, running these kinds of errands wasn't a bad gig.

"When did this Eco-Ella stuff become your life's mission?" he asked, watching FB chase a dragonfly. How often did her cotton-ball dog get into the wild? Brick could show FB a thing or two about bugs.

"I think it was always there." She played with her skirt, letting LK jump and toy with the hem. "I mean, you remember that I was into the outdoors."

"There's a difference between wanting to hang outside and taking off after college to go do what you did."

"Maybe."

His bullshit alarm chimed. Ella's passion generally evoked an ass-chewing or learning opportunity. The way she focused on her kitten said there was more to her transformation. "Why, Ella? I don't get it."

"It's important."

"It's air."

"*Exactly.*" But her focus never came off the playing cat.

What wasn't she sharing with the world? "I get it. We need it. To breathe. To live. Yada. Yada."

"It's also beautiful—"

Bishop pinched the bridge of his nose. "No, babe. You're beautiful."

Caught off guard, her chin tilted up, revealing her flushed cheeks.

Damn, totally beautiful. But his curiosity wasn't going to be appeased by her looks. "What I'm saying is—"

Ella stopped playing with LK and came closer. "Close your eyes."

His eyebrow lifted. "Why?"

"Do it."

"And if I don't?"

"Then you'll be even more of a stick-in-the-mud than I initially assumed, and all your dance moves from earlier will be for naught."

He laughed. "Assume all you want. You know—"

"Close your dang eyes."

There was that passion of hers. He chuckled again, letting her sass take charge, and he gave over to the request while grinning. "Closing."

"All the way."

"All the way. Now what?"

"Wait for it," she whispered.

"Ella—"

"Wait, Bishop. And don't open." She put a hand on his cheek, and the warmth of her skin had nothing on the goosebumps that jumped from her unexpected touch. Her palm lifted, replaced by a coolness where her hand had been. "Do you feel it?"

"I don't feel anything."

"You're lying. Try again."

The sunlight warmed his closed eyelids. The wind picked up, and his senses missed how close she had been with her fingers on his face. A sunny breeze picked up, and his muscles relaxed.

"It feels good, doesn't it?"

He dropped his head back, appreciating that she forced him far out of his comfort zone. She'd made him stand with his eyes to the sun and learn that he could feel a breeze on his cheek just by losing her touch. He'd sooner call that some pussy-ass shit, but when she was the catalyst…

"Now you get it." She stepped closer. "You felt it."

He opened his eyes and dropped his chin. "I understand enough."

Before he could think of the thousands of reasons he shouldn't, he pressed his lips to hers and felt her sigh into his kiss. Her lips parted, and his hunger took that slip of permission and consumed her mouth. This was out of the bedroom. A kiss that couldn't lead to sex was problematic.

Ella's hands slid up his chest. The tips of her fingers slowly moved up his neck, as though she needed to feel his pulse, until her arms locked around him, and he held her close. Their distance was gone, and their bodies fit together in perfectly carved hooks and grooves. Her hold on him was fierce. She talked about light and air, but when they collided, there was fire and combustion. *Smoke*.

He drew back, and her eyes were wild, her skin flushed. He cupped her face, and his thumb outlined her kiss-reddened lips. And it was slow—the act of tearing himself off her. "Damn."

"Damn," she repeated.

The curves of her breasts were still so close to his chest, and he wanted the taste of her tongue again. A stray strand of hair taunted him, and he pushed it aside. "Are you going to tell me the truth?"

Ella's face fell. Hell, everything about her did. She dropped her chin, pressing her forehead to his sternum. "It all started because of…Brie."

Gone was the sun. The warmth had frozen. Bishop's heart lay down to weep. "*My sister?*"

"My *best friend*. It's like you always forget that."

He wanted to push Ella away, but he'd done so much of that over this anguish that he couldn't. Even now, like this, his arms could've been cement pillars for how heavy they hung by his side.

Pain had coated each of Ella's words, and how much of a bastard did he have to be to disagree with her, to prove to her that his pain was worse, that blood trumped friendship.

Years in the military had taught him that was wrong—blood didn't make brothers. Experience did. If Ella had had a connection to Brie anywhere near as deep as he'd had with some of his teammates, then…it wasn't his place to disagree.

"What about her?" His raw throat barely managed the simple question.

"When you watch your best friend take her last breath…" Ella trailed off. "It's possible to become obsessed with the very thing that she didn't have anymore."

His chin dropped too, and Bishop didn't need to see Ella's face to know silent tears fell. He didn't want to look because he couldn't trust his unshed tears that threatened to descend. Fuck that awful day when their world had crashed.

"We're lucky to be here," she whispered. "And I like what I do. I feel strongly about so many things. But the air… When it's gone, it's gone."

Brie couldn't take another breath in. The ambulance hadn't gotten there fast enough. There had been other things wrong too. When the car crashed, Brie's chest had been crushed.

Shit… Bishop fought through the concrete hold that cemented his arms in place and folded them around Ella. Something he should have done a long time ago.

"It's okay." He'd never said anything like that to her before. Maybe he should have. Maybe if he had, he wouldn't have left, leaving Ella and pushing away the final memory that was too painful to hang onto. At the time, it would've been a lie. He hadn't thought anything would ever be okay again.

Secure in his arms, Ella sobbed. In all the time he'd known her, he'd never seen her fall apart, not even at Brie's funeral. They were both too strong for that. Felt too guilty. And that was what had destroyed them in the end.

LK meowed for attention. Ella wiped at her face, and Bishop quickly ran a hand over his cheeks.

Sheepishly, she shook her head, scooping up the kitten. "I don't really talk about that. I never have."

He nodded. "That's personal."

Sniffing, she petted LK. After a moment, she took a deep breath and switched topics. "I forgot. My folks called, and they're headed on vacation to some island. I think it's a great time to get away. They asked if I wanted to join them."

"You could use some down time." And he needed to process things away from her, like what had happened last night, and the decision to kiss her for no goddamn reason. And now, saying Brie's name, thinking about the accident, talking about it, even if only for thirty seconds, when they'd never talked about what had happened. It was all too much.

"Yeah." The kitten purred. "So I guess you have a vacation without me while I'm gone. No stalker will know where I am, ya know?"

"Sure." He cleared his throat. "I'll tell my powers that be. I'm sure they won't care." And maybe he would even get temporarily assigned to another gig, which would be a huge bonus. It would help clear his mind, and he would get to do what he had wanted to anyway.

"Bishop?"

"Yeah, babe?"

"Enlisting in the army, was that your Eco-Ella? Your escape after Brie?" Ella's eyelashes were still damp from her tears. They stuck together. Splotches marked her skin from crying so hard.

Bull's-eye. He couldn't answer. Instead, he leaned over and kissed her forehead. "Thanks for letting me feel the air."

CHAPTER 22

SPORTSCENTER PLAYED ON THE big screen, and Bishop's head pounded. He buried his face in his arms as Locke sat two chairs over and swiveled in the chair, tossing a baseball from hand to hand. Having a few days off should have been a good vacation, except he wanted a good gig where he could shoot things or track down whoever Titan called an enemy.

Hell. Really, Bishop's problem was Ella. Had it been the right move to let Ella leave the country without security?

Everyone agreed she would be fine. Completely off the grid. No one but her family, the FBI, Jared, Rocco, Locke, and himself knew where she was. Her "team" had a rough idea of when she would be back, and the more Bishop thought about her team, the more he decided they stunk like dead fish on a hot day.

The war room door opened, and he propped his chin on his forearm as Nicola walked in. He hadn't seen her much since the bathroom incident, but the short-term encounters they'd had in briefings had been quick-witted and smart as hell. He liked how she could assess situational data as well as she could read a team dynamic. "Hey, Nic."

"Nicola." Locke stopped bobbing in his chair and threw the baseball to her.

She caught it, tossing it to Bishop. "You two are cordially invited to Mia Winters's tonight."

He caught the ball, lofting it to Locke.

Locke palmed it and went back to the hand-to-hand. "Thanks. I might have plans, though."

Nicola smiled tersely. "Change 'em, Locke."

Interesting because Locke didn't say much to begin with, and Nicola made it sound as though social functions were a requirement.

"You too, Bishop. Be there."

Locke lifted his chin, accepting the invitation for what it was, an order of sorts, and Bishop did too. Though he planned a pit stop first to check on Manny. "Titan orientation 101 is not what I'd call *normal*."

BISHOP STOOD ALONE IN FRONT of a large white colonial house. Colby and Mia Winters' home was badass to the max. It had lots of land like the home Bishop had found when he settled back stateside, but the security had been tricked out. The place was an estate, and it screamed Titan. A row of huge trucks and SUVs lined the horseshoe driveway. Music played from the back of the house, and even from the outside, he could smell deliciousness.

But he wasn't actually alone. He just felt it, semi-wishing he knew his teammates better. That was likely the point of all this. Locke walked in step with him as they took in the place.

"Like the first day of school," Locke muttered before he banged on the door.

New team. New places. New everything.

The door flew open, and a girl, not quite a teenager, stood with dark hair and even darker eyes. She spun with another little girl, about half her size and very blond, attached to her waist. "*It's a new guy!*" yelled the dark-haired girl.

Well, all right then.

"Two of them!" corrected the blonde. "One, two. One and one is two."

"There are kids." Locke took a step to the side and held his hand out for Bishop to go first. "Didn't expect that."

He didn't either. All right, Winters had kids. That made sense. He guessed several of the guys did. Both girls wore camo and tutus. The younger one also had on a cape. They seemed covered on all bases, no matter what imaginary apocalypse loomed.

Then another kid tore through the room. *Holy crap.* This one was a little boy, who seemed dangerously unsteady on his feet, wielding what Bishop was certain were toy rocket launchers.

"We should follow the smell of food coming from the kitchen," Bishop offered.

"Roger that."

They rounded the corner, and there was the team. Thank God for people he knew. Adults. Bishop could handle that. In addition to his coworkers were what looked like significant others...and babies. Bishop did a quick once-over, rubbing the back of his neck, and could place almost everyone. This wasn't like his last team.

"Hey." A familiar woman's voice caught his attention. "If it isn't my favorite man with the ropes."

Bishop would know that voice anywhere, and he turned to Sugar, Jared's wife. He'd had a tiny misstep with her when their paths had crossed before he signed on at Titan. All had worked out for the best, but not before he'd tied up Sugar—who was very pregnant at the time—with a jump rope just in case she was a Russian mobster. "Hey, you had the baby."

"Or was I really pregnant?"

He faltered for a nanosecond. That woman had screwed with him from the words "hands up," and she had been pregnant. That, he knew without a doubt. "Congratulations."

Jared walked into the hallway, holding a very small infant. "Gentlemen, meet Violet."

"Nicely done, Sugar," Locke said.

She beamed. "Thank you."

"Don't forget who signs the paychecks," Jared grumble-laughed.

Sugar rolled her eyes. "Absolutely. Far be it from me to bear and birth the fruit of your loins only to exclude your contributions to this baby-making process." She was a handful, perfectly tailored for Boss Man.

Bishop laughed as a toddler ran through the room, followed by a kid who was a little older. "There are a lot of kids here."

"There are a lot of kids in Titan," Jared explained as though Bishop was a few rounds short.

Sugar caught the toddling child by his hand. "This way, Jacian. You too, Ace. Move boots. Round you go." She raised the hand. "This one is Rocco's; the loose one is one of Winters's."

Right. Was he supposed to remember that? Bishop looked at Locke as though he might have that answer. He needed Ella to handle the ebb and flow of this chaos. She would handle this, easy. But Ella was thousands of miles away in the tropics with her family, and that was a good thing. She was safe. And that was all that mattered.

He reached for a deep breath, following as Ace led their hallway contingent to a large kitchen.

Beth held a small child in her arms. Roman and Cash had a sniper rifle on a kitchen counter, examining what looked to be new hardware. A dark-haired woman with legs up to her neck called to Jacian. She sat next to Parker, who had a blond biker chick on his knee—oh, Bishop knew her.

"Hey, Lexi," Bishop said. The biker-chick look was vastly different from the workout clothes she had donned in the Sugar-jump-rope fiasco. Definitely a complete one-eighty.

Lexi bound off of Parker. "I've been waiting for you."

After a quick hello and introduction to Locke, Lexi scanned the room. "Who don't you know? Caterina, wave."

The leggy dark-haired woman lifted her hand, giving an accented, "Hello."

"Rocco belongs to her, and she knows how to torture people. No joke. Pretty much never upset her. Ever." Lexi pivoted. "You know Beth and Roman. That's Brady, the baby. Super cute."

A petite woman walked in under Winters's arm, holding another baby. *So. Many. Babies.*

"And that's Mia holding Ryan—Cash and Nic's." Lexi turned to them. "You bachelors overwhelmed and confused yet?"

"No comment." Wanting to belong to a team who was *family* in more than one way confused him.

"Not a bad answer," Lexi said.

Locke just laughed, and Lexi peeled away as Mia slid from her husband's arm and made a beeline for them, pushing her free hand out. "I'm glad you're here."

They all shook.

"Now let's never do that again." Mia made a face at their handshakes. "Get a beer. Eat some food. Get to know everyone."

"Yes, ma'am," Locke said.

She bounced the baby. "And never call me ma'am."

"All right, then." Bishop gave Locke a look, and they bumbled toward the beer outside on the back deck, each grabbing a bottle and twisting the top.

"Hey, man." Locke nodded to the group as they milled, going in and out, from the kitchen to the deck.

"What's up?" Bishop asked.

"Doing okay?"

"This shit is insane. Not what I thought a Titan barbecue was all about." Funny, though, the comradery was something he'd been craving since he'd been without a home base.

"Not what I'm talking about." Locke took a long pull from his beer bottle. "About Ella."

Hell. Bishop waited to answer until he had downed that first swallow of suds. "Ella."

His buddy lifted his chin, reiterating the conversation topic with a silent *go on.*

Well, shit. It meant something if Locke had honed in on Ella as a topic. Gossip and bullshit didn't seem like Locke's cup of tea, so if he felt that Bishop needed checking on, then he needed to get his ass in check.

"Yeah, man, I'm doing good. She's in a safe spot."

Locke nodded. Bishop nodded. Good, that was the extent of their conversation. Bishop rolled his shoulders back and cracked his neck.

Locke followed up. "Yeah?"

Maybe the conversation wasn't done. "I've never worked a TV star's detail before. Wild, right?"

Locke lifted his bottle and took another pull. "Hmm."

Bishop joined him in hiding behind the beer and avoiding the discussion. What was it about some things that pulled at the strings in his chest and made him want to hide? And how damn pussy was that? Enough to get the attention of his Titan employment, that was for sure.

The group, from the babies to the boss man, made their way outside. Thankful for the distraction, Bishop watched the team that he would one day blend effortlessly in with. Amazing how loud they all were, how interspersed the ladies were with the men. Some he knew were spies, while others were artillery experts. Some were ready for battle, while others looked a few notches underdressed for a cookout. The whole thing worked, and damn, he liked that he was with Titan.

Mia shouted to Cash to run back inside and get more napkins. Caterina tore chunks of food onto a plate—a lot of food—and handed it to Rocco, who whistled for his kid. That sent Winters's dogs running and set everyone howling.

Bishop moved into the mix of things as he grabbed a plate and worked his way down the long buffet. The food smelled killer, and he grabbed a seat on a bench next to Roman.

Across from them, Bishop realized that Beth was nursing a baby, something he had never in his life been around. But no one seemed to notice, and that made sense. Guess that kid had to eat too.

He dug into the chili, and—*damn.* "This is great."

"Right," Roman said with a mouthful. "Never miss a Mia Winters event."

"So noted."

The two oldest kids burst back onto the deck. The older one led the charge, with the younger one still hanging on her back, and walked up to him. "Hi."

"Hey," Bishop said, swallowing. "Thanks for letting us in."

"I'm Clara," the blonde piped up. "This is Asal. We're the welcoming company."

"*Committee.*" Asal rolled her eyes in a goofy kid way.

"Committee. That's what I said."

"No, it's not."

"*Yes*—"

"Thanks, welcoming committee."

Just as fast as they had arrived, they took off, grabbed plates, and cleared what they needed for food. Roman pointed his fork at them. "Two peas in a pod, despite the age difference, and literally always attached at the hip."

"Future Cash and Roman," Beth volunteered. "Though I don't know which one is the spotter and which one will be the sniper."

"Cute." Everything here meshed. Once these people had joined Titan, their lives had interwoven to the point that their kids' lives were interlocked.

Had he thought about kids before? No. But if he were to have any, he would want them running around in a world as tight-knit and loyal as Titan.

Bishop searched the deck, the grass, and back inside the house, looking for…what? It wasn't that something was missing. It wasn't that he'd only been on the team for less than a couple weeks and hadn't become this close. That would come; he could tell.

It was that some*one* was missing. He missed Ella. Simple.

Locke joined them, pulling a chair next to him. "Unknown, coming in slow and steady, nine o'clock," he said quietly.

Over Beth's shoulder, Jax made his way over, small-talking through the group. While Bishop and Locke had started on together, this guy was likely their third. Conversationally, he'd been lumped together as part of the new recruit trifecta.

Jax stopped short, doing a double-take as Beth pulled the baby from her boob. Bishop stood, stuck his hand out, and introduced himself, followed by Locke.

With a quick hello, Beth put the baby against her shoulder. "I'm Beth."

"You know me," Roman said.

Jax joked about something and dropped to the bench on the other side of Roman—and that baby let out a belch with reverberations as Beth patted its back. Bishop, Locke, and Jax froze, and he couldn't speak for the other two, but he was floored. There were grown-ass men who couldn't pull that off after shotgunning a six-pack.

"Go eat, Beth." Roman grabbed the little monster.

"Nice meeting you, Jax." She tossed Roman a cloth. "Here."

Roman walked off, kind of bouncing as he went, with his kid in one hand and a beer in the other.

"Well, fuck me," Jax breathed out. "Wasn't sure what to expect. This wasn't it."

Locke took a swig of beer.

"No kidding," Bishop agreed. There they sat, the three new recruits, surrounded by people who had been together for years, maybe decades.

Jax twisted the cap off his beer and flicked it at Bishop. "I heard that your job is keeping eyes on a hottie. Nice."

He shoveled a spoonful of chili into his mouth, wanting to answer "she's pretty smart too," but opting to stay as silent as Locke.

"I'd stay with that gig as long as possible, brother." Jax tipped back his beer. "Not that it wouldn't be fun to head out and blow some shit up, but paid to sit back and hang with some bangin' chick?" He whistled. "Yeah, I'd do it."

Bishop cracked his neck, catching Locke's glare. They were all the new guys, but this was *their* new guy, and his first impressions were crashing, kamikaze-style. "So you have any assignments?"

"Nothing that has me trailing a set of tits and an ass like whoa."

His fists curled. Jesus Christ, Bishop wanted to lay into him. Too overprotective? Yeah. Maybe. His collar felt as though it were strangling him, and he shifted, needing to get the hell out of this conversation before Jax said too much. Bishop couldn't stand much of the bro'd out bullshit.

"Man, have a little respect," Locke snapped.

Jax's beer froze midway to his mouth.

Bishop should've said that before Locke had, but he was glad it'd been done. Paranoia that he was too close to Ella had caused him to stay quiet. So, fuck, now he was second-guessing and not reacting the way he should, not wanting to speak up when he normally would. *Damn it.*

This was why he shouldn't screw the job. But really, it was why he shouldn't have kissed her when there was no chance of taking her to bed. *That* was a game-changer.

Bishop gave Locke an almost-imperceptible chin lift—a thanks for having his back when he couldn't figure out how much was too much.

Nicola walked over. "Your next assignment, should you choose to take it…"

Thank God for Nic's unknowing break in tension.

"You're in charge of Titan orientation?" Jax asked.

"Brother." Nicola pivoted, glaring. "For all you should care about, I'm in charge of your world."

Mental fist bump to Nicola. There was a definite hierarchy that Bishop needed to figure out. If Rocco was second-in-command and Parker handled operational logistics, it seemed that Nicola told them where to be when it came to team-building.

"Report to GUNS tomorrow." She turned, looking over her shoulder. "It's like Candyland for operatives and agents but better."

Just like the world knew of Titan, GUNS was world-renowned. Nicola, in his mind, might have been in charge of team-building, but she had just elevated herself to being in charge of fun.

CHAPTER 23

GUNS. THE MECCA. THE HOLY grail. The end-all and be-all of gunsmithing. Bishop's skin tingled with each boot fall in the parking lot. The wrought-iron gate swung heavy when the impenetrable door clicked open. Security cameras followed every movement as he and Locke stepped inside a place that Bishop had seen in magazine spreads and read folklore about for years.

No one was in the entryway to meet them, though someone had to have seen them coming. "Eyes in the sky maybe?"

"There were enough cameras to have known we were out a mile away." Locke's footsteps followed on the polished wood boards behind him. Locke sounded as in awe as Bishop felt. "This place…"

"Right?" They were both field grunts by blood, Special Forces by design. What stood behind these walls was the stuff that starred in their wet dreams.

Bishop ran his hand over the glass cabinets that housed beautiful handcrafted weapons. State of the art. Historic. Everything in between. Hot damn, he could get a hard-on over firepower.

Footsteps pricked his ears, and a lady who looked slightly out of place, with freckles and wearing a non-Sugar-like outfit, appeared. "I've been waiting for you three—two?"

"Jax will be here..." Bishop had no idea where that guy was. "Soon, and hell, we've been waiting too." Bishop extended his hand. "Bishop O'Kane."

"Sarah Gamble."

"Locke Oliver."

Sarah swooped her hand out. "Pretty, huh?"

"Gorgeous," he agreed.

"Want to see the real beauties?" she asked.

"Hell yeah," Locke said.

Apparently, Locke wasn't silent when it came to weaponry, just as when it came to defending what was right. He was moving farther and farther into Bishop's good-guy column.

"Move boots, boys." Sarah turned, hustling down the hall. There was something inherently badass about a Titan chick. It didn't seem to matter if she could field strip an AK or breach an insurgent weapons hold, or if she had a baby stuck to her boob at a barbecue or simply showed them down the hall at GUNS. Titan women had a strength about them that was Titan strong.

"Welcome to the workshop." Sarah stepped aside, and his pulse jumped.

Locke didn't wait for an invitation. Bishop trailed him, gulping in the sight. The ceiling had to be eighteen feet high. Straight ahead, the GUNS logo greeted everyone who came into the room. A large hammered metal display of dueling pistols was transposed over the letters G-U-N-S. Working around that were rows of automatic rifles, stacked with variations, carbines to the left, handguns to the right. The spread rippled in size, shape, and brand along the length in a stunning view of armaments.

"I've died..." Everywhere he looked, something unbelievable caught his eye.

Workshop tables took up the floor space, and opposite walls held shelving. Parts containers seemed expertly organized, and they were standing in a gun connoisseur's dream come true.

"As you probably know, this is Sugar's place." Sarah walked around a table, rubbing a non-existent speck of nothingness away. "It had a few versions of its usefulness over the years, but it's always been the best of the best and always has been GUNS."

He and Locke nodded like little puppies hoping to be released to the great outdoors. Any second, camo-covered elves would appear as if this was Santa's gun-making workshop. The place was simply more than he could comprehend, and Bishop had had high hopes.

"GUNS being Sugar's, and Titan being Jared's, means you two, or three when Jax finally arrives, can basically write your shopping list. On the table, the catalog is filled with possible customizations, etcetera. Just let me know everything you want. From what you'd like stocked for your everyday carry, to what you consider necessities, what's on your dream list…" Sarah paused and let that sink in. "*And* what you think might be impossible."

"Impossible?" Locke asked.

"The woman loves a challenge. Tell Sugar something doesn't exist, and you might just get it."

Bishop could attest to her loving a challenge, and damn, making his dream list? While on the payroll at his dream job, standing in his dream store? *Solid.* And he'd been working with his own dream girl—well, whoa. That was a bit much. He shook his head. That barbecue had thrown him off course.

Bishop recalibrated and focused on the workshop as Sarah tossed pens and a set of keys onto the table. "Enjoy."

"We'll do that." Locke scooped up the key ring and went to the secure shelves, while Bishop paged through the catalog and listing options, eyeing customizations.

Locke dropped a box of rifle grips on the table, then more carefully, laid out scopes. "So."

"So." Bishop pushed the catalog aside and stepped to Locke. Talk about tactical optics for the win. This would make any buildout badass. "What are you looking for?"

"How's your girl's trip?" Locke asked instead of gun talk.

"Our girl?" Bishop countered. They were both working Ella's protective detail.

"Not what I meant." Locke let his response hang. "The few times that I've worked with her, seen you two together…" He shrugged. "I don't miss much."

"Didn't think you did," Bishop mumbled.

"You heard from her?"

"Not much. Other than a check-in that she landed safely. Maybe a couple other times. I don't know." But he did know. Texting Ella, using the job as an excuse—that had happened more than it should.

"That's all we're going to say on her?" Locke raised his brows but slowly let them drop as he pulled out a container.

Bishop ran his tongue along the inside of his mouth. "We used to know each other. Years ago."

Locke *hmmed.*

"Dated in high school and college."

No response from Locke again, but he stepped to the table, crossed his arms, and waited.

Bishop reached back for the catalog and aimlessly flipped a few pages. Locke didn't budge. That was a good, and momentarily bad, thing about the guy; when Locke gave his attention, it was one hundred percent.

Bishop had to do the same. "We went different ways. Too young to know what to do with…" Love and devastation. Tragedy. "She wasn't the same crazy person riling up fellow lunatics."

Locke rubbed his chin. "She's passionate. Love or hate what she says."

"I don't hate what she says."

Locke nodded.

Bishop rubbed his sternum. "And hell, she was never that reserved to begin with."

"I like her," Locke said. "She keeps things interesting."

"No kidding," Bishop grumbled. "Hell." He could use a beer for this conversation—or any conversation having to do with Ella and Brie. "Do you have a woman?"

"Not anymore."

"Right…" The way Locke said that made Bishop hope he could trust him with more than the surface-level BS answers he'd given for years. "We made it complicated by doing nothing at all… Shit. I don't know. History blows, man."

Locke's forehead creased. "You'll have to believe me when I say that I get it."

No one *got* what they'd been through. Then again, he'd never given anyone a chance to prove him wrong. Maybe that was a pussy belief, but it was his. Even to this day, he could still hear the tires screech. He could never forget the crunch of glass and the dull thud Brie had made at that first impact. She couldn't even scream after it had happened. Still alive and unable to shout how they were losing her.

"Ella and I were in an accident with my sister." A grenade-size lump lodged in his throat. He'd said the word out loud. *Accident.* Admitting it was like pulling the pin, and now that it had been said out loud, the knot threatened to detonate years of unvoiced issues.

"They can be brutal."

"My sister was also Ella's best friend," he said quietly, admitting that just as she had when she'd sobbed into his shirt days ago. Why had he needed to explain that? It wasn't part of the damn story.

Locke waited him out, and Bishop drew in a painful breath.

"It was a blur. Ella and I'd had drinks. Ya know, but we were being responsible. *We thought*. Because Brie hadn't, and she was behind the wheel." They had tried to be good kids. They had taken turns suffering through nights as designated drivers. That was the rule, right? What would have kept them safe? "Brie and Ella were texting about me. I egged them on. We were just having fun. So stupid. Thought we were so funny and invincible."

"One of those recipes for disaster, huh?"

"Back then, no one ever thought not to do that. It was all 'don't drink and drive. Don't get stoned and get behind the wheel.'" Bishop shrugged, though he was anything but indifferent. "The text never made it out. The car flipped. She died."

That last part he said with the perfunctory abruptness of a grocery store order, because that was the only way he could get through it.

"Goddamn, man." Locke shook his head. "And you two, you and Ella?"

Wasn't that part of their problem? "Barely any scrapes and bruises. Isn't that some fucking shit?"

And they never spoke of it, never dealt with it, never grieved together, and never forgave one another for that night. "We were young, didn't know how to deal. We buried Brie and acted as though life moved forward." Failing miserably…

Teammates always knew the deepest and darkest secrets, but even his Ranger team was only aware that he'd lost a sister. Not when or how. Not like this. And nothing about Ella.

Funny, too, was that Bishop blamed that fucking phone, their need to connect at that damn second. It was stupid and emotional, but it was the truth, and maybe one of the reasons he couldn't believe where Ella's career had taken her: into the belly of the beast that had destroyed their lives. That monster was still hungry.

He couldn't help but make the connection. Ella posted videos and blogged, and now a stalker had his sights set on her. Bishop's blood ran cold. He could lose both to the same destructive force.

"Wish there were reasons when life tries to ruin us." Locke slapped him on the back and went back to the shelves, sorting through the other options. "But if she's yours, deal with your shit, and never let her go again."

Heavy advice that sounded just like a warning. Bishop bit his lip. Ella was a new woman. She even came with a new name. But when they connected, all things were the same. They belonged.

It wasn't a matter of possession.

Just fact.

Eloise Lewandowski, or Ella Leighton, or whatever the hell she wanted to be called, belonged to him. And he was *hers*.

Jax ambled in. "Sorry I'm late." He whistled. "The door clicked open, and I wandered into paradise."

"Hey." He ran a hand over his face, wanting to forget how losing Brie and Ella shredded him.

Jax did a full circle, taking in the enormity of the workshop. "This shit is wild."

Locke had gone back to silent mode, and Bishop filled Jax in on what Sarah had said they could get into.

Jax and Locke were lost in the world of GUNS, silently working. Bishop too, but his mind wasn't entirely in that room. It wasn't just thousands of miles away. It was walking the outskirts of a cemetery that he hadn't set foot in since Brie's funeral, and man, what a piece of shit did that make him?

CHAPTER 24

ELLA DUG HER TOES INTO the wet, cold sand. There was something about the evening as the dark skyline merged into the inky ocean. She listened to the calm. The lapping waves and the deserted beach gave her space to let her mind drift. It had been so long since she had been at peace, and she hadn't realized it.

For the time she spent playing down her stress, the only true respite she'd had recently was in Bishop's arms. Funny how it took traveling thousands of miles to make that realization. He'd said she needed to relax, asked her when was the last time she'd been silly.

"I didn't believe him," she told the waves.

Furry Baby and Little Kitty were wonderful distractions. Vlogging and live chatting with Eco-Ella fans couldn't be more fun. But pets could only do so much, and work was actually work.

The beach had always been her safe zone, even when filled with bastards who only thought about their bank accounts. What an adrenaline rush that had been and—

Sea grass swayed with a breeze. It shifted more than the dune weed should. She knew footsteps approached, and Ella's toes dug deep into the sand. It wasn't smart to be out there without a weapon. The second they'd arrived, Ella had dropped her bags and slipped out the door. Neither of her parents had called after her, maybe knowing that she needed to re-center at the edge of the water. Now that she barely came back, she hadn't thought two seconds about what to do if she stumbled upon some of her old *friends*, the poachers and pilferers. Though the location was all wrong.

Her stalker couldn't know where she was now. Right? Fear tickled the back of her throat.

"Sweet pea?" Her mom's gentle nickname carried on a breeze from a nearby dune.

Relief crawled through her like the ocean gust off the waves. "Hey, Mom."

She'd gone to a dark place, only serving as a reminder that it was good she was off the grid, trying to secure serenity.

Her mom's sandy footsteps recalibrated, changing direction under the guidance of a faint flashlight. She stopped at Ella's side. "Dad and I noticed you were gone longer than the last few times you checked in with us. I wanted to see if you were okay."

"Sorry," she said. "I lost track of time."

Burdening her parents always made her feel as though she was a baby. Starting back when they'd first lost Brie, her parents, particularly her mom, made it their goal to make sure that Ella was fine. There was nothing they could do to lift the guilt. When they'd realized that, it hurt all of them.

Blogging had made her better. Smiling in videos made her mom trust that things were improving. *Fake it 'til you make it.* Maybe that idiom had worked, because Ella had become a sunny person again, eventually. She'd climbed out of depression, gained weight back, slept more. There were so many reasons that Ella did what she did with the blog.

"Don't be sorry." Her mom clicked off the flashlight and gave her a shoulder hug. "That's not the reason I trudged down here in the dark."

"Oh, everything okay?"

"With everything going on, we realize that ditching your phone and not updating Eco-Ella has probably been hard."

"It's different, not informing the world of my every move." She lifted a shoulder, snuggling into her mom, and offered a self-deprecating laugh. "I'm joking."

"*But* you haven't been blogging, and when you've had your phone, it..." Her mom leaned in, and together, they let the wind roll over them. "It has not gone unnoticed that you smiled in a way that a mother would *want* her daughter to smile."

Heat crawled up her neck and flared into her cheeks. Thank goodness for the cover of the near-moonless night. "I wasn't smiling long."

"El, honey. You picked up your phone, you read something, and you smiled. I liked the way you smiled. I haven't seen that smile in so long."

Bishop had checked in. Not only had Bishop texted, but he had stopped by to see Manny, following up on her pets—the things that meant something to her, and that made her insides melt.

"What would you say if I met someone?" Ella asked.

Her mom patted her bicep, giving what almost felt like a hopeful squeeze. Only the waves hitting the shores responded, mixing with the sound of nature. It was a lyrical symphony.

Mom took in a deep breath and let it out slowly. "I would say that whomever this lucky person is, please give him a chance."

"A chance?"

"Yes, honey, a chance. Work is a good thing. Your father and I both understand that. We wouldn't have this life if we hadn't worked hard. But more importantly, we had each other. That is worth so much more than a job."

She stiffened. "It's more than a job."

"It pays the bills. It provides income. It puts a roof over your head. You might love it; it might be your passion, but it's also work. Nothing wrong with loving your work; just respect what it is."

"Understood." Sort of…

"If somebody has you smiling, El, then think about the last time it happened. When was that?"

She didn't have to guess, and it would be a lie to say that any of her time with Jay had produced any of the same feelings. "It's Bishop, Mom."

"*Bishop*?"

"Yes."

"Not that there are a lot of Bishops walking around, but are we talking about Bishop O'Kane?"

"The one and the same."

Mom pulled Ella around face-to-face and put both hands on her shoulders, manicured fingernails pressing into her skin. "Then I think some second chances are meant to be."

BRICK LAY ON THE FLOOR, running in his sleep, probably chasing a squirrel. It'd been a good day at GUNS. With Locke's words in his head, Bishop sat in bed, propped against the backboard with his cell pressed against his ear, because fuck it, texting wasn't doing the job anymore.

"Hello?" Ella answered groggily.

He should have said good night. Her mumble had been sleepy and soft. "Hey. Just checking on you. Go back to bed."

"I don't want to." Her voice rose, waking. "Don't hang up."

His stomach jumped, and fucking hell, he dropped his head back, because when she said that, he was stoked. "Beach treated you well today?"

"Not too bad. I went snorkeling and went to a wildlife preserve."

"Fun."

"There's this place back at home. It's honestly my favorite place in the world, at Seneca Park. There's this little hut."

"Yeah?"

"Well, I guess that's it. It's just a hut. But it reminded me of here somehow."

"Nice."

"Maybe I could show it to you."

"Sure."

"Nah, that's silly, actually. You'd be bored out of your ever-loving mind."

To this point, none of their excursions had been boring. Even the boring-sounding ones, which were all of them. If it was her favorite place in the world? "Likely won't be boring. Add it to our to-do list."

"Okay," she whispered. "I will."

"You need to go back to sleep?"

"I… I talked to my mom about you."

"Oh?" He faltered at the unexpected conversation twist. "Talked, how?"

"Mother's intuition or something. I don't know. She wondered if maybe I was…seeing someone? *Or* interested in someone."

Ella was work. They hooked up. They had a past. Her *parents* were the reason Titan had the Eco-Ella job. One phone call from her dad, and his ass was out of a job. But fuck it; he didn't care. What was her answer? He shifted in his bed, repositioning a pillow behind him. "What did you say?"

Ella didn't respond. What did that mean? What did he want her to say? Kissing the girl and making her come as though it was his God-given talent was one thing. But seeing someone, seeing him…dating him—that was an entirely different level.

"Ella."

"I told Mom it was you."

Whoa. That wasn't just admitting to someone. That was a different level and then some, the weight of which hit him broadside in the chest. There might be serious repercussions, to which he planned on strenuously defending himself and lobbying to keep his damn job. "Good. Okay."

"Yeah?"

"Yeah, babe."

"Good."

Goddamn, there was that cute, sleepy voice again. He wanted to hear it while she was plastered against his chest. "How did that go?"

Considering he was the asshole that had walked away from her years ago, there was no telling what her folks thought of him. They were good people. He'd always admired them, even after the time her dad had nearly killed him in high school for getting too serious with Ella. But her dad's intentions were spot on, and from this vantage point, so many years later, he could absolutely see his perspective.

Fabric swished on the other end of the phone. "You know."

"No threats of violence?"

"It was never like that."

"Maybe once or twice." He laughed. "The way things ended with us before—"

"I don't want to talk about that," she said.

"No worries." Not a conversation he wanted to have either. Considering they were both pros at not tackling important topics, they might never have to talk about their non-breakup where he had walked off the face of the planet.

"My mom said something interesting."

"And that was?"

"Oh." Ella giggled in his ear. "It was all said in the secret confines of girl talk. I can't let you in on specifics."

"Not fair, babe. You brought it up."

"Are you curious?"

"Everything about us has me curious."

"I like that you said *us*."

He grunted a non-answer.

She let that hang in the air. "Do you think it's peculiar? The way we ended up back in the same orbit together when we are so…"

"Complete and total opposites," he offered.

"Ha! I wouldn't call it that!"

"Maybe not total and complete. I'm digging those flowy skirts and dresses you've got going on. The hippie look suits you."

"Maxi dresses and my skirts aren't a hippie look!"

"Looks it to me."

"More like romantic chic. Beachy boho."

"Whatever you want to call it, El, you grew out of the T-shirts and mesh shorts that, don't get me wrong, I used to totally appreciate."

She laughed. "Shut up."

"You look good no matter what you wear."

"Thanks." She paused. "Bishop, I missed you—and I wish you were here right now."

"Yeah, babe. I wish I were there too."

She sighed. "I always missed you…"

Silence ticked the seconds away. Was this the entry she wanted into that conversation about how he'd left her? That was a conversation better had in person. She would cry, damn it. He'd hurt her. But he'd never meant to…never meant to.

"Okay," she said. "I'll talk to you later, maybe."

Maybe. This was where their conversation would be lost. On the battlefield, except this was a phone call, and he didn't know how to handle it. He couldn't get a read on the past and didn't know how to deal with her feelings.

"G'night, Bish—"

"Ella, I missed you too." Too simple and not enough. "I promise. Everything about you. Every day, I missed you too."

"Thanks," she whispered. "I needed to hear that."

Ella hung up, and who knew if his response had done any good, but hell if it wasn't the truth.

CHAPTER 25

TICK TOCK.

Tick tock.

Jay couldn't stop watching his clock app as he sat in his car catty-corner to Ella's building. He tried to play chess on his phone, but all he could do was beat the game or wonder if Bishop would know the difference between chess and checkers. *Likely not.*

Ella's flight had to have landed hours ago, and she should have been home. Her vague schedule said she would be home today. The last flights from all the local airports were mostly in. Where was she? And since when did he not get specifics on her travel?

People say the best relationships could make you a better person. Over the years, Ella had pushed him to dig deep. Jay was a better conservationist for the cause, a better evangelist for the environment, and now he was more focused, more logical, more studious. All because of Ella.

Growth wasn't easy, though. The more she tested him, the more he had to remember what was important. *Them.*

Jay snorted. One more minute had dragged by and—was that Bishop's truck?

Did Ella have that Neanderthal in his gas-guzzling behemoth

pick her up from the airport? What, she was too good for the metro or rideshare now?

He leaned closer, his ears aching to hear through the two vehicles' steel frames. What was happening? They just sat there! Idling! Ella idled? In what world did she allow fumes to pour from a tailpipe?

Pounding tension crept down his neck, cramping his shoulders. The Bishop situation had gone on long enough. For crying out loud, Jay would call her father tomorrow and explain that he would be personally responsible for Ella's security and safety.

No one would get to her! No stalker!

Of course, there would be no *stalker*. *He* was the man behind the confusion. Why did it feel as though they were two different people?

Jay rubbed his temples. This mass hysteria was his creation. There was not another person to actually protect her from. *Think. Remember*.

Titan could go to hell, and Bishop could disappear to the fringes of everything that Jay and Ella hated.

But still, that truck idled. Its red taillights mocked him. "She hates you!"

But shouting did no good when the truck didn't move.

Helpless rage made Jay nauseated. The passenger door opened, and Ella slid into view. Ah, there she was. He could breathe better now. The streetlights cast an amber hue, but despite the orange glare, she radiated.

Jay wrung his hands on the steering wheel, happy to have her close again. "Happy to be home?"

Wait. The taillights went out. Had the truck shifted into Park? Because Bishop wasn't pulling away. Jay's stomach churned and—*what the*… Jay growled. Bishop got out.

Okay, it was just to remove her luggage. That was okay. He could handle that.

Maybe.

Maybe not. Because Bishop didn't head back for the driver's door.

Jealousy scored through his body as Bishop moved the bags to the sidewalk but didn't let go. "Leave!"

Jay wondered if Bishop had a gun holstered on his side, and wild, wonderful fantasies danced. The different places that Jay could place a bullet. Different things he could say to Bishop before ending the problems that had cropped up with Ella recently.

In all of the years that Jay and Ella had teamed up, together they had outmaneuvered protesters, outsmarted poachers, and outplayed corporate assholes. This one man had become more dangerous than all of those other encounters.

Bishop put his arm around Ella.

"No!" Jay growled. "She's mine!"

Neither turned around, and Ella didn't flinch at Bishop's touch. Far away, across the busy street, Jay pushed out of his car, choking on the stale air and desperation. Hours of waiting, for this? No. He stalked several cars closer, obsessing over Bishop's hand on her back.

A sliver of space separated Bishop and Ella. *Finally*. Jay took a ragged lungful, gasping in relief as sweat trickled from his hairline. Exhausted, he propped against a stranger's car, watching from a perch on the street as they disappeared into her building.

It would take five minutes for Bishop to drop off Ella's luggage. Then Jay would confront him. A solid plan. He would explain that the situation was now under control. That conversation plus talking to Ella's dad, whenever he managed to figure out what to say, would erase Bishop.

Five minutes crept by, and his muscles started to cramp. Each slow second took its sweet time to torture him.

Jay had left his phone in his car as the next five minutes, then ten minutes, he guessed, passed just as painfully.

What was happening in Ella's condo?

Surely, his sweet Ella would not let that disgusting slab of meat put his hands—*no*. Of course not. But still. Chatting, laughing?

Jay's molars could have fused coal to diamonds. His head killed. A massive headache begged to be a migraine.

He crawled against the car, pressing his body to the cool metal while kneading his temples. The man with the gun was alone with his girl. A problem Jay had caused, but one he could fix.

Soon…

Or later…

How long would this take?

He needed to scream, to escape, to put Bishop's bullets through his own head.

A sadistic smile crept onto Jay's face, which relaxed for the first few moments in a very long time. An easy breath coaxed its way out, and he pinched his eyes, controlling the spiraling attack that had seized him.

At war with the darkness, maybe the only thing that could help was to embrace more violence so he could find peace.

"Yes." His heart beat slower. Everything calmed. His eyelids drooped with each deep breath in and out…

THE RIDE FROM THE AIRPORT had been quiet, but the tension was palpable. It was an odd combination of Ella talking to Bishop as if they were a couple and then running away from a deep conversation with him. Their unspoken truce about Brie remained intact.

Could she ever admit out loud that she had almost killed him by abandoning him when he needed her the most? *Two* O'Kane deaths could have been her fault. Would he have enlisted if she hadn't left him?

And if he'd died in war? After his sister died in that car? Ella would have died too. That was all she could think about.

Bishop guided her inside her condo building, and now that they were closing in on the small space of the elevator and then the very personal quarters of her unit, she felt eager for private time with him again as much as she feared the guilt he might ask her about.

Bishop rolled her bag, ushering her to a stop, and he called the elevator. "You've been silent since wheels down."

"Have not," she whispered.

They entered the elevator, and he backed her into the corner, dropping her suitcase handle the second he entered. With both hands on her cheeks, he brought her face to his and kissed her. His mouth immediately opened, hot and hungry, and she finally felt at home. His weight pressed her into the corner, and his tongue stroked hers. As strong as the kiss came on, he ended it, lingering. "Should have done that when I first saw you."

"I…" had no words, apparently.

He stepped back, pressed the button for her floor, then moved back to the same spot and kissed her again. This time, she kissed him as ravenously as he had done her.

When the doors opened, he led the way to her unit and took her keys from her, unlocking the door and disarming her security system. "Stay put for a second."

Back to reality. Ella's stomach cramped at the thought that something might be there waiting for her return. But there wouldn't be. The cameras, the doorman… This was a safe place.

Instead, she focused on Bishop, not impending disaster. "I'm just going to watch the view."

He turned to see her overtly gawking at his backside, but he went about his business, though shaking his head and smiling while checking for danger that lurked.

His back was broad, and his ass was tight. Bishop was a specimen of physical perfection. If someone was going to jump out of a corner and end it all, she was going to go out studying his butt.

Ella rolled her lip into her mouth. It hadn't been a mistake to tell him how she felt, and his reaction had been…what? Good? Not bad. That wasn't great. She'd kind of thrown it at him. Saying it had seemed brilliant in her sleepy head, until he stuttered through the rest of the conversation. *Hell.*

"Looks good, babe." But he faltered. "What's wrong?"

Wrong? Nothing was wrong. Or everything. "Just tired, I guess."

"Bullshit." He closed the distance in the small living room. "I can still tell when you're lying."

"I just want to feel you." She took a step forward and put her hands on his abdomen. It was too intimate a touch for where her head was, yet maybe it was what she needed. Touch him, hold him, try to say the things she needed to without words. Those tricky suckers weren't coming to her, at least not the right ones. She slid her hands under his cotton shirt, and his warm skin gave her a rush. "And I want you to feel me tonight too."

He took a step back, grimacing. "Not that I don't want in you, babe. 'Cause I do. But not when it's as a subject change."

Damn it to hell. "Didn't realize that was what I was doing."

"So spit it out."

"I don't know." She turned, not sure—

He grabbed her forearm. "Seriously, El. Ass on the couch, and your mouth better start moving."

Her eyes bugged. "*That's* a little bossy."

"You just forced me to turn down sex in order to be an upstanding dude. I'm not thrilled."

"Ugh." She swallowed a groan and plopped onto the couch. "It's stupid."

"Obviously. But yet…" He gestured. "My boots aren't moving, babe."

With a deep breath, she dug into the problem neither of them had talked about since they first were catapulted back into each other's lives. "I'm…*sorry*."

"Er…" His jaw flapped for a moment before he rebounded. "Okay. But what for? Not that I'll refuse the rare apology from you."

"God. Never mind." She rolled her eyes and tucked her legs underneath her, searching for Furry Baby, and remembering that Manny had her pets while she was gone. They would at least snuggle her right now as all of the emotion that she hadn't touched in fifteen years began to climb up her throat and leak out her tear ducts. *Shit.* She quickly wiped the corners of her eyes.

"Ella. Calm down. Kidding." He strode over and sat next to her. "You're sorry. What for?"

Sniffling, the past crept back so quickly. All the hopes, all the regret. "I should have called." Just saying that out loud was enough to let the tears loose. "Heck, I could've written you an email. Texted. Walked into your dorm. Gone home. Gone to you. Something. Anything."

"Shit, El…" Bishop dropped back against the couch, his head falling so he stared at the ceiling. It was forlorn enough to make her sob. They were in love, and she was the weak link.

"I know we had different majors, were at different sides of campus." She wiped her cheeks. "But most of the time, we were literally twenty minutes apart. Literally, the same city. I just couldn't handle it…"

He'd needed her, and she had been so lost in her own grief about Brie that all she could think about was herself. What kind of lonely hell had he been living in when she abandoned him?

"Tell me"—Bishop reached behind her and pulled her into his lap—"that's not what you think."

Of course it was. What else was there to think? One day, everything was fine; everyone was alive. The next day, there was silence. Silence morphed into depression that became separation until she wasn't there.

Bishop stroked the back of her head. "I didn't hunt you down as much as you didn't come to me."

"She was your sister."

Without looking, Ella felt him nod. "Yeah."

"You don't blame me?"

"For Brie dying? Yeah. I did. Both of us. A lot…" He cleared his throat. "If we hadn't been playing. If we hadn't been drinking."

Ella stifled a sob. "I know. I mean…" She took a shaky breath. "I mean with us. You and me. Do you blame me for us? Breaking up. Because, I'm sorry."

"*Ella*." He shook his head. "Never occurred to me."

"Why?"

"Babe—" His brow furrowed, and he pinched the bridge of his nose. "Babe. *I left you*. I enlisted and never looked back. Couldn't."

Dumbstruck by that paradigm shift, she sat there, letting that weigh on her. "I didn't know."

"I didn't offer."

"We were so far gone," she whispered.

"It was bad."

She nodded. "And you thought all this time that I…knew? That *you* left *me*?"

Bishop rolled his bottom lip into his mouth. "Makes me a pretty solid piece of shit, huh?"

"We were so young. And we just sat there, holding her hands, and she *died*." Ella remembered how Brie's unresponsive hand had turned lifeless. How they'd each held one. Each begged her to be okay, told her that help was coming. She remembered the littlest things, like glass in her kneecaps and the wail of the sirens that were too late.

"Ella, take a breath." Bishop hung onto her. "I've got you."

She trembled as hard as her heart and buried into his chest. "I know you do."

"Good, babe. Good."

"You and me?" she murmured against his shirt. "It's happening again. Except this time, we're adults, and I just said things I've never been able to say out loud."

He kissed the top of her head.

"I'm falling for you all over again."

His heavy arms tightened, enveloping her in a safe cocoon. "When you stop falling and simply understand, let me know." His chin rested on top of her head. "Until then, don't rush it. You have a lot going on."

She would've melted away if he hadn't held her tight. This was more than just seeing someone…

Today. That moment. This was the start of them. They had been in love before; they could do it again—

The doorbell rang, and his hold that had been as easy as an angel's caress transformed into steel. "Expecting anyone, babe?"

This late at night after she'd just come home? No heads up from her doorman? All of her shook. "No."

"That motherfucker."

Fear woke every nerve as Bishop deposited her on the couch and unholstered his gun. "Go into your bedroom. I'll be back in one minute."

She scurried up at the sound of what had to be his gun clicking into action and his boots heading for the door.

IT WAS MORNING? AND WHOSE voice was that? Jay rubbed sleep from his eyes, feeling an awful crick in his neck.

"*Sir?*"

He blinked, more awake but still disoriented. The rising sun shone brightly. Wildly, he searched for the moon and night's sky. It was gone, replaced by the brilliant purples and yellows of dawn falling into morning.

"*Hey!*"

Jay turned, putting the pieces together. He was on the ground, pushed up against a car, with his legs half in the grass.

"Get off my car or I'm going to call the cops."

A tire had been his pillow. Not his worst sleeping conditions. "What time is it?"

"Christ. Six a.m."

Oh, shit. He'd been asleep all night. "Sorry, I—" He had no explanation, and when he looked up, Bishop's truck was gone. "Shit!"

Jay scurried to his feet, unsteady and unsure. He rushed toward his car. If Ella saw him now, he would have no explanation for her, either.

What did it mean if he was losing control? If he couldn't see the differences between himself and the stalker, of spiraling to sleep on a sidewalk?

Jay quickly closed himself in the safe confines of his car and checked his phone. There was a voice mail—not from her—and text messages from Ella. She had not even told him she was back at home. He pressed play on the voice mail.

"Hello, Mr. Graff. This is FBI Special Agent Angie Byrd. Sorry for the late-night call, but I'd hoped to catch you. I'd like to learn more about Eco-Ella and get your insight on Miss Leighton. My schedule is open tomorrow. Please call."

Jay hit save, and his pulse raced at the opportunity to enter the conversation. Whenever she wanted to meet, he would be there.

An opening from the FBI to see what they had, and still, he had nothing from Ella.

Jay opened the sun visor and stared at the mirror. "What does that mean?" No calls? "It means you need to gain control of Ella. Quickly."

CHAPTER 26

THIS WAS SOME BULLSHIT. JAY tapped his fingers nervously on the metal table. But it was all in the name of Ella's safety. He glanced around the FBI waiting room. When he'd agreed to chat with Special Agent Byrd, he thought it would be a conversation. Jay had envisioned coffee and a meeting of the minds, where they sat around a conference table, working out all of the possible threats against Ella, all of the headaches and concerns she'd received over the years, starting when they took on their first corporate challenge and reaching its zenith when she was the star of reality prime-time TV.

His eyes tracked to the two-way mirror and dropped to the scarred table. This wasn't the right setup, and he wasn't thrilled to be waiting to help. Jay pushed back the heavy metal chair, not comfortable in any position, and drummed his nails on the table again.

Tap, tap.

Tap, tap, tap.

"Anyone around?" How long had he been in there? He didn't have his cell phone on him—security had forced him to leave it at the building check-in—and Jay could feel eyes on him through the mirror. Was this what Ella felt like? Eyes boring into her.

Was this not a friendly visit? Were they smart enough to study him closer? He'd hunted Ella, and now maybe they considered hunting him?

No. Not possible. His planning had been too clean. His alibi was airtight, his schedule flawless. Even with the questionable one-time use of Tara into his well-orchestrated plans, it didn't matter. They could have at him for hours…days. He would play.

"Hello? I don't have all day." Confidence was a declaration of innocence, a simple challenge.

The door handle jiggled before it opened, and in walked a dowdy lady.

"Mr. Graff." She wore a pantsuit and blocky black boots.

That was Ella's agent? Not even a smear of makeup, but she was unlike that of the all-natural, Eco-Ella crowd. This woman seemed as if she didn't care.

"Good morning," Jay said.

"Thanks for coming in." Her chair scratched across the tile floor, and she did nothing to stop the jarring scrape until she took a seat and made official introductions.

Jay gave the smile that worked on most women. "Nice to meet you."

The agent opened a portfolio, turning over a scribble-covered page that had lines and circles, arrows and asterisks. She rolled a cheap pen between two fingers, dropped it to the page to test for ink, then put it down before glancing up as though she didn't give a hoot that he'd put on his most charming smile. "I had a few questions to clarify."

Bitch. "Anything to help Ella."

She didn't smile. No twitch of her lips, no dip of her head. Nothing. The woman gave up zip and probably killed at poker. Though not chess, where a person had to think.

The agent remained silent, but the pen began to write. What

could she possibly have picked up and thought important enough to jot down in the last two seconds?

"You've had a working and personal relationship with Ella for several years? Would you say you're close?"

Irritation sharpened its claws against his chest, and Jay ran his tongue along the inside of his lower lip. "No one knows Ella better than me."

"No one else?"

Certainly not Bishop. "No."

"Not her family?" the agent asked.

"Outside of family," Jay conceded. "She's close with her parents. But friends and lovers are the family you pick."

Would she understand that? Some people couldn't comprehend friends and lovers. And how *special* could this special agent be? She had no reaction when Jay basically offered her the encyclopedia of intelligence.

The agent flipped to a new page and wrote feverishly. She tore it free and pushed the straggle-sided note to him.

"What's this?" he asked.

Her blank face remained even. "You tell me."

His eyes dropped to a list of dates that he had memorized and planned around. He was visibly, physically nowhere near Ella at those times. More often than not, Tara was with him, and she was exceedingly visible, which made the best alibi. Jay read the list of days Ella had been *stalked.* "What is this? Dates of when things happened to Ella?"

The agent's passive face didn't flinch. "Can you please check your calendar against these dates? Then let me know where you were?"

"They wouldn't let me bring my phone upstairs, but sure, I can get that to you." He offered his trademark pearly white smile. It had helped him time and time again, whether he and Ella were on the beach and needed to get in good with the locals, or they needed to sweet-talk the secretary of a corporate CEO.

Agent Byrd didn't notice. Jay tilted his head and deepened the smile. Still no reaction from the agent. He leaned back, assessing his opponent. She didn't retreat.

"Just in case, I had it brought up." She gestured at the mirror, and the door swung open.

An older man walked in with Jay's phone outstretched, and a trickle of concern ran along the back of his neck as he snagged the device. "Fine."

Scrolling through his apps until he found the calendar, Jay pulled up the details. They were perfectly scheduled for this exact situation. By his estimation, it would take approximately an easy two minutes to fill anybody in. "Ready?"

"By all means."

He spoke, but she didn't write anything down. The pen remained by the notebook. Jay's calendar items were pinpoint precise, and what did she do? *Nothing!*

"All right. Thank you for your time. That will be all."

He seethed. "That's it? That's all you have to ask?" He bunched his fists, standing, and ground them into the cold table. "That could've been handled on the phone or in an email. You didn't write anything down."

The agent showed a flicker of emotion for the first time. She looked triumphant. "No. It couldn't. Do you have anything else you want to add, Mr. Graff?"

Had he been set up? Was this hunter better than he realized? Jay pulled himself back; the realization of what had just happened slapped him across the face. "No."

She smiled. "Good day."

The woman in the ugly boots and ugly suit, with no makeup and bad hair, who didn't succumb to any of his charm and didn't flinch or flirt with a smile, pushed out of her chair, letting it scrape, then turned on her flat heels. She left him with his mouth agape.

Jay fell back in his chair, shocked. This was all wrong. He was the master of situations, certainly the master of Ella, like a fisherman who'd thrown his net and was pulling his girl back.

All of these things—the FBI, Titan, *Bishop*—they had all messed up his plan. His lungs hurt as he held his breath. Nothing seriously wrong had just happened. Simple damage control might be needed, but nothing major.

The phone-bearing agent reappeared, and after a few short words that Jay didn't process, Jay warily followed. He got his wallet back from security—where his phone had been—and pushed out the heavy doors, passing the security guards who had searched and scanned him.

The sun hit his face, and Jay jogged toward the parking garage. The building loomed next to him as if it might reach down and pull him back inside. His jog became a run, until he was at the garage, taking two steps at a time in the stairwell. Jay sprinted to his car.

Once in the safety of his Prius, he pulled Ella's name up and hit the button. It rang once, twice.

"Hello?" Her sweet answer soothed his soul.

Gasping, he squeezed his eyes shut. "Hey, Ella, what are you up to?"

"The same old. You?" She sounded distracted.

"Actually…" He fumbled blindly for the start button, needing the AC to cool him down. "I just spent time with your FBI agents." The air hit him, and he opened his eyes. "You have a good team. Whatever's going on, they're going to fix this. Don't stress about it."

"I'm not stressed."

"You're not *stressed*? Everyone's running around, dealing with it, and you're *not stressed*?"

"I—"

"You should be."

"Jeez, Jay. I'm trying to live my life. I have Bishop and Locke to run around and *deal with it*. Okay? I'm glad you talked with them and all, but—"

"Bishop and Locke are assholes." He slammed a fist onto the center console. "That Titan Group stands for everything that we don't. You and me, Ella. *We're* the team. We have our beliefs. They are a blip in time."

"Titan allows for whatever you believe in. That's a simple fact."

He sneered. "Excuse me?"

"Whoever's doing this? Screw that person. They're trying to control my life."

Damn. Fucking. Straight. Control her and bring her back. "You don't get it, Ella—"

"*No*. You don't, Jay. Last night, I dropped something out of my purse, and my neighbor stopped by to bring it over. You have *no idea* how scared I was just because my doorbell rang. You have *no clue* what I went through from a simple doorbell."

Finally—but she didn't call, and he had woken up on the street. How could his plan have failed so miserably? A migraine clouded at his temples.

"And no matter what I do or what I believe…" She trailed off, and he couldn't manage to speak any words to fill the gap. Ella continued. "Or what I want to fight for? As long as it's for the greater good, Bishop and Locke, Titan? They're behind me. That's my team. The Eco-Ella team, which you're supposed to be A-number-one cheerleader on. So get over it, Jay, and get back on *the* team. Or get a new job. I am done with the fighting."

A new job? His ear must be lying. No other reason, except… "Did you sleep with him?"

"*Are you out of your*—forget it."

"Did you sleep with him?"

"Jay!"

"Did that 'roided-up buffoon touch you?" Jay spat into the phone.

"You know what? I'm so done with this. You're fired."

The phone clicked, and the silent line screamed louder than his demons.

Chapter 27

The rage finally left Jay's shaking hands. Forty-five minutes later, he handed Tara a no-foam soy latte and took a burning sip of his. Together, they walked out of the coffee shop. Tara didn't have her quick-footed gait, and the corners of her mouth hadn't perked up, even with the promise of caffeine. She had nothing to complain about, though, given she hadn't been *fired*. Jay planned on wringing Ella's neck if she didn't call him back in the very near future and beg for forgiveness.

Tara worried him, though. The FBI didn't call her up and schedule an appointment. They'd dropped by her office, wanting a tour of her conference room, even though that had happened weeks ago and Titan had reported everything. She was a jittery mess.

He tugged at his collar.

"Jay—"

"What did they ask you?" They navigated the pocked brick sidewalks on Capitol Hill.

"Where was I, who I was with, what did I think about what was happening to Ella." Tara's bossy-bitchy, always so-sure candor wasn't there. Her lips rested on the lid of the coffee cup as they paused at a crosswalk.

"That's not a big deal." Encouraging her worked for both of

them. That one little stunt he had looped her in on wasn't his best move, but she had no idea the extent to which he had played with Ella. Tara had held his letters, looked at his pictures, talked about his doings *with him*, and had no idea. Everything would be fine. "It's a good thing to hash it out with them. It'll keep her safe."

But the heat had been set to boil. The game would have to end *now*. Ella had changed the rules; the FBI might be on the right trail. If Ella took him back, the stalker would go away and the game would be done. Everything would go back to normal, and their life would move forward.

The crosswalk sign changed, but Tara only moved the cup from her lips. "Wait—Jay. Every time and date they asked me about, I was with you."

Interesting that she thought that was noteworthy. "We're always together."

"Not always."

"I thought the same thing about you." He laughed, arching an eyebrow. "Do you have a plan to drive ratings with a stalker?"

"*No!*"

Perfect reaction. She was accused of pushing the envelope so often that she would be defensive. "We're together all the time. Throw a dart at the calendar, and we'd be together."

"Right… Does this have anything to do with what we had—"

"No." He cut her off abruptly. "Absolutely not. That was totally separate. It was just a thing. It's not even worth bringing up."

"Okay, because they asked if there is anything else that I could think of, and—"

"Did you mention that?" Because everything banked on the fact that Tara was unscrupulous enough to play a little with her clients, nothing illegal, and not mention it if questioned.

"No. It just seems silly," she stuttered.

"Exactly. We *were* just playing games. Now that everything else has happened, no one would find it funny. Context is everything."

"You're right," Tara said.

"You'd lose all your clients if that got out." Jay was going to have to pull off something big when he wasn't with Tara but still had an alibi, especially if this "you're fired" bullshit didn't wrap up.

Tara bit the edge of her cup, her silence agreeing with him. Nerves were contagious, and he drummed on the side of his coffee cup as they came upon Tara's office. What kind of event would force Ella his way and ensure he and Tara didn't have an issue with their identical calendars?

The taste of excitement mixed with his coffee. "Don't worry, Tara. Everything will be fine."

"Sure," she mumbled.

"Good news is Eco-Ella has never been so hot. Did you see the numbers from the last few nights?"

She stopped chewing on the edge of her cup and shined. "I did."

When all else failed, he could throw ratings out to pacify Tara. Mission accomplished.

ELLA SWIRLED THE STRAW IN her smoothie cup, unable to stop fidgeting. She had torn the team apart, and now it was time to tell Tara, who was always an advocate of the Ella-Jay dynamic duo.

"You're ruining your smoothie," Tara offered. "It's already a soupy mess. Consistency is half the battle."

Exactly. Consistency. And that was Tara—consistent. She'd always been there with the truth whenever Ella needed to hear it, never wavering, even if the delivery hurt. But that was one of the reasons why Ella appreciated Tara's insight. She would tell Ella if firing Jay was the wrong move.

"Jay met with the FBI today." Ella stilled her straw. "Then he sort of…crossed the line." His attitude problem had to be jealousy-based. Everything had been fine until Bishop showed up.

"I did too," Tara offered.

"Oh. Good." Everyone played a part in nailing the bastard that was screwing with her. Didn't Jay see that? Each person was part of the team, playing their role. "But with Jay…he's got a problem with Bishop."

"No shit, chickadee."

Ella's eyes bugged. "Well, if you know that—"

"Honey, the whole world knows that. I'm surprised even fans aren't commenting on that." She smirked. "Well, if Bishop would ever go on video, they would."

"That's not his role in all of this."

"And what is his role?" Tara sucked on the straw, tilting her head, waiting for gossip.

"I fired Jay."

The straw fell off Tara's bottom lip as it dropped. "You did *what*?"

"He asked if I was sleeping with Bishop."

"Well…" Tara's cheeks blushed. "I kinda did too. Are you going to fire me?"

"He did it in an angry way. Like he threw it in my face and yelled it a few times."

Tara pulled the straw back into her mouth. "Well, shit. When did that happen?"

"Right after his meeting with my agent."

Tara sipped the smoothie then chewed on the straw. "Hmmm. How about that shit?"

"I wanted to let you know, so that, I don't know. This is awkward. I just thought you should know."

"It's not awkward. Bishop's hot. You're single. I get it."

Ella blushed. "I always thought you wanted me back with Jay."

"No." She put her cup down. "You and Jay are ratings gold. When you two do a video, it's like whoa." Tara tossed jazz hands. "I'm a ratings whore. You know that."

"You're not pissed?" Ella asked.

"God…fuck me sideways. You're going to fire me, anyway. Let's get it over with now."

"What?"

"When you two first broke up, Jay asked me if I could help play matchmaker in getting you guys back together."

Ella blinked. "Meaning what?"

"You had some red-carpet event you were going to, and he wanted to escort you. You'd had some nutso fan letters within the couple weeks before that event. So…he wrote one up, and I let you see it."

"Tara!"

"It was nothing." Tara cringed. "Super poor timing, considering you had a real loose cannon out there. Look, I'm sorry. It was stupid. It was one of your first big events after the breakup, and I didn't know how it would go without him on your arm, and—I'm sorry."

Her mind reeled. "I don't even know what to say."

"Please," Tara whispered. "Don't say I'm fired. I do all kinds of publicity stuff for you. I lumped it in with that. Didn't think twice."

"That's so…so…"

"Manipulative as shit. Appalling. Categorically fucked up." Her brow furrowed. "I legitimately didn't think it was a big deal at first, and I have been letting it eat me alive every day since. I'm sorry."

"And Jay was in on this?"

Tara nodded. She bit her lip, tears welling. "I'm sorry."

"You guys are my team. My friends," she whispered.

"I really am. I made a mistake. It was just a letter, just for one event." Tara shook her head. "I don't mean to downplay. At the time, it didn't seem big. Now? With everything going on? My perspective has changed. And maybe, what I do for ratings too."

"This…really hurts."

"Are you going to fire me? Maybe you should. *You shouldn't.* But maybe you should…" She sucked in a breath and whispered, "Please don't."

Ella closed her eyes. "No."

"Are we still friends?"

"If that's what you call us…"

Tara wrapped her arms around Ella. "I'm going to be a better friend."

"And a nicer publicist?"

She pulled back. "I'm nice."

Ella choked on a laugh. "You should read back some of your text messages. They can be harsh."

"Really?"

She nodded.

Tara pulled her chair closer. "I'm team Ella. I love working with Eco-Ella, and I hope you're banging the brains out of Bishop."

"*Tara*!"

"I value you. I'll make it up to you. But first, I have a phone call to make."

"To who?"

"The FBI."

That caught Ella off guard. "About this?"

"About a couple things that popped to mind while we were

sitting here. Drink your melted smoothie and do a video—and God help us, don't post that thing until we walk out the door. As hot as your bodyguard is, I don't want him breathing down my neck."

It looked as though Tara had been on the receiving end of Bishop's "how to be safe in the age of the Internet" conversation. "He has a strong argument."

"I think he probably has a strong *everything*."

"Tara!"

"What? Dirty girl. I didn't say anything like your face just said. Who knew it'd take a beefcake like him to turn Eco-Ella into—"

"Don't finish that." But Tara was not wrong. "Make your phone call, then I have to go home."

Because now Ella had her own calls to make.

CHAPTER 28

JAY PACED THE APRON OF the Lewandowski driveway. Ella's parents weren't home. Big surprise. They traveled too much, and her father wasn't returning Jay's phone calls and texts. What kind of dad didn't do that when his daughter was in the middle of this dangerous situation?

He pulled out his phone, trying one more time. It rang and hit the third chime. Voice mail was a moment away. Again.

"Hello?" her father grumbled.

Jay startled. "Hi. Hello. This is Jay."

"I know, Jay."

His forehead wrinkled. Then why wasn't he answering? "I needed to speak with you about the security group you hired for Ella."

"This isn't a conversation that we're going to have, son."

See! Even her father still acted as though they were family, as though he and Ella were still a couple. "What you don't know—"

"Jay, I'm not meddling in my daughter's affairs."

"Exactly!"

"What's between you and El is between you two. I'd like to stay out of it."

"I'm trying to explain about the ineptitude of her security."

"Hmm." The sound drew through the phone. "I'm quite pleased. Thank you for your concerns, Jay. Take care."

The call ended, and he raged. "*Fuck!*"

BISHOP WATCHED SPECIAL AGENT ANGIE Byrd walk out. Rocco shut the door, one hand resting on it, while he shook his head. With Rocco's back turned toward the room, Bishop hadn't been able to get a read on his team leader's face, which had remained impassive throughout the entirety of the briefing. This was not going to be a slam, bam, thank you ma'am fast job. No, this was nothing more than gut instinct and a lack of evidence.

Rocco turned around. His gaze first went to Winters, and they exchanged a nonverbal conversation that Bishop wished he'd been at Titan long enough to read. Roman and Cash seemed to understand every word, their body language agreeing with a nod. Nicola and Beth had come in for the briefing, sitting side by side near Winters. While on maternity leave, they'd only come in for the most important of intel jobs, and Bishop didn't know what to make of their intense focus or the etched worry radiating from them as Nicola twisted her fingers and Beth remained eerily still.

Locke and Jax mirrored him across the table, both eyeing their teammates without making their moves obvious.

"Goddamn it," Jared growled from the head of the table.

All the attention shifted to him as Rocco dropped back into his chair next to Boss Man.

Rocco ran his hand over his face. "They don't know which way is up, which way is down."

"They do," Jared disagreed. "And aren't telling us shit."

Winters shook his head. "They didn't say that."

Bishop glanced at Locke then Jax. Disagreement in the family. Surely it happened, but they'd never seen it. Across the table, Roman and Cash were harder to read. Nicola and Beth were not.

Roman leaned back in his chair. "It's definitely not someone who gives two shits about Vamanato." He rubbed his chin. "It's someone she's close to."

"Byrd didn't say that," Cash pointed out.

Roman raised an eyebrow. "Didn't *not* say that."

"It's either the crazies—" Nic volunteered.

"Or the ex-boyfriend," Beth finished.

"My money is on the ex-boyfriend," Bishop volunteered. "Dude's a gallon short of a full tank."

Rocco gave Bishop a hyper-questioning look.

Screw that. Bishop's certainty wasn't based on his past with Ella. Even if the FBI agent had said that Jay's schedule was solid and his alibi airtight, Bishop's gut said that was bullshit.

"The guy is possessive; that's for sure." Locke eased their team leader off Bishop a bit.

Roman leaned forward, putting his elbows on the table. "Maybe if the cops took her seriously from the start…"

Around the room, everyone nodded.

"We don't deal in coulda, woulda bullshit." Jared cracked a knuckle. "We deal with problems."

It wasn't as if Titan wouldn't continue the protective detail. "We keep at her side," Bishop said.

Jax laughed. "Bet you'd like that, huh?"

Bishop's gaze swung to the asshole across the room. "What the fuck is your problem? Lay off the woman."

"Chill out," Rocco ordered.

Jared's ice-cold glare brought the room down a dozen degrees. "Rocco."

"Yes, sir."

"Your thoughts?" Boss Man asked.

"They are no closer to figuring out how to end this than they were when we first made contact. We agree with everything they explained: the situation is spiraling. It's becoming more chaotic."

Spiraling chaos. That upped Bishop's anxiety. He rolled his lip into his mouth, having nothing to offer to the conversation and hating that fact.

Jared's jaw flexed. "Parker is working everything he has to augment their data."

That should have helped alleviate some stress, but it didn't.

Jared rubbed a hand over his face. "It's a matter of time. Mistakes will be made. They'll figure it out."

"I think they know," Beth said. "I think they don't have shit for evidence, but like Jared said when she left, they aren't telling us. That was a woman who gave us everything she could show us except for what she couldn't."

Boss Man nodded.

"Bishop has a feeling," Beth continued. "Locke noticed something. We heard the profiles of Jay and Tara, both who give me the heebie-jeebies." Beth paused. "That agent doesn't know us from anyone else. But she does know we're going to sit here and tear apart what she says the second she leaves." Beth pointed her finger around the room. "Like hell would she tell you guys what her gut says, when not one of you asked her about it."

Bishop raised an eyebrow. No, they hadn't.

"We remain the course," Jared grumbled.

Then his intense glower rested on Bishop. "We're still loyal to the job, to her, to her family for however long this takes. This is our new normal. Bishop, Locke, you're still primaries. But depending on how this shit show continues to roll, consider yourselves all her white knights, dead set on ensuring her long-term survival. Understood?"

“The Knights of Titan,” Cash murmured.

Good thing Cash could drop humor when it was most needed because Bishop wasn’t sure how much more of Jared assessing him he could take while staying quiet.

“It’s the boyfriend,” Beth said.

“Or that batshit crazy publicist,” Winters countered.

“Doesn’t matter. Don’t care.” Jared stood up. “Keep our woman safe. Do what it takes.”

Chapter 29

Losing Jay from the team was a nightmare. Not because Ella missed him, but because he did a lot of work with content, running with ideas, and controlling hers. Right now, she had a thousand ideas and was running short on time for her project. Her anxiety was at an all-time high, and it wasn't even past breakfast time.

"Bishop's about to swing up here," Locke said. "I'm headed out."

"Thanks for pulling an overnight guard duty. I know there's a thousand things more fun than patrolling my front door and couch." She liked him. Sometimes, Locke said a lot when he said nothing at all. "I made fresh, non-wheatgrass smoothies, if you didn't notice me take tons of pictures to post later."

"No big deal, and"—he laughed—"I did notice. Very red-looking."

"I'm going to be insulted if you don't try one sometime soon." The door opened, and Bishop walked in, accompanying Manny. "Hey, guys!" She turned back to Locke. "Now you're off the clock. Go try one."

"Working didn't keep me from trying one, Ella."

Having chosen the pictures she wanted to post and rereading the recipe, she tossed her phone on the counter. "Now I'm insulted."

Locke's eyes widened a fraction, and dang it, he was too nice to screw with. That she would leave for Bishop. "Kidding. Kidding."

He smiled, which didn't happen nearly often enough. "All right, I'll try one."

Ella beamed that finally she had worn him down. Bishop was next on her list, though her goal was to get him to drink something with wheatgrass in it. That would be considered a trophy-win.

"Hey, El."

Two words, one reaction. Swoony-smiley. That was how Bishop made her feel when he turned his green eyes on her. "Hi."

Locke spun toward her blender and poured the strawberry power blast into a glass as she picked her phone back up and scheduled it to go live later.

He stirred the cup. "Smoothies of champions."

"Cheers." She prayed he would love it. Surely he would. Right? Who in their right mind wouldn't?

"Ella!" Manny pointed his thumb. "So me and Muscles—"

Bishop glared. "*Excuse me*?"

"What? If she can call you that, why can't I?"

Locke choked on his smoothie, laughing, covering his mouth, and heading for the sink.

Bishop's eyebrows almost hit his hair. "Muscles?"

"What?" Her cheeks were on fire. "You've heard me say that before."

He glowered. "I didn't know this was a common thing."

Locke howled in laughter, not that he was finished choking on her smoothie, which he had spit in the sink, dang it.

Manny tried to help. "Oh, come on. You've got big muscles. What other nicknames should we call you?"

Locke rejoined the conversation, wiping his mouth with the back of his hand, still chortling. "Yeah, Muscles."

"Screw you." Bishop shook his head, trying not to laugh, but

Ella could see that he could at least appreciate the entertainment value.

"He calls you Crazy," Locke offered.

"Still?" Ella sobered. "That's not fair. Or nice. At least Muscles is nice."

"And true," Manny said. "Ella's not crazy."

"She's had a few moments, Manny." Bishop clapped as though he were done and signifying that everyone else should be too. "What's on the agenda today?"

"I'm not crazy."

"She's passionate," Locke offered.

"Unorthodox," Manny added.

Ella smiled. "I'll take those."

He smiled and winked. "They're not as fun to call you."

"O-M-G, Bishop, please," Manny begged and fanned himself. "God, have mercy."

"I can't handle this shit." Locke laughed. "I'm out, folks."

"You didn't finish the smoothie!"

"Well, I—it was good."

"Make a to-go cup," Ella ordered.

"Definitely good enough that I'll do that."

"Thank you." She pointed at Bishop. "You should take notes, Muscles. He's better at this than you."

"Crazy, your nickname's going to morph into batshit if you're not too careful."

God, she hadn't laughed and had fun like this in so long. Just relaxed and—an idea sprang to mind. "Manny, want to do a video with me?"

He could do the bees-and-herb vlog with her. Then she could get it all finished and be done with it. In production, she could chop it up and make it into several short vlogs, maybe a webinar or something. Tara could work with that.

"Are you joking?" Manny's mouth hung open. It was a big task. Manny touted to everyone and anyone that he was personal assistant to the stars and an Eco-Ella super fan, but this was way more than that. His head bobbed, accepting before he even knew what the task would incorporate.

"You know that gorgeous park over in Seneca?" She pulled the pieces together on the fly, turning to Bishop. "Where we were the other day?"

"Um, yes," Manny answered for him. "Your favorite spot in the whole world."

"Not the hut, but the park, that big hill."

"Yeah, yeah, yeah!"

What a beautiful treescape that would make in the background. "We could set up a tripod and just talk. Do a few candids into the phone. I want to wrap the lavender and mint project up and pimp the urban beekeepers. It's such a good thing, but I'm losing the focus right now."

"I *love* what you're doing with that, though," Manny gushed.

"Which is why you're the perfect guy to help me."

"Ella, I would be so honored," he prattled. "I will do everything. I've always wanted to be your helper bee. No pun intended. *Yes, pun intended!* Oh, my gosh, I'm going to die."

"Sweet! We'll go do that today. That's our to-do list." She tilted her head to Bishop, questioning if he was onboard.

"Nice." Locke nodded. "Seneca is gorgeous."

"You should join us." Manny clapped. "Like a big team event. It's my first on-air production."

"I gathered," Locke added, letting Manny have his moment.

"He's off work," Ella explained.

Manny rolled his eyes. "That doesn't mean he doesn't want to hang out with us."

"I think it does." Not putting Locke in a super-awkward spot would be awesome. "He probably has other people to save and protect."

"Eh." Locke shrugged. "I'd be down to see what you guys do."

"Yes." Manny put his hand in the air, searching for a high five from Locke. "You will love this."

"Or not." Ella worried that Locke had been guilt-tripped into a yes, and that Manny was *maybe* idealizing this more than he should. "It'll be a little boring. We'll map out what we'll say, shoot the video, probably have a few bloopers. It'll be cool—"

"Nothing with Muscles and ol' Locke and Key over there will be boring."

Shit. Her cheeks flared again.

Bishop tilted his head. "Lock and Key?"

Manny nodded. "You know, for the strong silent type."

"I like it." Locke slapped Manny five.

"How often do you two talk about us?" Bishop's inquisitive look bounced between her and Manny.

"Never," she said.

"All the time," Manny countered simultaneously and giggled as though he wanted the nickname Crazy. "You two are the best thing to come along since the camera crew for *Under the Roof*."

AN HOUR LATER, BISHOP AND Locke were posted on the side of a steep hill, far enough away that Ella felt confident their voices would not be picked up by her video recording. Whatever supersonic speakers she had on her audio set were a bit much, but far be it for him to question *the process*. At the base of Seneca Park's longest hill, the woman was on a mission with a tripod, a boom speaker, and two video recorders for different angles. And apparently, it required a significant amount of distance, as he and Locke watched from afar.

"Boring," Locke said.

"Yup," Bishop agreed.

"I like it here, though. Good to get out of the condo and into fresh air."

"Amen." Bishop thought her place made him feel like sardines packed into a tiny container, especially when the four of them had been standing in her living room.

Manny had driven his van, which apparently was outfitted with everything FB and LK could dream about needing—food, water, snacks, poop bags. Who knew pets needed so much? Brick didn't need shit. When he was home, Bishop let his dog run around outside then threw some scoops of chow in a bowl and filled up another bowl with tap water. When he couldn't get home, Bishop's neighbor did what he would've done on his behalf. There was never a plan, certainly not a van stocked full of necessities.

Locke and Bishop had driven separately, Ella with him, and their vehicles were lined up in the lot on top of the hill. Somehow, all this had happened without much of a carbon footprint lecture.

The gray sky was scattered with angry clouds.

Locke tore at a piece of grass, and Bishop watched a trail of ants on the bench that they'd kicked back on, choosing to rest with their boots on the seat. They both leaned forward, elbows on knees, watching Ella and Manny gesticulate, smile, and laugh. They would hold up the plants and pass them back and forth.

"Man, they are super into it," Bishop muttered.

"Yup." Locke reached down, tearing out another long piece of grass, and went to splitting it.

Watching Ella work, while not riveting, was pretty cool. Just as cool as the bikini video from Costa Rica, because her passion bled through even from over here.

Manny and Ella donned headsets, sitting on the ground, pointing back and forth between the screen and something, almost as if they were disagreeing, or maybe searching for something on screen. Who knew? They were *into it* in a major way.

"I don't get it," Locke said. "Have you ever been that excited about anything in your life?"

Maybe about getting her back into bed again soon. "Nothing that I'd share with you."

Locke laughed. "Right."

Bishop rubbed his face. When she had come home, he'd spent all night with her. Every minute of that time had been spent wide-awake, reminding her that she had been missed.

Something moved in his peripheral. He turned as Locke did too.

"What the hell?" Bishop jumped up, and Locke muttered the same as he bound up also.

Manny's van moved in the parking lot at the top of the hill. Slowly at first. Enough that both he and Locke stared, stupefied. Then the slow roll turned into a rush. The hill was steep, and Ella and Manny sat in the van's path with their backs to it, staring at a screen and wearing big fuzzy headphones.

Bishop and Locke sprinted forward. Bishop's mind was racing. "Ella!"

"Who's in there?" Locke shouted.

Bishop's eyes narrowed, but the angle made the windshield hard to see. "No one!"

He veered toward Ella and Manny, who were still oblivious. "Move!"

Neither did. What were those fucking headphones? Noise cancelling? How loud was their audio?

"Go," Locke shouted, but Bishop was already pivoting downhill. Locke angled toward the van as it gained speed. What was Locke going to do? Climb in and divert?

"Ella!" Bishop charged down the hill, arms pumping and thighs burning as he hollered for them to look up. How did Ella not see the commotion in her peripheral? That screen in their laps—they were glued to it. "Manny, move!"

But they were too far away. *Fuck it.* Two choices: get them out of the way or make them move. He pulled out his sidearm and fired into the air. Ella and Manny startled and spun, seeing the van.

They froze. Fuck it. They froze.

Flight or fright, and those two chose the wrong fucking thing to do.

"No!" Bishop powered as fast as he could. "Move! Move, now!"

His heart was in his chest. His lungs pounded. He couldn't run any faster. Locke stopped short out of the corner of Bishop's eye. His teammate had his gun in hand and—*bam, bam, blast*—the back tire blew out, trajectory and speed only slightly altered and not enough.

That shocked Ella to stand up, but Manny didn't. She clung to him, was right by his side, both of them shouting and yelling.

These had been the longest seconds of Bishop's life, and the last two were an eternity. Bishop wanted to scream, "leave him," but neither he nor she would.

Bishop threw his arms out, praying to God, and dove for them. He caught Ella by the waist, twisting and spinning, throwing her out of the way, grabbing Manny by the shoulder, and—*slam*.

Bishop went down. Cold metal hit him like a football team clad in armor. He spun, losing his grip. Losing himself. His face hit the ground, dirt and grass in his mouth. When he realized where he was, he opened his fists—and his hands were empty.

Rolling over—*hell, that hurt*—his head spun.

"Don't move," Locke said from somewhere to somebody.

His elbow reached behind him, pushing up, and a splitting headache made the skyline tilt sideways. "Eloise—Ella?"

"Stay down, Bishop," Locke ordered.

No, thank you. Fucking hell. His head spun, and his stomach roiled. Where was she?

Hands cupped his face. "Bishop? Are you okay?"

Relief rolled through his confused mind. "Yes." *Thank fuck.* He dropped back, needing to catch his breath. Now he could stay down. Now... Panting, he just needed to know she was fine.

"Promise me!" Ella demanded.

"Yes, babe. I promise." Bishop wheezed, catching the breath that had been punted out of him by a van grill. "Give me a minute."

Squeezing his eyes shut once more, all he could remember was Ella's scared face the microsecond before the impact. All he could see was his world coming to an end as terror screamed in her eyes and her mouth gaped silent.

Bishop blinked away that nightmare, and she was gone when he opened his eyes again. Ignoring the soreness around his ribs and hip, he gritted his teeth and propped on an elbow to push up. Ella and Locke were perched next to Manny.

Shit.

"Locke, help him," Ella said.

"I—uh," Manny sputtered. "Oww."

Manny's eyes were closed, and Locke stood with his phone to his ear. "We need an ambulance." He pinched the bridge of his nose as he explained and gave their location.

Bishop turned toward the base of the hill, where the van had crashed into the trees. Ella's video equipment was strewn the remainder of the way down the hill, and the van's front end was demolished by the force of the impact. FB ran circles around them, and Bishop had no idea where LK was.

"Got Manny?" Locke asked.

Bishop nodded, knowing what was on his buddy's mind. They

were under attack, and somehow they'd missed it. What were the chances that Manny had forgotten to set his car in Park? Or that it had slipped out of gear? Impossible.

"Ella," Manny moaned. Tears leaked down his cheeks.

"Help is coming. Hang on!" She cried with him, holding his hand. "I'm so sorry."

"I'll be back." Locke sprinted up the hill.

"Is he going for the ambulance?" Ella asked. "I don't hear sirens."

No, babe. He's hunting. "We need to keep Manny calm."

How had Bishop missed this? They were in a wide-open park. They would've seen a car coming up to the parking lot. How long would it have taken someone to follow them? Or hike on foot? Too long. But nothing was impossible. They sure as hell didn't have tracking devices on their vehicles…or did they? Manny's van was the new item in the equation and a constant around Ella. They couldn't search everyone in contact with her…

An ambulance siren blared in the background. Locke jogged downhill, his head shaking. Once he was by Bishop's side, they watched as the ambulance made its way up the drive to the parking lot. Any car would have been visible, a point the ambulance just confirmed. "You're probably thinking what I'm thinking."

"Affirmative."

"I'll call in to Titan. Stick with Ella."

He wasn't going far from her. He almost hadn't made it in time. The memory of cold steel slamming into his body made him shudder. Ella could've been roadkill in a beautiful park that she'd sworn was her favorite place on earth. Guilt tightened his lungs, and he cleared his throat.

A medical team ran down the hill with a gurney and packs. They crowded around Manny, and Bishop scooped Ella into his arms. "I'll take you to get checked out." Truth was, he didn't want her to hear Manny when they immobilized him. It was better if Ella missed this.

"I want to stay with him."

"I know you do, babe. But I promise, they have him."

He ground his molars at the pain from his own bruises and cradled her. Ella sucked in a breath, reacting to an injury too.

She dropped her head against his shoulder. "How did I let this happen?"

"Same question I'm asking," Bishop mumbled. They were both hiding bruises, and both asking the same questions. Every time he least expected it, he found out they were the same. This time, for the first time, it was for the worst.

Chapter 30

The germicide smell of hospitals made Ella sick, and she itched to leave. Her room made her anxious, and the lack of Manny updates exacerbated that tenfold. Bishop and Locke hovered in the room like two ginormous, out-of-place soldiers in a dollhouse made for tender, breakable things. Their glares were hardened and angry, and their conversations were whispered back and forth, except when they were telling her to get back into bed.

"Can everybody stop fussing over me?" Ella barked at Bishop and Locke. "Because I am done with this! Done. Done. *Done!*"

Locke took a step back, and Bishop took a step forward. But neither said anything.

"Nothing is wrong with me." Her irritation level reached an all-time high at that very second. "Manny was the one who was hurt. Hurt because of *me*. I get that he's going to be fine, but I'm already fine. I have a few bumps and bruises. I have a headache, which I'm sure is from stress more than being run over by Manny's van."

Bishop crossed his arms, apparently none too thrown that she kept insisting on the truth. "You didn't cause that."

"Bishop's right, Ella," Locke repeated.

When these two decided to stick to a script, *man,* they did.

They never deviated and never stopped pushing their agenda.

She turned puppy dog eyes to Bishop. "Can you get me out of here?"

"Not yet."

Maybe they would work on Locke. "I'm appreciative for the checkup. But I don't understand the holdup."

A nurse walked into the room—the same nurse that had read Ella the riot act before. *Shit.*

"Observation, Miss Leighton. I thought that we had gone over this, but if you need to review it again, I would be more than thrilled to do so." Her tone said anything but. The woman didn't like her; that much Ella knew.

Locke's eyebrows bounced, and Bishop barely stifled a laugh. *Jerks, all of them.*

"Observation, I understand. Can't one of them observe me? They're paid a lot of money to make sure that I don't drop dead. And I'm still alive."

Bishop grumbled, and Ella took a mental note. Bishop was taking this hard, placing blame on himself as much as she was, maybe. "You guys know what I mean."

"I'm sure they have other things to do," the nurse said.

"That is literally their job. They are doing it here, and they can do it anywhere." She turned to Bishop and Locke. "Surely you two people have enough pull with"—Ella gestured wildly—"whomever to get me released from here."

Both of them twisted their mouths and tilted their heads as though she were right, but neither of them made any move to comply with her wishes. Maybe there was another way. *Hello!*

"Release me against medical wishes, or whatever it's called. Either way, I'm out of here. I'll just hitchhike my way home."

Bishop's brow furrowed. "You're not hitchhiking anywhere."

Locke just shook his head as though he were glad he was

secondary on her assignment. Truth be told, she was probably not the easiest person to work security for.

She laser-focused her attention on Bishop. "I will hitchhike all night, searching for big rigs and gas-guzzling trucks. Does that tell you how bad I want out of here?"

"Christ, come on already. Can't you just chill and relax? Listen to what you're supposed to do?" They faced off in a staring contest until Bishop blew out his frustration. "What do we have to sign to get her out of here?"

As though the nurse had been prepared for the conversation, she picked up a clipboard from the end of the bed, which she refused to sit on, flipped the pages, and handed it over. "Sign where marked. You're leaving against medical advice." She clucked her disapproval. "Good luck. I'll give you a printout of what to be aware of. If those things pop up, come back to the emergency room."

Ella scribbled her name where indicated. "I'll be fine."

"Sure you will." She waited for the signatures then walked out of the room.

As soon as the door shut, Ella stifled a thousand comments about how she was fine and that everyone's overreactions were causing her more issues than what had happened. "I'm not sure why she was hell-bent on hating me."

Bishop grumbled. "People either love you or hate you, babe. We're here because you've enraged a tree hugger."

"Ella." Locke worked his jaw back and forth. "First answer that comes to mind. Don't think. Just answer. Who is it?"

Jay.

Her eyes rounded, and she dropped her chin, staring at the floor, shocked. Where had that come from? Sure, she was mad as hell at him. He'd lied to her, played games with her, and he'd clearly crossed the line about Bishop and with Tara. But never had she once thought Jay was creeping on her, not even in the back of her mind.

"Ella?" Locke pushed.

She pulled her gaze off the floor and sought comfort in Bishop's eyes. His stare wasn't entirely what she needed. Or maybe it was. Fiercely protective and equally angry, the man wanted vengeance and blood. He wanted to make the hell she'd been through stop, and wipe away her suffering. Amazing, she got that all from a glance.

"Fuck, I thought so," Bishop growled. Fury flexed in his jaw. Even the way he breathed flared his nostrils with hostile intention. If Jay had been in a thousand-yard radius, Ella would've been worried for his life.

"The FBI is all over Seneca, but whatever you just thought," Locke said, his tone as serious as Bishop's face, "you tell Angie Byrd if you won't tell us."

Years of happy memories, tough times, hard work, and future goals disappeared as she fought to find the simple words. During the last hours spent under hospital observation, she'd been fine. Now, Ella shook like a lavender sprig in a summer storm.

"It's Jay, isn't it?" she whispered.

They remained silent, but their menacing, hardened features said her opinion matched theirs. Bishop had pushed her to question Jay before, and she had pushed back. Locke, though, had no reason to pull a jealous ex-boyfriend card, and truly, neither did Bishop. He wanted her safe. She knew that. He wasn't the jealous type. A man like that needed no comparison and had no competitors.

Ella had to realize it on her own, and the process took Manny's injury to do so. Hot tears slipped free. "I need to talk to Agent Byrd now."

Chapter 31

Bishop had offered, but Ella had taken Locke up on the ride to the FBI appointment, needing to be away from the deep emotions and reactions that bubbled up when Bishop stood close. He acted as though he understood why she wanted Locke to take her to meet the FBI, and hopefully, she hadn't hurt his feelings.

And now that she was here… This wasn't what Ella thought the conference room would look like. A man about her age, wearing a suit and tie, had offered her water or coffee, maybe trying to make her comfortable, but nothing could.

The door opened, and Agent Byrd walked in as perfunctory as ever. Her face was an odd combination of comfort and let's-get-down-to-business.

For the next thirty minutes, Ella poured her guts out. She recounted every thought, concern, and suspicion. She relived every second guess in vivid detail, explaining Jay's changing behavior and her changing attitude toward him.

None of it was evidence. Nothing she shared had been informative, but it was cathartic. Agent Byrd occasionally picked up her pen and took a note, but mostly, she listened. When Ella came to a stop, her agent leaned back in the chair, put the pen down, and rubbed her chin.

"I'm going to be honest with you, Ella. There's nothing concrete here."

"I know." Still, everything inside her felt shattered. "I just—"

"But," Agent Byrd continued. "We're on the same page. And I think he's who we're most interested in."

The truth hurt.

"But Ella, you know this. Jay is smart, and the thing is, technology? It can be hard to trace. We need to have that one string in the sweater to pull, then that's our in. We're not there yet, but we're looking. Until then, you need to be vigilant."

"What do I do? And…what are you doing?" Ella asked quietly, feeling like a traitor.

"We need something to pinpoint him on, but we're just shy of an arrest." Agent Byrd clacked her teeth once in thought. "I'd say get a restraining order. There's nothing to tie him to any of this. There's nothing to tie it to anybody. You need to stay safe." Agent Byrd sighed. "The problem with stalkers—and I need to be honest with you—the problem is that when things go bad, they go very bad, and there's not much I can do beforehand."

"Fantastic," she mumbled.

"*You* have to be aware. You have to stay away. Extract yourself from the situation."

"Which I've done," Ella explained. "I broke up with him. I fired him." All of which she already had said.

"On the surface, yes. But this is a whole new breed. There are online trolls. Online stalkers. Harassers. They know how to use technology and create profiles, hop IP addresses, use multiple SIM cards. The list goes on and on. It's so cheap. Readily available…" She shook her head. "What we're most vigilant about is the transition from the online fixation to real-life violence."

"But he *has* done things in real life. Manny was hurt."

"And now that he's done that, and he's spiraling, losing

control, he's going to make a mistake. But he's also getting more dangerous. This was an attempted homicide. An attempt on your life. On Manny's. We're no longer talking about online games and hiring college kids. We're talking about harming you. He wants the last word, and it's murder."

To hear those words come out of her mouth… Nobody had put it in those terms before, and she hadn't even thought about it like that. *Jay had tried to kill her.* Tears leaked, and Ella wiped haphazardly at her cheeks and chin. Agent Byrd reached across the table and grabbed the tissue box, sliding it toward her.

"It's just when you said that…" Ella sniffed. "I'm not sure how much more I can take. Everything I've understood about my world just changed."

But was it really Jay? Or was her mind so clouded now as to reach for the improbable? Because *murder*? They had traveled the world together, saving animals, saving the innocents. "None of this makes sense. It's just not like him. That's not his personality. It's not who he is to hurt another. What if I'm wrong?"

"Maybe you are." Agent Byrd acknowledged that very possibility, which only served to confuse Ella further. Then the agent signaled to the window. "That's why this is an investigation. Evidence trumps guesses as much as I rely on my instincts."

"What do I do now?" Ella balled up the tissue. "I can't keep *Agent Byrd* on my list of favorites forever."

The door opened, and the person who had escorted her in dropped off a cup of water. Agent Byrd pushed it to her. "You can call me Angie, Ella."

She sniffed. "Okay."

"You grieve." Angie laid it on the line. "You grieve the changes that you can't control. The loved ones and friendships that you lose. When your world alters, and everything you think you knew may be wrong? And the people who are most loyal to you end up delivering the most pain?" She paused. "You grieve that loss but then grab onto your strength. You find it, and you rise."

Ella wanted to believe she could do that. She breathed deep and swallowed a sip of water, trying to handle the pain in her throat.

"I've studied you enough, Ella, to know that you have an inner strength. Everyone has it. Some more prevalent than others. But it's always there. You find it and move forward."

CHAPTER 32

ELLA WAS NERVOUS WHEN SHE saw Bishop's truck idling, waiting for her. But the nerves were for naught. He asked her one question: "Do you want to talk about it?" Then he easily accepted her succinct answer of "no."

Angie's words about strength stayed with Ella, and she appreciated that Bishop let her be alone with her own thoughts.

The drive took a long time, and she used that time to drift in and out of self-pity and question if she was wrong.

Bishop slowed down and turned off of the two-lane road onto a tire-track-cut driveway.

"We're here?" she asked.

They rumbled over the uneven pathway. "Home of Bishop and Brick."

This was exactly the kind of place she thought he would like. Trees made a canopy on both sides of the driveway. They wrapped around the corner and opened up to green space with a house sitting on top of a hill. A large dog tore out of the house.

"That's Brick, right?"

"That is."

"Did he come from inside?" Bishop had a doggie door? She

wouldn't think that was very secure. It seemed to her that he would've had a tougher security system.

"He has the run of the place."

"What about an alarm? Doesn't he set that off?"

"Like a security system?"

"Exactly."

Bishop laughed. "Brick *is* the security system."

Oh… It took them another minute to roll up the driveway, and a few moments to unload and for her to meet Brick. He gave her a lot of love, but she could tell he was every bit the security system that Bishop had called him.

They walked into his house. The last time she'd actually been in a place that Bishop called home was when they were in college. This place looked like him. It was comfortable and practical, with homage paid to his dog and his time spent in the army. It was bigger than she thought it would've been and had more green space. And it was very clean, even though he joked about her place being cleaner than his. Maybe a little sparse, but nothing unexpected. This house was real grown-up Bishop.

"I'm going to go check something upstairs and be back in a minute. You need anything? Shower? TV? Bourbon…?"

"No, I'm going to nurse my water and nose around."

"Good. Snoop all you want. I thought you'd say something like you needed to talk to Tara—"

"Well, that too."

He shook his head. "Sometimes, I think you're a masochist." Then he walked down the hall.

Ella took a sip of her water and put it on the counter. She'd carried that cup of water all the way from the FBI headquarters, focusing on it instead of her phone. Now it was time.

She pulled out her phone and saw that Tara had texted.

TARA: Huge response online today. It leaked that you were in an accident. So always an upside.

Ella threw her phone into her purse only to dig it out and slam it back in. Not responding to Tara would adequately convey how she wanted to wring her publicist's neck. But she couldn't because she was too busy wiping away tears. Frustrated ones. Angry ones. There wasn't an upside to this! She was overwhelmed and didn't know what to do.

She drank the remaining water and went to throw the cup away. Ella opened the cabinet and froze. She expected some ugly black industrial trash can, but what met her gaze were two receptacles, including one labeled "RECYCLING."

She blinked, dumbfounded, as the cup she'd held onto since she left the FBI field office crushed in her hand. Almost in a state of shock, she slid the recycling bin forward and faltered at the contents. Crushed cans. Bishop had crushed all his cans. She couldn't look away. It was so stupid, so simple. The guy gave no craps about landfills, not two shits about the size of the cans if he were going to recycle. But there it was, staring back at her.

The paper cup fell from her hand and landed in the pile of cans. She couldn't help herself. She grabbed her phone and took a picture. Some people had keepsakes from first dates. This was...well, he wasn't exactly involved in this moment, but it showed he cared. Right? Her heart sang. Because, yeah, it did. And after the day she'd had, this was what she needed.

She shut the cabinet, backing against the counter with her hand over her mouth. There was a grin hiding behind her fingers.

He'd *definitely* done that for her.

She pulled out her phone, needing to share how cool this was with the world. Eco-Ella peeps would die, just like she was. They would totally get the moment. Quickly, she typed and loaded the picture, reading back the text for typos.

> That moment when HE recycles when you're not looking. ;)

Tara would go nuts. People would flock to figure out who *HE* was.

But *HE* would hate that.

Ella stared. It felt wrong. Too private. Too not him. But he wasn't actually in the picture… *Shoot, no.* She hit the delete button instead of publish, watching the message float away.

That wasn't meant to be a publicity stunt. It was a gift he unknowingly gave her. Ella bit her lip and slipped her phone into her purse.

It was *so* ridiculous, but she took one more quick peek under his sink. The warm fuzzies came back in full force.

Bishop walked into the kitchen. "Hey."

She jumped, slamming the cabinet shut and spinning. "Hi."

He chuckled, eyeing her suspiciously. "You doing okay?"

"Yes, I, um, I like your recycling container."

He lifted his chin in acknowledgement and went to the fridge. "Hungry?"

She came up behind him and wrapped her arms around his torso. "Thank you."

"Sure, babe. It was nothing."

God, now he was downplaying it, only making her hug him tighter. Even if he thought she was crazy, she didn't care.

He closed the fridge, turning into her hold, which was apparently not as strong as she would've guessed. "Ella, seriously."

Her eyes blurred with tears, and they threatened to escape over crushed beer cans. "I can't help it."

"Come on. We're not hanging out in the kitchen if you're crying over my trash."

"Recycling," she corrected.

"Potato, po-tah-toe."

"Wait." She pushed onto her toes and planted a kiss on his lips. "It means a lot."

He grabbed an orange from the counter then locked an arm around her neck. "You mean a lot to me, babe. See how that works?"

"I see." Her heart spun in a circle. "What are we doing?"

"Gonna relax and go to bed. We'll find FB and Brick. Make sure they haven't killed each other."

"Brick isn't going to hurt FB."

"I'm not worried about my boy. I'm more concerned that your city-dweller dog is going to be led to the wild side of dog food with meat in it."

She elbowed him. "I feed my dog meat."

He unhooked his arm. "So it's just you who's the tortured vegan."

"Vegan for life, Muscles. That I can't change for you."

He tossed the orange in the air and caught it. "I didn't change for you. I stomped on some Bud heavies. Brick ate my last trash can, and I thought of you and everything you spout when I went to buy another and was walking up and down the aisle. There's a shit ton of options, and one looked better than the rest. I don't want you to change, El. I love all that crazy shit you do. Keeps me on my toes."

"Really?"

He tore the skin, peeling the orange. "Mostly."

"Yeah?"

He popped an orange slice in his mouth. "Yup."

"Have a favorite?"

"When you kissed me at the bar, and I made every excuse in the world just to kiss you back."

Swoon. Thud. She was so done.

OVERHEAD IN THE DARK BEDROOM, the fan quietly spun. This wasn't how Bishop had pictured their first time in his bed, but as he gathered Ella under his arm and pressed her to his bare chest, he wouldn't change that she was here now. Her soft hair tickled his skin, and her quiet breaths fell in time with his fan. They'd been lying in the dark for what seemed like forever. He was just letting her process the day, and there had been little left to say.

More than just a physical attack, there had to be pain associated with that type of disloyalty. No matter that Jay was clearly fucking nuts, psychological excuses or not, it still had to hurt.

Another good-bye.

Not that he compared himself to Jay, and the similarities ended quickly, but he had left Ella, and now Jay had hurt her too. She didn't deserve this crap.

"We've both been awfully quiet," she whispered.

Guess she wasn't asleep. "I'm letting you process."

He had a lot to think about too, like how possessive he was when it came to her. While Titan was a new job, acting as a protector was an old routine. The military had taught him that. Actually, he was born with it, and they'd honed it. His sister's death had been a catalyst for change in his life, setting the course for him to be a better man, a tougher one.

But was he handling this situation well? He and Locke had both missed how the van was set in motion. That killed him.

Ella shifted to her hip. "Are you processing?"

She wore one of his oversized T-shirts. The cotton swallowed her, and even in the dark, he could make out an outline and see her shadowed face. "Yeah, babe, processing."

"What's in your head?" she asked.

"Don't know. Not much." Which was bullshit.

"I'll show you mine if you show me yours."

He squeezed her. "I go first, huh?"

"Since you just volunteered, that sounds great."

He chuckled quietly. "All right. Let's see how this goes." He rolled his shoulders, shifting as he felt her waiting. "Sucks not to have seen that coming—"

"Angie explained that the park had too many blind ways for someone to come to that lot on foot—"

"Appreciate it, babe." And noteworthy that Special Agent Angie Byrd was now just Angie. Even if Ella hadn't wanted to talk about it, it was obvious that her comfort level with her FBI POC had increased. "And logically, I know that. Doesn't mean I can't feel like shit for not seeing it."

"Short of putting me on lockdown, which I won't agree to, you guys couldn't have stopped what happened."

"Better location." They could've been closer. He could've insisted on no headphones, that she and Manny face him at all times. He could've been a complete dictator in how the production had gone, in how she'd done everything, hovering over every facet of her life, always expecting an incoming assault. But hell, what kind of life was that?

"It's where I wanted. My favorite place. *And* I'd still like to show you my favorite place."

"'Kay." Maybe he and Locke needed to gel better. They were two new guys working together, and perhaps that had been the problem. Defenses down because, other than the parking lot, they'd been in the wide-open park.

"I'm serious. I'd like to take you there. Maybe tomorrow. There's a little hut, and it looks like nothing, but somehow it's *everything*. If what it's seen and been through—"

He wished he had that spark she held onto despite everything that had happened. "You know what is so great about you?"

"Hmm?"

"You get so damn excited about whatever you're passionate

about." A hut? It was probably cool, in some nature-walk way, but had anyone else on earth gone on about how badass it was? Likely not. Bishop pulled her close. "Your turn. What's on your mind?"

Ella placed her hand on his bare stomach. "Well…"

It wasn't a sexual move, but they were in bed together, and he didn't have a shirt on. Hell, he was a guy. Everything in life could be construed as a sexual move. But that wasn't an excuse he'd ever used before. Her simple move pushed at his sanity. Good thing the lights were off, because if he'd been watching her casually tease the shit out of him, the suffering would have been unbearable.

"I should've listened when you pressed me on Jay." Her fingers spread. "I don't know. It's weird to think that he would do this."

"People are weird." Jay was likely weird before all this, but that was another conversation.

"All of a sudden, it hit me like *whoa*."

"Gotta trust your gut."

"I just don't get why." As if her tone hadn't punctuated her frustration enough, Ella dropped her weight against his arm.

He wanted to wrap her tight, peel her shirt away, and hug them together until she didn't care about Jay's reasons. Bishop wished there wasn't that hurt in her voice or the tinge of confusion in her words. But fuck it, what he really wanted was the scent of her shampoo in his nose, her hair dangling around his head. Instead, he contained an urge to taste her skin. The woman needed comfort, not the start of the erection he was trying to ignore.

Ella's fingers flexed, her nails lightly grazing above his belly button, and he sucked in his cheeks, ignoring his groan…or trying to.

"Are you okay?" she asked. "I can scoot."

He tightened his arm around her, refusing to let a micrometer of space come between them. "Don't."

She rested her chin on his shoulder. "Good. I didn't want to."

The tickle of her warm breath in the dark could drive a man mad. She turned her hand over, letting her knuckles softly drift over his abdomen, and it was too much. His dick jumped at the barely-there touch. His lungfuls were slow, deep, and purposeful. He couldn't stop how turned on she made him. "El..."

Her hand drifted down, grazing the waist of his boxer briefs. "You smell good." Her lips hovered next to his cheek.

It was a lethal combination that couldn't be ignored. He turned his head and took command of her mouth in the dark. Voltage as hot as she was rushed down his spine, igniting in his fingertips as he lifted her on top of him. This is what he was made to do—be with this woman.

Electrified and alive, it was as though emotions existed only when they connected. Everything amplified. Intensified. Wordlessly, he found a way to make everything better. "*This*. This is what we needed."

Nodding into his mouth, kissing and moaning, she agreed. "Yes."

Her knees pinched to his sides and her hands gripped him as though she had been drowning. Bishop flipped them over, sliding her under him and caging her head to his pillow with his forearms. "Everything will be okay."

"It will.

He reached over and turned on the light. A low, easy light cast over his bedroom, and when he looked down, all was as it should be. The most beautiful woman he'd ever held, the only woman he had ever loved, stared up, trusting, with hair spread over his pillow, while she wore his favorite shirt. This was the kind of thing that made the world go round.

He dropped a kiss to her forehead, her cheek, slid his lips to hers, and sank his tongue deep into the hot cavern of her mouth. She came alive, wrapping her legs around him, rubbing her hands against his chest, flicking her thumbs against the discs of his nipples, and tugging at his chest hair.

"Your heartbeat feels like mine," she whispered.

He agreed with every gasping word. "How's that?"

"Needing."

Bishop inched back, cupping a hand under her chin. "Yeah, babe. I need you." He slid his thumb down, toying with her lip. "Primal, possessive need."

She nuzzled into his palm. "I know. I love that about you."

"Hell, woman, I love *you.*" He leaned closer. "And after the hell of today, you need to know."

Shock widened her eyes, and Ella tilted her head. Hell, if she was going to have a disheartening, disloyal revelation about Jay, she could hear one that was the polar opposite.

"Why did you say that?"

He inched closer. "Because you deserve to hear the truth occasionally. Unvarnished, no bullcrap. I'm in love with you."

Her lips parted.

"*Again,*" he added. "Some things have a way of coming back."

Ella ducked under his arm and rolled out of bed. "Give me a minute."

"Uh…" Not that he had planned this conversation, but that didn't go how he thought it might. She rushed out of his bedroom, and Bishop had no clue what to say. "Hey…"

A second later, she walked back in with a smile that reached her eyes and a piece of paper in her hand. "Angie asked me to write down the only thing I knew for certain."

He took the paper she held out and unfolded what had been made into a tiny square. Each move amped his anticipation as he smoothed the paper. On the center of the page, she'd written one sentence in certain block print and underlined it in pen:

I'M IN LOVE WITH BISHOP O'KANE.

His heart jumped as his laugh rumbled. "You're crazy."

He wrapped an arm around her waist, tugging her into bed. A mixture of relief and adrenaline, of arousal and anticipation, spun inside his chest. "Good." He put the note on his nightstand. "Threw me for a minute, running out of bed."

"But seriously? That's kind of crazy." She crawled across the mattress, kneeling and eyeing the paper. "I mean—"

"Ella?"

"What?" Her chin tilted up, as she was still apparently amazed they'd had the same thoughts today.

He dropped his voice. "El." He read it, but damn, he wanted the words to burn in his ears.

"*Bishop.*" She crawled back, walking up his body, and into his arm. Her tongue traced up his neck, and she kissed his earlobe, whispering, "I'm in love with you, Bishop O'Kane."

It hit him everywhere.

Ella raked her nails down his chest. "I don't want to go to sleep. I'm done processing. I've done everything I'm supposed to, and I've said the magic words. Now I want to play."

Like there was any turning back now. "Rule book says your shirt has to go."

"Absolutely." She lifted her arms, and he pulled it off, tossing it over the side of the bed.

She kissed him, letting her tight nipples sway against his chest, and he couldn't keep his hands away. Palming both breasts, he rubbed the peaked tips between his thumbs and forefingers, watching color rise in her face. Gone was her playfulness, making room for straight-up arousal. He pinched, and she sighed, heady and hot. Then he squeezed and plucked her deep cherry red nipples again.

"Feel good, El?"

"Mm-hmm." She squirmed as he increased the pressure, her head dropping back. "Yes."

Releasing the tweak, she relaxed, almost buckling, and he slid his hands down her stomach, watching a trail of goosebumps erupt. "If you read carefully, it says these have to go too."

"I was hoping so." She lifted her hips, and he snagged the sides of her panties, dragging them down her legs, and dropping them over the side of the bed.

"God, I like this game." Her hair drifted over one shoulder. Her breasts were swollen, and Ella's eyes drifted closed as though she couldn't have been more relaxed, more turned on, more in the right spot.

"And I like that you're mine."

***"ME TOO."* ELLA'S EYES FLUTTERED.** Sitting over his thick thighs, very aware that his engorged erection was a layer of fabric away, she couldn't fathom how possessive and careful he could look at once. She traced his jawline. His scruff scratched her skin, and she teased down his throat. "I like that you're—"

"Can't say *mine*. I already took it." Playful, even when his intensity could melt a glacier.

Ella licked her lip, shifting and smiling as she teased against the bulge in his boxer briefs. "Sexy."

Bishop's hand shot behind her, and he flipped them over. "Too generic."

She shouldn't have teased him like that, except *wow*. His massive weight brushed on top of her naked body—*oh*—and her shaky breath couldn't be hidden as his powerful thighs spread hers.

"Try again, babe."

"Mmm." Out-of-this-world provocation wasn't good for thinking through answers. "I like that you're strong. You're ripped."

"That doesn't compete with *mine*." He stroked the length of his hard cock against her, and her mind short-circuited.

"Shit," she moaned at the pressure on her clit. "That's so nice."

But the pressure evaporated, and she whined a little until he dipped his mouth to suck on her nipple.

"*Bishop*, please." Please, what? Please, everything.

"Last time, Ella. You like that I'm…"

Oh, God. The wet heat sucking on her nipple went back to work, and the powerful flow of his body worked against hers.

"I… I like that…" She gasped. "I like that I…*can't say no to you*." She moaned. "Ever."

"Good answer." He released her nipple and rewarded her with two fingers that quickly stroked and speared her.

"God!" She dropped her head back, arching as he sunk his fingers in, knuckles deep. "Yes."

"Damn." Holding himself up, Bishop's mouth took hers with power reserved for a nuclear explosion, and he pumped and curled his fingers.

Ella cursed a thousand times as his mouth made love to hers, whisking away her obscenities before they left her lips.

"Want to come, babe?"

"Yes!" She clung to him. "No!"

Questioning her with a look, though he didn't stop the insane onslaught building, he decided for her. Yes, she would come, and thank God, because she was on the edge and had no idea how Bishop even had a string of sanity.

Her climax hit as he pulled the fireworks from deep inside her, lighting every nerve ending until they exploded. But it wasn't enough. Clinging to him, Ella begged, "I need you inside me. Need to feel you. *Now*."

Carefully, he withdrew his fingers, and she winced, sitting up, almost reaching for him. Maybe she should have rolled with the climactic wave and not been greedy, but as Bishop shucked his boxer briefs, and his beautiful length came into view, the millisecond of regrets vanished.

He opened the drawer of his nightstand and grabbed a condom. Lightning fast, he came back to her. "Lie on your back."

She complied, and the massive hulk of a man loomed. Calculating, he began his descent. His palms ran over her breasts, down her hips to her thighs, where he spread her legs farther apart. Open to his stare, she could've felt vulnerable, but instead, she felt safe, secure, …desired.

Hands resting on top of her thighs, Bishop squeezed her then leaned in for a kiss between her legs.

"Oh," she moaned as his tongue ran along her seam and his lips suctioned her clit.

Her butt lifted off the bed as his hands clamped her in place. "*Fuck*, you taste good."

Too much to think about, she couldn't handle his tongue, the words, but he slowed his kiss and eased up, tearing open the condom. "And if I didn't need to come so bad I was going to die?"

She shuddered.

He sheathed himself and crawled up her body, nudging the head of his cock against her entrance as he sucked on her bottom lip. "I'd lick you."

She breathed through the first thrust of his intrusion. Foreplay did wonders, but size was size, and Bishop's cock was thick and long. The heavenly sensation of him entering her was *real*. Ella flexed her hips, trying to accommodate him.

"Kiss you," Bishop continued, inching in, tangling his tongue with hers. "Suck that perfect, fucking little clit."

God. She tossed her head to the side. "Please."

"Damn, I feel that." His low voice shook, growling into her mouth.

"Me too," Ella gasped, needing more and pulling away. "More."

He didn't stop rocking until he was balls deep. Ella dug her nails into his back, crying that she loved him.

Bishop froze, his chest heaving. "Love you too, babe."

Then he went hard and fast, not stopping. With each collision, she came closer and closer to reaching the stars again.

Her pussy clenched, and she held onto him as he pushed her to fly. "Bishop!"

A relay of excitement, one nerve ending to the next, shot up her arms and down her spine. She couldn't breathe, didn't think. He held her, and that was all that mattered as her climax erased the worst parts of the day, shattering every memory except for *I love you.* All she could do was exist. The only person in her world was Bishop. Him in her. On her. Making her feel as though together, they were invincible.

Emotion caught in her throat. Something from history and something from today. Words bubbled but wouldn't come out. Whatever it was, it weighed heavy. She wanted to say something, needed to explain that she was grateful, explain that there was a *thank you* to be shared.

"Are you okay, El?"

She simply nodded against his cheek.

"Good." He had slowed through her orgasm to a gentle roll. Slow and steady. A beacon of strength in the wild—so very Bishop. "Give me your leg, Ella."

Numb legs like jelly didn't matter. He would get anything he asked for. She shifted, and he grasped behind her kneecap. With their new angle, all thoughts left her head as he stroked, unhurried.

"This is…" *Paradise.*

He captured her in a kiss, his tongue slow, dancing as fast as he made love. Lazy and languid, but still deep and dangerous, building her to the edge in the most undercover of ways.

Again, the wave of orgasm teased, toeing her to an insatiable end. "*I am…*"

"Yeah?" His hot breaths gasped as he amped up the piston of his hips. Every second passed with a more powerful pace. Even as he spun them to dizzying heights, Bishop controlled the maddening chaos until she could've sworn she was the center of his world, and he lived to bring her to that point.

His thrusts hit deep. Her pussy spasmed, rippling on his cock as she came. He groaned, his body quaking and possessing her in a way unlike she had ever experienced. Their orgasms slammed together. Their gulps for air mixed with exhausted, sated lip-locks until they were slumped into two heaving bodies, coming down from a high as one.

"*Thank you.*" The words had finally come.

His green eyes opened, and he gave her a chin lift. With a light kiss, he released her leg, pulling away. Separate but still touching, they continued to catch their breath. Bishop let his fingers wind with hers.

"This was a good way to end a shitty day." He squeezed her hand before rolling away and walking toward his bathroom.

She tossed her arm over her face. A million reactions ran through her head. But most notably, today had the worst, but now also *the best,* memories.

CHAPTER 33

THE FARMERS' MARKET WAS PACKED. Row after row of vendors hawked their fresh fruits and vegetables, sold their lemonade and baklava, and displayed their farm fresh eggs and homemade items.

"Are you ready for tomorrow night?" Locke asked, tossing an apple back and forth.

Two days spent with Bishop, then she'd surfaced for air when Manny called to say he had been discharged and was at home. She wanted to pick up some items to stock his kitchen, and Bishop needed to report in to his boss, so Locke was back on bodyguard duty. Truth was, she'd missed his no-nonsense way of telling her how it was—and how he could sometimes do it without saying a word.

"Sure." The three of them—well four, if she counted Tara—were headed to New York City. *Road trip.* It should be fun. But the last red-carpet event had had its own set of hiccups, and whenever cameras were involved, Tara's stress level made the New York City skyscrapers look teeny-tiny. Plus, she would have to abandon comfy clothes and be Spanxed into something lean and mean. "It'll be fun."

Locke grunted a disbelieving laugh. "What about now? You good?"

Ella waved to a woman she knew at a booth and stopped to buy a loaf of cheese bread for Manny. She snapped a quick picture, scheduling it to post later, when Locke repeated the question.

"I'm fine." *But definitely jittery.* She glanced around, itching under the scrutiny she couldn't place.

"You bought that for Manny, but you won't eat it?" he asked.

"Why do you guys think just because I won't touch certain things, that I won't let others eat them?"

"Well…" Locke shrugged. "I dunno."

"Manny's home and recovering. He needs food. I might not be the one who buys him ground beef—"

"Because that's different than buying him something with cheese in it?"

"Animals used for meat and their *byproduct* is an industry that has undergone changes over the years, from inhumane practices to more compassionate ones. There are many reasons I don't eat meat, and many more why I'm a vegan. But mostly, I'm disturbed that there was and in some cases, still is, an industry that is indifferent to the pain and well-being of animals, seeing them as nothing more than dollars on a spreadsheet, when they are livestock with beating hearts. It literally makes me sick." She smiled at a familiar face and glanced over her shoulder to see if there was someone else she knew. No one caught her eye. "I'm not here to regulate what Manny eats, but I am happy to help him get better. Free-range chickens didn't exist that long ago. Now it's a term people are willing to pay for. That helps the chickens and the famers by trickling more money back into an industry that has seen new growth."

Locke nodded. "I like that about you."

"What?"

"Everything's a lesson."

She blushed. "Well, I didn't mean it like that."

"My turn."

"Hmm?"

"Fifth time."

"For what?" she asked.

"I think you already know."

She bit her lip. "I'm looking around?"

Locke nodded.

"Do you feel anything…weird?" she asked.

Locke cast a lazy glance over the crowd and shook his head. "If I did, we wouldn't be here." His eyes continued to scan the crowd. They never stopped moving, like Bishop's, when they were in public. "But"—he rubbed a hand over his jaw—"there's something to be said for intuition. You've been in the crosshairs. Anyone who's been there before, especially more than once? They know the feeling."

"I know that feeling," Ella whispered.

"It's not a club that I welcome you into. But you're a card-carrying member."

"I—"

Anger tightened Locke's face in a way that she never could've expected. His eyes beaded as his nostrils flared, and a low growl emanated from his chest. "Son of a bitch."

Stepping quickly, he tucked her behind him, and she followed the direction of his ire. There was Jay. Her stomach turned. Angie had told her that she would consider him a person of interest, that Ella should consider him dangerous.

"Ella," Jay said loudly, closing the distance as though he couldn't see Locke in front of her. "We need to talk."

She took a step back as Locke intercepted. "Ella's good, man. She doesn't want to talk right now." Locke became a wall.

"What the—Ella. We need to clear some things up." Jay tried sidestepping Locke and failed. When he moved the opposite way, Locke blocked him again. "The hell? *Ella.*"

"We were just leaving." She turned toward the baker's booth. If anything, she could stand with a familiar face until Locke took care of this. What was Jay doing there? And how long had he been at the farmers' market? What did he want to clear up? Her mind spun too fast, with too many puzzle pieces desperately trying to slam together.

At the baker's booth, she clung to the table.

"Ella, are you okay?" the woman who had sold her the cheesy bread asked.

"I just need to—" She refused to sound weak. "I told a friend I'd meet him here."

"Here I am," Locke's deep voice said. "Ready?"

She nodded and grabbed onto his arm, needing to stabilize herself. "I know it was him. I know it now. How are they ever going to prove it?"

Locke's tight jaw confirmed her biggest fear. They weren't. Her best option would be something like a restraining order.

"Let's go." He hustled her toward the parking lot, weaving them through the rows of booths.

A cold chill ran over Ella, and she glanced over her shoulder. There Jay was, glaring. This was that same feeling she'd had for months, when she had no idea who her stalker was.

BISHOP PACED ELLA'S HALLWAY, LISTENING to Locke as he summarized the final few moments of the interaction with Jay at the farmers' market. This was why he wasn't in law enforcement. Bishop didn't have the patience for this cat-and-mouse bullshit. He wanted back in the mountains, back in the military, back to what Titan was supposed to offer. Orders. An enemy he could destroy. Not some jackass they had to pussyfoot around and play wait-and-see with.

"Man, you need to take a breath." Locke put his arm out. "You walk in there like that, you're going to scare the crap out of a girl who's already trying to keep it all inside."

Right. Ella didn't keep much inside. She talked. She posted. She *vlogged*—if that was actually even a goddamn word. "I'm fine."

"You're anything but."

"I'm—" His phone buzzed, and Bishop wanted to throw the damn thing against the wall for the headaches technology brought on. How else would Jay have even known where Ella was going to be? Locke surely hadn't left a breadcrumb trail. TITAN HQ appeared on his screen. Bishop rubbed a hand over his face. "Yeah. Hello?"

"Yeah, hello to you too, peaches."

He sealed his teeth and squeezed his eyes. "Sugar. What's up?"

"Not a good time?"

"No. It's fine." The last thing he needed to do was piss off Boss Man's wife. "Need something?"

"We think you do."

"*We*?"

"Lex and Cat are with me on speakerphone."

"*Spectacular,*" he said, barely opening his teeth. "What do you need?"

He hadn't put in a GUNS order, but with the three of them on the phone, Sugar didn't sound as though she was calling about an order or a job.

"We want to meet your girlfriend."

"I don't have a girlfriend." At least not one that he was going to admit to on the phone with the boss's wife.

"Oh, for God's sake. She's cute as a fuckin' button."

"Seems smart—"

"That was Lexi," Sugar said. "No one on this phone cares if you're nailing your detailee."

He pinched the bridge of his nose. "Is this really why you're calling me?"

"Get used to it," Caterina said—Bishop knew her accent. "Sugar is in everyone's business, and the second she smells sex, she's making calls, playing matchmaker, and butting in like you would not believe."

"That's terrific. Really." He kneaded the hollows by his eyes then rubbed a hand over his face. "But I need to get back to work."

"Exactly. That's *why* I was calling. Jeez. You'd think I didn't have a point."

"And that is…"

"We were watching her just now—"

"Just now?" Bishop turned toward Ella's condo door.

"And you need to remind that woman, do no harm *but take no shit*."

"Loud and clear." He saw red. "I gotta go." Then he turned to Locke, nodded good-bye, and let himself into Ella's unit with Locke's warning to chill out burning in his ears.

"El?" Where was she making a video in real time? When Jay was out there, stalking her *in real time*. What was she thinking? She wasn't. Simple. Jay was thorough. Shit, that man was a predator, and Ella was making it easy for him, even if he already knew where she lived. It wasn't the point.

Bishop scanned the living room and kitchen. No Ella. "Ella?"

Not in the laundry.

He tapped the ajar bathroom door. Not in there.

Stomach churning, he headed to her "fake" bedroom. Empty. Flawless. The covers were smooth, not even recently sat on. There was only one other place in this condo. But she wouldn't. No. Right? No way would Ella make a video from the only slice of privacy she had.

His molars smashed together as he approached the door. Light escaped from underneath it. Stupid move. Really? No. First, she went live, and second, from in there? Anger pounded in his chest that her recklessness was endangering the one thing he cared too much about: *her*.

Bishop crashed into the room, letting Ella's bedroom door slam against her wall. It hit so hard, the door bounced back, and he knocked it again with his elbow.

There she was, in the center of her bed, phone still in hand and tablet by her knee. "You can't even put the damn thing down."

Her wild expression tracked to the door and back to him. "What?"

"What were you doing?"

"Oh." Ella pulled her knees under her and dropped the phone, avoiding his glare. "My job. Like always."

"Wrong. Not like always. Look around you, babe. What's different? When is it different? *Things are different*."

She shrunk back into the row of pillows. "I know."

"What were you thinking?"

"I just felt so lost. And alone."

"So you turned to a million strangers? Pick up the phone, Ella. Talk to a real person."

"I did, and Tara said—"

"Tara? *Tara?* You could've called me. You could've talked to Locke." He stormed forward. "But no. *Tara*. And Tara said what? Tell people about your pain? And you thought, 'okay, that's so stupid, but why not?' Tara said, 'sure, your life's in danger, but let's give it a whirl.' Yeah, why don't you call and do whatever that loony-tunes woman with ratings-for-brains thinks."

"Stop with the name-calling." Ella buried her head in her hands. "I know you're upset. It made me feel better."

"Really? You know it now, or maybe you thought I'd lose my shit like I'm doing and did it anyway?"

She sniffled into her hands.

"Yeah, you knew it and still did it anyway. Awesome, El. Because I was hoping that maybe you were just being irresponsible and forgetful."

"Really, Bishop." She lifted her tear-streaked face. "You don't have to be so serious all the time. It was a live stream. Simple."

"For the purposes of ratings and likes and drama and whatever else that you and Tara can orchestrate."

"Seriously, it's one video. One time. That's all it was."

"In here! In your sanctuary. In this safe zone. The DMZ. Your green zone. The place where I shouldn't have to worry about you, and you do something as stupid as my sister did."

Ella's head snapped back, and her eyes went as wide as her mouth. "Screw you."

He hadn't even expected to say those words, but it was the God's honest truth. "She didn't have to pick up the phone, and neither did you."

"Everything is one impending disaster after another. And this room can't save me from lunatics—"

"Impending disaster?" he snarled, hurling her words back at her as though he finally had the grenade launcher he'd been searching for. "Only *one video*. Just like it was *one text*. You've simplified it, thinking that we're in some sacred space of your bedroom where no harm can be done. Same as with Brie, driving sober, when there were no other cars on the road. She still flipped that car. Brie still *died*, and it's like you're trying to find the same path."

"*Bastard*."

"Whose only fault is trying to keep you from the same fate."

"Go to hell, Bishop."

"Not until you understand the full effect of your actions, then I'm on my way there."

Her eyes bugged. "I just wanted to feel better. I wanted some semblance of my old normality before we head to New York, and Tara agreed—"

"Goddamn Tara." His head throbbed. Ella didn't get it, no matter what he said or how he explained it. "She's just like Jay. Do you hear yourself? She's the misconception of everything. She's using you like he does." Bishop threw his arms out. "Screw it. This is the same conversation. *Recycled*!"

"Cute. How long have you been waiting to use that?" Ella pushed her lips into a thin line and bunched her hands in her skirt. Then she dropped her head, letting her hair fall down, hiding her behind a curtain of strands. "I thought you'd catch me when I fell for you again. You said you would. How stupid was I?"

He stared at the woman that he wanted so desperately to care for, who wouldn't let him. This argument was the epitome of everything that he disagreed with. His throat burned because what he wanted most kept pushing him away.

"Ella, you have to *want* me to catch you. You have to fall when I have a chance to catch you. Hell, you have to fall near me, and we are not in the same universe. We're not orbiting in the same galaxy when you pull shit like this."

"I'm falling." She ran her hands over her face, threading her fingers into her hair, pulling at the locks before she released them. Her pained expression killed. "No, I fell for you, and it shouldn't matter where or how. Why don't you see that?"

"Jay was there today. Why don't *you see that?*"

"I do," she whispered. "More than anyone on earth."

"Then goddamn it! Why are you baiting him?" His eyes fell to a picture of Brie on her shelf. It was so small, he'd missed it last time he was in there. "I'm telling you. This is like watching Brie pick up the phone in slow motion. But you keep doing it over and over, and one of these days, it's going to kill you."

"Stop," Ella whispered, her voice shaking.

Each vibration struck him like the reverb from a mortar strike that, at this second, he almost missed. Anything was better than this pain. "I'm out."

"You're leaving the job? Or…me?"

A surge of bile stole his throat and his breath. "If it's not Jay today, then there's a half dozen psychos tomorrow, and you keep giving them the roadmap."

Her bottom lip trembled. "That wasn't an answer."

"It was, babe." And he was dying inside. "Locke's not far. I'll get him back here. I can't handle this right now."

"You're an asshole." Ella's voice had changed—still heartbroken, but *angry*. She was as mad and as ready to fight as he was. "You never make mistakes, Bishop? You never do things to blow off steam with the guys? Your job? That's something *we've* never talked about." Flames shot from her narrowed, tear-reddened eyes. "That same job, where you run around with a *gun* on your hip, and who knows what you'll do next after you're done working with me. You act like I'm the only person who has to be perfect not to die! You ran from Brie straight into a *war zone*. Now here you are, working for some company that still might kill you. Screw you for not admitting that too."

His fingers went numb as her truth hit him like a sledgehammer. His body followed suit, and last to go was his mind, suffering at her argument. "I'm out."

"That's the truth."

Ella is right… Bishop rubbed his face. The entire time he'd been on her job, he craved the adrenaline rush that put him in danger. He'd been trained, disciplined. Though at the moment, it would be impossible to tell.

"You know what?" Didn't matter if she was right or wrong; he still refused to watch her walk a gangplank of stupidity. "Forget it. You, me. We don't work. This is done."

The heaviest steps of his life took him out of that room that millions of people had now seen.

He trudged through her condo, and damn, the grip on his lungs was enough to crumble him to his knees. Or infuriate him to the point of punching a trail of holes in her wall. That would shout how much she meant to him, and she could *vlog* the shit out of it.

He just couldn't watch her self-destruct.

Bishop dragged his hand over his mouth, throwing open the front door. Locke stood, waiting. Thank fuck for his buddy, who knew what might happen and stood ready and waiting as backup without even having been asked.

"Man, you good?" Locke asked.

"No."

"You leaving?"

"Yes," Bishop growled.

"It's going to be okay, brother."

Bishop turned around, sweeping one last look over Ella's condo. He didn't buy Locke's line of bullshit for a hot minute. He let the door slam. Whatever else Locke had to say would have to wait. There were less than twenty-four hours until they needed to be in New York City for the Capri Awards with Ella and Tara, and the thought of wearing one more tuxedo was enough to make him lose his mind.

CHAPTER 34

THE FABRIC WAS TOO RED, the waist was too tight, and the V-neck dropped way too low between her breasts. Ella couldn't stop cringing at the mirror in the hotel room suite, and Tara couldn't stop beaming. The Capri Awards were tonight and packed serious star power. A little bit of Hollywood, the who's who of television, and Tara was in her element.

"What is with your face? You're never this blotchy." Tara grabbed powder that the makeup artist had left. "She had to airbrush you to hell and back. You do know that, right?"

"Obviously, I know that." Ella tried not to sound as though she had cried all night while sucking down mint tea to counteract the effects of love-torn devastation.

Tara and the makeup girl had spent an easy ten minutes analyzing her puffy, bloodshot eyes before coming up with a *course of action*. Who knew makeup needed such things?

Tara pressed her hands together and rubbed them back and forth, sizing up Ella. "Everything about this dress is perfect. Do you know how hard it was to get this thing? It's going to photograph perfectly. Your curves are va-va-voom—"

"I hate—"

"Blah, blah, blah. I get it, I get it. But the boho chic does nothing for you in the big leagues. Black tie, not beach-and-bonfire. Trust me, this is the look you need."

"I trust you." But did she? Should Tara have been the voice of reason and reminded her to stay on point with Bishop's rules? *No*. Tara had never been the voice of reason, and Ella was responsible for her own decisions on whether to post live or not. Plus, Tara knew clothes and red carpets.

"Of course you do. This is what you pay me to do. You'll easily be on every best-dressed list. This is *Malia Sava*."

Designers were not her thing. "Wheeeee…"

"Your stories get more coverage if *you* get more coverage." Tara repeated the mantra that Ella had come to know during award-show season. "Think about how this dress will look when you're holding a Capri."

A mantle full of awards didn't get Ella that excited. "I can get coverage without my boobs being on display."

"Ehhh. I don't know." Tara put her hands on her hips as though she were scolding Ella. "You've got some killer tits, and there's nothing I like more than a dress that says *cover me*."

Ella knew she didn't mean that in the literal sense. She meant press coverage. "Understood."

The door opened, and in walked Bishop, ripping into a piece of beef jerky. *That asshole*. Ella swallowed a gag. Gone was the fresh heartache that made her want to cry again. That was how he walked in here? Screw him. His message was sent to her loud and clear. She'd cried all night for no reason. Clearly, she had fallen in love with a jackass.

Tara continued her lecture. "It's sexy. Sex sells. I sell you. See how that works?"

Bishop stopped, mid-rip into the jerky. That face said it all. The dress was *sexy*. Soon as he kicked back into gear, he managed to look everywhere around the room and also straight at her simultaneously.

Served him right, and suddenly Ella *loved* this dress. The jerky still made her want to puke, but she would own it if it made him act like that—and she hoped it hurt. Oh God, now the tears wanted to come back. *No*. Ella wouldn't let that happen again, and she sucked down a long breath.

"Monkey suit looks good on you," Tara said without turning. "What is going on with you, Ella? More powder…"

Tara was right about the blotchy spots on her cheeks and about Bishop in a tux. Locke wore his well too. Both men were big, broad, and built to wear custom-tailored fits. Battling head-to-head with half the people walking the rope line and red carpet tonight, Locke and Bishop would easily blow the competition away. And she would have to ignore it all. *Deep breath in, deep breath out.*

"What do you think?" Tara nonchalantly asked Bishop. "On a scale from one to can't-keep-your-hands-off-her, where's our girl land?"

Ella gasped. "*Tara!*"

Bishop cleared his throat, walked straight into the hotel room's kitchenette, and got a glass of water as she stared a hole into her publicist's face.

"Don't say that," Ella whispered, feeling embarrassed heat spring all the way to the top of her ears.

Tara grumbled. "See, that proves my point. Red-blooded male. You're hot, but this dress makes you on fire."

"You have no idea. That look has nothing to do with the dress." The blotchiness was back tenfold, and as Tara reached for the makeup again, Ella didn't think this night could get much worse.

Bishop had been in the room for all of one minute, and she was dying inside as much as she wanted to walk over and throw herself into his arms—to explain and to punch him in the chest. But instead, she took Tara's offered hand and slipped into the heels that waited her.

"Perfect," Tara crooned. "Now those shoes turn your butt into a booty."

Bishop choked on his water and slammed the glass into the sink. Ella remained as silent as the wind rolling off a bay.

Tara went into analyzing mode, her eyes bouncing between the both of them. "Are you no longer banging his brains out?"

"*Tara*," Ella hissed.

Bishop raised his eyebrows, clearly hearing that. Spinning away, he headed for the bathroom.

Tara watched the door slam before her entire animated personality flew into top gear, wide-eyed and mouth agape. "What is going on?"

"I crossed the line, and he told me so."

"Why?"

"I made that video we talked about."

"Yeah? You didn't say anything in that—"

"I did it from my real bedroom. It was too much for him."

Tara pursed her lips. "That's the stupidest thing I've ever heard."

"He has his reasons. It struck too close to home."

Tara crossed her arms and tapped her expensively clad foot. "That's some bullshit." That was one thing about Tara—she was fierce and didn't hold back. Ella could see how she got her way with as many reporters as she did.

The bathroom door opened, and Bishop walked out, adjusting his earpiece. Tara straight *growled* at him, and Ella didn't call her off.

Bishop didn't flinch. "Schedule says we hit the road in two minutes. Limo's waiting downstairs. Ready?"

"Of course we'll be ready," Tara snapped. "It's what we do."

"Glad you have your game face on." Bishop tugged at his wrist, pulling at a wire in his sleeve. "You run offense, I'll stay on D, and then, in the end, we'll see what was worth it."

Great. Tara versus Bishop wasn't what she need before the big event.

Tara turned to the table and gathered items into a bag, while Ella walked to the giant picture window and stared out into the city. The afternoon light painted New York in a beautiful, albeit overpopulated, glow. Nerves always tickled before events, and this one had a new twist for her: an award presenter. Maybe she would pick up an award too, but mostly, the purpose of tonight was to garner buzz and keep relevance, all of which made Tara so, *so* happy.

Tara spun to her. "Ready?"

"Yup." She stared at the bustling traffic below, trying not to bite and chap her lips too badly before the cameras zoomed in.

"Great. I'll be in the hall." Bishop stormed out, letting the door slam behind him.

With him went an air of tension, and Ella could suddenly breathe better. She dropped her head back—

Tara whistled. "Holy. Shit. Woman. What on earth did you do to that man?"

"Nothing I hadn't done before." No matter what he had explained or what she'd said, they had an impasse as big as the gap in their history. "We should go."

Chapter 35

The limo eased up in the line, waiting for the red-carpet exit. Ella's nerves jumped in her throat as she watched the coverage of the event on her phone. With the volume on mute, she saw a reporter in front of the Jumbotron, which was adjacent to a bleacher full of fans. Then Alia Bardi, someone who Ella would totally fangirl, exited a limo, waving to the crowd. A moment later, the rumble of cheers roared from outside the limo. It was unreal to watch and live the live coverage—very meta. Ella may never get used to this world.

Locke was already inside the event, and Bishop sat across from her. At least her emotional tailspin had numbed while sitting near the brooding, angry, tux-clad badass.

"Four vehicles until us," the driver said.

"All right. Smile," Tara ordered, doing the final social media prep.

Ella did, letting her snap a few photos that they all agreed would be uploaded in real time because obviously, everyone knew she was at the Capri Awards, and part of her job was to hype up her fans.

"Now, random candids." Tara asked for different poses.

Ella glanced out the window, in her purse, at Bishop… He had shifted to watch her, and their eyes locked. *Shit.* One glance held too long, and the waterworks threatened to ruin hours' worth of makeup.

Tara noticed too. "Nope. Cut that shit out, you two. Dab your eyes, Ella. Come on."

Whatever his intense look had been, it wasn't a nice mushy one, but it still sliced deep inside her heart. Ella dropped her chin and blankly held her phone. "It's nothing."

"Then don't mess up that eyeliner or those lashes." Tara rifled through her bag and pulled out a tissue. "Cry or kill each other later. Not until I have this event done."

These drop-off lines took forever. Four limos didn't seem like much. But pulling up, waiting, the big exit, the pull away—even though they ran it like a machine, there was still time, and it ticked by like molasses on a frigid day.

Her phone burned a hole in her hands, and hell, she needed to talk to him before all of this started. Ella flipped to her text messages. Rarely was Bishop one to text. Not unless she was at the beach or dropping location updates. Definitely not for conversations, but now he was going to have to figure it out.

ELLA: Is this how it's going to be? All night?

ELLA: ???

BISHOP: I'm working. You are too.

ELLA: HA. Good thing social media is part of my job. As you reminded me.

BISHOP: Low blow, babe.

ELLA: YOU BROKE UP WITH ME OVER A VIDEO

BISHOP: If that's why you think I can't deal, then you need to think again

Tara cleared her throat, obviously catching on that she and Bishop were texting. "One limo up, one in the hole. Only two, Ella. *Two* in front of you, so don't screw up your makeup."

"Got it." Her thumbs hovered, ignoring Tara. Bishop was right. She knew it wasn't the video.

"One and then us," Tara whispered. "Head up and game face on. You have an exclusive almost immediately with GreenTV."

"Got it," Ella mumbled to appease Tara.

Bishop didn't walk away over the video. It was Ella's words, her location, the actions after all his warnings, and what was common sense. She'd never set foot in that room with a live feed. What had she been thinking?

"Ma'am," the driver said as he paused.

"That's my cue." Tara reached for her phone. "Hand me whatever you want me to carry inside."

> BISHOP: If that's all you came up with? Blaming the video? That *sucks*. I loved every second hanging with you though. Least we can say we tried.

Now he could channel emotion via text? Dumbstruck, Ella couldn't fathom a response. It didn't matter. Tara was scooting, and Bishop too, pocketing his phone and readying to exit the car. Numbly, she handed over her cell to Tara.

The limo eased up and paused again, and Tara pulled her credentials, emblazoned with "publicist to Eco-Ella," around her neck. She popped up as her door opened opposite the red carpet. "See you on the inside."

Bishop—who was clearly the muscle and didn't need a badge hanging around his neck—said zip, leaving out the same door as Tara.

"Ready, Miss Leighton?" the driver asked.

"Yes, sir." This was work. She was a professional. The tears could come later when she could find a bathroom and fall apart privately at a better time. Until then, she would fake the next few hours, even if she couldn't see past the pain and distraction that made her arms numb and her legs drag.

They eased to another stop, and the red-carpet security opened the door. The Jumbotron's camera zoomed in on her face, and she beamed, as happy and carefree as Eco-Ella could.

Chapter 36

The red carpet had been a blur, and the green room was supposed to be somewhat calming.

Ella sipped water and watched Tara upload behind-the-scenes pictures online, cross-posting everywhere. The category that Ella was presenting came early in the awards show, so she'd been immediately whisked backstage.

"That was easy." Finished, Tara dumped the phone into her purse and moved behind Ella, rubbing her shoulder as though she was readying an athlete for a match. "One of the best red carpets you have ever had."

"Thanks, Coach." Disagreeing took energy. Ella had simply delivered the talking points that Tara had drilled into her head. They had flowed like water, mainly because they were based off of issues that Ella was a true believer in, but having had the verbiage crafted for her was, for the first time, a gift from Tara that she'd used. "I aced the rope line and didn't fall flat on my face."

"And you gave details on the lavender and mint project. Rallied the Vamanato haters. Fist-bumped the beekeepers and easily reminded prime-time viewers that the environment is as trendy as your dress. And *everyone* is talking about this little number. That's what teamwork is all about."

Tara had prepped several reporters about the incident at Seneca but also had given them *tons* of backstory on Eco-Ella projects. So even as Ella had ignored the drama-filled questions about the accident—no mention of the stalker and little of Jay—she could finally boast about the venture that had nearly killed her and Manny.

"I appreciate it. Really."

Tara gave Bishop a placating thumbs-up. "And you kept us safe. Way to make sure this holding cell of a green room is super safe from hostile takeovers."

He grunted his non-amusement, not lessening the uncomfortable tension in the air. Bishop had remained either ten feet in front or behind her, even between pressers and photo ops, never once adding to the conversation with Tara. He'd behaved like any other security detail that was assigned to *actual* celebrities.

Internally, this event had ginned up a lot of what she liked to call impostor syndrome. Because there was no way in the world she was supposed to be there. Though with how her notifications were blowing up after Tara had just posted those pics…

"Thousand likes already on this one," Tara mumbled. "And thousand plus thumbs-up over here on this vlog. Plenty are tuned in."

Bishop's phone buzzed, which was different than him talking into his wrist, which he had been doing since they left the hotel. "Hey, Locke."

He turned to the wall so she couldn't hear, not that she wanted to anyway. But why was he on the phone?

Tara narrated from hers. "Tonight's trending pretty much everywhere."

Everyone was on their phones, and Ella felt naked without one. But for the purposes of making a point, she didn't ask for it from Tara. "Great."

Bishop handed the phone to Tara. "Locke needs to talk to you."

Ah, that was why it wasn't a wrist-and-earpiece convo.

"Perfect." Tara paced. "Yes, I want to see that."

She hung up and handed Bishop his phone back.

"You want to do more behind-the-scenes video or pictures?" Tara asked, perhaps trying to saw through the pressure and keep her limber for the stage.

"Not really." Ella had morphed into a machine, but it was exhausting, and she needed to save all the faux candor for the stage.

"Right. So what would you like? A candle?" Tara opened a drawer against the wall, peeking around the corner at the vanity and couch. "They have incense."

"Actually, I'd just like to be by myself. Can I do that?" She turned toward Bishop. "Is that allowed?"

"Sure. The talent gets what the talent wants."

"Oh, for Christ's sake, you two." Tara rolled her eyes. "Yes, Ella. Bishop and I can stand outside the room. Not a problem. Do you want to stick with still water, or I can find you sparkling?"

"Really, I'm fine." There was a mini fridge if she suddenly couldn't handle flat water, and she could get it herself. "I just want to be alone."

Tara touched her arm. "All right."

"We'll be right outside the door," Bishop said, stiffly moving to the door and holding it open for Tara.

Ella paced back and forth in the tiny, L-shaped room then dropped in a chair in front of the vanity. "Keep it together."

She pictured the beach, calming waves, and she pulled in a breath, letting it drift. When she opened her eyes, the woman staring back at her was hard to recognize, but that was still her. "Just makeup and hairspray. It all washes away."

At the base of the mirror sat an envelope with her name

elegantly scrawled across it in calligraphy. It leaned on a small gift box. How had they missed this?

She picked it up. The cardstock was heavy and expensive. She rubbed its textured paper between her thumb and forefinger, tilting the card until the sharp edges scratched her palm. She closed her eyes, trying to relax, turning the card over and over… How had everything gone so wrong with Bishop? And so fast?

Again, she stared at her airbrushed and processed reflection in the vanity mirror. *Just make it through tonight.* And to do that, she needed to put Bishop aside.

Ella slid the little box forward, surprised by its weight. She batted it between her fingers on the counter before letting it slide to a standstill. "You're strong. You've always been that way. Sometimes, it's harder to find that strength, but it's in there. Even when you don't recognize yourself."

She tore the expensive envelope open, ripping the thick paper, and slid the card out.

Dear Ms. Leighton,

We would like to thank you for your participation as a category award announcer this evening! We're pleased to have you and the Eco-Ella powerhouse brand as part of the show. Please accept our token of appreciation with this small gesture.

With our sincere thanks,

Your Friends at the Capri Awards

How thoughtful. Normally, Tara intercepted gifts and cards, and she only learned about them after the fact. Ella picked up the box and removed the decorative cardboard. It was pretty, though a completely unnecessary waste of resources. *Not to be unappreciative.*

Nimbly, she opened the top of the box and—well—not her style, but staring up at her was a beautiful bracelet.

It had an intricate design and was unlike anything she'd seen—very abstract art-looking, she guessed, very New York City. Ella lifted it out of the clips, peeling the unneeded plastic wrapping off of the thick, ornate metal band, and held it out on her fingers. The ornate clasp was even a work of art, and she wrapped the bracelet around her wrist, locking it on.

Definitely gorgeous and absolutely not something she would normally wear. But really, it was fashionable, and maybe even matched what she was wearing.

She held her arm out then dropped it against her dress. The bracelet didn't move much and was fairly tight on her wrist. Was she expected to wear this tonight? What were the social rules on these things? She didn't know. This was a time that it would be helpful to have other "celebrity" friends. What was there? A message board where they could post questions? An Ask Abby of online personality protocol?

Or was the gift part of a sponsorship, and she was expected to wear it as part of her speaking tonight? Tara sometimes made arrangements, and Ella was supposed to wear certain gifts and borrowed items from designers. Like this dress—a *Malia Sava* original. How many times had Tara dropped that phrase into conversations, and Ella too, as instructed?

"Hey, Tara?" Ella called over her shoulder.

The bracelet definitely didn't match with anything boho chic that she owned. If she was ever to wear it, it would probably be tonight. Fumbling at the clasp, she couldn't undo it, as if she needed evidence that this wasn't her type of jewelry. If they had given her something handmade of beads and hemp, Ella would have been a happy camper.

"Come on..." But—*ugh*—she was going to chip her nail

polish, and Lord knew if she did that, Tara would give her hell. Sometimes, her publicist could be like a mom—a helicopter one that leaned to the bitchy side and needed to have a glass of wine. But right about now, she needed that mom to undo this bracelet. *Shoot. Never mind.*

Ella stood up and looked in the mirror, posing at various angles. The combination looked good, though. "Tara?"

She waited for her publicist to burst in and immediately drop the gauntlet with the fashion decision before Ella could ask the question. But no dice.

It wasn't as if the place was soundproof. She walked to the door and twisted the knob, only to find Bishop alone. *Dang it.* "Where'd Tara go?"

"She went to find Locke and stake out your seat." Green eyes crawled down her dress, drifting over every curve and pausing too long in that deep V between her breasts. His throat bobbed before he turned back toward the empty hallway.

Ella stared at the opposite side of the empty hall, still feeling his gaze. "Is she coming back?"

"Probably not. Event staff will find you before your time. Why?"

He didn't sound as if he was asking because he cared, more that he was asking for work. They were back to the beginning, when she was a job. And he was good at his job, which she should be thrilled about. The best of the best was watching her butt. Almost quite literally, except it had been her boobs.

She turned back when she felt his gaze again. "I had a question about jewelry."

He raised his eyebrows and bunched his lips, obviously assessing if fashion at an awards show was serious. "Is it an emergency?"

"No, it's not." Ella held the heavy bracelet out. "The Capri Awards gave this to me. I…never mind."

The metal clung to her skin tighter than she liked but then again, she was used to beach wear. Even these hellacious shoes were foreign to her, and she was pretty sure that after this event was over, Tara had them ready for a charity auction. At least two fashion reporters had asked her about them, one even remarking about her spectacular *toe cleavage*. To which, Ella had kept her stupefied *what the hell* to herself.

Bishop let his eyes drift down and back up, and it would have been a total lie to say she didn't feel every inch of his inspection.

God, she hated this feeling. Hated the distance between them, figuratively and literally.

"Ella Leighton," a man called from down the hall. "Lights, camera, action!"

She jumped, spinning toward the man's voice and almost killing herself in the shoes and skirt combo while making that move.

A young man came swiftly down the hall. He was dressed in black, wearing a headset attached to two electronic packs on his waist, and carrying a clipboard. "Your turn. Let's go, my dear. If you need anything, say it now or forever hold your peace."

Her stomach catapulted as he breezed past them, motioning for her to follow. She didn't need anything. "I'm great. I got the card. The bracelet—"

"Little faster, honey," he called over his shoulder.

"You're good, Ella. You walk as fast as you want," Bishop countered protectively.

The man ahead laughed. "Sure, whatever security says. Or you can listen to me. We're live on TV."

CHAPTER 37

BISHOP TUGGED AT HIS EARLOBE, repositioning the earpiece until it moved into the least uncomfortable spot. It had just been him and Locke, but any moment now…

"Hey, I'm here," Parker said from Titan HQ home base.

"Hey, buddy," Locke said.

Bishop brought his wrist to his mouth. "Hear me okay?"

"Loud and clear," Parker responded. "Just logged into their systems, and everything looks good. Video feed's up. Let's get this one in the can and call it a night."

"Roger that," Bishop mumbled as he followed Ella. They maneuvered around the shit ton of people backstage. There were teams of staff, clipboard-holding, headset-wearing directors, and random folks that made him uncomfortable. There were people who *looked* important, surrounded by those who reminded them of that fact constantly. Bishop then passed someone who seemingly had once been important, but had drowned that memory in a bottle, and was currently being babysat by what he could only assume was the intern of someone important. Backstage was a clusterfuck.

Ella followed behind the clipboard man until they came to a stop on the side of the expansive stage. Throughout the entire labyrinth of hallways and people, she had opened and closed her fist as though she was trying to work out tension and anxiety, nervously twisting that bracelet.

"One minute," their stage escort said amidst the flurry of people spinning backstage.

The auditorium erupted in laughter, and the booming voices from the sound system surrounded them. How was Ella getting away with only a simple twist of her hands as an outlet for all of her nerves? Bishop had no idea.

If he was about to go onstage in front of hundreds of people? No way. And knowing that it was a live broadcast? Hell no. More power to her for being able to handle that kind of pressure. Not that he'd made it any easier for her.

Two women dressed in black strode over, one carrying an envelope. He had expected them, as per Tara's very specific instructions. The envelope contained the name of the award winner that Ella would announce. Watching her take it all in stride was spectacular. Hell, she was spectacular. Beautiful, smart, and all he wanted to do was tell her that—yeah, he was starting to realize how big he'd fucked up and needed to get a fast grip on his goddamn issues.

"Thirty seconds," clipboard man said.

Ella closed her eyes and let her head drop back, elongating her neck in that daring dress that had been driving him insane since he walked into her hotel room. Between the dress and not knowing what the shit he was doing at an awards show, he itched at the unknown—and his chest needled.

He swept his gaze backstage, always on patrol. Nothing popped, but his skin prickled at an unknown he could sense. What was he missing?

Bishop brought his wrist to his mouth. "All good?"

"Eyes in the sky have nothing to report," Parker said.

"Nothing front side," Locke added.

Damn. Give him a grenade launcher, and he would feel at home. Put him in a monkey suit at a prime-time awards show, and he was lost. Lost and…his senses tingled.

What was it? Something…

"Ella," Bishop whispered.

Startled, she abruptly turned to him. And maybe he should've talked to her way before she went on national television.

With wide eyes, her bottom lip dropped open, and she again started her new nervous habit of twisting her wrist. "Yes?"

Damn it. Her voice was too quiet. It shook. And since when did she fidget? He shouldn't have said a word before she went onstage. What had he been thinking?

She fiddled with her bracelet rather than further acknowledge his existence. He couldn't blame her.

"You're going to do amazing. I'm really proud of you." It was the only thing he could do. He had to save the moment. He had to do that for her.

Semi-smiling, maybe reassured, she refocused back on the stage as though that was what she needed to hear. She certainly didn't need him asking, *Are you okay*? *Do you feel weird*? *Does anything seem off?* Because those were irresponsible things to say. And he couldn't tack on *I'm a fucking asshole; I'm mad but not done.*

The man with the clipboard raised his hand and pointed his finger. "And you're a go." The music crescendoed as the lights swayed up then dropped down. The announcer boomed the names of Ella and her co-presenter to a huge round of applause.

Cold chills competed with his proud enthusiasm. She was stunning, graceful, and he would not have been able to handle the pressure of all those eyes and cameras. Even with her stalker and the stress between them, she was flawless.

That was the kind of person he wanted by his side, and as she walked onto the stage and into the homes of millions, he couldn't have been angrier with himself.

Still, every step she took exacerbated the feeling that something was off. The farther she got, the more he was concerned. Bishop's eyes tracked behind stage, seeing the expected chaos, but nothing out of the ordinary.

The hairs on his arm stood like soldiers readying for war. The ones on the back of his neck jumped to attention. His cold chill escalated, crawling across his shoulder blades, and sweat dampened his shirt underneath his tuxedo jacket.

Hesitant, he brought his wrist to his mouth again, chewing his bottom lip. "Locke, does anything seem out of place?"

"That's a negative."

"Parker?" Bishop couldn't see across the stage for all of the glaring lights. Then all went dark as the large screens showed a video montage about Ella's category. Something about best in documentaries on TV, but Bishop didn't give a crap about what was on the screen.

"Not that were seeing, buddy. What's up?"

What the hell was he supposed to tell Parker? That he had a feeling his girlfriend—his *ex*-girlfriend—was in a bad spot? They already knew that. He probably just had nerves by proxy. He'd never felt so out of place before in his life. This was the antithesis of being on an Afghani mountain in the middle of nowhere on the back of a donkey while carrying a gun.

"Bishop," Parker ordered. "Spit it out."

"Something's wrong. I don't know it. I feel it."

"Feel what?"

Bishop shook his head, unable to explain. "Locke, is Tara with you?"

"Affirmative."

"*Shhhh,*" the guy with the clipboard hissed.

Bishop glared until the man shrank down even though he took a step back and focused on his conversation with Parker and Locke. "Ask about the bracelet. She's wearing a bracelet."

"Hang on."

Seconds felt like eternity until Locke came back. "Tara said that it is uglier than hell and she wants to have Bishop's ass for letting her walk onstage with it—And if that was his *I'm sorry* gift, she had things to teach him."

Both Locke and Parker chuckled, and if his guts hadn't bottomed out, he would have had something to say. "I didn't give that to her. Ella said it was waiting for her. Something from the awards show?"

Locke relayed that information and came back at breakneck speed. "Tara said no way. She would've known prior."

If his stomach had bottomed before, now Bishop's insides catapulted to a layer of remorse he'd never experienced—not in war, not since the realization that his sister had died and he could've prevented it. Ella had a piece of metal wrapped around her arm, and he couldn't place its origin.

"It was in her green room?" Parker questioned.

"Yes." Bishop's unease choked him tighter than the sashes around the giant velvet ropes along the stage.

"Staff, security, and talent..." Parker's voice trailed off. "Are the only people that had backstage access. I'm rushing through their surveillance footage. Give me a second for facial rec."

Onstage, the spotlight followed Ella as she met a Hollywood movie star that Bishop recognized. He watched the man guide her safely to a podium, where they smiled and laughed as if they had known each other for years.

Good job, El.

Ella mastered the audience, and she and the actor effortlessly flowed into their lines. They bantered back and forth, pausing perfectly and nailing their timing. Their presentation was scheduled to take five minutes, and they were less than a minute in.

"*Fuck.*"

Parker's one word stopped Bishop's heart. "What?"

"I don't know what the deal is with that bracelet, but I do know that Jay Graff is on video with the Eco-Ella credentials wrapped around his neck, walking into Ella's green room hours before you guys got there."

CHAPTER 38

OH MY GOD. **ELLA'S WRIST** burned as though it was on fire. Now was the wrong time to have an allergic reaction to the bracelet, as she stood in front of Hollywood, New York, and cameras pouring live feeds into living rooms around the world. Their spot would be over in a flash, but it seemed as if hours had passed.

Joe Devlin, the hunky actor at her side, put his hand on her back, leaning close as she tried to hide a whimper of pain. *Shoot.* Ella blinked, focusing on the teleprompter, trying to find her place. *Okay, one simple line.* She licked her lips, trying for a smile. "And the winner is…"

But she couldn't move her wrist without crying out in pain and grimacing. Ella turned to Joe. Her arm shook as she handed him the envelope, going completely off script. Being the consummate professional that he was, Joe went with the flow. Everything else was a blur, and Ella bolted offstage as soon as she heard the room roar with applause for the winner.

Her eyes were on her own prize, and Bishop had his arms outstretched—an offstage safety net, ready and waiting.

His strong hands grasped under her arms, and he lifted her up, as her designer shoes couldn't carry her another step. "What's wrong, babe?"

"Get this off me," she croaked, clawing at the bracelet and tearing at her skin. The burn seared her fingertips. She'd always been hypersensitive, but this was intense.

In a deft move, Bishop spun her away from the prying eyes of stagehands and behind the makeshift privacy provided by the dark underbelly of backstage. Footsteps and whispers surrounded her, but she couldn't open her eyes to make sense of the burning pain radiating from her wrist.

"I've got you. Easy."

"My wrist. This bracelet. Something's wrong. I swear, it's eating through my skin. Help me get it off!"

Someone said they were on a commercial break, and another groused that she had lost her mind.

"I'm not overreacting. This hurts."

"I need some light." Bishop lifted her hand up.

"Ow. Don't do that," she pleaded.

A dozen cell phones must've lit up with their flashlight accessories, and several people gasped. Ella blinked, forcing her eyes open through the tearing mascara—*no!* Red, irritated skin marred her arm near the bracelet.

"That's like a chemical peel gone haywire," someone behind her muttered.

"Ew, God," said another. "Poor thing has the shakes."

A cameraman appeared, shoving the lens as close to her wrist as Bishop's face was.

"Get that out of here." He elbowed the man, dropping her hand.

"*Bishop*," Ella cried. When he let go and her hand fell, the pain quadrupled.

"Shit. Get that asshole out of here!" He knelt back down, and together, they ignored the network staff's arguments for and against why the camera should stay. "Ella, how do we get this off?"

"I don't know. I couldn't get it off." Her teeth chattered. The pain began to push the limit of what she could handle without outwardly reacting. "I couldn't undo the clasp."

"Parker, Locke, are you getting all this?" Bishop asked as she started to cry. "Can someone find the house doctor already? It's starting to blister." He pivoted on his knees, inspecting and growling at the people hovering nearby. "Keep that camera away. So help me God. And get the goddamn medic already. Some water—"

"Yes, wash it off." Why hadn't she thought of that? She needed someone to get her a bucket of ice water to dunk her hand into.

Bishop pulled his fingers away, inspecting his hands. "No water. Hang on."

Behind her, people ran off. She could hear the scurry and feel the movement, but the localized intensity of her wrist drew her attention like a moth addicted to a flame. "I'm going to be sick."

"No, you're not," Bishop ordered, wiping his hands on his pants.

Her head swam as her stomach revolted.

"El, listen."

She looked up and found his green eyes. He had such fierce green eyes. They were angry, on fire. Just like she was right now. She whimpered. This was ridiculous. It was just a bracelet, but it was anything but. A collar. A trap. A torture device.

Gasping, she couldn't catch her breath, couldn't understand why the agony wouldn't plateau. Ella pinched her eyes closed.

"*Look at me, babe*," Bishop said, attempting again to get her attention.

Shaking, she sought his green eyes once more. Those were always her lighthouse. "Trying."

"Jay's here somewhere."

A layer of panic fell over her, smothering her in disbelief. "*What*?"

"He was in the green room. This bracelet, whatever's on it, he has something to do with it."

She recoiled. "No."

"Think. What is it?" Bishop growled over her shoulder. "Back up. Give the girl some room."

"Jay wouldn't... Could he?" Pain engulfed her thoughts. "I'm not allergic to anything."

"I know, babe. This is...corrosive," Bishop whispered. "This shit's locked on you. I've never seen anything like it." He brought his arm to his mouth. "Parker, what's the ETA on someone to cut through metal? Med tech won't be able to deal with this."

Locked on her...almost like a leash, a collar. Almost like... *Oh God.* "I have..."

"You have *what*?" Bishop paused from the conversation happening in his earpiece. "Ella?"

She closed her eyes. "I don't remember where..." But she couldn't forget the slave bracelets that she had seen years ago, a continent away. She hadn't known things like that existed—burning bracelets attached to wire, leashed so that slave laborers remained locked overnight, so they wouldn't struggle or try to escape. The more they moved, the more the liquid would rub and seep.

Jay had been by her side.

"CAN YOU MOVE FARTHER BACK please?" a woman clipped at them. "It's been a solid two minutes. There are other places to have this problem."

Bishop thought of a thousand ways he could explain how they weren't going anywhere, but truth was, he wanted off backstage and out of New York City so bad that he couldn't stand it. "You good to stand up, El?"

And if not, he could carry her.

She nodded, sweating in pain. "Yes."

"Ten seconds until we're live again," a man said, walking behind stage. "Ten seconds."

Music cued. LIVE boxes lit again.

Bishop watched famous people onstage do what they do best, walk. And—*damn it!* Jay strolled up to the middle of the stage.

Bishop gaped. "Holy. Fuck."

"What's this?" The woman next to him asked, along with about half a dozen other people, who apparently were all tuning into whatever was coming into their headsets.

Security rushed onto stage and—stopped.

"Wait. Why are they stopping?" Bishop turned to the woman, stunned.

"This is great TV," she said, eyes wide. "Guys upstairs are going to let it go to see what this guy does. We're on five-second delay if he does something whacked."

"That's Jay Graff. He *is* going to do something whacked."

She shrugged. "Don't know the name."

"FBI knows the name. Tell that to the people upstairs."

She shrugged again. "Buddy, I just take orders and deliver. I don't tell them shit."

"Already on it," Parker advised in Bishop's ear.

Only half of what Bishop thought was an appropriate amount of security and law enforcement for this type of event hovered nearby.

Jay walked to the middle of the podium and stood awkwardly between the actor and actress who tittered and stepped back. "Good evening." The entire auditorium lulled quiet. Eerily so, almost as if they recognized him as not quite a B-lister and couldn't figure out what kind of career suicide was about to happen during this prime-time production. "I have a story for you."

"I would've guessed he had a political statement to make," the woman with the headset mumbled.

"No. He's insane," Bishop said.

Ella propped herself up, leaning on him. "Oh… God." She sniffed, her breaths catching. "What is Jay doing?"

Bishop's enemy was close. He had a gun on his hip, one on his ankle, and a knife on his side. He was armed to the teeth, but the weapons didn't matter. The deadliest things on him right then were his hands.

"Let's not stop the show." Jay played to a captive audience. "Have you met Eco-Ella? Ella Leighton? If not, you shouldn't waste your time. I spent years with her. *Years*. And what do I have to show? *Nothing*."

The woman next to Bishop shifted. "You're Ella Leighton?"

"Tonight's Ella's big night," Jay continued, gesturing with his hands. "Every night is Ella's big night. But this is Ella's very big night."

"Everyone's on the same page now," Parker said in Bishop's ear.

A second later, security must have received the message from the network producers to cut Jay off. En masse, they started onto the stage at once, circling him.

"Hold on now." Jay smirked. "There's a loose piece missing somewhere. Part of the game unaccounted for. Or do you have it under control, Bishop?"

Loose piece?

Bishop's pulse stuttered at his name. He glanced about, having no idea what the lunatic was referring to, but he stepped closer to Ella.

"Ah, Eco-Ella fans," Jay said as Bishop lost sight of him to security. "Maybe you don't know who Bishop is. I think it's time for you to meet him—"

The sound system cut off, but several security guards abruptly jumped away from Jay.

Ella went limp against Bishop's side. He took his eyes off the stage to help her. "Sit back down, El."

"Heads up," Locke said. "Tara's gone. Who the hell knows where? Piss-poor timing for her to go missing."

"What the fuck?" Parker growled. "Nothing's coincidence now. Searching this huge-ass place."

"Missing how?" Bishop asked. Because if there was a *loose piece* missing, and Tara was MIA…

A few security officers simply walked off the stage as though they weren't paid enough to deal with the headache Jay caused. What was wrong with them? Watching Jay's arrest might be a career highlight for him if the officers would go on and cuff the dickhead. Then Bishop could go back to helping Ella.

"I'm sweeping everywhere," Locke said.

"Facial rec's running," Parker added. "This place has too many people, tunnels, and—Tara walked off with Jay just about the moment Ella went onstage. Wasn't a pleasant conversation between friends."

Bishop bet not. Tara was likely to throw a right hook if she got fired up.

More security peeled back. Jay was left standing center stage, holding what looked like a remote. *Motherfucker!*

All hell broke loose in the auditorium. Silence erupted into a chaotic war as famous people jumped out of their seats and rushed to every exit.

Bishop stared at the madness. "*Are you seeing this*?"

"Damn it," Parker growled. "NYPD should have a bomb squad on standby. But goddamn it!"

Two small clicks sounded in Bishop's ear. "I'm here." Rocco cleared his throat. "What a shit storm."

Backstage cleared in hysteria as two EMTs arrived. "What's happening out there?"

The people tearing out of the place had no idea. When they saw others run, they hauled ass too. These first responders were cut from the right cloth, not giving two shits about actresses in fancy dresses, feigning worry when they didn't know why.

Locke rushed to join the newly arrived EMTs and Ella. "We need to get you three out. We're evacuating."

Cops appeared where celebrities had been seated, but they hung back. The onstage security officers who remained acted as though they were a heartbeat away from attacking. But everyone waited.

"Why are they *evacuating?*" Ella gaped. "What is going on?"

The two EMTs exchanged a brief good-bye and hustled out.

"Locke, get her out of here," Bishop pushed.

Jay walked toward their side of stage. "I want to see Ella. If she leaves, I'll trigger the switch."

Enough! Bishop charged in front of the backing security force. "You goddamn asshat."

"I've been waiting for you. Say hi."

Locke, Parker, and Rocco debated in his ear about whether or not Jay was bluffing and whether that remote was set to detonate anything. Would Jay be so stupid? *Yes. He absolutely would.* Would he kill himself and take out everyone in the awards hall? Bishop wouldn't put it past the guy. All those murder-suicide news reports came to mind. He didn't know one thing from another when it came to psychology of the broken-hearted, but he did know that Jay was off his fucking rocker and had a creative mind that was warped enough to end it all.

"There's bomb-sniffing dogs and hostage negotiators on the

fast track," Parker reassured him. "But do what you gotta do."

"Damn it. You don't know if there's a dead man's switch," Rocco said, reading Bishop's mind. "This would be some good fucking TV if not for everyone about to die on my fucking job."

Bishop turned, momentarily aware of the cameras and not caring. "Walk offstage, Jay."

"No way." He looked over Bishop's shoulder. "Unless she's still over there?"

"What's on her wrist?"

Jay stopped searching for Ella. "The fun part of vlogging every part of her life has been working with her fans. They haven't had a chance to meet you. Say hi, Bishop. You're spending all your time with her now. They deserve to know who you are." He pulled his phone out, running his thumb over the screen. "Yup, they're asking about you."

"Walk offstage."

"Say hello."

"You're hurting her. Make it stop. If you ever loved her."

Jay laughed and looked down. "It's real time. The cameras are rolling, and this is the man they're meeting? Big, angry, shouting Bishop. Not someone that should be with Ella." Jay clucked, and Bishop wanted to put his fist through the guy's face. "This is a great live stream—are you looking for Tara?"

His stomach dropped as the earpiece clicked again.

"Jared here. I'm read in. Stay steady, Bishop."

That didn't do much for his plummeting stomach.

"Hey," Locke broke in. "Ella wants to talk to Jay."

Goddamn it!

"No go, Locke," Rocco ordered. "Stay with her."

"No shit," Locke muttered. "Just looping you in."

Parker rumbled a low curse. "Found Tara."

"Where?" Locke asked.

"Bomb dogs have her pegged in a room directly below stage. Waiting on bomb techs to arrive."

Ella wouldn't leave. Tara was directly below stage. Too much was happening. "Ella's who you care about, Jay. Let's talk about her."

Jay held out his arm. "I always wondered if we could create pandemonium online like we just did in here."

Then he tossed his head back. "Now, Bishop. Stakes are higher. You showed up, thinking Ella was queen of the castle. But then there's Tara. What's your move? Are you the queen's Bishop, or do you play defense another way? Tick, tock. What to do?"

"Jay," Ella cried out from offstage. "Why are you doing this?"

"Where is she?"

"Damn it," Jared growled. "Locke, let her onstage, keep her close."

As Ella came onstage, Jay twisted, studying her in such a detached way that Bishop's blood slowed. The man was emotionless except for his focus on proving his issue to the camera and the Internet. The complete tunnel vision was terrifying.

"Ella," Jay droned, unaffected by her hair clinging to her temples and the black streaks of makeup that marred her cheeks. "You had so many opportunities to do the right thing. I gave you so many chances. And now you've come to a point where you're going to look back on your life and realize that you had a decision, and you messed up. You're going to regret it for the rest of your life—however short or long that may be." He looked at his phone and watched for several seconds. "Wow, they loved that line."

Jay was watching the reaction on social media? *What. The. Hell.*

"I don't know who you are right now," Ella cried. "But this person? Whoever you've become? You're nothing to me."

"Wrong, Ella. You're always wrong."

"Bomb tech crew is with Tara," Parker reported. "Keep him talking. This is almost done."

Bishop rolled his tongue along the inside of his mouth. "This is what you want, Jay? Me to look at camera?" He waved. "What else you got, man?"

"Want to know something?" Jay asked.

"Not really, dickhead. But shoot."

"The second that the hydrogen peroxide dissolves through the layer in the bracelet's clasp—*kaboom*." Jay's fist splayed and his fingers wiggled overhead. "You should know a thing or two about that from your military days. One of those things suicide bombers put in their vests." Jay chuckled. "It doesn't take a lot, does it?"

No, it didn't. Bishop's gaze dropped to Ella's hand and back to Jay.

"Now that's *worry* on your face." He checked the phone. "Everyone agrees."

If what Jay said was true… "Don't move, El."

"What?" she asked.

"Babe. Don't move." He pulled a breath through his teeth. There couldn't be enough chemicals packed in that bracelet to blow up the stage. But it would be enough to kill her.

Where was the bomb squad? With Tara? Bishop wanted them upstairs. Was he going to ask that of Titan? When there was a camera on his face and the world watched?

"Ella, babe." With each punch of his heartbeat, Bishop teetered on the edge of destruction. "Careful as you can, walk off-stage with Locke."

"You want her moving?" Parker asked. "It's unstable."

"You want this playing out on TV?" Jared demanded.

Parker's keyboard clicked in the background. "Network cut broadcast already."

"What the fuck are people watching?" Jared snapped.

"Fucking hell, I don't know. There's at least two cell phone feeds from the auditorium livestreaming onto the Internet."

"Cut them!"

"We'd lose our connection. And I can't magically make a jammer appear where there's not already a device."

Bishop couldn't listen to the back and forth at HQ. His pulse tumbled in his throat. Sweat soaked his tuxedo shirt. How much longer would she have before whatever bullshit liner completely dissolved?

Jay stared at his phone. "Definitely some complaints about the use of the word *babe*."

"And no complaints about the bombs?" Bishop spat. "Isn't that interesting?"

Jay smirked.

"Ella, go," Bishop calmly tried to urge.

"No." Her hoarse voice damn near killed him.

"I love you, Ella, and I'm telling you, I need you to walk off this goddamn stage." Sweat trickled down his neck. "Now."

She sobbed. "Bishop, not without you."

"*Please* don't move like that," he begged. Sobbing and crying and shaking caused too much movement with an unstable compound on a device already lined with a chemical corrosive.

"Or else kaboom," Jay whispered.

Bishop was going to murder the fucker.

Locke came to Ella's side. "Come on, El. We need to do this."

Hatred flashed in her eyes. "I hate you, Jay. Right this second, I'd rather die."

Bishop growled, terrified as soon as her lips closed. "Goddamn it."

"So be it." The coldness in Jay's voice had never been scarier.

CHAPTER 39

"GO," JARED DEMANDED IN BISHOP'S ear. "You have a go!"

"Take down your target," Rocco ordered.

Bishop went high, his right hook swinging hard and making contact as his left hand connected with Jay's, transferring the remote. Locke dove behind Jay, ripping his free hand behind his back. If they did this wrong, and there was a dead man's switch, Tara was dead.

But they wouldn't do this wrong, because he and Locke were in step. What had happened at Seneca Park was a fluke. They were a team. He might not be able to see Locke eye to eye, but he had to trust his brother-in-arms.

"Got the bastard," Locke grunted.

Bishop had the remote, fumbling and gaping. Best he could tell, there was a detonation trigger and no dead man's. The next seconds lasted a lifetime. He waited for the report of a blast, braced for the reverb.

It didn't come. *Thank fuck.*

Bishop advanced. "Let him go."

"I made her," Jay spat.

Locke let go, and Jay bound to his feet.

Bishop let his right hook fly. The resounding crack of his fist into Jay's jaw didn't feel a tenth of how good it would feel to get back to Ella, but damned if he wasn't glad to have taken the punch.

Locke snagged the still rebounding Jay, and Bishop didn't look back. Those precious seconds he'd taken to hit Jay were selfish. *Fuck it.* They were needed, but selfish.

Ella stood semi-frozen onstage, her arm hanging awkwardly, her face twisted in pain as shocked, sad tears mixed with her makeup. Bishop sprinted to her, immediately stabilizing her arm.

"Babe, please stop moving." He ignored Jay's muffled shouts in the background.

"Ella needs to stay put. Bomb techs hustling ass up the stairs," Parker reported. "A minute, tops."

"Bishop," Rocco's low voice warned. "I've got to tell you to walk away from her."

"Fuck that, boss."

"Understood."

Ella shook in pain, and Bishop tried like all hell to keep her arm still. If this bracelet was blowing up, he was going with her. That minute was the longest sixty seconds of his life.

Finally, two people in bomb suits rounded the stage corner. Ella's lips chattered with nerves and pain.

"It's almost done," he said. "Then we can go get Furry Baby and Little Kitty. Take them to hang with Brick. They'll have fun."

"You said their names," she whispered hoarsely.

Because Lord knew he was trying to do whatever the hell it took to keep her still and thinking happy thoughts. "You picked up on that."

The techs assessed the situation as they took the remote detonator from him and pulled out their tools. "You need to move, sir."

"Not a chance."

"We don't have the time or equipment to protect you."

"I give zero fucks. Get this off of her."

A man holding a tool grimaced. "It's going to hurt like hell considering what her skin looks like."

"Do it."

"Fast," Ella whimpered. "Please."

One tech cut the bracelet, while the other readied a box for the device.

Ella's screams curled Bishop's toes and brought tears to his eyes as the men manhandled her raw, blistered flesh. Then it was done. They moved fast, and so did he. Up and into his arms, he took her, moving quickly as Parker directed him to an ambulance—then a gunshot rang out.

Ella jolted, and he twisted his head, not slowing, but wondering. "Locke?"

"What the hell?" Rocco demanded.

"Goddamn it!" Locke shouted simultaneously.

"All right," Parker interrupted. "Locke's fine."

"What happened?" Bishop asked.

"Jay got his hands on a service weapon while in NYPD's custody. Blew his brains out."

"Shit," Bishop whispered, downing the stairs toward the receiving bay, where the ambulance waited.

"What was that?" she asked.

"Nothing but a checkmate."

Chapter 40

Ella rubbed the sleep from the corners of her eyes with her good hand, sure that she had accidentally double-dosed her pain medicine.

Gone was the constant noise of the hospital. Too much of her time had been spent in that room. She really didn't do well in medical facilities, but the outpouring from the public had been overwhelming. Even Vamanato had sent her flowers, and that made her smile while dealing with the burn treatment.

But she wasn't there anymore, and unsure of what she'd just seen, Ella tried to open her eyes again, only to find herself face-to-face with Brick. He could stand on the ground and rest his head on the bed.

"Good morning," Ella whispered, letting the scent of coffee pull her further awake. Brick licked her face, and she wrinkled her nose, using her good hand to wipe it dry. "Yup. I'm awake."

Confident that she was not "on" painkillers, she shifted to look away from Brick.

Bobbing across from the foot of the bed was a ginormous balloon with the words "I'M A DICK" printed in bold lettering. It was also shaped appropriately well, given the message. "I was not dreaming."

She had to laugh, and Brick licked her face again.

Bishop walked in. "Hey."

She angled toward him and propped herself up. "Hey."

She bobbed her eyebrows, not pointing to the big floating cock balloon in the room, but letting it speak for itself. "That's an interesting way to wake."

"I was told that maybe I should say I was sorry."

Ella propped herself against his backboard. "You saved my life, while I basically refused to leave." Where did she get a balloon that said she was a moron? "You almost died in the process."

"Not even close," Bishop blustered.

"You could've."

"Titan strong, baby."

She laughed, shaking her head. "Am I going to hear that a lot?"

"Yeah, probably." He threw himself on the bed, flopping down. "More than that, *I'm sorry.*"

Now fully awake but with a sore wrist, she could carefully snuggle against him. "Don't apologize but apology accepted."

"Good. Because this is what I figure."

"You've been figuring?" she teased.

"Babe? Once you work at a place like Titan, with ladies like Sugar and Cat? Nic and Beth? When they drag you to a place that has cock balloons and don't blink when you ask to put 'I'm a dick' on it? Yeah, I've been figuring."

Ella snort-laughed. "Oh boy."

"Once in a lifetime, you meet a person who changes everything. Tell me I haven't changed everything for you. Because you have for me."

"You haven't."

"Bull, Ella. Bull a thousand times over."

"Bish—"

"You're supposed to fall in love with the person who forces you to enjoy your craziness, Crazy. And woman, I enjoy it. Need it. Love it. I love you, babe. Don't you get that?"

"You didn't change everything. You set the bar. And when you weren't there, the world fell apart. Now that you're back, everything, for me, has gone back to as it should."

"Well…"

"Does that work for you too?" She rubbed her cheek against his chest. "It's kind of the same thing. What'd you say once? Potato, po-tah-toe."

His hand threaded through her hair. "Same thing, then. Works for me."

"Good," she sighed. "Because being with you feels like a million butterflies high on the sun and racing through the air."

"Yeah, babe." His thumb rolled strands of her hair between his fingers. "Nothing like I ever would've said, but…me too."

"Bishop." Ella propped her chin on his chest, letting his fingers slide down her cheek. "Do you love me?"

"Always. Never stopped. Not for some stupid argument. Come here." He tugged her up and let his lips brush hers. "I see you and know you're mine. But, El, when I kiss you?" He teased her mouth, lingering. "It's more. It's the future. The next, what? Fifty, sixty years of our lives." His whisper tickled her sensitive skin. "But if you keep saving the world and making it a better place to live, maybe longer than that."

Ella stared into his deep-green eyes and believed every word he'd just said. "What's bigger than love?"

"Us."

Chapter 41

Bishop had his first *REAL* Titan job under his belt—the first one outside of Ella. It had felt like coming home. But the second that helo had touched the ground and they'd loaded up their gear and debriefed, Bishop hauled ass home. *That* felt like coming home too. Even though he knew today would be rough.

Ella had been fine while he was gone, handling the fact that he'd gone dark for days in a danger zone surprisingly well. Now, there they were. He shifted his truck into Park and glanced at Ella, who had her fingers tied in knots, much like his gut.

He pulled the keys from the ignition, nervous. "I always liked how this place looks." Some folks went about getting approval to get engaged in a more traditional fashion. He and Ella weren't traditional, so there they were, walking into a conversation that no one could prepare for.

She fidgeted. "Mm-hmm."

"Are you ready?" Because he certainly wasn't.

Ella had her bottom lip tucked between her teeth and was rolling a piece of hair on her fingers. "Are you?"

"I don't think anybody's ever prepared for this type of conversation, but this is—" He shook his head. "Let's do it."

They opened their truck doors, jumped out, then let them shut.

The thud echoed in the very quiet afternoon. The peaceful day had little more than a slight breeze as Ella joined him at the front of the hood, letting her fingers wind with his. Her long flowing skirt picked up on a gust and brushed against his legs.

Trees swayed. He hadn't been back here in years. So much time had passed that it almost looked like a different place, having grown up as he had. The landscaping was the same, but the bushes and trees had matured.

His stomach was in his throat. Nerves, emotions—things he hadn't felt in a very long time—jumbled. He didn't have the words as they walked on a path, until they came to a stop.

"Here we are," Ella said quietly.

Thank God she could talk because standing at his sister's grave killed him.

"Hi, Brie." Ella paused, losing her composure. "It's been too long since the three of us were together."

Tears pricked Bishop's eyelids, and he had to stare away at the sky. It wasn't just that it had been too long since the two of them had been there; it had been too long since he had. Years had passed since he stood there, and how awful of a brother did that make him?

Ella squeezed his hand, and he squeezed back.

"Hey, sis." Because that was about all he could manage.

"I guess you probably see this already. Us," Ella wondered aloud. "Or maybe you don't. Who knows how it works? But Bishop and I found our way back together." Gently, she swung their hands.

Somewhere, a bird carried a tune, and Bishop took a stabilizing breath, standing stoically for Ella and Brie. They might never know that right now was one of the hardest moments of his life, but he would sooner fall down and die than let them both down again.

"Brie and I knew that it would always be like this. Right,

Brie?" Ella laughed quietly. "It took Bishop some time." Ella tilted her chin, a gentle smile waiting for him.

"Not that long," he offered.

She gave him a side eye, and it made him laugh—which he tamped down. Laughing at a cemetery felt wrong. Everything about this was weird. They had talked about closure. Ella felt very strongly about having this conversation with the three of them. But actually *talking* out loud? And laughing? While Brie was gone? This was a place of respect.

Hell. This was what Ella wanted and maybe he even needed. Either way, he still found his way back to his sister, who loved to laugh and smile with them. They were the three musketeers.

"I think…" Bishop studied the grave. Brie O'Kane. "That girls figure these things out before the guys do. *But* I figured it out." He held Ella, pulling her in front of him and wrapping her to his stomach. "And I'm gonna marry El one of these days. That's one of the reasons why we're here."

"All those years of doodling his name in a heart paid off."

He laughed, shaking his head. "I promise not to be such a stranger anymore."

Bishop leaned on Ella in so many ways as the breeze picked up her skirt, brushing against his leg as it always seemed to do. She leaned back, and they stood, letting time float by, until he gave her a squeeze.

"This is good," he said. "I think we've done more for us and Brie today than we have in years."

"WELL, LOOK AT YOU." BISHOP couldn't hide his smile as Ella pulled his truck in front of his house. "If I knew any better, I'd assume you were a natural-born, diesel-driving, road mama."

Ella rolled up the window and opened the door, hopping out. "Ha, ha. Let's not get carried away." A quick whistle, and Brick followed her out of the truck's cab. She reached in and helped out FB and LK. "We had a video to shoot, and I thought it would be best by that creek."

He met her halfway down the front path. "You're using Brick for his good looks and charming personality."

"Brick stole the show. His ratings compete with mine."

Bishop grabbed his dog's head. "Don't become a celebrity," he said to his dog. "I can only handle one at a time."

"Oh, shut up." She jumped up for a hug.

"Sure, sure. Boss all your people around. FB, LK, Brick, get the talent something for dinner."

Ella kept her arms wrapped around his neck. "You're horrible. If I weren't starving, I'd say that was just mean. But since I am, I'm wondering if Brick has amazing vegan dinner-making skills."

He pulled away from the hug. "All right. Go inside; do whatever you have to do. I have the rest of the day planned."

Ella's eyebrows rose. "Really?"

"Yes. Go."

She scooped up her cat and went inside, with Brick and FB following suit. They'd swung by her condo after stopping by Brie's grave, and he'd directed her to pack a bag—which in reality meant *bags,* but that was all part of the process. And today was a hell of a process. Bishop waited patiently, crushing cans and chucking them for Brick, who was less patient. He had given up and returned after thirty seconds. Eventually, despite however hungry she claimed to be, Ella popped out his front door.

She twirled at the top of the stairs, letting her skirt swirl around her waist. "I'm ready for my date."

"Who said it was a date?" He chuckled, throwing another

smashed can for Brick. It didn't matter how long she took. When that woman spun in that skirt? They would be lucky if they got off the front porch, because it was about to be hiked around her waist.

"Well, what did I have to get ready for, then? And it's time to feed me."

"You sound like Brick." He met her at the base of the stairs and took her hand. "Let's go, babe."

"Where to?"

"Surprise."

"Definitely a date."

He guided her to his truck and opened the door. "In you go." Then he turned to Brick and FB. "And you guys go inside."

They barked and whined but listened. Ten minutes later, he and Ella were hauling ass down the road.

"Um, Bishop..." Ella's shaky voice was unexpected.

Maybe this was a bad idea. No, it wasn't. This was a bad*ass* idea, and he was going to own the shit out of it.

"Why are we headed here?"

"You said this was your favorite place. Short of heading to the tropics, this is the place you said that you loved most."

"It *was*."

"You cried and said you would do anything to replace that day."

"True." She sighed. "My happy escape was ruined. I hate that." She reached her hand to his. "Are you going to walk around, kick-start this place with new memories?"

He nodded. "Thinking about it. Good plan?"

Her fingers squeezed his. "Excellent plan."

Bishop pulled off the road and drove into Seneca Park. Ella was distant as they pulled into the parking lot near where she and Manny had had their accident—but then he kept driving.

"Wait a minute," she whispered excitedly. "Do you know where—"

"Maybe…"

"You looked up my hut!"

He laughed. "Roger that, babe."

"You did! Oh my God. No one on earth looks up that hut."

"Trust me, I know." He'd practically had to call in a favor with Parker to look up freaking old park guides. *Abandoned* natural park guides.

Bishop pulled off the road and parked near the path he'd scouted, having been there earlier that day. They jumped out.

"If I had any idea we were doing this, I would've worn something besides a skirt."

"It's not a hard hike. I just want to look at the place. Then we can get some food."

They meandered down the easy path to the old hut.

"Here we are! You're going to love it." Her good hand gripped his tightly, pulling him the last few yards. "If you don't, that's fine. I won't hold it against you. Well, maybe a little. It's pretty amazing."

He followed her lead, almost surprised she didn't break out her cell phone and video a quick Eco-Ella spot. They walked up the old rickety stairs. Each one of his boot steps made the entire building groan, and if this was not her favorite place, he might never have noticed the old nature stop.

"Oh—" Ella froze halfway in the door.

Bishop came up behind her, wrapping his arms around her waist.

"Bishop," she whispered.

A blanket lay in front of them. Her favorite, most requested vegan foods were chilled in containers on ice.

"You made me a picnic?"

He leaned close to her ear. "Yes, ma'am."

"In my silly hut." Shaking, her voice dropped even quieter, and her hands found his arms that were crossed over her stomach. She clung to his forearms, her bandaged wrist on top. "You did all of this just to make my favorite park mine again?"

That was affirmative, but it was so much more than that. He spun her around in his arms. "Is it working?"

"Yes." She nodded, and her eyes welled. "This is beyond thoughtful. I am…speechless."

For that, he had to grin. "I've done the impossible."

Ella went on her tiptoes and kissed him. "You're too good. Thank you."

"This is the thing, Ella. I think you're too good for me." He tilted his head toward the picnic blanket. "I want to give you that. This park. Your hut. I want to give that all to you because even if I don't get it, *I get it*. If it makes you happy, that makes me happy. Simple."

"You do. You make me really happy."

After this day—after the chaotic months she'd been through and their lifetime getting to this spot—knowing that was a damn good thing. Bishop kissed the top of her head then her forehead. "Good. I love you, Ella." He took her healing wrist and kissed that too.

"I know." She snuggled into him, making him feel like the most important man in the world. "Love you more than you will ever know."

He pulled away and held her outstretched in his hands. Everything he cared about, he held between his palms. "Talking about the rest of our lives this morning, about marrying you… You're mine," he promised. "I need you to know that."

"I know."

He had no magical ways, no magical words, just the truth in everything he wanted to say. Bishop let his hands slide down her arms. Her bandaged wrist straight *killed* him, and he vowed never to let anything like that happen again as he bent onto one knee. He removed a ring from his pocket and gazed up at the pure shock on Ella's face. "Not what you expected?"

Slowly, she shook her head.

"Ella, *nothing* about you is what I expected." He laughed. "Trust me. But we have one truth. And you know what that is."

Nodding, she was already mouthing, "*Yes*."

"I'm supposed to be by your side, watching you fight like all hell when you believe in something, and—"

"And when you refuse to leave me when you think I might blow up." She half-laughed, half-cried. "*Don't you ever do that again.*"

"Ella, marry me."

She sank down, sitting on his knee, and cupped his face. "You did all of this for me?"

"Everything is for you."

"Yes." Her hug might have been the tightest one he thought she could manage, then she stepped it up a notch.

Lesson learned—never assume anything from his soon-to-be wife. "You get a ring for putting up with me." His low laughter rumbled as he took her hand, sliding the ring on her finger.

Her sweet intake of breath was all the approval he would ever need as she took in the ring. A loose sculpted braid of four gold strands that mimicked vines arched around a classic solitaire. It combined parts of both of them—her free-flowing style and his traditional manner.

"All right. Want to eat? Surely, something is edible in one of these containers." He winked and pulled her onto the blanket.

"I kind of want to take a picture. This is really beautiful."

As she should. This was an important day for both of them. "Do it. Nothing exists unless it's Eco-Ella posted."

"That's not what I meant!" She laughed. "Wait. Are you talking about the picnic or the proposal?"

What the hell? Why not. He shrugged, tickled. "Your call."

Excitement brightened her face with the permission to post either the picnic or the proposal. "Thank you!"

She took one photo—no video—of her bandaged left hand in front of her vegan picnic, then quickly typed before handing her phone to Bishop for him to read.

The picture was totally badass, not that he was one to give himself too much credit on the setup. Though it was a killer job. Then he read her status.

I said yes.

"Okay?" She bounced with eagerness as though maybe trying to appreciate that he was a social media avoidant.

Bishop gave his approval. "Works for me."

Ella pressed publish and watched for a moment before looking up. "It's live."

"Watch out, Tara." They both laughed, and he could picture Tara throwing her hands in a Thanksgiving prayer. Right after she threatened to kill him for lack of a heads-up. "Think you should call her?"

"She owes me for something. This is turnabout but nicer."

"All right."

"One more thing." She held her finger on the screen and powered off her phone.

Bishop's eyes went wide. "What are you doing, babe?"

"I turned my phone off." Ella tossed the phone over her shoulder and dropped next to him on the blanket. "All done for the day."

"I can see that." He howled with laughter. "That's all I had to do to get you to turn off your phone? Just propose?"

"Oh, shut up." She play-punched his bicep then kissed him quiet.

He couldn't stop laughing. "I'm never going to be able to top this."

She kissed him harder. "Take off your gun. Literally, nobody in the world can find us until one of us decides to surface."

And with that, all the vegan food was a distant memory.

THE END

About the Author

Cristin Harber is a *New York Times* and *USA Today* bestselling romance author. She writes romantic suspense, military romance, new adult, and contemporary romance. Readers voted her onto Amazon's Top Picks for Debut Romance Authors in 2013, and her debut Titan series was both a #1 romantic suspense and #1 military romance bestseller.

Learn more about Cristin at http://cristinharber.com

Connect with Team Titan on Facebook
http://www.facebook.com/groups/TheTitanSeries/

Join the newsletter! Text TITAN to 66866.

Made in the USA
Middletown, DE
28 October 2016